# A Mother's Love

# A Mother's Love

## CHARLOTTE HUBBARD

KENSINGTON BOOKS
http://www.kensingtonbooks.com

KENSINGTON BOOKS are published by

Kensington Publishing Corp.
119 West 40th Street
New York, NY 10018

All Kensington titles, imprints and distributed lines are available at special quantity discounts for bulk purchases for sales promotion, premiums, fund-raising, educational or institutional use. Special book excerpts or customized printings can also be created to fit specific needs. For details, write or phone the office of the Kensington Special Sales Manager. Attn.: Special Sales Department. Kensington Publishing Corp, 119 West 40th Street, New York, NY 10018. Phone: 1-800-221-2647.

Library of Congress Card Catalogue Number: 2016955146

Kensington and the K logo Reg. U.S. Pat. & TM Off.

ISBN-13: 978-1-4967-0844-1
ISBN-10: 1-4967-0844-X
First Kensington Hardcover Edition: April 2017

eISBN-13: 978-1-4967-0845-8
eISBN-10: 1-4967-0845-8
Kensington Electronic Edition: April 2017

10 9 8 7 6 5 4 3 2 1

Printed in the United States of America

# A Mother's Love

## Chapter 1

Rose Raber looked away so Mamma wouldn't see the tears filling her eyes. As she sat beside her mother's bed, Rose prayed as she had every night for the past week. *Please, Lord, don't take her away from me. . . . I believe You can heal my mother's cancer—work a miracle for us—if You will.*

Tonight felt different, though. Mamma was dozing off more, and her mind was wandering. Rose had a feeling that Mamma might drift off at any moment and not come back.

"Was church today?" Mamma murmured. "I don't . . . recall that you and Gracie . . . went—"

"We stayed here with you, Mamma," Rose reminded her gently. "I didn't want to leave you by yourself."

Her mother sighed. As she reached for Rose's hand, Rose grasped it as though it could be a way to keep Mamma here—to keep her alive. They didn't speak for so long, it seemed Mamma had drifted off to sleep, but then she opened her eyes wide.

"Is Gracie tucked in?" Although Mamma's voice sounded as fragile as dry, rustling leaves, a purpose lurked behind the question.

"*Jah,* she is, but I'll go check on her," Rose replied, eager for the chance to leave the room and pull herself together. "All that fresh air from planting some of the garden today should make her sleep soundly."

"Gracie was . . . excited about doing that. She asked me . . . how long it would be before the lettuce . . . peas, and radishes shot up." Mamma chuckled fondly, remembering. Then she gazed at Rose, with her eyes fiercely bright in a face framed by the gray kerchief that covered her hairless head. "When you come back, dear, there's something we . . . must discuss."

Rose carefully squeezed Mamma's bony hand and strode from the bedroom. Out in the hallway, she leaned against the wall, blotting her face with her apron. Her five-year-old daughter was extremely perceptive. Gracie already sensed her *mammi* was very, very ill, and if she saw how upset Rose had become, there would be no end of painful questions—and Gracie wouldn't get back to sleep.

The three of them had endured a heart-wrenching autumn and winter after a fire had ravaged Dat's sawmill, claiming Rose's father, Myron Fry, and her husband, Nathan Raber, as well. The stress of losing Dat had apparently left Mamma susceptible, because that's when the cancer had returned with a vengeance, after almost thirty years of remission. The first time around, when Mamma was young, she'd survived breast cancer, but this time the disease had stricken her lungs—even though she'd never smoked.

With the family business gone, Rose and Gracie had moved into Mamma's house last September. Rose had sold her and Nathan's little farm so they would have some money to live on—and to pay Mamma's mounting bills for the chemo and radiation, which had kept her cancer manageable. Until now.

Rose had a feeling that this date, April third, would be forever emblazoned on her heart, her soul.

*Little Gracie has lost so many who loved her,* Rose thought, sending the words up as another prayer. She composed herself, took a deep breath, and then climbed the stairs barefoot. She peeked into the small bedroom at the end of the hall.

The sound of steady breathing drew Rose to her daughter's bedside. In the moonlight, Gracie appeared carefree—breathtakingly sweet as she slept. Such a gift from God this daughter was, a balm to Rose's soul and to her mother's as well. For whatever reason, God had granted Rose and Nathan only this single rosebud of a child, so they had cherished her deeply. Rose resisted the temptation to stroke her wee girl's cheek, feasting her eyes on Gracie's perfection instead. She'd seen some religious paintings of plump-cheeked cherubim, but her daughter's innocent beauty outshone the radiance of those curly-haired angels.

Rose quietly left Gracie's room. Standing in her daughter's presence had strengthened her, and she felt more ready to face whatever issue Mamma wanted to discuss. Rose knew of many folks whose parents had passed before they'd had a chance to speak their piece, so she told herself to listen carefully, gratefully, to whatever wisdom Mamma might want to share with her. Instinct was telling her Mamma only had another day or so.

Pausing at the door of the downstairs bedroom, where Mamma was staying now because she could no longer climb the stairs, Rose sighed. Mamma's face and arms were so withered and pale. It was a blessing that her pain relievers kept her fairly comfortable. When Mamma realized Rose had returned, she beckoned with her hand. "Let's talk about this before I lose my nerve," she murmured. "There's a stationery box . . . in my bottom dresser drawer. The letters inside it . . . will explain everything."

Rose's pulse lurched. In all her life, she'd never known Mamma to keep secrets—but the shadows beneath Mamma's eyes and the fading of her voice warned Rose that this was no time to demand an explanation. Rose sat down in the chair beside the bed again, leaning closer to catch Mamma's every faint word.

"I hope you'll understand . . . what I've done," Mamma mumbled. "I probably should have told you long ago, but . . . there just never seemed to be a right time—and I made promises—your *dat* believed we should let sleeping dogs lie."

Rose's heart was beating so hard she wondered if Mamma could hear it. "Mamma, what do you mean? What are you trying to—"

Mamma suddenly gripped Rose's hands and struggled, as though she wanted to sit up but couldn't. "Do *not* look for her, Rose. I—I promised her you wouldn't."

Rose swallowed hard. Her mother appeared to be sinking in on herself now, drifting in and out of rational thought. "Who, Mamma?" Rose whispered urgently. "Who are you talking about?"

Mamma focused on Rose for one last, lingering moment and then her body went limp. "I'm so tired," she rasped. "We'll talk tomorrow."

Rose bowed her head, praying that they would indeed have another day together. She tucked the sheet and light quilt around Mamma's frail shoulders. It was all she could do. "*Gut* night, Mamma," she whispered. "I love you."

She listened for a reply, but Mamma was already asleep.

Rose was tempted to go to Mamma's dresser and find the mysterious box she'd mentioned, but desperation overrode her curiosity. She couldn't leave her mother's bedside. For several endless minutes, Rose kept track of her mother's breathing, which was growing slower and shallower now, as the doctor had said it would. He had recommended that Mamma stay in the hospital because her lungs were filling with fluid, but Mamma had wanted no part of that. She'd insisted on passing peacefully in her own home.

*But please don't go yet, Mamma,* Rose pleaded as she gently eased her hands from her mother's. *Stay with me tonight. Just one more night.*

Exhausted from sitting with Mamma for most of the past few days and nights, Rose folded her arms on the edge of the bed and rested her head on them. If Mamma stirred at all, Rose would know—could see to whatever she needed.

In the wee hours, Rose awakened with a jolt from a disturbing dream about two women—one of them was Mamma, as she'd looked years ago, and the other one was a younger woman Rose didn't recognize. They were walking away from her, arm in arm, as though they had no idea she could see them—and didn't care. Rose called and called, but neither woman turned around—

"Oh, Mamma," Rose whispered when she realized she'd been dreaming. Her heart was thumping wildly and she felt exhausted after sleeping in the armchair beside her mother's bed. She lit the oil lamp on the nightstand. "Mamma? Are you awake?"

Her mother's eyes were open, staring straight ahead toward the door, but they didn't blink when Rose gripped her bony shoulder. Mamma's breathing was so much slower than it had been yesterday, and in the stillness of the dim room, the rasping sound of each breath was magnified by Rose's desperation.

Rose stared at her mother for a few more of those labored breaths, trying again to rouse her. Mamma's expression was devoid of emotion or pain. She was unresponsive—as the doctor had warned might happen—and Rose curled in on herself to cry for a few minutes. Then she slipped out to the phone shanty at the road.

"Bishop Vernon, it's Rose Raber," she said after his answering machine had prompted her. "If you could come—well, Mamma's about gone and I . . . I don't know what to do. *Denki* so much."

Rose returned to the house with a million worries running through her mind. Soon Gracie would be awake and wanting her breakfast and—how would Rose explain that her *mammi* couldn't talk to her anymore, didn't see her anymore? How could she manage a frantic, frightened five-year-old who would need her constant reassurances for a while, and at the same time deal with her own feelings of grief and confusion? All the frightened moments Rose had known this past week, when she'd thought Mamma was already gone, were merely rehearsals, it seemed.

"Oh, Nathan, if only you were here," Rose whispered as she walked through the unlit front room. "You always knew what to do. Always had a clear head and a keen sense of what came next."

Rose paused in the doorway of the room where Mamma lay. Her breathing was still loud and slow, and the breaths seemed to be coming farther apart. Rose hoped it was a comfort to Mamma to die as she'd wanted—even though it was nerve-racking to Rose. There had been no waiting, no doubts, the day she and Mamma had returned from shopping in Morning Star to discover that the sawmill had caught fire from a saw's sparks. The mill, quite a distance from any neighbor, had burned to the ground with her father and husband trapped beneath a beam that had fallen on them. Their men's deaths had been sudden and harsh, but quick. No lingering, no wondering if she could be doing some little thing to bring final comfort.

Once again, Rose sat in the chair beside Mamma's bed, and then rested against the mattress as she'd done before. The clock on Mamma's dresser chimed three times. It would be hours before the bishop checked his phone messages. Rose didn't want to rustle around in the kitchen, for fear she'd waken Gracie, so she placed a hand over her mother's and allowed herself to drift. . . .

*Chapter 2*

Rose awoke from a doze to realize someone was knocking on the front door. By the time she roused herself, Bishop Vernon Gingerich and his wife, Jerusalem, were entering the front room. Vernon's rosy face, usually lit with a beatific smile, appeared solemn.

"Rose, I'm sorry you're having to deal with your mother's passing alone," the bishop said as he reached for her hands.

Jerusalem hugged Rose hard. "We came as soon as Vernon heard your message," she said. Jerusalem felt warm and stalwart, as though she'd dealt with death enough times that she no longer feared it. "Maybe Gracie would be better off with me today—seeing's how you have no family members close by to keep her until your vigil is finished."

Gratitude filled Rose's heart. Her only remaining relatives lived in Indiana. "That might be best, *jah*. She's still upstairs asleep—"

"I'll get her dressed and tell her what a *gut* time we'll have today," Jerusalem said with a smile. "Don't worry about her, Rose. We have goats and cows and newly hatched chicks and all manner of distractions at our place."

"*Denki* so much," Rose murmured. Vernon had recently remarried, and Jerusalem had been a *maidel* schoolteacher until she'd met him—always ready with a game or a song when kids were around—and Gracie adored her. As the steely-haired woman started up the stairway, Rose glanced at Vernon. "Mamma's in this room, Bishop. She'll be comforted to know you've come."

The bishop hung his black hat on a peg near the door and followed Rose into the back room. He stopped a few feet from the bed to observe Mamma, who lay staring straight ahead, unseeing. Vernon stroked his snow-white beard as the sound of her breathing filled the room. "We can be grateful that your mother's beyond her pain," he said softly. "Her soul has heard God's call and her body is preparing itself so she can go to meet Him. It will all happen in the Lord's *gut* time, and our job now is merely to wait. They say the sense of hearing is the last to go, so let's pray for her, shall we?"

Rose joined Bishop Vernon at the bedside, bowing her head as he took her hand and placed his other hand on her mother's shoulder.

"Dear Lord and Father of us all," he intoned, "we give thanks that You never leave us, and that You are caring for Your daughter Lydia, preparing her a place with You in Heaven. Bless Rose with the strength and wisdom she'll need to wait and watch, and to tend to her burial. We thank You for the *gut* life Lydia lived, and for the promise that she will soon ascend to be with You. We pray these things in Jesus' name. Amen."

Rose let out the breath she'd been holding. Upstairs, she heard Gracie talking excitedly to Jerusalem, and it made her smile.

"Do you want me to stay with you?" Vernon asked. "Some folks get uneasy, being alone with a loved one who's about to die."

The sound of footsteps coming down the upstairs hallway—some of them quick and some slower—determined Rose's reply. "I'll be fine, knowing that Gracie's with you," she said as she started for the doorway. "If you take her with you now, she won't be frightened by her *mammi*'s condition."

Vernon nodded and followed her from the room. Rose put on a bright smile and held out her arms when she saw her daughter bouncing down the stairs, wearing her favorite yellow dress and a fresh white pinafore. Wisps of strawberry-blond hair escaped Gracie's *kapp* and her smile lit her entire face.

"Mamma, we're gonna milk the goats!" Gracie cried as she launched herself toward Rose's arms. "And we gotta count the baby chicks—"

"You'll have the best time ever with Jerusalem and the bishop," Rose said as she held her daughter close. "You can say your alphabet and your numbers—"

"And play games!" Gracie added. "And maybe bake cookies!"

Rose smiled gratefully at Jerusalem as the older woman reached the bottom of the steps. "It'll be a wonderful time—because you'll be a *gut* guest while you're at the bishop's house, *jah*?" Rose asked purposefully.

"*Jah*, Mamma," Gracie said as she wiggled to get down. "We're havin' French toast for breakfast, so we better get goin'!"

Jerusalem chuckled as she took Gracie's hand. "We'll gather some fresh eggs first, and it'll be the best breakfast ever. But you'd better stay sharp at the table, Gracie, because Vernon *loves* French toast and he might try to snatch yours!"

"Nuh-uh!" Gracie exclaimed. At the doorway, she turned to wave to Rose. "Bye, Mamma! Be a *gut* girl while I'm gone!"

"You too, missy," Rose replied. She walked out to the porch with Bishop Vernon, and his gaze expressed his silent wish for her strength and consolation. She watched the buggy take off behind a fine bay mare, waving when she saw Gracie looking out the rig's window.

When the vehicle reached the road, Rose went inside and dropped into the nearest chair. The house was too quiet. The hours would crawl by without the sunshine of Gracie's presence; yet Rose believed she'd done the right thing, letting the little girl go with two dear adults who would keep her busy— and who would answer Gracie's questions about her grandmother's condition in a wise, patient way. When it came to matters of the soul and practicality, nobody was more gracious than Bishop Vernon Gingerich.

After listening to a couple more of Mamma's labored breaths, Rose left the bedroom doorway to brew a pot of strong tea and slather a couple slices of bread with butter and jelly. She returned to Mamma's bedside with her breakfast tray, and turned the armchair slightly so Mamma's eyes wouldn't be fixed upon her while she ate.

Rose poured a cup of tea, muttering wearily when some of it sloshed onto her tray because her hands were shaking. As she took a bite of the buttered bread, a sob escaped her. She drank some tea and sank back into the chair, wondering how long it would be before her mother passed. Already the waiting weighed heavily upon her.

After she'd finished the slices of bread, Rose set aside her tray and turned to check on Mamma. Her mother's face was still frozen in a slack, emotionless expression as her eyes continued to gaze at nothing.

*Or do you see God?* Rose pondered. *Do you see Dat and Nathan, awaiting you in Heaven? Do you realize how much I already miss you, even though you're not yet gone?*

Rose turned again, unnerved by Mamma's unblinking eyes and the sound of her lungs filling with fluid. She desperately needed something to keep her busy. She was tempted to look for the box her mother had mentioned, but she didn't feel strong enough to deal with whatever—or whomever—Mamma had mumbled about last night before she slipped into this coma.

Rose fetched her yarn bag and began crocheting colorful granny squares for an afghan she'd started when Mamma had become bedfast. The repetitive motion, paired with familiar crochet stitches that required no real thought, lulled Rose into a meditative state. It was mindless activity, exactly what she craved after dealing with so many difficult situations these past few days.

When Rose realized she hadn't been paying attention to Mamma's breathing, she turned in her chair. She waited a long time until her mother took another gurgling breath. The clock on the dresser—which Dat had given Mamma as an engagement gift—chimed noon. The morning had somehow slipped by. Rose felt so tired she might have cleaned out all the closets instead of merely crocheting a stack of multicolored squares. She wondered what Gracie was doing. And she was painfully aware that her mother hadn't inhaled for several seconds.

Mamma did breathe again, shallowly. Rose waited, watching for the slight rise and fall of her mother's shoulders—listening for the sound that had tugged at her heartstrings all morning.

Mamma's next breath didn't come.

"Ohhh," Rose murmured as she stuffed her yarn and crochet hook back into her bag. "Oh, Mamma. It's over and
done with now, isn't it?"

Rose gently closed her mother's eyes, and sat down in the
chair again. She knew there were dozens of things she must
do, yet she could only stare into space with tears streaming
down her cheeks.

Rose didn't know how much time had passed before she
was able to go to the kitchen to start a list of things she needed
to do. She called the bishop again, asking him to contact the
undertaker before he and Jerusalem brought Gracie home.

Then Rose waited and prayed.

# Chapter 3

Rose realized it might be a while before Vernon and Jerusalem would bring Gracie home, so she went to Mamma's dresser and opened the bottom drawer. There, beneath darned black stockings, old shoestrings knotted together, and other odds and ends her mother couldn't bear to throw away, Rose found a box—the kind that inexpensive stationery came in. She carried it out to the front room, away from Mamma's presence. When she lifted the box's lid, she saw some letters tied together with a piece of faded blue ribbon.

With shaking fingers, Rose untied the ribbon. The top envelope simply said *To Rose* in the loopy penmanship of a schoolgirl who hadn't quite mastered cursive writing. Rose gingerly removed the letter. The lined paper was from a tablet like Mamma kept in the kitchen for her store lists. The ink was splotchy here and there, probably from a cheap ballpoint pen.

Rose realized she was focusing on these minute details to brace herself for whatever she might learn when she read the words. As she skimmed the first few lines, her chest got so tight she couldn't breathe.

*My Dearest Rose,*
*If you're reading this, it means your mother Lydia*
*has passed on and I am so sorry for your loss. When I*
*gave you to her, you were but two days old, and half of*
*my heart and half of my name—Roseanne—will*
*remain with you when I leave. Please understand that*
*I'm only sixteen, in love but unmarried, and your new*
*parents will give you the stable home I can't provide.*
*Myron and Lydia Fry are dear people who have*
*allowed me to live with them so I can nurse you until*
*you're weaned.*

A strangled sound escaped Rose as she rose from the sofa. She forced herself to suck in some air as her thoughts spun in accelerating spirals. She'd had no idea that she wasn't her parents' biological child. How many times while she was growing up had folks remarked that she was built like her mother and that she had Dat's tan complexion?

Rose paced, overwhelmed by so many unexpected emotions. Anger. Denial. Shock. Betrayal. If Lydia and Myron Fry weren't her birth parents, that meant everyone in their extended families knew about this; yet they'd never once hinted about the real circumstances of her birth. Had her entire life been a lie?

*It was my parents' place to tell me about this. That's why no one else spoke up.*

Rose took a deep, shuddery breath as other uncomfortable thoughts occurred to her. Her birth mother hadn't been married. As the Old Order saw it, Rose had been conceived and born in sin—

*"Do not look for her, daughter. I—I promised her you wouldn't."*

*"Who, Mamma? Who are you talking about?"*

Rose felt so bewildered—so hurt—she wanted to storm into the back bedroom and shout loudly enough to waken Mamma from death. She wanted to demand the whole story from the woman who had kept a vital truth from her all her life.

*But then, so had Dat if he'd wanted to let sleeping dogs lie. And what a lie it was—they could have explained this sometime while they were alive, but no! They've left me to struggle with this discovery alone.*

Rose stared out the window, stunned, grasping for clarity as she gazed at the bright pink-purple blooms of the redbud trees. What about the girl who'd written that letter—Roseanne? How could she give away the baby she'd nurtured inside herself for nine months? Rose couldn't imagine handing newborn Gracie over to anyone—

*If Roseanne had really loved me, wouldn't she have found a way to keep me? And if Mamma—Lydia—had really loved me, couldn't she have told me about this sooner? How am I supposed to handle this news of my birth and Mamma's death all at once?*

Feeling desperately alone and overwhelmed, Rose dropped back onto the couch. She'd opened the box—this can of worms—so there was no closing it now. There was nothing to do but read on, hoping the rest of Roseanne's letters would answer some of the questions that were whirling frantically in her head. Rose reread the first paragraph and then kept doggedly on, determined to make sense of what this letter was telling her.

*I am so in love with your father, Rose! Joel Lapp is*
*a handsome young man with beautiful green eyes,*
*auburn hair, golden skin, and the passion of an artist.*
*He loves me, too, and he begged me to jump the fence*
*with him—he intends to take art classes so he can im-*
*prove his natural talent and become a professional*
*painter. But of course even though we're both in our*
*rumspringa that sort of vocation is forbidden in the*
*Old Order settlement of Clearwater, where we both*
*grew up.*

Rose swallowed hard. Had she gotten her green eyes, red
hair, and skin that tanned easily from Joel Lapp? If so, why
had people said she took after Lydia and Myron—and why
had her parents let her believe them? She'd been a trusting little
girl, delighted when others had said she resembled her mother,
because she and Mamma had always been so close. . . .

Weren't daughters supposed to believe what their parents
told them? Of all the people in God's wide world, parents
were the people children trusted most.

Rose sniffled loudly and decided to keep reading. Lament-
ing the truth her parents hadn't told her wasn't helpful.

*Being an obedient daughter, I reluctantly stayed*
*home when Joel left our neighborhood and our faith. I*
*was naïve, however, trusting in Joel's love—and*
*unaware of the facts of life. When I discovered I was*
*carrying his child—you, Rose—I was at once terrified*
*yet grateful that I had a precious part of Joel growing*
*inside me. My parents didn't see it that way, of course.*

*They sent me away to Aunt Nettie's in New Haven,*
*telling the neighbors I was helping an aging* maidel
*aunt.*

Rose stopped reading. If Roseanne and Joel had grown up
in Clearwater—just up the road from Cedar Creek—and she'd
gone into seclusion at her aunt's in New Haven, Roseanne
hadn't traveled far from her disapproving parents or the
neighbors' curious questions. But maybe Roseanne's parents
had made up a different aunt in a different town so no one
would discover what had really happened to Roseanne.
Maybe parents were more inclined to alter the truth than
Rose had ever imagined.

*Poor Lydia Fry has been bravely fighting her breast*
*cancer after undergoing a double mastectomy. She'd*
*been to a checkup at the New Haven hospital when*
*Aunt Nettie saw her sitting on a curbside bench in*
*front of the grocery store, crying. The two of them*
*struck up a conversation and Aunt Nettie brought*
*Lydia home—arranged for your adoption not an hour*
*after Lydia first laid eyes on you, Rose. Lydia immedi-*
*ately took on a brighter disposition and couldn't thank*
*us enough for answering her fondest prayer, when*
*she'd believed she would never hold a child.*

Rose sighed. She'd never thought of herself as the answer
to Mamma's prayer. Her heart softened a little.

As a child, Rose hadn't questioned her mother's flat chest,
which was somewhat disguised by her loose cape dresses
and aprons. Mamma had always seemed absolutely perfect
to her back then. When Rose had gotten old enough to de-

velop breasts, Mamma explained about the cancer that had robbed her of so many feminine features most women took for granted. The subject was never belabored—not until last fall, when the doctor had confirmed that Mamma's cancer had returned to attack other parts of her body.

When this diagnosis had forced them to think about the cancer again, Rose was surprised that Mamma had considered such a radical procedure as mastectomy years ago, because Old Order Amish believed that a person's health—or illness—was a result of God's will. Rose had been even more surprised to hear that Dat had agreed to the surgery because it offered the only real chance that Mamma would live—and that Mamma's parents, the Borntregers, had paid for the expensive procedures, medications, and postsurgical treatments. They had been relatively well-off, and none of their other children had lived to see their first birthdays, so they'd spared no expense to keep Mamma alive. They had passed on within days of each other a few years ago, so at least their Lydia had survived them.

Rose pulled herself out of her musings to continue reading.

*I can't tell you what a blessing it has been to stay with Lydia and Myron so I could nurse you—so Lydia and I could share the first incredible eight months of your life, dear daughter. You have no idea what a gift from God you are to both of us. It will sadden me greatly to leave you behind—I'll have a huge hole where my heart has been—but I know you'll have a secure, happy life with two generous, compassionate parents who already love you as though you are their own. From now on, my name will be Anne, for I will have left my Rose behind.*

Rose let out a sob. Her birth mother's loopy handwriting resembled a young girl's, but there was no doubt about it: Roseanne's message packed an eloquent, emotional punch. It would require a lot of fortitude to read Anne's other letters, if they were anything like this one.

> *I have to go now, but I will write again, dear Rose. Never doubt that I will think of you every single day of my life, hoping you are well and happy—hoping you know how much I will always love you.*
> *Your mother,*
> *Anne*

Feeling wrung out, yet too intrigued to stop reading, Rose slipped the first letter back into its envelope and opened the next one. Surely her *dat* had been unaware of the letters his guest of eight months had left behind, or he would've disposed of them—and it surprised her that Mamma had secretly kept them, too.

When Rose unfolded the single page, she forgot everything else. This page was a full-sized piece of white paper, and the head-and-shoulders watercolor of a young brown-haired Amish girl made her gape. The facial features were so much like her own—and when Rose looked on the back of the page, she found a brief message:

> *This is a portrait of me that Joel did before he went off to art school. I thought you'd like to have it.*

With shaking fingers, Rose held the picture closer to the lamp to study it. Such a happy light shone in her birth mother's green eyes, and freckles danced across her pale, slender nose. Joel Lapp's talent was evident in every line and brushstroke. He had rendered Roseanne with tendrils of brown hair escaping her white *kapp*, looking so lifelike that she appeared ready to speak. Roseanne gazed at it for several moments, discovering herself in this likeness of her birth mother—in the cheekbones, nose, a facial shape that resembled her own.

Rose realized she would have to hide these letters carefully so her daughter wouldn't discover them. She'd been hard-pressed to explain the changes in Mammi's body and the loss of her hair to five-year-old Gracie, so delving into this bewildering issue of birth mothers and adoption was something Rose hoped to avoid for a while. She and Gracie had enough other trials and tribulations to muddle through.

Aware that her little daughter might arrive at any time with the Gingeriches, Rose reached for the last envelope in the box. It had been postmarked twenty years ago in Clearwater, addressed to Mamma, and the letter was written on another lined sheet of tablet paper. The handwriting appeared tighter and more mature.

*Dearest Rose,*

*I have met a fine man and am delighted that he's courting me! Saul Hartzler is a pillar of his church, a deacon. He's giving me a chance at a new life and a new family, so I hope you'll understand why this will be my last letter to you, dear daughter. By the time you're reading this, you'll be old enough to understand why I must ask you—must insist—that you not seek me out or try to find me. Saul's a wonderful fellow, but he has no idea that I have borne another man's child.*

"*Jah*, he'd be shocked," Rose muttered. "I know the feeling."

> *While I stayed at your parents' home, Lydia and I became close friends who would do anything for each other—so I know she has honored my request not to tell you about me until she passed away. The way I see it, your mother gave both you and me a chance at a normal life without the shame our faith would've heaped upon us because I had you out of wedlock. Please don't think too harshly of me for giving you up—or of your dear mother for not telling you about this while she was alive. We were both doing the best we could at the time.*
>
> *Live in love and peace, as I hope to do. You'll be in my prayers every day, Rose, and I will love you forever.*
> *Your mother,*
> *Anne*

Rose stuffed the letters and the painted portrait back into the stationery box and hurried upstairs to her room. As she stashed the box on the closet shelf above her dresses, where Gracie wouldn't find it, her thoughts spiraled tightly, angrily. Her birth mother had had no idea about the impact this news would have on Rose, no matter how honorable her intentions had been when she wrote those letters—and when she swore Mamma to secrecy about the adoption.

"Don't think too harshly of you, indeed," Rose muttered. She felt like a teakettle on a high flame, ready to boil over and whistle shrilly with its buildup of steam—

"*. . . or of your dear mother for not telling you about this while she was alive. We were both doing the best we could at the time.*"

Rose blinked. Her breath caught and then she began to cry again. How could she be so angry with Roseanne—her real mother—and yet succumb to her plea for compassion? How had Roseanne known exactly what to say in her letters, to make Rose react so vehemently one moment and then burst into tears the next? Mamma had fallen so ill these last couple of weeks—had battled her cancer with everything she'd had—so how could Rose even think of staying mad at her?

"I'm such a mess," Rose murmured as she gazed around the room she'd had when she was growing up. Everything looked the same as when she'd lived here at home—the same quilt covered the twin bed, the same furniture sat in the same places, the same sun-streaked curtains hung at the window. In the haven of this modest room, Rose had matured over the years and had discovered the young woman she was meant to become—yet, in truth, she'd had no idea who she really was.

Would she now reexamine every relationship, every family event, looking for hints that others had wanted to take her aside and tell her the truth? Had anyone ever considered how vulnerable and shocked poor Rose would feel if she found out she wasn't Lydia and Myron Fry's daughter—especially after they could no longer answer to her?

When news of Lydia Fry's death got around, would anyone try to tell Rose about the circumstances of her birth? Most of the families she knew had lived in Cedar Creek for generations, so they surely had to know she was adopted.

*Pull yourself together,* Rose thought when she saw Bishop Vernon's buggy pulling into the lane. *You can only deal with one hard truth at a time—and you'll need all your strength to explain to Gracie why that hearse coming in behind the buggy will be taking her* mammi's *body—*

Rose sucked in her breath. Vernon Gingerich had been the

bishop of the Cedar Creek district since before she'd been born. When Mamma's cancer had returned last fall, he'd talked with her about when she'd had cancer as a young woman—so he had to know Rose wasn't her biological child. He'd probably even met Roseanne when she'd lived with Mamma and Dat—and perhaps knew where she'd gone—

*Don't even think about that. She's Anne Hartzler now and she wants nothing to do with you. She told you to stay away.*

## Chapter 4

Rose went downstairs, steeling herself for the difficult sight of the undertaker taking Mamma's body away. Gracie's questions and tears would make the moment even more difficult. As she stepped out onto the front porch, Vernon's rig pulled into the yard and stopped near the side of the house. The hearse remained in the lane, however, and the driver stayed inside it.

Gracie hopped from the buggy and bounded over to Rose, her face set with childlike purpose as she grabbed her mother's hand. "We're gonna show 'Rusalem the garden we planted," she insisted. "She wants to see if maybe the peas and lettuce and stuff have sprouted!"

Rose sensed she shouldn't protest, because she noticed the same purposeful smile on Jerusalem's face as the older woman started toward the garden plot. Vernon was making his way toward the house, removing his hat.

"We've made the arrangements," he said gently. "If you'll run along with Gracie, Parker and I can handle this part."

Gratitude filled Rose's heart as she waved to the undertaker, doing as Vernon suggested. Parker Conrad ran the funeral home in Morning Star, and he had overseen the preparations for Dat's and Nathan's funeral last fall. Once Mamma's body was prepared, Rose would dress her in new white burial clothing, along with the apron Mamma had worn at her wedding. The visitation and funeral would be held here at the house. Rose tried not to think of all the cleaning that needed to be done—not to mention sewing Mamma's burial dress—as she scurried to keep up with Gracie's eager jog.

"How was your morning with Jerusalem and Vernon?" Rose asked as she managed a smile for the bishop's wife. "I hope you were a *gut* little guest?"

"The best company we could've asked for," Jerusalem replied. "We gathered the eggs, and Gracie counted the new chicks in the barn—"

"Thirty-eight!" Gracie exclaimed.

"—and then we made French toast—"

"And I ate two whole pieces!" Gracie crowed. "With maple surple and fried apples."

Jerusalem stopped at the edge of the tilled garden spot, and when she held out her hand, Gracie raced over to grab it. "And we played hide-and-seek with Vernon, too, didn't we, dear?"

"*Jah,* but I found him every time!" Gracie replied. "He thought I wouldn't see him under that tarp, but his big butt was stickin' out!"

"Gracie," Rose chided. "This is our bishop you're talking about. Be polite."

Jerusalem chuckled. "She speaks the truth. Hiding isn't Vernon's best talent, I'm afraid. But he was a *gut* sport about it when Gracie found him right off."

"See, 'Rusalem?" the little girl said, pointing to the mounded rows in the garden. "We put the lettuce on this end, and the peas down this way. Mamma said we could plant an extra-long row of those, coz they're my favorite."

"Nothing's better than a bowl of creamed peas with new potatoes," Jerusalem mused aloud. "You might see the little green shoots sprouting up by next week, warm as it's been."

Gracie turned to gaze up at Rose. Was it her imagination, after studying the painting of Roseanne, or did Gracie's strawberry-blond hair look redder today?

"Know what, Mamma? Mammi went to Heaven today," the little girl said matter-of-factly. "She's with Jesus and Dat and Dawdi now. And when we see her in that—that box thing . . ."

"Her coffin," Jerusalem said gently.

"*Jah,* her coffin," Gracie continued, "she won't be able to see us or talk to us coz she's not in her body anymore. And she's not sick anymore coz she's in Heaven."

Rose blinked back tears. She'd been so concerned about how to discuss these matters, yet her child had spelled it out for her instead. "You're exactly right, Gracie," she said softly. "I'm glad Jerusalem and Bishop Vernon explained that to you."

"I'll call the neighbor ladies and we'll be here tomorrow morning to help you clean," Jerusalem said. "We're all in this together, Rose. Your mother was well-loved, and she's left you and Gracie in our care."

When Jerusalem stepped toward her, Rose entered her embrace gratefully. As she cried against Jerusalem's sturdy shoulder, she wished this compassionate woman had been around when Mamma and Roseanne were together—but an insistent patting against Rose's thigh pulled her out of those thoughts.

When she reached down, Gracie wrapped her little arms around Rose's neck. Rose held her daughter close, both of them

enveloped in Jerusalem's hug. It was a sweet moment of re-
lease and relief. Behind them, an engine started. Rose closed
her eyes, pressing her cheek against Gracie's until she no
longer heard the crunch of gravel beneath the hearse's tires.
When she sensed Vernon was approaching the garden, Rose
eased away from Jerusalem's arms.

"I would invite you in for a bite of something," Rose said
apologetically, "but I don't know what it would be."

"Cookies, that's what!" Gracie said as she wriggled down
to the ground. "We made a big pan of cherry pie bars, and
chocolate chip cookies, too!"

"My word, you were busy bees this morning," Rose said
as her daughter took off toward the bishop's rig.

Vernon smiled and squeezed her shoulder. "Gracie's a busy
girl. I suspect she'll keep you from getting too depressed as
you adjust to your mother's passing."

"She has a soul made of sunshine and a mind as sharp as a
tack," Jerusalem remarked as they started toward the house.
"She'll be *gut* company, *jah,* but if you need some quiet time,
don't hesitate to give me a ring, Rose."

"You've already been so much help. *Denki* for all you've
done," Rose said. She crossed the porch and held the door
open for Vernon and his wife—and then for Gracie, who was
carrying a lidded pan chock-full of goodies. After Rose put a
fresh percolator of coffee on the stove to boil, she joined the
others at the kitchen table, where Jerusalem was pouring
glasses of milk.

"Here, Mamma," Gracie said, placing two cookies in front
of Rose. "I put *lots* of chips in these, just for you."

Rose had to chuckle. "*Jah,* you sure did. I think these are
mostly chocolate chips and nuts held together by a bit of
dough."

"Chocolate's *gut* for the soul—and they say all those antioxidants make it a health food, too," Jerusalem teased.

When Rose bit into her cookie, the chips were still soft enough to ooze over her tongue. A sip of cold milk soothed her, too. Except for the gurgling of the percolator, the kitchen was quiet as the four of them savored their treats.

"This being Monday," Vernon said quietly, "I've set your mother's funeral for Thursday. If you'll give us a list, we'll call all the out-of-town folks that need contacting. Parker will have her ready for you to dress tomorrow afternoon."

Rose's mind filled with all manner of details she needed to see to in a very short time. "I—I hope I'll be able to afford his fee, and the coffin and—"

"I'll take care of those matters, Rose," the bishop assured her. "Your *mamm* mentioned to me that she suspected her chemo and medications were running through your money, now that your menfolk aren't providing an income. Our district's aid fund will cover any expenses you have until you decide where to go . . . who will look after you."

"Mamma, we're stayin' right here, ain't so?" Gracie piped up with a worried frown. "This is our home now, coz you said so—and coz we've got garden growin'!"

Rose suddenly felt weary to the bone, and the thought of becoming dependent upon any of the men in Nathan's faraway family tied her stomach in a knot. With a napkin, she dabbed at a blob of chocolate in the corner of Gracie's mouth.

"*Jah*, this is home, sweetie," Rose stated. She held the bishop's gaze as best she could. "Nathan's family—his *dat* and older brothers—would have a hard time providing for Gracie and me. They made some large investments in what turned out to be a swindle, and they haven't recovered," she explained. "And you might recall that Dat's family resented his marrying a Missouri girl—accused him of leaving Indiana for the Borntreger family's money. So we've not heard from them in years."

"That's how your *dat* told it." Vernon reached for a cherry pie bar. "As I recall, Lydia's folks did quite well with her *dat*'s furniture factory before they passed on."

"*Jah,* and Mamma inherited a nice chunk of money because she was their only surviving child," Rose replied softly. "But we've gone through it. We kept hoping the chemo would kill off the cancer this time, like it did when she was younger."

"It'll all work out in God's *gut* time," Jerusalem said, fetching the percolator from the stove. "You've got a lot on your plate these next several weeks, Rose. We'll not let you girls fall through the cracks."

"*Denki,*" Rose murmured gratefully.

Jerusalem nodded as she poured their coffee. "I spent the first several years of my adult life managing my own affairs—my sister, Nazareth, and I were schoolteachers," she added with a wink, "so I know you'll find a way to get by, Rose. You'll figure it out."

Rose sipped her coffee, smiling. She suspected Jerusalem's independent streak was sometimes a challenge to Vernon's Old Order mind-set, yet he smiled indulgently at her.

"God's will be done," he said before taking a big bite of his cherry pie bar.

*And that's how it'll be,* Rose thought. *If I believe God will see me through, He will.*

# Chapter 5

After the Gingeriches left, Rose braced herself to enter the downstairs bedroom so she could tidy it. As she stepped through the door, she was grateful that either Vernon or Parker had made up the bed after they'd removed her mother's body.

Behind her, Gracie sighed loudly. "So Mammi really is gone? Did she want to be in Heaven more than she wanted to stay with us?"

Rose reached for her little girl. "Oh, no, sweet pea, never think that your *mammi* wanted to leave us," she insisted as she lifted Gracie into her arms. "But when the cancer made her stop breathing this morning, she went to a better place, where she won't be sick anymore. I like to think she's watching over us, looking down from Heaven."

Gracie gazed at the ceiling as though seeking a sign that this was true.

Rose pondered how parents made up little feel-better stories to protect their children from truths they were too young to understand. She wanted to believe Lydia Fry's soul had ascended to Heaven, but how were they to know, really? It was a matter of faith—words spoken from one generation to the next as folks they loved passed on.

Rose realized she might cave in to a grief that would render her helpless—useless—unless she got out of this room. It was tidy enough to suit her, anyway, so she set Gracie on the floor. "Let's go to the mercantile. I need to sew Mammi's burial dress today, because tomorrow we'll have lots of ladies here helping us clean the house. We're going to be very busy these next few days."

Gracie brightened and skipped ahead of Rose. "Can we maybe get fabric for a new dress for *me* at the mercantile, Mamma? Or maybe some chalk and a chalkboard?" she asked eagerly. "Me and 'Rusalem—"

"Jerusalem and I," Rose corrected gently.

"—played school and it was fun, writin' my letters and numbers on her chalkboard. Can we, Mamma? Please?"

Once again, Rose was amazed at how many ways Jerusalem and Vernon had entertained her daughter this morning—and what a sight it was, when Gracie's face lit up with her love of learning. "We'll see what we can find," she replied. She didn't often give in to Gracie's yearnings, because she was watching their money, but her daughter asked for so few things.

A short while later, the two of them were strolling down the unpaved road toward the Cedar Creek Mercantile, carrying a few canvas totes for their purchases. "I like to walk to town, Mamma," Gracie said. "It's a lot simpler than hitchin' up the horse."

"Especially when we're only going after a few items," Rose remarked.

As the county road came into view, along with the two-story mercantile, Rose realized she would have to break the news of her mother's death when she entered the store. Preacher Sam Lambright, the proprietor, would need to know about the Thursday service because he and Vernon and their other preacher, Abe Nissley, would be preaching.

Rose's heart clutched. Now that she'd left the haven of their home, she had to deal with her loss in public—and she hoped she wouldn't cause a commotion by bursting into tears. She was already tired of crying, and her grieving had just begun.

Gracie jogged toward the blacktop road, stopping at its edge. "C'mon, Mamma! We *love* the mercantile—and maybe Sam'll give me a stick of candy!"

Rose caught up, grasping Gracie's hand. "Look both ways," she instructed. "We don't see any cars, so now we can go. And don't pester Preacher Sam for candy, all right? It's supposed to be a gift he gives you."

"Preacher Sam thinks I'm special, Mamma. He likes my smile—he told me so."

Rose bit back a laugh. It amazed her that Gracie had already learned how to charm her way into other folks' favor. As she opened the mercantile door, Rose was glad the parking lot was almost empty and that the aisles in the dim store weren't crowded with folks who'd want to know the particulars of Mamma's death. The jangle of the bell above the door made the man at the front counter look up.

"Rose and Gracie, it's *gut* to see you. I'm so sorry about your *mamm*'s passing." Sam Lambright smiled sadly at them from behind the checkout counter. "Vernon stopped by and told us about the service on Thursday—and to make things easier for you, my *mamm* has offered to set up tables in her greenhouse and host the lunch afterward."

Rose's eyes widened. She hadn't even *thought* about the meal that would follow the funeral. "But Treva's in her busiest time of the year, selling bedding plants and garden—"

"She and Barbara and Abby are already calling gals, organizing the food," Sam insisted with a smile. "Won't take us long to set up tables—we've done it for weddings and other funerals, after all. And it's a lot handier for folks to come here, just up the hill from the cemetery, after the graveside service instead of having to go back down the road to your place again."

Relief washed over her. "Sam, that would be a wonderful gift," Rose said. "I came to get fabric for Mamma's burial dress today, because I don't know when else I'll have time to sew it. We're cleaning tomorrow and—"

Sam leaned his elbows on the counter, silencing Rose with his patient gaze. "To everything there's a season," he reminded her, "and somehow—with the help of God and our friends—everything gets done, Rose. It's our time to give and yours to receive."

Rose managed a smile. "*Denki,* Sam. I'll get that fabric and we'll head back home—"

"I found the chalk, Mamma!" Gracie hurried down the center aisle of the store, pointing excitedly behind her. "And there's cute little chalkboards, too—just like 'Rusalem's! We're gonna play school, Sam!"

Sam laughed as he came out from behind the counter. "I bet you're already pretty *gut* at learning, too, Gracie. Will you be old enough to go to school this fall?"

"*Jah!* I'm ready *now,*" Gracie insisted. "But Mamma says I have to be six."

"And mammas make the rules, *jah?* My *mamm* still tells me what to do," the storekeeper remarked. He led Rose to the rear of the store, where the shelves were filled with bolts of colorful fabrics for sewing and quilting. "Just got in a new bolt of white poly-cotton. Most gals choose that because you don't have to iron it—just hang the dress on a hanger after you wash it."

"I'm all for saving time and effort," Rose agreed.

Gracie was tugging at Rose's skirt, gazing up with wide green eyes—*Eyes like Roseanne's?* she wondered. It was no time to be comparing her daughter's looks to the painting of her birth mother, but such details would probably jump out at her now that she'd read Roseanne's letters. "While you're cutting me three yards of the white fabric, Gracie and I will pick out something for a little summer dress," Rose told Sam.

Gracie jogged down the aisle, her shoes beating a quick, light tattoo on the wooden floor. "This blue is pretty," she said, grasping the loose end of the bolt's fabric. "It's like the summertime sky."

Rose agreed, yet she wondered if she was giving in to Gracie's demands too quickly. Once the funeral was over and life settled into place again, they couldn't spend money for anything other than necessities—and she had to reestablish the difference between *want* and *need*.

Sam smiled at Rose as she laid the bolt of blue fabric on the cutting table. "Why don't you ladies choose your chalk and chalkboard while I finish cutting this?" he suggested as he deftly guided the shears through the white fabric, along the cutting trough. He lowered his voice as Gracie took off to find them. "They're my gift to you—something to keep her occupied while you prepare for the funeral and need quiet time afterward."

Rose's mouth dropped open. "Sam, I can't accept—I don't need—"

"I want to do this for you, dear," he insisted. "Gracie's blessed with a bright mind and I want to encourage her learning—not to mention help you out. You've shouldered quite a load since last summer, Rose."

Rose's head drooped. "*Denki* again, Sam," she mumbled. "I'm ever so grateful."

*You have no idea about the new load I've taken on,* she thought as she went down the aisle to help Gracie. Her daughter was pointing to a small charcoal-colored board.

"This one, Mamma," Gracie said. "And see? This box has white chalk and colors. I can write my letters and draw pretty pictures, too!"

"That will be fun," Rose said as they returned to the front of the store. Had her daughter perhaps inherited an artistic flair from Joel Lapp? It was another of those questions that would probably go unanswered.

As she stood at the counter while Sam rang up her purchases, Rose felt overwhelmed by his kindness—as well as the many things she needed to accomplish before Thursday. The secret about who she really was weighed heavily on her, too—but this was no time to ask Sam what he knew about Roseanne staying with Dat and Mamma for the first eight months of her life.

After Rose paid Sam, she divided their purchases among the tote bags, allowing Gracie to carry the one that held her blue fabric and the box of chalk. When Sam handed a stick of pink-and-green-striped candy over the counter, Rose envied her little girl's delight. Would such simple pleasures ever make her smile again? Would she ever feel so overjoyed that she couldn't help squealing?

"*Denki*, Preacher Sam!" Gracie exclaimed. "I'm glad you're my friend."

"I'm glad, too," the storekeeper replied. "You girls be careful walking home. Cars sometimes come around the bend too fast."

Rose nodded, already thinking ahead to the cutting and sewing she would do this evening. She wondered if she should have bought some cheese and lunch meat—it seemed her head didn't hold nearly as much necessary information these days as it once did. She glanced at Gracie, who had slung her tote over her shoulder so she could unwrap her candy stick.

"Come on, sweetie," Rose urged as she strode toward the door. "I'll help you with your candy when we're—*Ach!*"

The door burst inward and a tall fellow stepped inside just as Rose was trying to go out. Her totes flew every which way, sending the little chalkboard and the white fabric to the floor and knocking Gracie's candy from her hand.

"I'm sorry," the man said as he quickly stooped to pick up the totes and their contents. "I should've been paying attention—"

"I wasn't looking where I was going," Rose insisted, mortified that she felt like bursting into tears. Her emotions went on a roller-coaster ride as she numbly watched the fellow refold the white fabric for Mamma's dress. He put the blackboard back in the other tote and handed them both to her.

"What can I do to make up for running into you?" he asked earnestly. "I'm really sorry."

"It's all right. No harm done." Rose glanced away shyly. Then she saw the stricken expression on Gracie's face, and her quivering lower lip.

"Sweetie, it's okay," Rose said as she reached for her little girl. "We'll get you another stick of candy."

"No, *I* will get you another stick," the man insisted as he picked the pieces of pink-and-green candy from the floor. "Is watermelon your favorite? Or shall I lift you up to the counter so you can choose your own?"

Gracie nodded hesitantly, wide-eyed as the man crouched in front of her.

"My name's Matthias," he said gently. "I'm really sorry I knocked all your stuff—and your candy—to the floor. Can I be your friend, anyway?"

Gracie handed her tote to Rose. Then she nodded at the man again.

"Will you tell me your name, honey?" Matthias asked.

When he opened his arms, Gracie stepped into them, smiling as he hefted her up against his broad shoulder. "Gracie," she said sweetly. "And Mamma's name is Rose."

Rose felt her face turning three shades of red when Matthias gazed at her. He was probably six feet tall, broader than Nathan had been, with a brown beard and brown hair and laugh lines fanning out around his hazel eyes. It was nice, yet a bit alarming, that her daughter already seemed so comfortable with this stranger. Gracie wiggled happily as he walked to the candy display on the counter.

Sam was watching them as though plans might be forming in his mind. "Matthias Wagler has a harness shop in Willow Ridge," he told Rose. "He stops in every now and again for supplies. If I were to choose anybody for you and Gracie to run into, it would be Matthias."

Rose's cheeks burned. What on earth did Sam mean, making such a remark? In her embarrassment, she couldn't get Gracie out of the store fast enough. Not only was her daughter delighted to be sucking on a fresh watermelon stick, she clutched four other flavors in her little hand as they stepped out into the bright sunshine.

"Matthias is nice," Gracie said as they strode toward the road.

"*Jah,* whatever," Rose muttered. She looked both directions for traffic.

"He likes you, Mamma," Gracie prattled on. "I think he likes everybody—like Jesus does! Matthias looks just like the picture of Jesus in my Bible storybook."

Rose stopped in the middle of the road to stare at her daughter. Where did Gracie come up with such wild ideas? "Let's get home," she insisted, walking faster. She'd never seen Matthias Wagler before, and she didn't care if she ever saw him again.

# Chapter 6

Matthias caught his breath, noting how the sweet fragrance of watermelon candy lingered in the air. He was glad the store was quiet, so nobody except Sam Lambright had witnessed his run-in with that poor, startled woman. "So who was that?" he asked Sam. "Does she always look like a deer caught in somebody's headlights?"

A smile softened the storekeeper's face. "Rose Raber lost her mother early this morning. That white fabric was for the burial clothing she's going home to sew."

"Oh, no," Matthias said with a sigh. "I chose a lousy time to upset her, but I couldn't help noticing—"

"Rose lost her husband and her *dat* last summer. Their sawmill burned down with the two of them trapped inside it," Sam continued.

"—that she's a redhead who's not pale and freckled." Matthias blinked as Sam's words sank in. "*Jah*, I remember hearing about that nasty fire. So little Gracie and Rose have no men around, and now Rose's *mamm* has passed as well? Wow. That's really sad."

"The funeral's Thursday. We'll be hosting the lunch at my

*mamm*'s greenhouse after the service," Sam said, slipping his thumbs beneath his suspenders. "Rose has never been one to seek sympathy, but, *jah,* she's in a bad way. I don't think it's hit her yet—how difficult things might get as she's raising little Gracie alone."

"What can I do for her?" Matthias asked earnestly. "I asked Rose, but I got no answer." He had no intention of pestering Rose for a date—*And where did that thought come from? I haven't gone on a date since Sadie died*—but he felt bad about running into her.

He waited patiently as Sam considered his question. Matthias didn't know the storekeeper very well—he only came to the Cedar Creek Mercantile because Willow Ridge had no such store where he could buy supplies for his shop.

"What with no brothers or uncles nearby," Sam said softly, "Rose doesn't have anyone to dig her mother's grave—although the funeral home would take care of that detail if—"

"Nope, that's exactly what I'll do," Matthias declared. "I'll buy a shovel while I'm here, and I'll let the undertaker know that task is covered."

"I'll call Parker right now while you do your shopping," Sam said with an approving nod. "I need to chat with him, anyway."

Matthias smiled, recalling the news he hadn't yet shared. "Take your time, Sam. I've got a long shopping list today," he said as he slipped the piece of paper from his pocket. "I'm relocating my harness shop—and myself—to Morning Star. Just found a little place on the outskirts of town, and I'll be moving there soon."

Sam's eyebrows rose. "That's quite a shift, after living in Willow Ridge all your life. What brought this on?"

Matthias shrugged. He was still getting used to the idea of

this major change. "When my brother Adam married, his new wife moved into our place with her five younger siblings, and the house got a little crowded—plus a lot noisier," he added with a chuckle. "And now Annie Mae's had twins—"

"So a place of your own sounds like a fine idea, I bet," Sam said. "He's a *gut* man, your brother, taking responsibility for all those kids."

"Adam's the best," Matthias agreed. "And Morning Star's a fine town—has more businesses, Plain and English alike, so my harness shop should do even better there than it's done in Willow Ridge."

"Change is a *gut* thing sometimes," Sam agreed as he stepped from behind the counter. He gazed at Matthias for a moment. "Do I remember correctly that you lost your wife a while back? Maybe Morning Star will offer you more opportunities to meet somebody special."

Matthias sobered. "My Sadie's been gone a little more than three years," he murmured. "I like to think she knows I'm moving—and that she'll believe I'm moving forward now as well."

"You're young yet. It'd be a shame if you lived alone much longer, Matthias," Sam said as he headed for the phone shanty "I'll call Parker and be back in a few."

As Matthias grabbed a shopping cart, he thought Sam Lambright was taking an intense interest in his personal life. Was it because Sam was a preacher, who advocated marriage for all adults? Or was he watching out for Rose Raber, thinking of her future?

Matthias shook his head at this notion. Rose was attractive and little Gracie was a charmer, for sure, but he had to remain focused on moving to his new home and setting up his new shop.

*The baby Sadie was carrying would've been nearly three by now . . . a bit younger than Gracie. We wanted that child with all our hearts.*

Matthias pushed his cart toward the back of the store, where the hardware and tools were. He hadn't thought lately about Sadie and their unborn child—considered it a blessing that he'd finally emerged from the heavy fog of grief, which had enveloped him for so long. Meeting Rose seemed to be kicking some memories loose.

Hundreds of times he'd chided himself for not being home when his wife had succumbed to an asthma attack. Afterward, the doctor had told him Sadie had probably gotten morning sick after Matthias had left on an errand, and then her asthma had flared up and she'd suffocated on her vomit. Nowadays Matthias could believe her death wasn't his fault, but the grief—Sadie's absence from his life—still haunted him on nights when he couldn't sleep.

Matthias focused on his shopping list. He stuck a sturdy spade and a blue tarp in his cart. A few aisles over, he found sandpaper, Spackle, putty, and white latex paint—all of which would come in handy when he moved into the house he'd bought in Morning Star. The older folks who'd been living there couldn't maintain the place, so a lot of windows and walls needed repair before he painted all the rooms. He was glad his brother had offered to help with some of these tasks. Adam ran a home-remodeling business—and had some tools and skills Matthias was lacking.

The jingling of the bell above the door, along with the sound of voices, told Matthias that other folks were entering the store. He quickly put a new mailbox in his cart, along with a sturdy wooden post to support it. He still had a few items on his list, but his cart was full so he pushed it up to the front to check out. Two young blondes—he thought they might be Sam's daughters—nodded at him and disappeared into the workroom behind the front counter, where Sam was resuming his place.

"My word, Matthias, you've got your work cut out for you," the storekeeper remarked as he assessed the contents of the cart. "And on that same subject, Parker Conrad sends his thanks for your digging Lydia Fry's grave."

"Where's she to be buried?" Matthias asked as he began placing his smaller items on the counter. "In the cemetery right down the hill from here?"

"*Jah*, it's right alongside the pasture where the sheep are grazing," Sam explained as he rang up the putty and the Spackle. "Take the second dirt road into the cemetery and along the fence, just past the biggest oak tree, you'll find where Myron Fry's buried—that's Rose's *dat*. Her husband, Nathan, is on one side of him, and we'll bury Lydia on Myron's other side."

"Should be easy enough to spot." Matthias held up the mailbox so Sam could see its price. "Might as well tackle that job while I'm here in town. I've posted a sign on my shop door in Willow Ridge about being away today, so folks won't be expecting me."

"You'll be doing Rose a real favor. Not trying to play matchmaker, you understand," the storekeeper said, "but you could do a lot worse than Rose Raber. *Gut* solid woman. Devoted to her little girl, her parents—and to her Nathan when he was alive."

Matthias refrained from rolling his eyes at Sam's obvious ploy to fix him up. "Rose will probably go to live with a brother or an uncle, if she's got no husband to support her."

"Rose is an only child. Her *dat*'s family lives in Indiana, and her *mamm*'s family is gone," Sam explained. "When

Nathan and Myron died, Rose sold her husband's place and moved back home with Lydia—and Lydia's chemo and other treatments have surely eaten into their savings. Not trying to make you feel sorry for Rose—nor will she appreciate your pity," Sam added emphatically. "I'm giving you this information so you can sift through it."

"Food for thought," Matthias said. He was glad to be paying for his items, because other folks were entering the store—and he didn't want Sam discussing his personal life in front of strangers.

As Matthias wheeled his cart outside and loaded his purchases in his wagon, he reminded himself that Rose wasn't his immediate concern. He was simply going to dig her mother's grave, and then he'd head back to Willow Ridge. As he prepared to move to Morning Star, he felt his life was too busy these days to even think about dating.

Matthias vaulted up into the wagon seat and clucked to Ed, his gelding. It only took a couple of minutes to reach the Cedar Creek Cemetery. When he spotted the big oak tree, Matthias drove along the dirt path, past rows of identical cream-colored round-shouldered headstones. He parked in the ancient tree's shade, unhitched Ed, and tethered the horse so he could graze.

Matthias grabbed the spade. After he confirmed the names on Nathan Raber and Myron Fry's stones, he paced off a space that would accommodate a plain pine coffin, marking boundaries in the grass with his spade. He spread the blue tarp on the ground beside the grave.

As he began to dig, Matthias was grateful that the earth was soft from recent rains and that the oak tree shaded him. After he'd cleared away the rectangle of grass and the first layer of dirt, the digging became grunt work. . . . His hands and arms took over and his mind wandered. The grave got deeper and the dirt pile on the tarp got higher. He thought back to when he and Adam had buried their parents, and to the times he'd dug graves for other folks as a favor to their families.

When Rose Raber's face came to mind, Matthias couldn't help smiling—and recalling Gracie's little arm around his neck as she chose sticks of candy. Now that he was an uncle to Adam and Annie Mae's twins, as well as his sister-in-law's little siblings, Matthias was used to settling squabbles and wiping tears, singing songs and telling stories. It had been a real pleasure to gaze into Gracie's wide green eyes and to see the freckles sprinkled across her nose as she sized him up—and decided he was worthy of her trust and could be her friend.

Matthias was hip-deep in the grave when a voice behind him brought him out of his thoughts.

"Hey there, Matthias! Dat thought you might like a cold drink and a snack."

Matthias flashed a grateful smile as the two young ladies he'd seen at the mercantile approached him. The older one carried a pitcher of lemonade and her sister held a plate of goodies. They wore matching lavender dresses and their smiles resembled Sam's.

"Now that you mention it, I could use a break." Matthias stuck his spade into the loose dirt and levered himself out of the grave. "You're Sam's daughters, *jah?*"

"I'm Gail and this is Ruthie," the older girl said with a nod. She appeared to be in her late teens, while her sister was considerably younger. "We heard Dat talking to you about Rose Raber, and about how you're helping her out—"

"So we took a break from filling bags in the back room," Ruthie continued, "because visiting with you sounded like a lot more fun than working."

"Ruthie!" Gail muttered, elbowing her sister.

The younger girl handed Matthias her plate, which was filled with cinnamon rolls and chocolate chip cookies. "It's true," Ruthie insisted. "Where would *you* rather be on an April day, Matthias? Out in the sunshine, or cooped up in a storeroom full of barrels and boxes, scooping macaroni into plastic bags?"

Matthias laughed as he accepted a glass of lemonade from Gail. "Can't say as I'd be much *gut* at scooping macaroni—"

"But you're a *gut* fellow to be helping Rose Raber," Ruthie put in, gazing directly into his eyes. "Bishop Vernon's always telling us we're to be the hands and feet of Jesus here on earth. I'd say you're His muscle and backbone—and His kind heart."

Matthias swallowed his lemonade carefully. "That's a very nice thing to say, Ruthie."

The young blonde nodded emphatically. "I'll be sure Rose knows it was *you* who dug her *mamm*'s grave, too," she said. "Rose doesn't like to be beholden to anyone, so I'll bet she offers to cook you a nice supper in exchange for—"

"Ruthie, stop!" Gail whispered in exasperation. "You're taking this too far."

Matthias glanced away, aware that his face was probably red—and that Ruthie would know he wasn't flushed from digging the grave. He had a feeling that by Thursday's funeral, everyone in Cedar Creek would think he was chasing after Rose Raber. "I appreciate your kind words, Ruthie," he said, "but after I ran into Rose and knocked the bags out of her hands, I suspect she'll be steering clear of me—and that's all right. You really don't need to match us up."

"*Jah*, you're embarrassing me as much as you are poor Matthias. Let's get back to work, Ruthie." Gail smiled apologetically at him. "You can bring the dishes to the store when you're finished. We'll leave you in your peace and quiet now."

Matthias chuckled as the girls strode down the dirt road, their lavender skirts swishing and their *kapp* strings drifting on the breeze. Gail was giving her sister a talking-to, while Ruthie was stubbornly looking the other way. He gratefully gulped the cold lemonade and set the plate of treats on the back of the wagon bed.

"What do you think, Ed?" he asked when his horse glanced at him. "It's a *gut* thing we're moving to Morning Star, instead of Cedar Creek, *jah?* Sam and his girls seem determined to fix me up with Rose, no matter what Rose and I might think."

Ed nickered, showing his big teeth in a mocking grin. Matthias took it as a sign that the jokes and teasing were just beginning. It was probably best that he had no inclination to attend Lydia Fry's funeral. Whatever gossip and romantic remarks the Lambrights might spread would fall flat if he simply stayed out of the picture, away from Rose Raber.

After he'd eaten a couple cookies and a soft, chewy cinnamon roll, Matthias finished digging the grave. He put the last shovelful on the tarp laden with soil—men with equipment from the funeral home would move it before the graveside service—and hopped onto his wagon. When he slipped inside the mercantile to return the pitcher and plate, he was glad to see that Sam was busy with a customer in the plumbing department.

Matthias drove back to Willow Ridge, happy that he'd done a good deed for Rose—and that he had so many things to fix at his new place, he'd have no reason to return to Cedar Creek anytime soon.

# Chapter 7

As Rose walked slowly behind the horse-drawn hearse on Thursday, she felt exhausted, lost in a blur of suspended time and motion. The sky was a bright blue with wisps of white clouds, the grass alongside the road was deep green, and the redbud trees were loaded with purple-pink blooms, but the beauty of the day was lost on her. She felt emotionally drained and dead on her feet as she went through the motions of this difficult ritual.

Somehow in the past couple of days, she'd sewn her mother's burial dress, accepted the cleaning help of every woman she knew in Cedar Creek, and survived the ordeal of dressing Mamma's body and sitting beside her plain pine coffin while a huge crowd came to the house to pay their respects Wednesday evening. Her refrigerator and kitchen counters were overflowing with food the neighbors had brought. Local men had set up the pew benches and readied the house for the funeral. Rose couldn't recall much of what Bishop Vernon and Preacher Sam had said during the funeral service, but she was grateful for all the people who were supporting her with their presence.

*Hang on for a few hours more,* she repeated to herself. *After the funeral lunch, I can go home and collapse.*

Rose was grateful that Gracie had taken on the solemnity of this somber occasion rather than firing off curious questions or fidgeting during the service. Her daughter's hand, so small and warm, was the only tangible hold Rose had on reality as she led the other mourners on her mother's journey toward eternal rest. The folks in black behind her remained silent, walking two or three deep as they entered the cemetery.

"Look, Mamma—sheeps!" Gracie whispered, pointing toward the flock on the grassy hillside that adjoined the cemetery. "Are they the lambs of God, Mamma?"

Rose found a smile. "Those are Matt Lambright's sheep, sweetie," she replied softly, "but, *jah*, they're God's lambs, too. Just like you are."

As she and Gracie passed Nathan's and Dat's grassed-over graves, Rose's heart hitched—but the sight of the gaping hole beside Dat nearly undid her. The funeral home had provided a device to lower the coffin, but the braces and straps did little to disguise the grave that would soon swallow her mother. To keep from unraveling, Rose lifted her daughter into her arms and positioned herself where she could see those fleecy white sheep on the hillside, so serene and peaceful. She focused on the flock—spotted two black-and-white dogs keeping watch beneath the blooming dogwoods—as six men bore the coffin to the grave and placed it on the wide straps.

"Ashes to ashes, and dust to dust," Bishop Vernon intoned in a voice that reverberated in the crowd's stillness. "We commend the body of our sister Lydia to the ground and her soul into Your care, O Lord. . . ."

Rose closed her eyes against hot tears, resting her head

against Gracie's. The bishop's remaining remarks drifted around her, unheard, until she felt Vernon's hand on her arm.

"Come, Rose. We've finished with the graveside formalities," he whispered near her ear.

Rose blinked, suddenly aware that everyone else was watching her. Vernon offered his arm and she took it. She set Gracie on the ground and grasped her hand as Jerusalem walked on the other side of her daughter, away from the coffin poised above its grave.

*Do they think I'll collapse without their support?* Rose straightened, determined to carry on as Mamma would expect, while they walked the short distance up the hill to Treva's Greenhouse. The women in Sam's family would be serving the meal prepared in the nearby café. Countless other women had baked pies and bread after they'd cleaned her house on Tuesday.

Rose sighed. How could she possibly repay the kindness her friends had shown these past few days? She was too numb to think about it. Rose squeezed Gracie's hand, focused on putting one foot in front of the other until she got inside the greenhouse. She would fill a plate—mostly so Gracie could eat, because she herself couldn't possibly force any food down—and then sink into a chair . . . accept condolences by nodding and murmuring her thanks—

"Matthias!" Gracie suddenly cried, waving excitedly. "Matthias, hi! It's me, Gracie!"

Rose cringed, following the direction of her daughter's finger—as was everyone else in the procession. Sure enough, the man she'd run into in the mercantile was standing outside the greenhouse, studying the tomato and green pepper plants displayed on tables alongside the glass building.

*Surely, Matthias knows the greenhouse is closed today for the funeral. If he's shopping for plants, why is he dressed in black trousers, a vest, and a white shirt? He wasn't at the house for the service—*

When Gracie tried to wiggle free, Rose held her daughter's hand more tightly. "Gracie, hush," she murmured, "and don't you even think about—"

With a determined surge of energy, Gracie escaped Rose's hold. "Matthias! It's *gut* to see you!" she blurted as she raced toward him.

Walking beside Rose, Vernon chuckled. "Gracie's done very well today, Rose," he said.

"All that pent-up energy's got to get loose or she'll likely explode with it," Jerusalem remarked. "And it seems Matthias is as happy to see Gracie as she is to see him. Nice fellow, Matthias is. Got to know him when I lived in Willow Ridge, before I married Vernon."

Rose sighed. What would her neighbors think about her and Gracie chatting with a strange man? As she approached the greenhouse, she noticed Matthias had crouched to chat with her little girl—and he was gazing at *her* over the top of Gracie's *kapp*, his eyes full of questions and concern. There was no way around it. Rose had to speak with Matthias—hopefully, without everyone in the crowd eavesdropping.

"You folks go on inside," she urged Vernon and Jerusalem, including everyone else in her gesture. "Get your food while it's hot. We'll be in shortly."

Vernon went up to Matthias with his hand extended. "What a pleasure to see you here, son," he said. "I trust all's well in Willow Ridge this week?"

"*Jah,* far as I know. I've spent most of my time in Morning

Star." Matthias stood up, smiling, as Vernon pumped his hand—and as Gracie wrapped her arms around his legs—but he was looking at Rose as he responded.

"I—I almost didn't come today," he said apologetically, "but I realized that sorrow touches every one of us during our lives, so I wanted to be here. To be a friend."

"You and me, we're *gut* friends, Matthias!" Gracie piped up. "Let's go in and get dinner. I'm starvin' and you gotta sit with me, okay? *Please,* Matthias?"

Rose wished the ground would open up and swallow her. Her cheeks prickled. The last thing she wanted was to make small talk with this out-of-towner while her neighbors looked on . . . no matter how earnest and sincere he appeared. But if she brushed Matthias off—pretended that she needed to sit with other folks—Gracie would put up a fuss. And that scene would embarrass Rose even more.

"Nice to see you, Matthias," Gail Lambright said. She waved at him and then headed through the greenhouse door with the others.

"It was nice of you to dig Lydia's grave, too," Ruthie put in before ducking back into the line behind her sister.

"We'll catch up with you later, Matthias." With a knowing smile, Vernon took Jerusalem's arm and eased into the flow of the crowd that was entering the glass-paneled building.

Rose swallowed hard. There was no way around talking to Matthias now. "I—I had no idea you dug Mamma's grave," she mumbled as her heart began to pound. "What a kindness you've done for us. *Denki* so much."

Matthias shrugged, still holding her gaze. "You weren't figuring on me being here to eat, so if you think there won't be enough food—or if you'd rather I didn't stay—"

"You can share my dinner, Matthias!" Gracie blurted. "Let's get lots of chicken and mashed taters, okay?" She gazed up at him adoringly, still embracing his legs.

Rose sighed, hoping she didn't appear ungrateful. "No, no—there's more than enough food," she insisted. And because she saw no graceful way around it, she added, "We'd be pleased if you'd sit with us, Matthias. Gracie has been very quiet and respectful today. She's ready to see a smiling face and talk about something besides her *mammi*'s passing."

When Matthias opened his arms, Gracie reached up for him. He lifted her to his shoulder effortlessly, comfortably, as though he did this sort of thing on a daily basis.

"You, um, have kids of your own?" Rose asked as they went to the end of the serving line. She knew next to nothing about this man, so maybe she should be asking questions—before Gracie became so enamored of Matthias that there'd be no pulling her away, no matter what she might learn.

"My wife, Sadie, was carrying our first one when she passed," Matthias murmured sadly. Then he smiled at Gracie, eye to eye with her. "But my brother's got new twins now, and his wife's three little brothers and little sister—close to your age, Gracie—live with us. Plus Annie Mae's sister, who's a teenager. Having so many kids around keeps me on my toes."

Gracie giggled. "I wanna see you on your toes, Matthias."

"Maybe not now," Rose insisted before her daughter got too carried away. She was amazed at how happy Gracie looked, as though she'd known Matthias for years—*Or as though he were Nathan. She's not been this bubbly since her* dat *passed last summer.*

Recalling how her husband had held Gracie high above his head to make her giggle uncontrollably, Rose sucked in her breath.

They had almost reached the serving line, where the women were dishing up pieces of golden-roasted chicken, creamy mashed potatoes with chicken gravy, fried apples, green beans, and coleslaw—even as they were gawking at her and speculating about Matthias.

Rose forced herself to appear normal. She took two plates from the stack and grabbed two napkin-wrapped bundles of silverware—anything to act rational, as though she always had a handsome man holding her daughter, standing close enough that he almost touched her.

*Matthias* is *handsome,* Rose realized—but she concentrated on choosing food rather than thinking about him. "*Jah,* that chicken thigh looks perfect," she said as Treva picked it up with her tongs. "*Denki* for setting up tables in your greenhouse. You had to move a lot of things around—and during your busy season, too."

Treva waved her off before placing a big scoop of mashed potatoes on her plate. "Happy to do it for you, Rose. Your *mamm* was a pillar of this community. A friend to all of us."

"I want three chickie legs and a big ole bunch of taters," Gracie announced as she pointed to the food in the steam table. "Lotsa gravy, too—right, Matthias? Do you like lotsa gravy on your taters?"

"That looks like awesome gravy." Matthias smiled at the women who were filling his plate. "If I could have some on my chicken, as well as my taters," he said, winking at Gracie, "that would be wonderful. *Denki,* ladies. This is a fabulous meal."

As Rose gazed around the crowded greenhouse, looking for three empty chairs, she was very aware that folks were watching her—whispering about the man who followed her between the tables, carrying Gracie as though she were his. Rose wanted to announce, loud and clear, that Matthias Wagler was only here for the food.

*But they'll know that's not true. Just like I do.*

Rose's cheeks tingled with heat. She hurried toward the last unoccupied table in the back corner of the big glassed-in room, not meeting anyone's gaze. Settling into a folding chair, Rose sighed heavily as she gazed at the plate she'd filled. Why had she taken so much food when she had no appetite? Why had her attention wandered as she'd listened to Matthias's voice and watched him hold Gracie against his hip as though he'd done that dozens of times? She smiled weakly at him as he gently set Gracie in the chair beside hers. Because she couldn't think of a thing to say, Rose took Gracie's hand and bowed her head in prayer. She heard Matthias sit in the chair on the other side of her daughter.

*What have I gotten myself into, Lord? I've just buried my mother, yet I'm allowing this man I've met only once to sit with me and to entertain my little girl. This feels so improper—and everyone else is thinking I've wandered off the straight and narrow, too.*

Rose's eyes fluttered open. Was God displeased with her behavior? Had she really lost her way? Now that she'd given in to Gracie's fascination with Matthias, how could she tell him she wanted nothing more to do with him? She glanced at him and sighed.

*He's still in prayer before his meal. Gracie has put her tiny hand on top of his big strong one. How can that be so wrong when it looks so right? So sweet.*

As though Gracie had read her thoughts, she opened her eyes and beamed up at Rose. "Mamma, maybe Matthias will

go home with us," she whispered as this wonderful idea cap-
tured her imagination. "Maybe he could fix the screen door
and that window in my room and—"

"Gracie, hush," Rose whispered. Even though Matthias
had opened his eyes to gaze at her over Gracie's head, she
said, "Matthias is busy. He doesn't live here—"

"I'd be happy to help you, Rose," Matthias interrupted
gently. "Sam told me you've lost your husband and your *dat,*
and that your *mamm*'s been so ill that—well, I'm sure you
haven't had the time or inclination to repair anything under
those circumstances. You've had a lot of caretaking to do. A
lot of things on your mind."

*So Sam has taken it upon himself to encourage this
stranger's attention?*

Even as Rose's heart yearned for Matthias's compassion,
she couldn't let him repair things at the house. Her friends
were probably murmuring about the way she sat with a nice-
looking man whom Gracie seemed quite fond of—yet few of
them had ever seen Matthias. They had to be questioning her
morals, her apparent lack of respect for her recently deceased
mother—not to mention Nathan.

"Why are you here, Matthias?" Rose blurted, knowing before the words left her mouth that she sounded rude. However, she needed to know his answer so she could assess it.
Many chores around her parents' place had indeed gone undone for several months, but she didn't want to be sucked
into a relationship she might regret.

Matthias's wounded expression shot an arrow of remorse
into Rose's heart. He glanced away, and then used his fork to
keep Gracie's green beans from spilling off her plate.

Gracie smiled at him as she grabbed a chicken leg. "You're

here coz you're my friend, huh, Matthias? You know Mamma's been kinda fussy with me, coz she's been so sad she's forgot how to be happy."

Rose swallowed hard as her cheeks flushed. Everything Gracie had said was true, but that didn't mean she wanted her problems shared with Matthias.

"You've got that right, Gracie," Matthias replied pensively as he cut into his chicken. "I remember how sad my brother, Adam, and I were when our *mamm* died, and how fussy and sad I was after my wife died, too. I forgot how to be happy, just like you said. But I'm feeling much better now."

Matthias returned Gracie's smile. "I knew your mamma was feeling lost and lonely, Gracie—the way I used to be—so I wanted her to know she could talk to me about it whenever she needs to. And I'll understand if she just wants me to go away, too."

Rose clasped her hands in her lap and stared at them. Matthias was a man acquainted with grief, offering his support. She chided herself for being so blunt about his intentions. She'd heard nothing suspicious, but it still felt inappropriate to accept Matthias's offer of friendship and help. It was just too soon.

"I'm sorry," Rose murmured. "I'm so tired I can't see straight, and I feel like a blanket that's unraveling. I didn't mean to offend you, Matthias."

"No offense taken. And since this food's the best I've eaten in a while, I'm going to stop talking and enjoy every bite of it. Maybe you'll feel better if you eat some of your dinner, too, Rose. Just sayin'."

"*Jah*, Mamma, these taters are the best. And so are the chickie legs!"

Rose had to chuckle about the gravy on her daughter's chin, and at Gracie's gleeful enjoyment of her food. She didn't wipe Gracie's face yet, but she did take a napkin from the center of the table and tuck it into the neck of her daughter's best dark dress.

"It's *gut* to see you eating without Mamma having to pester you," Rose said, tweaking Gracie's nose.

Gracie paused with her second chicken leg in front of her mouth. "It was hard to eat when Mammi was so sick," she replied softly, "but I'm not worried about her anymore coz she's in Heaven."

*Isn't it just like Gracie to speak such a truth? Out of the mouths of babes . . .*

Rose blinked back tears, refusing to break down in front of Matthias. There would be plenty of time to cry after she returned home—and perhaps she *would* feel better if she ate some of this wonderful meal. She hadn't felt like cooking anything as elaborate as mashed potatoes and baked chicken for weeks.

*Your mother would be appalled if you left all that food untouched on your plate,* she cautioned herself.

The first bite of mashed potatoes and gravy made Rose realize how famished she was. The oven-fried chicken was crisp and moist; the fried apples swam in buttery juice and cinnamon; the green beans had been cooked with onion until they were soft and delectable. After she'd cleaned her plate faster than usual, Rose looked up to see Matthias and Gracie watching her.

"Pie, Mamma? Please can I have butterscotch?" Gracie asked wistfully.

Rose smiled. She did feel better now that she'd eaten.

When she turned to gaze at the table where Barbara Lambright was setting out slices of pie, she was amazed at the variety still available after most folks had taken a piece.

"What kind shall I bring you, Rose?" Matthias asked as he stood up. "Gracie gets her butterscotch, and I'm having apple—unless the cherry strikes my fancy when I see it."

"No one would mind if you took one of each," Rose pointed out. "I'd like peach—and *denki*, Matthias. I don't know how to act, being waited on, you know."

Matthias's face lit up. "Maybe I can change that, Rose. I'll be right back."

# Chapter 8

On Friday afternoon, as Matthias carried groceries into his new place in Morning Star, he shook his head. Other than milk, eggs, bacon, cheese, and hamburger, his food consisted of boxed mac and cheese, loaves of store-bought bread, cold cereal—stuff he could whip up without much effort. It was a far cry from the dinner he'd enjoyed yesterday at this time in Cedar Creek with Rose and Gracie.

*Was the food really so fabulous, or was it the company that made me so happy?*

Matthias set three heavy bags of provisions on his small kitchen table. "Yes, and yes," he mumbled, talking to himself yet again.

Living alone was going to be a huge adjustment, after sharing the home place with Adam, Annie Mae, her five siblings, and the new twins. Moving to Morning Star tomorrow was in his best interest, but Matthias hadn't realized how the rooms in this place echoed when he walked through them. His life would be very *quiet* from here on out.

*Gracie would bring this place to life in a heartbeat.*

Matthias smiled as he went outside for the last couple bags

of groceries. What a treat that little girl was! Somehow, he'd won Gracie's heart without even trying. The moment she'd called out his name and pleaded for him to eat with her and her mother, he'd been wrapped around her little finger. As Matthias unloaded cans of fruit, beans, and pasta sauce, he knew the truth, however: it was Rose he longed to get better acquainted with.

*You want to get a lot more than acquainted, Wagler. All of a sudden, you're feeling like a man after being without a wife for three years. It's like the sun's shining again, sending the birds and the bees into high gear.*

Matthias laughed. At first, he'd thought sharing the house with newlyweds Adam and Annie Mae had rubbed off—made him aware again of the intimacy men shared with their wives—but it was Rose who'd brought his needs into sharp focus. Matthias felt really good about this—downright joyful—even though spending time with a man was probably the furthest thing from Rose's mind right now.

*Patience is a virtue,* he reminded himself. *And cleanliness is next to godliness.*

Rose would take one look at this place and walk away—not that it was filthy, but the clutter was a sure sign a bachelor would be living here, come tomorrow. Matthias spent the next half hour finding places for the new dishes, silverware, and kitchen linens he'd bought—items he'd never needed until he'd left Willow Ridge. This would be the first time in his life he'd lived alone. And he felt uneasy about it.

Even though he'd prayed diligently on the subject of moving—and he knew that locating his harness shop near the Hartzler Carriage Company in Morning Star would be good for his business—Matthias now realized he'd have to make new friends, attend a new church district, and shop in different stores. He'd be fixing his own breakfast, washing his own dishes, doing his own laundry—chores he was perfectly capable of handling, but the prospect of spending his evenings alone weighed on him. He'd sometimes gotten impatient with the constant commotion Annie Mae's little brothers and sister created, yet he'd never lacked for company. He'd had Adam and Annie Mae to chat with, usually with a kid or two in his lap.

*Deal with it,* Matthias told himself as he walked through his nearly-empty front room. *If you say one word to Adam about being lonely, he'll remind you that he tried to talk you into staying home.*

Home. The whole concept was changing for him now.

"Redefine it. Start again," Matthias whispered as he prepared to go back for his last night in Willow Ridge.

*Start again with Rose. You can't give up on her, no matter how many times she turns you away. It's a real good time to be your hardheaded, persistent self, Wagler.*

As the sun slipped behind the hills Friday evening, Rose's spirits sagged. Gracie was at Matt and Rosemary Lambright's house for her very first sleepover with their daughter, Katie, who was four. The girls were constant companions at the common meals and visiting time that followed church services. Gracie had been so excited about staying at Katie's house—and taking her new chalkboard and chalk—that Rose hadn't had the heart to keep her daughter home.

So now she was alone. And she realized how much time she'd been spending at Mamma's bedside these past weeks, in the home where she'd grown up—the house she'd considered home until she'd married.

As Rose sat in the unlit front room, however, the house

closed in on her, smothering her in its silent grief as the dusk deepened. There was no getting around it: not only was she alone, but she was nearly broke as well.

The bills for Mamma's final chemo treatment and medications had arrived, and the total would all but wipe out Rose's bank account. Bishop Vernon had assured her the church's aid fund would cover these bills, but it still scared her half to death that she would be penniless after Mamma's funeral was paid off, with no income in sight.

Rose blinked back tears. "Enough crying already," she muttered as she headed for the kitchen. She smeared peanut butter on a slice of bread, and then jelly. The makeshift meal settled her edgy stomach, but it did nothing to satisfy her soul.

*You're not really alone, you know. You have another mother out there.*

Rose exhaled slowly. The past few days had been so crammed with activity that she hadn't thought about Roseanne—Anne Hartzler—but now the hidden letters beckoned her. What else did she have to do this evening? Mamma had told her about those letters for a reason, after all. Maybe rereading them would give her an idea of how to proceed with her life. She was grasping at straws, because both Mamma and Anne had insisted that Rose wasn't to go looking for her—

*If Mamma didn't want me to find my real mother, why didn't she pitch those letters? If Roseanne didn't want me to know about her, why did she write them?*

Rose hurried upstairs, grabbed the stationery box from her shelf, and lit the lamp on her nightstand. She plumped her pillow against the head of the bed and kicked off her shoes, determined to find some peace—or at least the purpose behind these letters—while she had time alone to reconsider them.

*My Dearest Rose,*
    *If you're reading this, it means your mother Lydia
has passed on and I am so sorry for your loss.*

Rose blinked back tears. She'd heard this sentiment so many times over the past few days, she should've been immune to it, yet words written by a stranger nearly thirty years ago made Mamma's death sting fiercely, all over again. Would Anne still feel sorry after all this time, if she heard about Lydia Fry's passing?

*Mamma's obituary will be in the* Cedar Creek Chronicle. *If Anne lives in this area, will she know Mamma's gone?*

Rose held her breath, wondering where such an idea would lead. Then another thought sent goose bumps up her spine. *Will Anne try to find me? If my birth mother still thinks of me every day, like she said in these letters, will she make an effort to comfort me? Even if she doesn't seek me out, she might write me another letter in care of the funeral home. . . .*

What an idea that was! Rose sensed it might be dangerously foolish to make assumptions—to succumb to wishful thinking—about how Anne Hartzler would react to Mamma's passing. Anne might have died or moved away from the area after she'd gotten married. Rose knew of Hartzlers that were scattered around this region, but she hadn't heard of any fellows named Saul.

Rose focused on the letter again. Her swirling thoughts were influenced by her exhaustion and loneliness, and she could easily fall prey to her romantic imagination.

*Please understand that I am only sixteen, in love but unmarried, and your new parents will give you the stable home I can't provide. Myron and Lydia Fry are*

*dear people who have allowed me to live with them so
I can nurse you until you're weaned.*

Rose blinked. Which room had her birth mother stayed in?
Her parents had always slept in the largest room at the front
corner of the house, and the room she was in now had always
been her bedroom. That left two other rooms—

*Why does that matter?* Rose chided herself. *What you really
need to know is whether Lydia and Myron treated Roseanne as
family while she was here. Did your birth mother hole up in
her room, or did she visit when the neighbors came over? Did
she attend church and get to know folks? Eight months is a
long time.*

Rose thought about this idea. Did she dare ask Barbara
Lambright or Beulah Mae Nissley what they recalled about
the girl who'd stayed with Mamma and Dat after she'd been
born? Instinct told her not to ask Preacher Sam or the other
men about it—but Barbara was a midwife, so maybe she
would understand Rose's need to know more about the
young woman who'd nursed her so long ago. Maybe Barbara
had delivered her—

*Barbara would've only been in her twenties then—awfully
young for a midwife. See how your tired mind is leading you
astray?*

Rose skimmed the rest of the letter, until she reached another part that made her stop and think.

*It will sadden me greatly to leave you behind—I'll
have a huge hole where my heart has been—but I
know you'll have a secure, happy life with two generous, compassionate parents who already love you as*

*though you are their own. From now on, my name will*
*be Anne, for I will have left my Rose behind.*

Rose unfolded the watercolor portrait and studied it carefully. Once again, she was drawn in by her mother's bright
green eyes, freckles, and the wisps of brown hair that escaped
her *kapp*. The girl's facial features resembled her own—

*And that's what she was when she wrote this letter—a*
*mere girl,* Rose reminded herself. *It sounds so romantic that*
*she changed her name, but isn't that really a sign that she was*
*confused—maybe caught up in her fantasies about Joel, still*
*hoping he'd come back for her?*

Rose took the final letter from its envelope—the one in
which her birth mother insisted that Rose shouldn't try to
find her because she was being courted by a deacon. The
twenty-year-old postmark and some mental math told Rose
her mother had been about twenty-six when she'd married
Saul Hartzler. A paragraph near the bottom of the page held
Rose's attention:

> *The way I see it, your mother gave both you and me*
> *a chance at a normal life without the shame our faith*
> *would've heaped upon us because I had you out of*
> *wedlock. Please don't think too harshly of me for giv-*
> *ing you up—or of your dear mother for not telling you*
> *about this while she was alive. We were both doing the*
> *best we could at the time.*

Rose sighed tiredly. In her heart, she knew that Anne and
Lydia had indeed done the best they could—and they had put
a tiny, helpless baby's welfare ahead of their own. They had

probably endured nosy questions and had become the subjects of nasty gossip because Roseanne hadn't been married. Some of the men might have quizzed Dat about why he would allow such a wayward girl to stay in his home . . . but Mamma's cancer had put a cruel end to the Frys' ability to have a family. So Lydia and Myron had taken the opportunity they felt God had brought them.

*And they did it for you, Rose. They loved you despite the circumstances of your birth—and they welcomed Roseanne into their home so her breast milk would give you a stronger start. They loved you so much; they didn't care what other people thought. It was all about you.*

With a little sob, Rose got off her bed. She had to move around, had to think about something else so her emotions would settle. She slipped the letters and the portrait back into the stationery box and carried them downstairs to the kitchen table. Tomorrow, in the light of a new day, she would read the letters again. Gracie wouldn't be home until midmorning—or later, if she was having a good time with Katie—so Rose would use that time alone to get her emotions under control. She would figure out how she really felt about Mamma and her birth mother, and what she would—or wouldn't—do next.

She would think about finding work, too. If she wasn't to become dependent upon the generosity of others, she had to find a decent job—and quickly.

*God helps those who help themselves.* The old saying ran through Rose's mind as she turned off the lamps and got ready for bed. *Becoming a charity case is not an option. Your parents always put your needs first, and you must do the same for Gracie.*

*Chapter 9*

The next morning, seated at the kitchen table, Rose was so busy writing out index cards that she didn't realize Bishop Vernon had arrived, until he called through the screen door.

"Rose, how's it going?" he asked in a resonant voice. "Thought I'd see how you and Gracie are doing."

"Come in!" Rose called out. "I'll put on a fresh pot of coffee."

Vernon entered the kitchen with a smile on his face and a plastic sack in his hand. He removed his black straw hat and smoothed his snow-white hair. "By the time you've got that coffee on, I'll have your screen door fixed. I noticed how the bottom was dragging the other day. A little persuasion's all it needs, most likely."

Rose watched the bishop pull a small mallet from the sack—one of the tools he used for building furniture in his shop—before he laid the sack on the table. She suspected Jerusalem had sent some goodies, judging from the way the plastic draped over a boxlike object inside it, and her stomach rumbled in anticipation. Vernon stepped out onto the porch. As she measured coffee into the percolator basket, filled the pot with water, and set it on the stove to boil, she heard a couple of sharp whacks and the bishop whistling "She'll Be Coming 'Round the Mountain."

"*Gut* as new," he announced when he returned to the kitchen. "Anything else need fixing while I'm here?"

Rose almost declined his offer—but if the bishop could get Gracie's window open, then her daughter couldn't pester Matthias about it anymore. "If you wouldn't mind looking at a window upstairs—"

"Consider it done. Which room, dear?" Vernon smiled kindly at her, as if he had the entire morning to devote to household repairs.

"The smallest one, at the end of the upstairs hall. We haven't been able to open the window on the north wall since Gracie and I came here to live with Mamma."

Vernon strode through the front room and up the stairs, whistling. Rose wondered if she should slip her index cards into a drawer—she'd been writing out some "job wanted" notices to post on the bulletin boards of Plain stores in nearby towns. Rose believed this was her best chance to generate some income, but she knew the bishop would object to her working away from home.

A steady pounding came from the room above her head, and then it stopped.

Rose braced herself, deciding Vernon might as well find out about her intention to look for a job. He was a staunch believer in Old Order values—but even if he lectured Rose, quizzing her about Gracie's welfare if she did take a job, he might think of an opportunity for her. Vernon was resourceful, and he knew an incredible number of people in this part of Missouri. Members of the Cedar Creek church district believed he was capable of bending God's ear and getting anything he requested—including miracles.

Rose sighed. She could use a miracle about now.

She heard the stairs creak beneath the bishop's weight. "*Denki* so much, Bishop Vernon," she said when he entered the kitchen. "It's very kind of you to look after us this way."

"Once I got the window loose, I used the bar of soap from your bathroom to lubricate the metal track. Wish all home repairs were as simple as yours." The bishop took a lidded container from the plastic sack. "Jerusalem's looking after you, too. She wanted you and Gracie to have some of these fresh cinnamon rolls—but it seems your little chickadee has flown the coop."

Rose took two small plates from the cabinet. "Katie Lambright invited her for a sleepover. I can just imagine how lively things must be for Rosemary with two little girls scampering around."

Vernon laughed. "Glad to hear that. It's important for Gracie to spend time with her friends—what's this?" he asked as he picked up an index card. He skimmed it, frowning. "Rose, your most important job is raising your daughter. Even if you didn't have Gracie, it's too soon for you to consider looking for work," he said sternly. "This tells me you're so upset about your mother's passing, you've lost sight of your priorities. Lost your perspective."

Rose steeled herself. If she'd learned anything from losing her parents and her husband this past year, it was that she had to depend upon her own strength—had to be resourceful—or nothing got accomplished.

"I'm being realistic, Bishop," she insisted in what she hoped was a respectful tone. "I appreciate the way you've offered to cover Mamma's burial expenses with money from the church's funds, but I can't depend on charity forever. Mamma and Dat raised me to be a giver rather than a taker. A doer, not just a talker."

Vernon placed the index card back on the table. He sat down at the place where Rose was putting his cinnamon roll and hot coffee. "What if we set a time frame—let's say five months—for the church to support you?" he mused aloud. "That would get you and Gracie through the summer and give you time to consider better options for employment. Meanwhile, I would also search out some reasonable ways for you to earn money from home. Gracie starts school in September, correct?"

Rose nodded. She kept quiet so Vernon would continue to spin out his plan for her—and so she wouldn't irritate him by refusing to go along with it.

"With the rest of her family gone now, your little girl will look to you for *everything*, Rose," he continued pensively. "It's crucial to Gracie's well-being that you be at home with her these next several months, preparing her to be a scholar and sewing her clothes. Being here to welcome her home after her day at school."

Vernon stopped uncurling his cinnamon roll. "Surely, you can recall how wonderful it was to return to your mother's kitchen after a school day, Rose—to feel welcome because she was home for you, and because she enjoyed your help and company as she prepared the evening meal for your *dat*," he insisted gently. "You owe Gracie the same love and security."

Tendrils of resentment and pain curled around Rose's heart. Even before she spoke, she knew she was getting herself into trouble. "*Jah,* my mother loved me and gave me everything she had, Vernon—including the truth, that she and *dat* weren't my birth parents," Rose whispered, tapping the top of the stationery box. "These letters from the girl who birthed me don't change the way I was raised—the thirty years of life I've lived in the Fry and Raber families—but they've made me reexamine *everything* I thought I knew about who I am."

Vernon stared at her. He put his cinnamon roll on his plate. "Oh, my. I counseled your parents to remain silent about your being adopted—because it really doesn't matter—"

"How can you say that?" Rose blurted defiantly. "How would you feel if you'd learned—from letters your birth mother wrote to you—the truth about your own circumstances? It was the last gift Mamma gave me. She told me about Roseanne's letters right before she went into her coma."

Rose stood up, hoping not to burst into tears. "I—I wish I'd had just ten more minutes of conversation with Mamma before she slipped away. I think she would've explained a lot of things that are agitating me now."

"Roseanne wrote you letters?" the bishop whispered. "Addressed them to *you*, Rose?"

"*Jah*—they're in that box," she replied with a wave of her hand. "Go ahead and read them—they're short. I know them by heart now."

As Vernon reached for the stationery box, Rose busied herself at the sink, wiping the countertop—anything to avoid watching him—until curiosity got the best of her. When she turned, the lines and planes of the bishop's face shifted as he set aside the letters. He studied the picture of Roseanne.

"My father did that portrait of her," Rose murmured. "He was an accomplished artist even before he left the Old Order to go to art school." When Vernon looked up at her, Rose said, "You knew Roseanne, didn't you? You met her while she stayed here for those eight months."

"Roseanne was a girl tossed upon the stormy seas of misplaced passion," Vernon stated. His blue eyes, ordinarily as clear as a summer sky, had frosted over. "Something tells me you're following in her footsteps, Rose. You want to find this woman and be drawn in by her romantic notions—and you expect this adventure to read like a fairy tale where everyone lives happily ever after. Don't even *think* about looking for her, Rose. Leave it alone."

Rose scowled. Vernon was saying exactly what she'd anticipated, but his attitude rankled her. "How can I just leave it alone?" she challenged in a stiff whisper. "The cat's out of the bag now and it's got claws—I've felt torn to ribbons ever since I found her letters. Of *course* I realize that Roseanne was only sixteen and full of fanciful ideas," she continued, pleading for the bishop's compassion. "But she's my mother, Vernon. Just when I've lost everyone else I've ever loved—except for Gracie—I've learned that I have another mother."

"Be very careful, Rose," the bishop warned solemnly. "Just as Eve listened to the serpent—believed him when he coaxed her to ignore God's commandment—you are falling for the alluring words of temptation. These letters spin a spellbinding fantasy, but your mother—Lydia—and Roseanne were right about one thing. Do *not* try to find her, Rose."

Rose wrapped her arms around herself. She didn't want to hear what the bishop was saying, but there was no stopping his lecture.

"For all we know," Vernon went on in a softer voice, "this woman has a houseful of kids and a loving husband now. Think of how you'll upset that family if you show up from out of Roseanne's unfortunate past. Think of how betrayed Saul will feel, knowing she lied to him—or didn't admit the truth about you, her love child—when he took her as his wife."

"Do you know Saul Hartzler? Do you know where they live now?" Rose asked in a tiny voice.

Vernon's blue eyes widened in disbelief. "Do you really think I'd tell you, after I've insisted that you leave this whole situation alone?"

Rose sighed. Vernon did know Saul Hartzler. She was sure of it.

"I can better understand now why you're looking for work—just how confused and scattered you're feeling after your mother's death," the bishop observed. He gazed at Rose with the love of a father who's disappointed about his child's attitude, yet won't give up on her or stop caring for her . . . the way Dat would've dealt with her. "Please consider my suggestion about waiting at least five months before you make any major changes, Rose," he pleaded. "After losing so many important people in your life in such a short time, you don't realize how vulnerable you are to . . . imprudent, hazardous fantasies."

Rose looked down at her arms, crossed over her black apron. Vernon was the wisest, most reasonable man she knew, but . . .

"Sit down, dear," he said, pulling out the chair next to his. "We'll pray on this together. It's the least—and the most—I can do for you, to wrap the mantle of God's love and protection around you."

After a moment's hesitation, Rose sat down beside the bishop and allowed him to take her hand as he bowed his head. His kindly features softened as he whispered words of encouragement and an invocation of God's presence and power in her life.

". . . and we trust, Lord, that Your will shall be done, for the benefit of our Rose and her little Gracie," Vernon prayed fervently. "Grant us all Your wisdom as we grapple with perplexing issues, that we may see the way You would have us go. In Your Son's name we pray, amen."

Rose quickly shut her eyes and bowed her head so Vernon wouldn't know she hadn't prayed with him—although she'd followed along without mentally protesting his words or challenging God to listen to *her* wishes instead. When Rose looked at Vernon again, he held her gaze.

"The choice is yours, of course. God has granted us free will," the bishop reminded her. He squeezed her hand before releasing it. "The consequences of our actions often go far beyond our anticipation—certainly beyond our control. Keep Gracie's welfare uppermost in your mind, Rose. I'm confident you'll do and say the right things for her benefit."

"*Denki,* Bishop," Rose said as he stood up to take his leave. "And *denki* again for fixing the door and the window."

Vernon smiled. "Doors and windows," he said gently. "'The Lord shall preserve thy going out and thy coming in from this time forth and for evermore,' just as the Psalmist told us long ago. Grace and peace be with you, Rose. Let me know how I can help."

Rose walked the bishop to the door and watched him drive away in his open rig behind a fine, prancing bay gelding.

*Gracie will indeed be with me, but peace? I'm not so sure about that.*

Even though there was no church on Sunday, Rose awoke early, still agitated after the bishop's visit. Sleep had eluded her most of the night. She dressed in her black clothes and white *kapp,* going downstairs quietly so she wouldn't waken Gracie. As the first ribbons of peach and pink lit the horizon,

Rose went to the barn and got fresh water and feed for Daisy, their mare. She wanted to plant more of the garden because she'd lost so much time during the past week, but that was more work than was allowed on Sunday.

*It's going to be the longest day of my life,* she thought as she walked back to the house. *Nothing to do. Nowhere to go. Just Gracie and me trying to muddle through.*

Once again, Rose realized how much time Mamma's care had required, and how all those hours stretched before her now, empty. It was the Old Order custom to visit with family on non-church Sundays, but even if she had any family left in this area, folks would understand if she and Gracie stayed home right after Mamma's funeral.

Rose sorted through the food on the countertop and in the fridge, because it would be a horrible waste if it spoiled. Loaves of bread, whole cakes, and pans of cinnamon rolls went into the freezer, as did the casseroles in disposable foil pans, which friends had brought.

*How much food do they think Gracie and I can eat?* Rose sliced the roasts, a ham, and a turkey, and put portions of them into plastic bags.

"Whatcha doin', Mamma?"

Rose turned toward the kitchen door and smiled. "You got dressed all by yourself. *Gut* job, Gracie," she said, even though her daughter's hair hung loose beneath her slightly crooked *kapp*, and she'd chosen her brightest pink summer dress. "I'm freezing this food, because there's no way you and I can eat it all before it goes bad."

Gracie scooted her little wooden stool closer to the counter and stood on it, surveying what remained. "Can we have turkey for breakfast? With cookies?"

Rose almost suggested something healthier than the cookies,

but what difference did it make, really? Nobody else would see what they were eating. "That sounds yummy," she said as she placed slices of turkey on a plate. "Here's some bread—"

"I'll get the mayo!"

"—and we'll have cookies and milk—and there's apple-sauce, too," Rose continued.

They were eating their unusual breakfast, talking about what they might do during their Sabbath day, when someone knocked loudly on the front door.

"I'll get it!" Gracie said eagerly.

After her little girl raced through the front room, Rose heard the familiar voices of Vernon and Jerusalem Gingerich. She sighed. While the bishop and his wife saw it as their duty to visit her today, Rose was still smoldering from Vernon's re-buff concerning finding a job—and finding her birth mother. She filled the percolator with water and coffee. Vernon had probably told his wife about Rose's concerns, so Rose would have to be especially patient if both of them started in on her. It might turn into an even longer day than she'd anticipated.

"We got all sortsa cookies, and turkey, and applesauce!" Gracie exclaimed as she led the Gingeriches into the kitchen. "It's a feast!"

"And you might as well join us," Rose added, finding a smile for their guests. "We've got so much food, I've been putting some of it in the freezer—"

"And here's your dinner for today," Jerusalem said, hold-ing out a foil-covered pan. "Easy enough to make you girls a pan of scalloped potatoes and ham while I fixed it for us yes-terday."

"Seems your friends have indeed looked after you," Ver-non remarked as he glanced at the remaining plastic bags of food that were ready to go into the freezer. "'Behold the fowls of the air, for they sow not, neither do they reap, nor gather into barns; but your heavenly father feedeth them,'" he recited in his mellow voice. "You won't need to buy groceries for weeks, Rose."

Rose turned to put more cookies on a bigger plate. She couldn't miss the sermon the bishop had tucked into their conversation before he'd even sat down.

"Come here, Gracie, and I'll coil your hair up," Jerusalem said kindly. "Your *mamm*'s been busy—"

"I got dressed all by myself!" Gracie crowed.

Rose pressed her lips together. Now the bishop and his wife were convinced she was a negligent mother, allowing her daughter to wear bright pink on the Sunday following her *mammi*'s funeral—and not winding Gracie's hair into a proper bun beneath her *kapp*.

"Even Solomon in all his glory wasn't arrayed like you, Gracie," Vernon quipped kindly. Then he gazed purposefully at Rose. "'Wherefore, if God so clothe the grass of the field, which today is, and tomorrow is cast into the oven, shall he not much more clothe you, O ye of little faith?'"

Rose bit back a retort, but then a reply sprang into her mind. "I was hungry and you fed me, I was thirsty and you gave me a drink," she paraphrased softly. "And I was sick at heart and you visited me, Bishop. *Denki* for all you and Jerusalem have done, but please understand that I'm weary and I might not be the most gracious hostess today—or the most tolerant lamb of your flock."

Vernon's unflinching gaze told Rose she'd stepped over the line, flinging Scripture back at him—even though she hadn't quoted it verbatim. Most bishops believed that members of their congregation should leave the reading and interpretation of Scripture to those whom God had chosen as leaders. Rose lowered her gaze, acknowledging her blunder.

There was no graceful way to say it: Rose was tired of Vernon's preaching at her. He wanted the best for her and Gracie, but she was in no mood to receive another heaping helping of his counsel today.

Somehow Rose endured another hour of the Gingeriches' company, and Jerusalem finally suggested that they should leave. Vernon led them in prayer, and they departed—but not before the bishop got in one last word.

"Pride goes before a fall, Rose," he reminded her as Gracie accompanied his wife outside. "Please don't assume you can shoulder your burdens alone, or that your way of handling them is the best way. Wait upon the Lord, dear. He never fails us."

Rose nodded, swallowing any sort of reply. As she watched the bishop's rig roll toward the road, she knew he was right—and she wished she could obey him without second-guessing what the future held.

*We're like sheep that have gone astray,* she thought as she watched Gracie bounding across the yard toward her. *Forgive me, Lord, for my prideful, willful ways and show me what to do. Spell it out in big, bold letters so I can't miss Your sign, and the direction You want me to go.*

# Chapter 10

Early the next morning, Rose hitched the mare to the buggy. She didn't have to coax Gracie to come along, because her daughter was bubbly and happy, still recounting the details of her sleepover with Katie.

"Where we goin', Mamma?" Gracie asked eagerly. "We walk to the mercantile, unless we need a whole lotta stuff."

"You're right, sweetie," Rose agreed as she clapped the lines lightly over Daisy's broad back. She reviewed the story she'd planned, and decided to go ahead with it. "But today we're driving to Willow Ridge, and to New Haven and Morning Star—"

"Wow! That's a lotta places!"

"—and first we'll stop at our mercantile, but *only* if you promise Mamma to do exactly as she says, right down to the letter," Rose finished. She held Gracie's gaze, watching her green eyes get wide and bright.

"What's letter *A*?"

Rose smiled. She was so blessed to have a daughter who already loved to recite her letters and numbers, and who adored little games. "Letter *A*, we go into the mercantile—"

"*Jah*, I'm likin' this so far," Gracie said with a nod.

"—and *B*, you ask Sam to help you choose a toy or game that costs less than two dollars," Rose continued.

Gracie's brow furrowed. "How do I know what stuff costs?"

"That's why you're asking for Sam to help you," Rose explained. "He'll show you how to read the price stickers, so you can decide which toy you can afford. He really likes teaching kids about careful shopping, and how much their money will buy. This early on a Monday morning, there won't be many folks in his store, so he can take his time with you."

Her daughter's bright smile rivaled the sun. "And what's letter *C*, Mamma? I like this game!"

Rose reached into the pocket of her black apron for two folded one-dollar bills. "*C* is for *cash*. This is your money, so you can learn to be a *gut* thrifty shopper. *Thrifty* means that you don't waste money on things you don't need."

Gracie took the money, gazing raptly at it. "Is this a lesson, Mamma?"

"It is. You'll do well, Gracie, because Sam's a *gut* teacher—which is one reason God chose him to be a preacher," Rose added as she watched for traffic on the county highway. "Geddap, Daisy! We're almost there, girl."

The mare trotted across the blacktop and into the parking lot, heading to the hitching posts along the side of the mercantile. Rose was pleased to see only one other buggy. As she strode toward the door, trying to keep up with Gracie, she prayed that her little plan would play out smoothly.

Rose opened the door and her little girl rushed inside. When Gracie spotted Sam restocking a display of cleaning supplies, she hurried over to greet him.

"Sam, I'm playin' a game and you're s'posed to help me—pretty please?"

The lanky storekeeper placed a few more sponges in the display's bucket. "What sort of a game, Gracie-girl? My *gut-ness*, and you've got a handful of money, too."

"C is for *cash*!" Gracie recited proudly. "Mamma says you'll show me how to read the stickers on the toys so's I can pick out somethin' fun for my two dollars."

"I'd be happy to do that, young lady." Sam flashed a smile at Rose as he followed Gracie down the aisle where the small toys and games were. "It's important for kids to understand the value of money—"

"And to be thrifty!" Gracie exclaimed. "So can we find me a toy that's fun, but it's somethin' I really *need*?"

As her daughter's chatter kept Sam occupied, Rose slipped over to the bulletin board near the door. She felt rather devious as she attached one of her cards to the pitted cork with a pushpin, because Preacher Sam would feel the same way the bishop did about her looking for work.

But hadn't Vernon admonished her to put Gracie first? *"Keep Gracie's welfare uppermost in your mind, Rose,"* he'd told her.

How could she raise her little girl without money? Rose had prayed earnestly, and had given a lot of thought to the bishop's five-month plan. God, however, had not shown her the big, irrefutable sign she'd asked Him for. And five months seemed like a very long time to depend upon the generosity of her neighbors—neighbors who earned their livings.

After all, Beulah Mae Nissley ran the café—Mrs. Nissley's Kitchen—and Rosemary Lambright sold baked goods there, which she made in her double oven at home. Sam's sister, Abby, had moved her sewing business into a bedroom of the

Graber house across the road after she'd married James Graber. Barbara Lambright earned money for her midwifing visits, while Sam's mother, Treva, ran the greenhouse. Other women around Cedar Creek didn't expect their men to be the sole support of their households. Rose had no doubt that if the married ones were widowed, they would continue in their businesses.

Rose glanced toward the toy section. Sam and Gracie were holding a serious conversation about the merits of flash cards versus paddleballs and books, so Rose focused on the notices posted on the bulletin board. Several ladies were willing to do sewing or laundry, or they offered to be caretakers for elderly folks.

The HELP WANTED section of the board wasn't nearly as full—and jobs in pallet-making shops and vinyl siding factories were suitable only for men. Rose was disappointed, but this was just her first stop. On her card, she'd written that she would cook and clean, but she was perfectly capable of doing other household chores, too, depending upon what a potential employer needed.

"Mamma, look what I got!" Gracie cried as her shoes beat a rapid tattoo on the wooden floor. "Sam 'splained about the dollar sign and the dot—"

"The decimal point," Sam said gently as he followed her up the aisle.

"*Jah,* the decimal point!" Gracie stopped in front of Rose, clutching a small book. "And if the number in front of the decimal point is less than two, it means I got enough money, right?"

"We'll have a lesson about adding tax later," Sam said as he winked at Rose. "She made a fine choice. Could've had a set of jacks, or flash cards, or animal stickers—"

"I got a book about Jesus!" Gracie chimed in. "We *need* Jesus, so I'm a thrifty shopper, huh, Mamma?"

Rose's heart rose into her throat. "You and Sam are a fine team—teacher and scholar. Let's go to the counter so you can pay for your book."

Rose lifted Gracie so she could transact her business at the tall counter. As Sam punched the numbers into the cash register, she almost felt guilty for using her little girl as a diversion—but she believed her motives were honorable.

"Tax—and a stick of candy—are on me today," the storekeeper insisted when Rose fished more money out of her apron pocket. "It's always a pleasure to see you in my store, Gracie. Next time I see you, you can tell me all about your new book."

"*Jah,* I will. Bye, Sam!"

"*Denki* again, Sam," Rose added as they headed for the door. She recalled running into Matthias in this spot, but she put him out of her mind. She had places to go, notices to post—and she'd heard nothing from him since Mamma's funeral. Maybe he'd just come to eat a free meal.

"Where we goin' now, Mamma?"

Gracie's eager question brought Rose out of her musings as she lifted her daughter into the open rig. "Willow Ridge is our next stop," she replied as she unhitched Daisy and stepped up into the buggy. "It's a long ride, so it's a *gut* thing you bought a book, *jah?*"

Gracie nodded, opening the cover. "See? Here's Jesus—and He looks just like Matthias, don'tcha think?"

As Rose focused on getting the rig safely onto the county highway, she wondered where her daughter got such notions—and why Gracie had grown so attached to Matthias so quickly. When Daisy was trotting along the shoulder of the blacktop, she stole a glance at Gracie's book.

"Oh, my," Rose whispered. The illustrations showed Jesus as the Good Shepherd, surrounded by fluffy white sheep. He was smiling tenderly; His golden brown eyes were alight, gazing directly at her . . . and indeed, with His reddish-brown beard and center-parted hair, Jesus could have been Matthias's twin—except His hair was longer. "Those look like Katie's *dat*'s sheep."

"Jesus needs a couple of sheepdogs like Panda and Pearl, for when the sheep go astray," Gracie remarked. "It was fun playin' with those dogs, Mamma. I wish we had a dog."

Rose was struck by the *"going astray"* part. What would she tell her daughter when they went into the next store? The way Bishop Vernon probably saw it, Rose needed more than border collies to herd her back onto the straight and narrow.

"And look at this page, Mamma. Why does Jesus have bright yellow lines around His head and body?"

Rose glanced at the book. "It says, 'Jesus is the light of the world,'" she replied. "Those are rays of really bright sunshine—like a giant halo surrounding Him. And that's the world He's holding in His arm."

"Wow," Gracie said softly. "Jesus must be really, really *big*! Way bigger than Matthias."

Rose laughed for the first time in days, grateful for this sunny day and for Gracie, who was the light of her life. Her daughter wore her favorite yellow dress today, a pleasant lift from the dark clothing Rose had been wearing since Nathan and Dat had passed—and Mamma's death would extend her mourning for another year. Only Rose's *kapp* was white, in the tradition of Cedar Creek's Amish community. All her clothing from her neck down had been dyed black after her husband and father had died in the fire.

As they rolled down the road, Rose set aside her concerns

to enjoy her daughter's curiosity. They read the entire picture book and talked about Jesus, so the next half hour flew by. There wasn't much traffic, and Rose was grateful for that.

As they approached Willow Ridge, Rose decided to explain what was going to happen when they reached Zook's Market and a couple of other stores. Gracie was far too observant to let Rose post her notices without asking questions that were best not answered with other people nearby.

"Gracie, when we stop at the stores in Willow Ridge and New Haven and Morning Star, we're not staying long—and we're not buying anything," Rose added gently.

Gracie's face puckered with thought. "If we're not buyin' stuff, why're we goin' to so many stores, Mamma?"

Rose owed her daughter an honest answer, after all their talk about how Jesus and God knew their thoughts and needs. "I'm posting cards on the bulletin boards, sweet pea," she replied, hoping she didn't sound desperate. "With your *dat* and Dawdi gone, we don't earn money from the sawmill anymore. And while we were taking care of Mammi, we spent a lot of our money on her medicine and chemo. So Mamma's looking for work that will pay her something."

Gracie considered this, her expression fluctuating as these concepts about jobs and money sank in. "Why can't you just be with me, Mamma?" she asked softly. "We got a garden, and we got Mammi's house for our home, *jah?*"

"*Jah,* we do," Rose answered in the strongest voice she could muster. She hated herself for making Gracie worry. "I hope to find work I can do at home, or at a place where you can come with me."

"But not when I'm gonna be in school!" Gracie protested.

"That's right," Rose assured her. "But school doesn't start for a long time—"

"And we gotta have money to get stuff from the store some-times—like peanut butter and macaroni, coz they don't grow in the garden," Gracie remarked pensively. "And we gotta be thrifty, huh, Mamma?"

Rose slung her arm around Gracie and hugged her tight. "I'm so blessed to have you, Gracie—and so glad you understand," she said in a wavering voice. "We'll be just fine, you and me together. Do you believe that?"

Gracie nodded solemnly. "I got you, and you got me, Mamma. And we got Jesus. It's all *gut*."

As Rose blinked back tears, she saw that Willow Ridge was only a quarter mile farther down the road. "Tell you what," she said in a lighter voice. "We'll post my notice in Zook's Market—see the store with the blue metal roof?"

Gracie sat taller, nodding.

"And then we'll get a fresh sweet roll or something at the café a little farther down the road," Rose said. "It's been a long time since we ate our breakfast."

"*Jah,* my tummy's rumblin'. Maybe a roll with cherry filling?"

"We'll see what they have. You're a *gut* girl, Gracie, and I love you," Rose said as she steered the mare over a narrow bridge. "Look at this mill with its waterwheel. That's a new place since last time I was here."

Gracie turned in the seat as they passed the mill, watching the big wheel spin slowly as it dipped water from the river. She slipped her hand around Rose's elbow. "I love you, too, Mamma. This is a fun trip, huh? We've havin' an *adventure*!"

"That's a *gut* way to look at it," Rose agreed.

# Chapter 11

When they'd parked beside Zook's Market, Rose reached for Gracie's hand. It only took a few minutes to post her notice and read the HELP WANTED notes—none of which offered work Rose could do. "Shall we walk down to the café—stretch our legs after riding for so long?" she asked as they stepped outside.

"*Jah*. Is that it, in that building there?"

"Uh-huh," Rose replied. "And there's a quilt shop on the other side."

The tantalizing aroma of roasting meat drifted on the breeze. Rose was tempted to suggest stopping for lunch—but there weren't any vehicles parked there. "Hmm. This café looks a lot newer—and bigger—than the one I remember," she said as they walked closer. "Ah, see, the sign says, 'The Grill N Skillet,' and it's open for lunch and supper now. The other café was open early for folks to eat breakfast."

Rose peered into the café's big plate-glass window. The clock on the wall inside said it was only five minutes past ten. The tables and chairs were unoccupied. "Well, we could go back to Zook's and get a package of rolls or cookies—"

"Let's wait, Mamma," Gracie suggested. "Store-bought rolls aren't as *gut* as fresh-made ones. We're bein' thrifty, *jah*? Only buyin' what we really need."

In a surge of emotion, Rose lifted Gracie to her shoulder in a fierce hug. She was more blessed than she'd ever imagined, having such a bright little girl. "You're absolutely right, sweet pea. Last time I bought a package of rolls in the store, it was a complete waste of my money. Let's go on to New Haven. It's only a few miles from here."

Once they were in the rig, Gracie opened her book again, smiling as she traced her finger around the pictures of Jesus. As they came to the edge of town, it occurred to Rose that she had been born here in New Haven . . . the old low-slung grocery store on the corner of the county highway was probably where Roseanne's aunt Nettie had first met Lydia Fry—although there was no longer a bench nearby.

Had Aunt Nettie lived in one of these homes in town, rather than out in the country, like most Plain folks did? The letter had made it sound as though Lydia hadn't had far to walk to Nettie's house, where she'd first seen Roseanne and her newborn baby.

Rose steered the horse carefully through the car traffic and off onto a side road. It was natural to wonder about Roseanne and Nettie and the day Lydia Fry had decided to adopt her, but Rose had much more pressing, present-day situations to deal with. She carefully composed her face so Gracie wouldn't ask what she'd been thinking about.

"Almost there," Rose remarked, pointing down the road.

The stop in New Haven didn't take long. The Dutch Bulk Store was busy, and as Rose posted her index card on the corkboard, she didn't see any HELP WANTED notices at all. Was this trip a waste of her time? Maybe English folks didn't look at the job postings in Plain stores these days. Maybe they found their employees on their computers.

"Want to see what's in the bakery case, Gracie?" she asked. "It'll take us about half an hour to get to Morning Star."

"But there's a pizza place there, *jah?* Can we have pizza for lunch, Mamma?"

Rose laughed as she took her daughter's hand and headed outside. "You never forget a *gut* place to eat, do you?" she teased. "Maybe we could get a big pizza and take home what's left, to have for our supper tonight."

"Pizza two times in one day! Let's do it!"

Rose set out again, and as the mare pulled them around the curving road, they met up with a big enclosed horse-drawn wagon. The driver waved—as most country folks did—before Rose noticed the yellow lettering on the side of the royal-blue vehicle: WAGLER REMODELING: PAINTING, PAPERING & REPAIRS.

She blinked. That Wagler surely had to be related to Matthias. Hadn't Sam told her Matthias had a harness shop here in Willow Ridge?

"That was a big ole wagon, Mamma!"

Rose smiled, but she didn't mention the possible connection it might have to Matthias. "The sign said it was a painting and wallpapering business—and up ahead there, see that big auction barn? That's where folks buy and sell cattle and horses and pigs."

As they approached Morning Star, they discussed the various places they saw—the white Mennonite church, the funeral home, and the Morning Star Senior Center were on this side of town as they drove in. Because it was the county seat, Morning Star had a lot of English businesses along the main streets. Rose passed a car dealership, a Laundromat, and the post office before they finally reached the Plain bulk store, which sat just down the block from the pizza place.

"Here we are!" Gracie sniffed deeply. "I can smell the pizza bakin', Mamma!"

Rose hitched Daisy to a post at the side of the white metal bulk store building. "I think I can eat a whole pizza all by myself," she teased. "What if there's none left for you?"

"Puh! I got fast hands, Mamma," Gracie replied without missing a beat. "I can snatch that pizza off the pan way faster than you can! Just you watch me!"

Rose laughed out loud, once again thankful for a little girl who gave such pleasure to her—such love and understanding beyond Gracie's years. Bulk stores fascinated Gracie. She loved to walk down the rows of shelves, gazing at the hundreds of plastic bags filled with spices, cookie sprinkles, muffin mixes, candies, cereals—and there were more varieties of bulk grocery items here than Sam carried in the Cedar Creek Mercantile. Rose posted her index card on the bulletin board; then she watched her daughter walk along the aisle where all sorts of pasta shapes and homemade dried noodles were bagged.

*Maybe Gracie had a point about going to stores without buying anything . . . and it's not like a simple treat will set us back much in this place.*

Rose joined her daughter at the end of the aisle. "Pick out a package of macaroni or noodles," she suggested. "We can do a lot of things with that—like mac and cheese, or—"

"Tuna casserole with peas?"

"*Jah,* we've not had that in a long time," Rose said. "And it'll be fun to eat if the macaroni is an unusual shape, don't you think?"

Gracie jogged along the aisle until a package caught her

eye. "Look, Mamma—these are orange and green and red and noodle color, all mixed together. And they're butterflies!"

"Perfect. We'll pay for them and head to the pizza place," Rose said as she took money from her apron pocket. "I'm so hungry I could eat a horse."

Gracie planted her fists on her little hips. "But not Daisy, right? Coz it's a *looong* walk home, Mamma!"

Rose paid for the pasta and they headed outside, hand in hand. As they strolled down the block, Gracie chattered about making a special picture with her colored chalk and the colorful pasta butterflies—until she sucked in her breath.

"Matthias, hi!" she called out, releasing Rose's hand. "We're gonna eat pizza now! Come with us!"

Rose held her breath as her daughter scampered toward Matthias, who'd just stepped out of the bank. He opened his arms, laughing as he effortlessly lifted the ecstatic little girl to his shoulder. What a sight, their two smiling faces—as though they'd been friends forever and hadn't seen each other for months. Rose's heart pounded as she watched Matthias delight her daughter—just as Nathan had done.

"Pizza?" he teased. "Why would I want to eat pizza with the likes of you, Gracie?"

Gracie giggled. "Coz you love me!"

Matthias planted a quick kiss on her cheek. "*Gut* answer, Gracie-girl."

Rose's hand fluttered to her chest. It was just like Gracie to blurt out the first thing that came to mind, but Rose hadn't expected the subject of love to come up. Matthias had reacted without a second thought, with a kiss. . . .

"Mamma says we can get a really big pizza and take some home for supper!" Gracie continued excitedly. "I'll be eatin' pizza two times in one day!"

"Sounds like a fine plan." Matthias smiled as Rose caught up to them. "If we order two really big pizzas—two different kinds—then I can have pizza for supper, too. How are you, Rose?" he asked in a lower voice. "What a nice surprise to see you girls in Morning Star."

"It's *gut* to see you as well, Matthias," Rose replied, hoping Gracie didn't blurt out the reason they were in town. "I— I don't know if it's proper for us to be eating with you, what with me being a—"

"I understand your hesitation," Matthias murmured, standing closer to her so the folks on the walkway could get past them. "And if you're uncomfortable eating with a man in public at this point, I'll leave you and Gracie to—"

"Nuh-uh!" Gracie protested. As she looked from Matthias's face to Rose's, her lower lip trembled. "We was gonna have a *gut* time, just eatin' our pizza, Mamma. I promise I won't talk real loud. *Please?*"

Rose sighed. Was she giving in to Gracie's whims and whining too often these days? Was she being unreasonably modest? Matthias's expression didn't match his words. He was saying he'd leave her and Gracie to eat their lunch, but his intense gaze told Rose he'd be very disappointed if he couldn't join them. "It's only lunch, I guess," she said softly. "Not much different from sitting with you at the funeral meal."

"Is that a *jah*, Mamma?" Gracie asked in a hopeful whisper.

Rose felt time stand still for a brief and shining moment. Gracie had hooked her arm around Matthias's neck. They were cheek to cheek, appearing so comfortable together— outvoting her doubt with their optimism.

"Let's go in," Rose finally said. "I'm probably causing

folks to stare at us more out here, stalling on the sidewalk, than if we just sat in a booth and got our pizza."

"I was hoping you'd see it that way," Matthias said. "May I buy your lunch to repay you for that fine meal we ate in Cedar Creek? Please?"

Was he treating this as a date now? Rose's heart pounded painfully in her chest, because only eight short months ago, in August, she and Nathan were so happy together, and it seemed too soon—almost a betrayal of the marriage to which she'd been totally committed. And if she saw anyone she knew, they would wonder why she was out and about, apparently *celebrating*, mere days after she'd buried her mother.

"He's helpin' us be thrifty, Mamma," Gracie said in a loud whisper. She nodded emphatically, coaxing Rose with her cherubic smile.

Rose held her breath, hoping Gracie wouldn't elaborate on their financial situation—or about her posting notes on bulletin boards—as Matthias held the door for her. "All right, I'll accept your offer," she said softly. "You're very kind, Matthias."

"Just like Jesus!" Gracie beamed at Matthias as they chose a booth near the back of the restaurant. "I got me a new book about Jesus today, and He looks just like you, Matthias!"

Matthias's eyes widened. After Rose scooted toward the wall, he gently set Gracie on the seat beside her and took his place across the table from them. "That's a mighty high compliment, comparing me to Jesus," he replied. "I'll have to be very careful now, to be sure my behavior measures up—except I'll never be perfect, like He was."

Something about Matthias's expression, his kind hazel eyes when he gazed at her, made Rose sparkle inside. She dismissed this sensation as hunger, glad when the young waitress came to the table with glasses of water. Gracie immediately asked for a double-cheese pizza and lemonade. When Matthias asked Rose to choose what the second pizza would be, she blinked. Nathan had always done the ordering for all of them—

*Matthias isn't Nathan. Give him an answer before he thinks you don't even know what kind of pizza you like.*

"How about sausage and Canadian bacon with lots of green peppers, mushrooms, and black olives?" Rose ventured.

"*Yes!* All my favorite ingredients!" Matthias smiled at the waitress. "Make those two large pizzas, please, and bring us a pitcher of that lemonade."

Rose felt a fluttery excitement inside, but again she chalked it up to the aromas of spices and baking pizzas making her hungry—*For food, not for Matthias's attention,* she cautioned herself. She was glad Gracie was chattering with him so she could just observe, rather than making intelligent conversation. It seemed she was perfectly capable of taking her future in hand and raising Gracie, but when it came to talking to a nice guy like Matthias, she was feeling . . . tongue-tied.

# Chapter 12

Matthias nearly cheered as they stepped out of the restaurant and Gracie spotted kids in the park across the road. The bright-colored swings, slides, and teeter-totters—and little Plain kids in *kapps* and suspenders playing on them—drew Gracie like a magnet. Maybe he would finally have a chance for real conversation with Rose, who'd been very quiet while they were eating their pizza.

"Mamma, *pleeeaze* can I go play?" Gracie asked eagerly. "Those kids're havin' a real *gut* time!"

"We could watch her from that bench in the shade," Matthias suggested as Rose gazed intently at the kids and the young women who supervised them. "The park's right behind the Mennonite school, so the teachers let their scholars play on the swings at recess."

Rose glanced at the white school building. "We're probably keeping you from your work, Matthias."

He shrugged, hoping she wouldn't shy away and take Gracie home. For Rose Raber, Matthias had all the time in the world.

"Truth be told, I just got moved into my house here in

Morning Star, and I'm setting up my harness shop," he said. "Spending time with you girls is a nice break from toting boxes and unpacking them—and then figuring out where to put things. Moving to Morning Star is the best thing I've done for myself since Sadie passed, but all that decision making can wear you out!"

Gracie took her mother's hand and then grasped Matthias's. He reveled in the sweetness of being *chosen* by this charming child as they made their way to the park. "The littlest kids are playin' tag!" Gracie said excitedly. "I can run real fast, so I'm gonna play the next game with 'em, okay, Mamma?"

Rose chuckled. "It'll do you *gut* to run off some of that pizza before we head home."

"*Jah,* I'm tired of ridin'," Gracie said. "Here I go—bye, Matthias! Bye, Mamma!"

Matthias watched the little blonde scurry across the grass toward the other children. "*Gut* for Gracie," he said. "She's not afraid to meet new kids and join in their games."

"When I was her age, I was still hiding behind Mamma's skirts when strangers came around," Rose replied. "Sometimes I wish I had her confidence—and her energy."

Matthias listened closely. Rose didn't impress him as a shrinking violet, but he took this as a warning to go slowly with her, to be her friend until she wanted him to be more. "Tell me how you've been doing, Rose," he said as they approached a wooden bench in the shade. "Are you adjusting to your *mamm*'s absence?"

Rose sat down on the end of the bench. She placed her pizza box beside her, focusing on Gracie as she played with the other children. It took her several moments to reply.

"I'm surprised Gracie didn't announce why we're in town," she began softly. "We've also been to Willow Ridge and New

Haven today, because . . . I've been posting notices. Hoping to find work."

Matthias perched on the other end of the bench, greatly surprised by Rose's admission. As he set his pizza box on top of hers, he realized why Rose had remained so quiet while they ate their lunch. The shadows under her eyes and the set of her jaw told him she was having a tough time with this situation. If she had to look for a job—

*Don't offer her money! You'll scare her off,* his thoughts warned.

"I bet that was a hard decision—something you'd never figured on having to do," Matthias murmured. He longed to squeeze her hand, but he knew better.

Rose focused on him with wide green eyes that shimmered like a springtime forest beneath her arched brows. Her auburn hair and golden complexion made an unusual combination, but it looked beautiful on Rose.

"*Denki* for seeing it that way," she said gratefully. "Bishop Vernon wasn't as patient. He expects me to accept the church's financial help for at least five months—until Gracie's in school—before I look for work. But how can I sit idle for so long? I need to *do* something."

Matthias bit back the impulse to look after Rose's needs. He would offend her by offering her money, and it would be presumptuous to think she wanted anything more permanent, more emotionally satisfying from him—or any man—at this point. "A mother's death leaves a big hole in one's life," he agreed softly. "I admire you, Rose. You've suffered staggering losses this past year, yet you're making plans instead of rolling up in a ball and hiding. That takes a lot of gumption."

Rose's breath escaped in a soft sigh. "I worry about finding a job that'll allow Gracie to be with me," she admitted, "but

I must trust God to show me what I'm to do. I'm both her mother and her father now. I—I feel funny telling you all this, Matthias," she admitted quietly, "but I have to keep a roof over our heads and food on the table. Vernon knows that, but he doesn't understand, really. He insists that the Lord will provide, while I believe in the old saying about God helping those who help themselves."

Matthias felt he'd been entrusted with Rose's deepest beliefs and most desperate longings. It was all he could do not to blurt out his newfound desire to take care of her and Gracie. "We all need a sympathetic ear from time to time," he pointed out. "Rose, if there's any help you need—anything I can do for you—don't hesitate to ask. All right?"

She looked away, searching for Gracie in the group of kids who scurried from the boy who was "it." Their laughter and happy voices rang out, sounding so carefree that Matthias envied them.

"*Denki,* Matthias. I'll keep that in mind."

Matthias sensed he'd reached the limit of what Rose would accept from him. He smiled at the way Gracie darted away from the older boy who was trying to tag her—so lithe and quick, she was, mentally and physically.

Would Gracie lose her easy charm, her eager smile, if Rose had to leave her in someone else's care each day? A part of him objected to this arrangement as unnatural, yet Matthias certainly couldn't offer to watch Gracie. He had a shop to manage—harnesses to cut and customers to do business with. Not that Rose would even consider leaving Gracie with him—

"Can I tell you something else, Matthias—while Gracie's playing?" Rose sounded scared and shy, but in need of a sympathetic ear.

"What is it, Rose?" he asked gently. "I know you have a lot on your mind."

"I found out, the day Mamma died, that I'm not her biological child," Rose said in a voice he could barely hear. "I—I know who my birth mother is. Now that I'm nearly alone in the world, I have these fantasies of finding her—"

"Oh, my," Matthias murmured. "That's quite a thing to discover at this point in your life. I—I guess I'd be curious, too, in your place."

Rose gazed gratefully at him. "My birth mother wrote me letters after I was born, Matthias. She told me about how she loved my father, but he left the Old Order to become an artist," she said with a hint of pride in her voice. "She also said she was getting married and that I shouldn't try to find her—not that I have any idea where she lives. But her husband, Saul Hartzler, has a name that's a bit different from most Plain fellows, because he spells it with a *U*—like the Saul in the Bible who persecuted Christians rather than as a nickname for Solomon. So maybe it wouldn't be so hard to—"

"It's one thing to be curious," Matthias blurted, "but it's another thing altogether to go butting into this gal's marriage. You'd better leave well enough alone, Rose," he warned. "I can't think that Saul Hartzler—or any man—would want to find out his wife had a baby before she married him and kept it a secret. He'd most likely order you out and then chastise his wife as well."

Rose's face fell. "You sound just like Vernon."

"I didn't mean to hurt your feelings," Matthias said quickly. "It's just that—"

"I—I'm sorry I bothered you with my personal problems, Matthias." Rose stood up, her movements stiff with disappointment. "Gracie and I should head home. *Denki* again for the pizza."

Without allowing him to reply, Rose grabbed her pizza box and strode toward the playing children. She signaled to Gracie and then grasped her daughter's hand. Gracie knew better than to protest, but her little face appeared tight with frustration. Matthias sat on the bench until they had crossed the street, heading for the bulk store parking lot. He'd been hoping for another hug from the little girl who'd won him over so easily.

*You told Rose the truth*, he said to himself as he walked home. *The truth shall set you free—but you're probably free of Rose's company forever now. She's like a moth near a flame, headed for a scorching you want no part of, Wagler.*

# Chapter 13

That evening after she'd put Gracie to bed, Rose chided herself for revealing so much to Matthias after lunch. What had possessed her to tell him she needed a job? And why had she mentioned learning about her birth mother? She'd had no intention of opening up to him—

*Matthias is a very considerate listener—and he seemed genuinely interested in my welfare, that's why.*

But when all was said and done, Matthias had been no different from Bishop Vernon. He had no idea how she longed to find her birth mother after losing Mamma . . . how her life loomed before her like an empty tomb—like the yawning grave that had undone her in the cemetery. Once she fell into that emptiness, Rose feared she'd never be able to crawl out.

*What if Matthias knows Saul Hartzler? Maybe he got snippy because he knew Saul would cause trouble for Anne if I showed up.*

Rose dropped into the recliner, thinking back to her conversation with Matthias. He'd seemed cordial and compassionate until she'd mentioned Saul's name. Then he'd sternly told her to leave well enough alone.

Rose sighed tiredly. Her life would be a lot simpler if Anne hadn't written those persuasive letters—or if Mamma had destroyed them. Surely, those two women had known she'd be tempted to search for her birth mother if she had any inkling of where to find Anne Hartzler—or Saul.

Rose yawned. She'd been on the road most of the day, doing what she'd considered prudent for her future, but now Matthias's mention of rolling herself up in a ball and hiding sounded like a pretty good idea. She could let the church district cover her expenses—could be obedient to the bishop and dependent on charity for the rest of her life.

*Or I could let God handle it tonight, and I'll try again tomorrow.*

On Tuesday afternoon, Matthias decided to do some investigating—which would not only answer questions Rose had raised, but would be a way for him to introduce himself as a new shop owner in Morning Star. As he walked toward the carriage shop on the outskirts of town, he planned what he would say . . . how he would figure out whether the Hartzler fellow who owned it was the man Rose had been talking about. Matthias hadn't lived in Morning Star long enough to attend a church service, or he would've already met Hartzler because he was the deacon. He knew of several Hartzler families scattered around the area, and he knew of a couple of Solomon Hartzlers who went by Sol.

But Rose was right. If the fellow who owned the Hartzler Carriage Company spelled his name with a *U,* he was probably the man who'd married Rose's birth mother. Matthias had heard the carriage maker employed more workers than anyone else in the Plain community, which made him a man to be reckoned with—quite possibly the wealthiest man in the Morning Star church district. Such a fellow wouldn't want any secret babies showing up. It would be a scandal—a heinous breach of trust—if the deacon's wife had borne a child out of wedlock. And if Hartzler took after his biblical namesake, persecuting folks, Rose—and her birth mother—would be in deep trouble.

Matthias slowed his pace as he approached the carriage shop. The white metal building was much larger than most Plain shops, with a modest sign on its side: HARTZLER CARRIAGE COMPANY. Amish and Mennonite families in the area had been buying their rigs, courting buggies, and farm wagons here for years.

When he stepped through the back door, Matthias paused to let his ears adjust to the racket of air-driven tools and the rapid-fire whine of bolts being driven into metal surfaces. At the back of the large room, several fellows attached the pieces of standard black buggies on a short assembly line. On the wall nearest the door, he noticed a list of names alongside time slots—the employees and their weekly schedule. The name above the list made him swallow hard:

HARTZLER CARRIAGE COMPANY—SAUL HARTZLER, PROPRIETOR

"What can we do for you today?" a male voice bellowed above the factory noise. "I'm Saul Hartzler. And you would be—?"

Matthias's hand got swallowed in a hearty grip that left his fingers aching. "I'm Matthias Wagler," he replied loudly. "Just opened a new harness shop here in town, and thought I'd introduce myself. *Gut* to meet you, Saul."

"You're a harness maker, eh?"

"*Jah,* and I also make custom-tooled saddles and special tack, for parades and such," Matthias replied. "Lived and worked in Willow Ridge before I came here."

Saul motioned for Matthias to follow him. After they crossed the impressively clean, well-organized shop area, they entered a separate workroom.

"Quieter in here," Hartzler remarked as he closed the door. He was a tall, burly man with thick, black hair and a dense beard framing his face. "What brings you to Morning Star? I hear Willow Ridge is quite the busy place these days, so I'd think your harness shop would do well there."

"*Jah,* it did," Matthias agreed. "But sometimes a man needs a change in his life."

As he explained how crowded the home place had become, and how he was hoping to expand his business, Matthias had the feeling Hartzler was sizing him up. Saul was nodding, following every word Matthias said. He gestured for Matthias to approach three of the most unusual carriages he'd ever seen.

"You've mentioned custom work, so I'll show you my latest special projects," Saul said with a wide smile. "English folks operate places they call amusement parks—like the rides at a county fair or a carnival, but on a lot bigger scale. Some of these places offer rides in fancy horse-drawn carriages—and I've been getting orders from far-flung places called Disney World and Six Flags, all over the country."

Matthias's eyes widened. "My word, this coach looks like a huge pumpkin—and this pink one, with the white wrought-iron curlicues and the grid of tiny wires around it—"

Hartzler's laughter filled the room. "Mighty exotic, ain't so? I'm going to install hundreds of wee little lights on those wires," he explained as he led Matthias around the three vehicles. "It's supposed to make little girls feel like a fairy princess—like Cinderella—when they ride in it."

Matthias imagined Gracie's delight at seeing this carriage, let alone getting to ride in it. Little Plain kids heard the occasional fairy tale, even though their parents were more likely to read them Bible stories. The third carriage reminded him of pictures he'd seen of stagecoaches, except it was very elaborate. All the supports, braces, and decorative details—even the spokes of the wheels—were painted sparkly gold.

"This one's for a place where they perform high-class weddings—*not* a church, most likely," Hartzler explained. "Can you see a Plain couple riding around in this after they got hitched? Hah! Bishop Jeremiah would be having none of that!"

Matthias laughed along with the man beside him. He'd heard Jeremiah Shetler was more progressive than other bishops in this region, but he hadn't yet met Morning Star's leader. As Matthias took another turn around the three vehicles, admiring the meticulous workmanship, he sensed Hartzler was still scrutinizing him.

"This custom work takes a lot of time," Saul said. "I do most of it myself, and it brings in several thousand dollars more per carriage than the rigs and wagons we make for our Plain customers."

"*Jah,* I can imagine." Matthias was itching to ask Saul about his family, but he didn't want to overstay his welcome—and he felt Hartzler should bring up that subject himself. He had explained his own family situation, after all. "I should let you get back to your work. I just wanted to stop by—"

"See you at church next Sunday. We'll gather at the Shetler place, just west of town." Hartzler reached for his hand again.

"I might be bending your ear soon, about providing harnesses and tack for some of my buggy customers. Let's keep in touch, *jah?*"

As Matthias stepped outside into the bright sunshine—and the relative peace and quiet, after being inside the shop—his head was spinning. If he could do some harness work for Hartzler, his name and reputation would get around Morning Star much faster than if he just worked in his little shop at home. It was something to consider, because it was obvious that Saul Hartzler made an impressive income and tolerated nothing less than the best quality work.

Saul would also tolerate nothing less than absolute loyalty—which was another reason Rose shouldn't contact her birth mother. Hartzler came across as jovial and enthusiastic, but his painfully firm handshake—his bearlike size and physical strength—told Matthias that anybody who messed with this man or intruded upon his fine life would regret it immediately.

*How can I warn Rose again to stay away from Saul's family, without her guessing I've met him?* Matthias pondered this. If Rose guessed that he'd found Saul so quickly, she would surely search out Hartzler's wife.

# Chapter 14

As Thursday morning wore on and her muscles grew sore, Rose forced herself to keep hoeing rows in the garden and planting seeds for carrots, radishes, and beets. Gardening had never been her favorite job. It had to be done, though—and in a few weeks, she needed to buy her cabbage, pepper, and tomato plants from Treva's Greenhouse.

Gracie had grown bored with keeping the proper distance between the tiny seeds, so Rose allowed her to sit in the shade with her chalkboard. She was singing cheerful songs, drawing all sorts of flowers and animals with her colored chalk.

"Look, Mamma! A butterfly!"

Rose slowly straightened her back, reminding herself to be patient. Gracie was good at entertaining herself, after all, and that was something to be grateful for. "Pretty colors," she said with a nod. "You're a fine little artist, sweet pea."

Gracie beamed at her and scurried back to her spot in the shade. As she wiped the board with an old washcloth and began to sketch something else, Rose wondered again if her daughter's artistic talent might've come from her grandfather, Joel Lapp. These past couple of days at home had given Rose a lot of time to think about her birth parents—and about her suspicion that Matthias and Vernon knew Saul Hartzler, but they weren't about to tell her where he and his family lived.

Was she being foolish, hoping she would meet Anne Hartzler someday? Should she just burn those letters and eliminate the temptation they were leading her into?

*Forbidden fruit tastes the sweetest,* Rose's thoughts taunted her. *Anne's words are already burned into your heart and soul, so setting fire to them would do no good.*

As she gazed down the seemingly endless row where she was planting green beans, her aching back urged her to take a break. But if she went inside and poured a glass of iced tea, her thoughts would again wander toward Anne Hartzler—or torment her about what she'd do for money if no one replied to the index cards she'd posted. Her mind was a whirlwind of what-ifs and second-guessing, and she was clinging to the hope that God would indeed provide some answers.

"Mamma! Here comes the mailman!"

"Stay out of the road until he's gone, Gracie," Rose reminded her daughter sternly. Bless her, Gracie loved to chat with anyone who came by, and she didn't always pay attention to traffic. Rose stepped carefully over the rows she'd planted, her bare feet sinking into the soft, moist soil until she reached the grass at the garden's edge. The mailman stuck their mail in the big metal box, said something that made Gracie smile, and waved before driving on. Rose waved back, watching her daughter open the box.

"Lotsa stuff, Mamma!" Gracie declared as Rose approached. "Here! You take the mail and I'll see if we got any phone calls."

Rose smiled. She remembered what an adventure it was, at Gracie's age, to check the mailbox and the phone, but her mood faltered as she flipped through the stack of envelopes.

The one from Gestner-Conrad Funeral Home was probably the bill for Mamma's coffin, the basic preparation of her body, and the closing of her grave. Even though the Amish didn't embalm their dead, Rose suspected the total would appall her. The Yoder brothers down the road had also sent a reminder about the load of wood they'd delivered last month. Ordinarily, they expected payment upon delivery, but they'd given her extra time because she'd been caring for Mamma. She couldn't stall them any longer—and she still had to pay the bill for Mamma's final chemo treatments, too.

Rose was ready to cry, wondering if she had enough in the bank to cover even half of these obligations, when Gracie hollered at her.

"Mamma! The message light's blinkin'!"

Rose composed herself so Gracie wouldn't see how upset she'd become. With a smile pasted on her face, she strode to the small white phone shanty.

"I'm gonna go draw some more with my chalks," Gracie said. "Can we have lunch after you listen to the messages?"

"*Jah,* that's a *gut* idea," Rose replied as she sat down in front of the phone. "I won't be long."

When Gracie ran toward the porch, Rose took a deep breath. Someone might be calling to remind her she owed them money, too—or Vernon might be telling her to forget about her birth mother and stay home with Gracie. She pressed the button and grabbed a pencil so she could jot a phone number on the scratch pad.

"I'm calling for Rose Raber," a woman's voice said. "I saw your notice on the board in the Morning Star bulk store, and I'd like to talk to you about cooking at the senior center. If you could call me—Sherrie West—as soon as possible—"

With a pounding heart, Rose scribbled the phone number.

Someone named Sherrie had seen her notice and wanted her to come to work! Maybe someday she could pay all these bills, after all!

*Don't count your chickens until they've hatched,* she reminded herself. It was one thing for a potential employer to call, and it was another thing altogether to land the job. With shaking fingers, Rose dialed the number. She'd never applied for a job, and she had no idea what questions to ask or—

"Hello, this is Sherrie West at the Morning Star Senior Center. How may I help you?"

Rose's mind went blank.

"Hello? May I ask who's calling, please?"

"*Jah,* it's—I'm Rose Raber, the one who posted the index card in the bulk store," she said nervously.

"Rose! I'm glad you called back so quickly." The woman spoke in a businesslike tone, yet she sounded patient and kind. "The lady who's been running our kitchen has become too ill to work anymore. Could you come sometime soon for an interview—maybe today? I'm eager to talk to you."

"Oh!" Rose's thoughts spun wildly in her head. She would have to shower and change clothes and drive all the way to Morning Star and—

"Are you still interested in a job, or has someone already hired you?" Sherrie prompted.

"*Jah!* No! I—I'm sorry I sound so *ferhoodled,*" Rose replied with a sigh. "I'm excited to hear from you, and I want to come talk to you, but can it be tomorrow? I've been planting my garden and I'm a mess—and it takes me nearly an hour to drive to Morning Star. But I want to come!" she added quickly.

Sherrie chuckled. "My previous cook was a Plain lady, and she was such a conscientious worker that I'd prefer to hire another Amish or Mennonite woman. Can you arrive tomorrow, by noon?"

"*Jah!* I'll be there!"

"I look forward to meeting you, Rose. Be careful on the roads." *Click.*

Rose flopped against the back of the wooden chair, stunned. Would Sherrie hire her if she'd be wearing black all the time? What if she seemed too nervous? What if the kitchen had electric appliances and she burned everything? What if she had no idea what to cook for the residents and they complained about her food?

"What about Gracie?" she said with a sigh. Rose was elated that she'd gotten a response to one of her postings, but reality was smacking her in the face. She had no choice but to take Gracie with her tomorrow, but what if she had to find a full-time place for her daughter to stay? What if Sherrie wouldn't hire her because she believed Rose should stay home with her child?

*I'll figure it all out. All things work together for gut to them that love God,* Rose reminded herself as she stepped out of the phone shanty. She would take this one step at a time. Her first step was to fix lunch. Then she would explain this new, exciting opportunity to Gracie. And then?

*I have to pull myself together so I don't sound mindless when I show up for my interview. Lord, please tell me what to do and say!*

Matthias was tapping the final shading designs into a black leather saddle when his shop door opened behind him. "Be with you in a sec," he called out. "I have to finish this section while the leather's damp."

"Take your time, Matthias. I'll mosey around your shop."

Matthias's eyes widened as he tapped the tool with his mallet. He was pretty sure it was Saul Hartzler talking, but the detailed work he was doing for a longtime customer had priority over visiting. "This saddle is for a cowboy who rides the professional rodeo circuit," he remarked. "I'm pretty excited that he's ordered a third one from me, along with a matching bridle and breast collar."

"The highest praise a customer pays us is when he orders more of our work," Saul said. He came to stand beside Matthias at his worktable. "Will it bother you if I watch?"

"Nah, I'm almost done." Matthias took a deep breath so his fingers wouldn't shake. Being this close to finished, he didn't want to ruin the intricate floral-and-star design that made this saddle so special. "I like to do this custom work when I can. Plain harnesses and tack are my bread and butter, but sometimes it's nice to have a little jam, you know?"

"That's why I take orders for those special carriages," Saul replied with a chuckle. "I can build a basic rig in my sleep. I like the challenge of making somebody else's designs and ideas come to life."

With two final taps, Matthias laid aside his tools and smiled up at his guest. "All done! It's *gut* to see you, Saul. What can I do for you?"

Saul leaned closer so he could study the detailed design on the saddle. "Beautiful work, Wagler," he stated. "Will this have some brass or silver ornamentation, like the saddles I saw in the Simple Gifts shop in Willow Ridge?"

Matthias's heart skipped a beat. Hartzler didn't impress him as a fellow who spent much time shopping, especially in gift stores. "*Jah,* this cowboy loves the flashy stuff," he replied, gesturing toward a nearby table where other pieces of the saddle were drying. "Almost every blank space will be covered with silver and rhinestones—lots of sparkly blue and white rhinestones. These pieces will be a lot fancier than the ones you saw in the gift shop."

"Stands to reason. You're selling those other pieces on consignment," Saul said with a nod. His bearded face creased when he smiled at Matthias. "I'll get right to the point. I mentioned earlier that I might want you to supply harnesses to some of my customers. Now that I've asked around in Willow Ridge, I've got a different proposition in mind. How about coming to the house for supper Saturday night?" he asked, gazing intently into Matthias's eyes. "We can get better acquainted over a *gut* meal. I think that's important for a new fellow in town—and even more important if we're to work together."

Matthias knew better than to hesitate. "I'd be pleased to come," he said as he stuck out his hand.

Saul shook it with another knuckle-crunching grip, pumping Matthias's arm. "Glad to hear it. I think we can do a lot of *gut* for each other, Wagler. See you around six."

"Looking forward to it," Matthias replied, hoping he didn't sound nervous.

After Hartzler left, Matthias paced around his shop to think about what had just transpired. He was going to have dinner with a prosperous Amish businessman—the deacon of his new church district—to discuss making some custom harnesses. It was an opportunity such as he'd not dared to dream of, after seeing the magnitude of the work Hartzler's shop produced.

*And you'll meet his wife—Rose's birth mother. This might*

*be the most important meal you've eaten in a long while, and you'll have to figure out what comes next—what you will or won't tell Rose when you see her again,* he reminded himself.

Matthias laughed as he put away his tools. After the way he'd upset her in the park, telling her to stay out of the Hartzlers' lives, Rose might not give him the time of day.

*But she'll be glued to my every word if I tell her I've met her mother. . . .*

# Chapter 15

"Mamma, tell me again. What's a *inner-view*?" Gracie asked plaintively.

Rose had to word her reply carefully, because she wasn't sure what to expect from her talk with Sherrie West. She gazed at her daughter, seated beside her in the enclosed buggy as they drove to Morning Star on Friday morning. Gracie was wearing the new blue dress Rose had sewn last night—a fresh spring color that might make her own black cape dress and apron look less faded and somber by comparison.

"I'm going to talk to the lady who runs the Morning Star Senior Center," Rose explained as she steered Daisy onto the county road that led to Morning Star and Willow Ridge. "She wants me to be the cook—"

"Can I help, Mamma? I like bein' in the kitchen with you." Gracie smiled up at Rose, holding her new book open in her lap.

Rose paused, thinking about how to answer. Her daughter was so precious, so trusting—and smart enough to detect a dodge. "I don't know, sweet pea," she replied. "I like having you in the kitchen with me, too, but we'll need to see what the rules are. If we find out you can't go with me, I'll ask Rosemary if she would keep you—"

"So me and Katie could play! Every day!"

Rose smiled. She probably shouldn't have mentioned that alternative before asking Rosemary if she'd watch Gracie—but a lot of their everyday activities might get tossed like a salad if she took this job. "We'll see," she said firmly. "We'll talk about this after Mamma's finished visiting with the lady at the senior center."

Gracie went back to gazing at her book about Jesus. As Rose drove the last mile, she reviewed the things she wanted to say to Sherrie, hoping she appeared competent rather than scatterbrained. "Here we are in Morning Star," she said when they came in sight of the park and the bulk store.

Her daughter looked out the window with a smile. "Maybe the kids from the school will be havin' recess when we leave that senior place," she remarked hopefully. "Can we play on the swings before we go home?"

"Maybe. We'll see what time it is when I finish."

Nodding, Gracie glanced down a side street with modest homes on both sides. "Where's Matthias's house? Will we see him today?"

"I doubt it," Rose replied quickly. "He'll be working in his harness shop."

"He's really nice, Mamma."

Rose glanced over to see that Gracie was gazing intently at her. "*Jah*, he is, sweet pea. But we've got other things on our minds—and there's the senior center up ahead. What's our *ABC* game for today?"

Gracie set her book on the seat. "*A* means *act like a big girl*," she recited. "*B* is *be very quiet*. *C* means *candy* from the bulk store, if I stay beside you the whole time."

Rose slung her arm around Gracie's little shoulders. "Exactly right! You're my best honey-girl, Gracie. We'll do just fine today."

"*Jah*, Mamma," she replied with a firm nod. "I got you and you got me. It's all *gut*."

As Rose steered the mare into the senior center's parking lot, she prayed that Gracie's positive attitude would fill her with confidence. It was true: she and Gracie had each other, and no matter what happened today, they would move into the future God had planned for them.

Rose hitched the mare to a fence post and took her daughter's hand. They entered the building through the front door, pausing to look around.

"Look, Mamma! There's little birds in this glass cage!" Gracie walked over to the corner of the lobby to gaze at the tiny, colorful birds, which gave Rose a moment to get her bearings. Sherrie's office—or a check-in desk—would surely be near the front door, but all she saw in the lobby area were clusters of upholstered chairs and tables with lamps, where folks could sit to visit. A big glass aquarium sat against one wall, and Gracie went over to look at the colorful fish swimming in it.

"Mrs. Raber? Hello!"

Rose turned to see a tall, slender Englishwoman with glasses and light brown hair in layers around her face. "*Jah*, I'm Rose—and this is my Gracie," Rose said as she gestured toward the aquarium.

"We have security cameras in the lobby, so I can watch who comes and goes from my office," the woman explained. "I'm Sherrie West, and I'm pleased you agreed to come, Rose. Would you like to look around before we talk?"

"That would be *gut*," Rose replied. "I've been to Morning

Star many times, but never in the senior center. Everything looks so bright and cheerful."

Sherrie gestured back toward the hallway. "We've recently repainted all the public areas and the dining room. We do our best to make the center feel like home for our residents—and we host craft sessions, card parties, and other activities that seniors from around town come to as well."

Rose nodded. She was about to mention that Plain families cared for their elderly members at home, no matter how ill or addled they were—but she sensed Sherrie might interpret such a remark as a criticism. "How many folks live here?" she asked instead.

"We have thirty-five small apartments, and right now thirty-two of them are occupied," Sherrie replied. "Our residents are ambulatory—they must be able to come to our dining room, although many of them use walkers or scooters to get around."

"*Scooters?*" Gracie piped up. "When I get bigger, I want a scooter!"

Rose squeezed Gracie's hand in warning, but Sherrie stopped in the double doorway of the dining room to look at her. "And how old are you, Gracie?"

"Five! I getta go to school pretty soon!"

Sherrie nodded. "It's good to be excited about going to school. Let's go this way and look at the kitchen, shall we?"

When they went through the double swinging doors, Rose's eyes widened. A huge stainless-steel stove and oven took up the center of the big room—and she was relieved to see that they were gas, like the stove at home. A large refrigerator and freezer lined the back wall, along with deep stainless-steel sinks and what she thought must be a dishwasher. "Will I be doing the dishes after I cook the meals?" Rose asked, gesturing toward the intimidating machine.

"No, my assistant, Alison, and our housekeepers take care of that. Mrs. Yutzy, who just left us, didn't want to run the dishwasher, either."

Rose nodded. "Mrs. Yutzy got ill, you said?"

"Yes. And before her multiple sclerosis limited her mobility, Frieda was with us for nearly ten years." Sherrie opened the big freezer so Rose could look inside. "She and I planned our menus a few weeks in advance and ordered most of the groceries from a food service. Do you cook mostly from scratch, Rose, or do you prefer to use box mixes?"

Rose's eyebrows shot up. "I can do whatever you prefer," she replied carefully, "but I'm used to making all our bread, and cooking what we have in our freezer and in glass jars— the vegetables we've canned from our garden."

Sherrie's smile made Rose feel like she'd given the right answer. "I think you'll know exactly how to prepare the good old-fashioned meals our residents prefer. We've kept a lot of favorite recipes in this box as well, so you'll have those to go by."

Rose nodded, encouraged. She opened one of the white metal cabinets above the back work counter, observing the neatly arranged baking supplies. "Who's been cooking since Frieda Yutzy left? I smell sausage and French toast, I think."

"You have a good nose, Rose," Sherrie said with a chuckle. "One of our housekeepers and I have been managing the meals, but we'll be glad to have someone who knows her way around a kitchen. Are you still interested in the position?"

"Oh, *jah*! I might make a few mistakes while I learn the routine, but I could do this job," she replied. She was about to ask if Gracie could come with her each day, when her heart sank. Her little girl wasn't in the kitchen anymore—and when Sherrie realized why Rose was glancing into the back corners of the room, her smile dimmed.

"Have you recently been widowed, Rose?" Sherrie asked gently. "I bet, like most Amish women, you're not comfortable leaving your child in someone else's care."

"I—I lost my husband and my *dat* last summer, and my *mamm* twelve days ago," Rose replied in a wilted voice. "I'll just go find Gracie—"

When Rose stepped out into the dining room, however, her daughter was nowhere in sight. She nearly choked on her disappointment. She'd just lost her chance at getting a good job she was capable of doing. When Rose heard a familiar little voice in the hallway, she spotted Gracie seated on a padded bench beside an elderly, stooped woman, not far from the aquarium. She was about to call out to her daughter, but Sherrie gently took hold of her arm.

"Let's watch for a moment," the director said softly, nodding toward Gracie and the elderly lady. "Gladys hasn't smiled this way for a long time. She's very withdrawn, probably because she never has any visitors. Her family lives a ways from here, and they seem to have forgotten her—except to send her payments."

Rose was appalled. It bothered her that English folks felt so comfortable dropping off their older relatives to live in a facility like this. Although she couldn't hear what the two of them were discussing, the happy tone of Gracie's little-girl voice rang in the sitting area.

Gracie spotted Rose in the doorway. "Mamma! This is Gladys," she called out. "We've been talkin' and she wants to be my new *mammi*! Can I come see her every day? Please, Mamma?"

Rose's breath caught and she swiped at a tear. "Oh, my," she murmured to Sherrie. "Gracie really misses her grandmother. I—I can't get her hopes up, though, about seeing Gladys—"

Sherrie was suddenly smiling brightly. She walked over to the bench, rubbing Gladys's stooped shoulder. "Looks like you've made a new friend, Gladys."

Rose approached cautiously, not wanting to interrupt this quiet conversation. When she opened her arms, Gracie slid off the bench and jogged into her embrace. "Mamma, I runned off, so I don't get C for *candy,* huh?" she whispered apologetically. "But I saw this lady sittin' all by herself—"

"I do have a new friend," Gladys agreed. She sat up straighter to smile at Gracie and Rose. "Such a sweet little girl, to talk to a lonely old lady. I hope I get to see you again, honey."

Sherrie turned toward Gracie, who now rested against Rose's hip. "Your daughter seems very comfortable here," she said. "Most kids shy away from our residents."

Rose held Sherrie's gaze, sensing this situation might turn in her favor. "Gracie's around older folks a lot at church. They love her sunshiny company," she said quietly.

"Gracie might be just the sort of sunshine we need around here," the director continued in a thoughtful tone. "We'll have to establish some rules about where and when Gracie can visit with our residents—"

"Oh, Gracie knows about following rules. She just admitted that she'd broken one by leaving me," Rose said as Gracie nodded. "She loves to make friends, and—and I would *really* appreciate it if she could come here with me—"

"I'll be real *gut* and stay with Mamma in the kitchen," Gracie said solemnly. "Me and Mamma, we're *together.*"

"I can see that, Gracie, and it's wonderful," Sherrie agreed. "Shall we go to my office and talk about the particulars of this job, Rose? Gracie, will you come with us? I have some magazines you can look at."

As they sat in Sherrie's office, Rose's thoughts whirled. The pay for this job seemed like quite a lot. She could work either five or six days a week—and she could start either tomorrow or Monday. After explaining what Rose would be doing, adding information about how the senior center operated, Sherrie complimented Gracie for sitting in a chair, quietly looking at magazines.

Gracie beamed. "I'm readin' about these deers and turkeys," she stated, pointing to the photographs in the magazine. "You gotta watch out, or deers will eat the plants right outta your garden!"

Sherrie laughed. "Yes, they will! That's why we have a fence around our garden in the backyard. Would you like to see it?"

Rose was still so excited she could hardly talk as they went down the hall. She was pleased to hear that the residents who were able could work in the garden with Sherrie's assistant, who did most of the planting and picking. "Looks like you'll be having peas and salad greens soon. I'm glad we'll have fresh food to work with," Rose added gratefully. "The longer I'm here, the more I like it."

"We'll see you both on Monday then," Sherrie said. "I'm so glad you've come to see us, Gracie. I think you'll make a lot of friends here."

"Me too! See ya!"

Rose's heart skipped happily as she and Gracie went out the front door—after Gracie stopped to peer into the birds' glass enclosure. The sun was shining high in the sky and Rose stopped in the parking lot to raise her face and soak up its bright rays. With the warmth on her face and a little hand in hers—and a way to make a living and support her child—Rose felt right with the world again.

"C is for what, Gracie?" she asked as she lifted her daughter into the buggy.

Gracie's eyes widened. "I get candy, Mamma?"

"*Jah,* you did really well at the senior center," Rose said as she unhitched Daisy from the post. "And *P* is for the pizza we can have, and *S* is for the swings you can play on for a few minutes before we drive home."

As Rose stepped up into the buggy, Gracie scooted across the seat and threw her arms around Rose's waist. "Candy *and* pizza *and* swings?" she asked gleefully. "Oh, Mamma, it's a happy day, ain't so?"

"It's a happy day," Rose agreed as she directed Daisy toward the street. "'This is the day the Lord has made. Let us rejoice and be glad in it.'"

## Chapter 16

On Saturday afternoon, Matthias closed his shop a little early. He'd met several local fellows who'd come in to check out his harnesses, and he'd taken a few orders, so he was in a fine mood when he went to the house to freshen up. He wanted to look just right for going to supper at the Hartzler home.

Matthias showered and carefully shaved above his beard, which he'd trimmed that morning. He chose his newest green shirt—he hadn't worn it since Annie Mae had ironed it for him—and his better pair of gray broadfall trousers. It occurred to him that he would soon run out of clean, pressed clothes, but he couldn't be concerned about that. Matthias focused on making a favorable impression on Saul, and on getting acquainted with Hartzler's wife—just in case he got to see Rose again.

As Matthias walked the half mile to the Hartzler place, he wondered again about what Saul had in mind, as far as the two of them working together. Would he want Matthias to make harnesses fancy enough for custom carriages, like he'd seen in the backroom of the shop? Or would Saul merely send some of his clients to Matthias's shop, as a courtesy? As he strolled up the Hartzler's packed-dirt lane, he prayed that the evening would be beneficial to everyone and that he would gain a new understanding of Morning Star's Amish deacon.

Saul was waiting for Matthias on the wide front porch of the tall, immaculate white house. He rose from the porch swing, his features alight. "Matthias, we're all looking forward to becoming *gut* friends with you," he declared in a booming voice. "Anne and my *mamm* have been cooking all our favorite dishes today, hoping you'll like them, too."

Matthias preceded Saul into the house. "I've never met a meal I didn't like—especially if somebody besides me cooked it," he added with a chuckle. "What a lovely home you have."

The front room was large yet cozy, with hardwood floors that glimmered and overstuffed chairs and two sofas upholstered in deep maroon. Handsome wooden bookcases flanked the stone chimney, crammed with books. Near the big front window, a quilting frame was set up to take advantage of the room's best light.

"I believe our meal's ready, so let's head on into the kitchen."

Matthias entered one of the largest kitchens he'd ever seen—it spanned the entire width of the house. A broad table was set for four in the center of the room, which was painted buttery yellow and had two white-curtained windows in each of its three walls. When a slender woman at the stove turned to smile at him, Matthias saw Rose Raber's face with fair, freckled skin and thinner eyebrows.

"My wife, Anne," Saul said, "and my mother, Martha Maude. Matthias says he's looking forward to your cooking."

"Welcome to our home," Anne said graciously. She and her mother-in-law began carrying large, steaming bowls of food to the table. "We didn't make anything fancy—"

"Just *gut* stick-to-your-ribs food, and lots of it!" Martha Maude joined in. She was taller than Anne and stockier—built a lot like her son. "We're always glad to meet new folks. God made every one of us different, with our own skills and preferences—and quirks," she added mischievously. "What would we be without our idiosyncrasies?"

Matthias chuckled as Saul pointed him to the chair at the right of the table's head. He sensed Martha Maude had read most of the books in the front room, as she had a more intellectual air than most Plain women he knew. "And half the fun of meeting new folks is figuring out what those idiosyncrasies are," he said.

When the two women sat down, everyone bowed for a moment of silent prayer. Delectable aromas of fried chicken, glazed carrots, and new peas creamed with potato chunks made Matthias's stomach rumble. He was thanking God for this glorious meal and the new friends who'd invited him to share it, when another thought struck him like lightning.

*I don't see a single sign of kids or grandkids. No toys, no noise, no high chairs, or pets.*

Saul cleared his throat, ending the prayer. They passed a basket of fresh, warm rolls, butter, and homemade jam. Along with the carrots and creamed peas, Anne had fixed a relish tray with pickled beets, green onions, radishes—and she'd made a bowl of wilted lettuce with bacon, as well.

"I'm guessing all these fresh vegetables came from your garden," Matthias said as he passed the relish tray to Saul. "My sister-in-law, Annie Mae, has expanded the garden at the home place in Willow Ridge, but I doubt I'll get anything planted this year."

Martha Maude gazed directly at him, her face warming with a smile. "Could be you'll become our personal mission project, Matthias. Anne and I always seem to plant a lot more food than we can possibly eat or need to can."

"We still have several jars of green beans, tomatoes, and other vegetables from last year, too," Anne put in warmly. "We'll load you up before you leave—"

"And we'll see that you get some fresh veggies as well," Martha Maude added with a decisive nod. "We can pick them after supper while you and Saul visit."

Matthias could hardly speak for the gratitude that welled up inside him. "*Denki* so much," he said, including Saul in his thankful gaze. "You're making me feel very welcome."

The meal proceeded at a leisurely pace. The ladies gave Matthias recommendations about the best places in town for shopping, and Saul spoke about the many Plain shops out in the country. They also talked about the businesses in Willow Ridge. Saul had apparently spent quite a bit of time there on Thursday, when his carriage shop—and a lot of other Amish businesses—closed because the men worked most of the day on Saturday.

"The new café there puts out quite a spread," Saul remarked as he sopped up his cream sauce with a piece of his roll. "I was glad we stopped there for supper."

"*Jah,* the Grill N Skillet does a lot of business," Matthias said.

Martha Maude laughed as she stacked their dirty dinner plates. "A pie in the hand is worth two in Willow Ridge, *jah?*" she quipped. "Our rhubarb plants outdid themselves last year, so we're using up what's in the freezer to make space for this year's crop. Hope you don't mind that the cake I made also has rhubarb in it."

"Cake *and* pie?" Matthias replied. "Hope I can roll myself away from the table!"

After dessert and coffee brought the meal to a satisfying close, Saul invited Matthias to join him out on the front porch. Dusk was settling over the pasture, where a herd of Black Angus cattle grazed. The dogwood trees along the fence were in full bloom, their pale blossoms glowing with the final rays of the sunset. Matthias stood at the porch railing to take in the gentle roll of the green hills, the freshness of the spring evening air, and the massive red barn behind the house.

"Are those your cattle?" he asked as he settled into the wicker chair beside the one Saul had taken. "They make quite a picture."

"I raise them for restaurants and butcher shops that specialize in grass-fed, organic beef," Saul replied. "We Plain folks, who don't cotton to fancy feed additives or growth hormones, are in a unique position. English pay top dollar when they know their beef, pork, and poultry are raised locally. But enough about my cattle," he added in a purposeful voice. "I would like to put a display of your harnesses and tooled leatherwork in my carriage shop, Matthias. I believe my customers will recognize the high quality of your work."

Matthias's smile felt so wide, he probably resembled an ecstatic little boy at Christmas. "I'd be happy to provide examples of my work for—"

Saul held up his hand. "I have another proposition of a more serious, long-term nature," he said, gazing steadily into Matthias's eyes. "I have no sons to carry on my carriage business, and no employees with enough acumen to keep the shop profitable if something should happen to me. I'd like you to be my business partner, Matthias," he stated without hesitation. "I've seen your work, and I've talked to a number of business owners in Willow Ridge. I'm convinced you're the man I've been looking for."

Matthias couldn't breathe or think. It seemed Hartzler had traveled to Willow Ridge with the idea that he'd partner with Matthias even though they'd just met earlier this week.

"I—I don't know what to say," Matthias stammered, although there was really only one reply to Saul's incredible proposition. "I'd be honored to partner with you, Saul. I'm amazed that you've made me this offer so soon after we've become acquainted."

Saul's dark beard shifted with his smile. "I'm rarely wrong about people's aptitudes and character. You impress me as a man who provides the highest quality of workmanship on an everyday basis—and not just for folks who can afford your pricier, specialized items. I respect that."

Bedazzled by Saul's offer and compliments, Matthias gazed out over the pasture to compose his thoughts. This was no time to say something that would come across as silly—no time for half-baked ideas. "What do you see as my role in this partnership?" Matthias asked softly. "I know very little about building carriages—and your shop is clearly more productive and profitable than my harness business. From where I stand, it seems like a very lopsided arrangement."

Saul's intent gaze expressed his agreement with Matthias's assessment, and his pleasure in it as well. "I can teach you the rudiments of carriage making, but I understand that working with leather is your calling, Matthias," he replied. "I believe if I introduce you to my men—and show you my customer records, and we discuss the business, in general—over time you'll get a firm grasp of it."

Matthias's eyebrows rose. "You don't want me to keep the books, do you? It's one thing to operate a little one-man shop, but it's something else entirely to manage a company that pays wages and ships carriages all over the country."

Once again, Saul smiled, as though he appreciated Matthias more with every question he asked. "My mother does the accounting," he said. "Truth be told, her sharp eye on the books has probably had as much to do with keeping me profitable as my own decisions about what projects I take on. Martha Maude can tell you to the last dollar what those three fancy custom carriages have cost me to build," he said. "I rely on her figures when I tell those big English clients what they'll be paying me for such specialized work."

Matthias considered this. It seemed a partnership with Hartzler Carriage Company might be more complicated than a gentleman's agreement made on a handshake—and it surprised him that Saul considered his mother as another partner, of sorts. "I don't mean to sound doubtful," he said cautiously, "but if something happens to you—and to your *mamm*—"

"Then Hartzler Carriage Company will belong to you, Matthias." Saul shifted in his chair, leaning toward Matthias to emphasize his point. "You've got it right. Martha Maude will remain in place as the company's anchor and accountant if I should pass first, but once we're both gone—or unable to conduct business—you will own Hartzler Carriage Company. I've prayed faithfully on this matter over the past few days, Matthias."

Saul settled back in his chair then, appearing totally serene and at ease. "I believe God wants me to take you as my full partner. And my mother knows better than to second-guess God," he added with a chuckle.

Matthias felt light-headed. Partnering with Saul Hartzler would be a monumental undertaking—a large, long-term learning curve. But what an opportunity!

"To make this more official, I'll write up an agreement that spells out the terms we've discussed," Saul said. "Once we've signed it, I'll put it with the company's records. Martha Maude already understands this partnership, but a signed document will spell out the details for any employees who might doubt my wishes, should my mother and I both pass on at the same time."

Matthias nodded, still in awe of the plan Hartzler had put into place so quickly. He'd never known a Plain businessman to plan so fully for the future by putting his wishes in writing—and he understood that Saul's implicit trust in him meant that there would be no attorney involved. Old Order Amish preferred to handle their own affairs and keep English lawyers out of them.

There would be no backing out, either. No changing his mind.

"*Jah*, the terms of our agreement should be on record," Matthias agreed. "I wouldn't be surprised if some of your long-time employees might figure they should take over the company if something happens to you."

Saul chuckled. "Make no mistake, Matthias. My mother and I are both as healthy as horses, and we plan to be on this earth for a long time yet," he said. "But a man without sons must make his plans—and provide for his employees. If the carriage company were to close down or go bankrupt, two dozen hardworking men would lose their jobs. You and I are even more responsible for their welfare than for the profitability of the shop."

"*Jah*, that's the main thing—making sure those families

don't have to scramble to keep food on the table," Matthias agreed. He couldn't help thinking of poor Rose, left to care for her mother and daughter after her husband and her *dat*'s sawmill died with them.

Hartzler stood up and stuck out his hand. "You've hit the nail on the head," he said as he pumped Matthias's hand. "Now I know several families in this town will continue to be taken care of, their men fairly compensated. That's part of my purpose as the deacon of this district, you see," Saul added. "All of the Amish in Morning Star are provided for, because we look after our own."

As Matthias followed Saul back into the house, rubbing his sore knuckles after another brisk handshake, he sensed he'd become a partner in a holy mission. Not only had the wealthiest businessman in town asked Matthias to work with him, but Saul had also invited him into the kinship of tending the flock. It was a high calling, a commitment to his new church district. Of course his harness business had just gotten a huge boost as well.

Anne and Martha Maude greeted him with bags of fresh lettuce, green onions, radishes, and peas—and a box containing a dozen quart jars of tomatoes, green beans, and beets. "This should keep you eating for a while, Matthias," Anne said with a smile. "We're so glad you came to supper—"

"And we'll have you back often," Martha Maude put in. She studied him intently, her facial features very much like her son's. "Partners are like family. They share our successes and failures, and when they become woven into the fabric of our lives, we are strengthened and brightened. Welcome, Matthias."

Matthias wasn't sure how he responded to Martha Maude's stirring words, and he probably only caught part of what Saul chatted about as he gave Matthias a ride home with his groceries. When he'd bid Saul good night and set the food on his kitchen table, Matthias stood at the back window.

*Lord, I'm grateful for this unexpected gift—this amazing partnership You've opened to me,* he prayed as the silhouettes of the trees against the night sky soothed him. *Help me as I learn Saul's business and tend to my own shop. And give me the right words when I tell Rose about this. Because You know I will.*

# Chapter 17

Rose sighed with satisfaction as she drizzled a powdered sugar glaze over two pans of warm cinnamon rolls. Because it took her a good forty minutes to drive here each morning, Sherrie had suggested that Rose could prepare the next day's breakfast before she left—at least to the point where Sherrie could pop it into the oven—and then she could prepare the noon meal and supper after she arrived. It was only Wednesday, but Sherrie had told Rose she was doing exceptionally well, and that several residents had complimented her food.

"What's for lunch, Mamma?" Gracie asked. She was seated, coloring, in a small school desk Sherrie had provided. "I hope it's that meat loaf I'm smellin'. Are we eatin' with Gladys again today?"

Rose smiled at her daughter. Gracie had adapted beautifully to being here at the senior center. "We can eat with anyone we want to," she replied. "Maybe you can take a look, after folks come into the dining room, and see if somebody needs a friend, Gracie. Even if they don't talk to us much, they'll like having you at their table."

Gracie considered this. She chose a purple crayon and con-centrated on coloring within the lines of the butterfly that filled the page.

"Oh, it smells wonderful in here!" Sherrie exclaimed as she entered the kitchen. She clasped her hands as she gazed at the pans of cinnamon rolls. "Tomorrow's breakfast?"

"*Jah,* and I'll fry some apples for you to warm up and serve with them," Rose replied. "Should I slice the meat loaf? It's nearly noon."

"Yes, and I'll go help Zelma and Flo to the dining room. They're a little slower these days. Gracie, would you like to come with me?" Sherrie asked. "Flo tells me you remind her of the little granddaughter she doesn't see very often."

Gracie skipped out the door ahead of Sherrie. Rose took the pans of meat loaf and hash brown casserole from the oven. She filled serving bowls with stewed tomatoes; then she fetched the bowls of gelatin salad from the refrigerator.

Alison, Sherrie's assistant, smiled as she came into the kitchen. She was in her late twenties, a plump young woman with thick glasses and a compassionate way about her. "Rose, this dinner looks wonderful," she said as she loaded the steam-ing bowls of food onto a wheeled cart. "I'm so glad you've come to cook for us! We were worried when Frieda had to leave, thinking we wouldn't find anybody else who could cook the way she did."

Rose glowed. "I'm grateful to work in a place where Gra-cie can come with me," she said. "You ladies have made us feel right at home—only at home, we don't have a big glass cage with lovebirds in it, or an aquarium."

Alison chuckled. "Gracie's such a sweetheart. All the resi-dents hope she'll come to their apartments with Sherrie and visit. I'll be right back for more food."

When the platters and bowls were on the table, and the residents were seated, Rose let Gracie lead her to the table she'd chosen. Rose introduced herself and met Flo, Zelma, and Ethan, all of whom greeted Gracie happily. After Rose and her daughter had bowed in prayer—and noticed that the other three folks had done the same—Flo spoke up in a voice that quavered a little.

"This is quite a feast," she said. She passed the stewed tomatoes with both hands because they were shaking slightly. "I don't know how you do it, fixing three meals a day for thirty-some people."

Rose put a slice of meat loaf on her plate and on Gracie's. "In Amish homes, it's not unusual to have twenty or more folks for family get-togethers," she pointed out. "If you're used to fixing food for a family, it's not that much more effort to feed a group like this one."

"We like it here!" Gracie said in a high, happy voice. "It's kinda quiet at home with just me and Mamma."

Rose felt a pang of sorrow, recalling that a year ago they'd had her parents and Nathan eating with them. "It's *gut* to be here amongst you folks," she agreed in the cheeriest voice she could manage.

"I remember being home alone after my wife passed," Ethan said wistfully. He adjusted his glasses and smiled at Rose. "I don't recommend it. We're all better off here, with activities and somebody to cook and clean and look after us."

*And being here helps me keep a roof over our heads, even if we don't spend a lot of time under that roof anymore,* Rose thought. She held the basket while Zelma chose a whole-wheat roll. It was good to be useful. Good to be busy. *Best of all, you're not at home feeling sorry for yourself, missing*

*Mamma—or feeling like a charity case. Gracie's got it right: it's all gut.*

On Thursday, as Matthias drove toward Cedar Creek, he thought about how to tell Rose he'd met her mother. He had signed Saul's handwritten agreement on Wednesday, so the deal was sealed. The more time he spent with Hartzler, the more positive Matthias became: Rose would really upset the apple cart if she insisted on meeting Anne. Such a visit would wreak havoc on Anne's marriage to a man who was used to being the head of the household, making all the decisions—and the partnership papers would probably be torn up if Saul knew Matthias had helped Rose find her birth mother.

Matthias sighed as he caught sight of the Cedar Creek Mercantile. He was buzzing with the excitement of seeing Rose and Gracie again—he missed them more than he'd thought possible. He'd repeatedly reviewed his lunch at the pizza place and those precious moments in the park, talking with Rose as they'd watched Gracie play.

*She has a right to know about her mother. I can't keep that information to myself,* he mused as he steered his bay onto the road that led to the Fry place.

As he'd thought back to the meal he'd eaten in the Hartzler home, it struck him that although Anne had married well, she seemed rather lonely—and wasn't Rose lonely, too? But while Rose had Gracie to brighten her days, Matthias sensed that Anne lived in the shadow of her more outgoing, outspoken mother-in-law, in a home built for children who hadn't arrived to bless her marriage. And wasn't that a puzzlement?

*Why wouldn't Anne want to meet her adult child—not to mention her grandchild?* Matthias wondered as he approached the Fry farm. He knew the revelation of Anne's secret baby would anger Saul—and it would be underhanded to arrange a reunion for Rose and Anne without letting Saul know. And yet . . .

Matthias sighed as he pulled into the lane. He'd seldom felt so torn about a situation. He wanted to please Rose by telling her about Anne, yet he didn't want to get Anne into trouble and he didn't want to kiss his shop's future good-bye by casting Saul's wife into a dubious light.

He sat in the open rig for a moment, looking around. The Fry house needed a fresh coat of paint—and the barn looked worse for the weather's wear, too. The fencerows needed trimming, and the grass in the yard looked ankle-high. Matthias had come to Rose's place with the idea of doing a few chores, but the larger jobs would take some planning and more time than he had today.

He pulled up to the side of the house, feeling vaguely uneasy. A few of the windows were open, so Gracie surely must've heard him driving up the lane. Still, he saw no sign of her—or her mother. A few dresses flapped forlornly on the clothesline behind the house, and Matthias wondered how long they'd been hanging there.

"Rose?" he called out as he stepped onto the porch. "Gracie? Anybody home?"

Silence.

Matthias sighed, glancing through the window. He saw a front room furnished with a couch that was covered with a quilt, and a couple of dolls on the floor near a saggy-looking upholstered rocking chair. He figured the door was unlocked, as most Plain doors were, but he didn't feel right about letting himself inside.

He walked around the house and then out to the small barn.

When he saw no horses inside, he realized that Rose and Gracie had gone someplace—and why wouldn't they? No one stayed at home all the time.

"Should've called her," Matthias muttered as he walked back to his rig. He'd driven for more than half an hour to get here, so he decided to stop at the mercantile before he headed home. Unlike some Plain merchants, Sam kept his store open on Thursdays, and Matthias was grateful for that. When he pulled up, the number of buggies told him several folks were shopping—so maybe Rose and Gracie were here. Her buggy resembled half of the ones he saw.

When Matthias stepped out of the bright sunshine into the store, the bell above the door jingled. He stood for a moment, allowing his eyes to adjust to the dimmer light. High up in the ceiling, gas-powered fans spun in lazy circles. The scent of grass seed in a barrel near the door tickled his nose and he sneezed.

"Hullo? If you need my help, just holler," a familiar male voice called out from the center of the store.

"Hey there, Sam. It's Matthias Wagler," he replied. "No need to stop what you're doing. I know my way around."

Matthias nodded to a couple of fellows in black straw hats who were looking at metal fence posts and big spools of barbed wire. He walked slowly down the center aisle, smiling at Plain women pushing shopping carts through the grocery section. He was hoping his voice had alerted Gracie to his presence as he glanced from side to side in the toy section, past the kitchen utensils, and into the large corner filled with colorful bolts of fabric. Behind him, he heard a chuckle.

"Out of your usual territory, ain't so?" Sam teased as he clapped Matthias's back. "But maybe you've taken up quilting in your spare time."

Matthias chuckled. "Truth be told, I'm looking for Rose and Gracie. I stopped by their place and they weren't home," he admitted. "Guess I'll grab a few snacks for the road and head back to Morning Star."

Sam shrugged. "Last time I saw those girls was Sunday, at church. No telling what they might be up to on such a fine day," he said as they headed toward the front counter. "What's new with you, Matthias?"

Did he share his big news, or keep it to himself? Matthias decided Sam was a good listener—and he might know the Hartzler family—so he quickly chose a bag of lemon drops, a bag of ripple potato chips, and a bottle of root beer from the big cooler full of ice on the floor. "I've taken on a partnership with the fellow who owns Hartzler Carriage Company," he said softly. "It was a big surprise when he asked me."

Sam nodded as he rang up Matthias's purchases. "From what I've heard, that carriage shop is quite a lot larger than my brother-in-law James Graber's, across the road," he remarked. "So he wants you to make harnesses and such for him?"

"That, and a few other things," Matthias hedged. He pulled money from his wallet and waited for his change. "Seems like a *gut* solid sort, Saul does. He's the deacon of the Morning Star district."

As he placed two quarters and a dime in Matthias's hand, Sam smiled. "Sounds like you're in for a big increase in business. Congratulations. You'll do well."

"*Denki,* Sam. I'm settling into my new hometown faster than I anticipated."

Sam stroked his gray-shot beard. "Don't know what else to tell you about Rose," he said in a faraway tone. "She didn't say much to me at the common meal after the service, but she had a big smile on her face. With women, that could mean a lot of things."

Matthias laughed along with the storekeeper and took his leave. As he unhitched his horse and vaulted up into his rig, he wondered what Rose's big smile might have meant. Had she come into some unexpected money? Had Gracie said or done something that made Rose feel happy again?

*Has Rose found another man?*

Matthias backed the rig out of its parking spot and urged his horse down the county highway at a quick clip. He twisted the cap from his bottle of root beer with more force than necessary, feeling flummoxed. He knew better than to read too much into what Sam had said about Rose's Sunday behavior, yet he felt suddenly anxious about his future with Rose and Gracie.

Were his dreams of having another family falling by the wayside like the horse apples scattered on the shoulder of the road?

Matthias shook his head to clear his thoughts. *Ah, but you know things about Anne Hartzler—information Rose would treasure if you shared it. Nobody else can give her such a gift.*

It was the wrong attitude to have. Matthias felt like a man who'd climbed onto a tall roof and watched his ladder fall to the ground. He was stuck—and no one but Rose could rescue him from his emotional predicament.

# Chapter 18

Rose gripped the lines, praying Daisy wouldn't be spooked by the jagged bolt of lightning that flashed across the sky on Friday morning. Rain pelted the enclosed buggy, so loud she couldn't hear herself think. Even though the orange triangular lights on the back of the buggy were flashing, Rose feared that the dark sky and the wet, shiny blacktop would distract drivers and they might crash their cars into her rig—or pass her in their impatience, and hit another car coming over the hill.

"Mamma, I'm scared," Gracie whimpered.

Rose reached over and grasped her daughter's little shoulder. "We're doing the best we can to get to Morning Star, sweet pea," she murmured. "If I pull over until after the storm passes, we'll be even later than we already are."

When lightning flashed again, Gracie squeezed her eyes shut and scooted against Rose's side. Her little body was shaking. When she was at home, Gracie simply went to her room and pulled the curtains during a storm, but out on the road she had no place to hide.

Rose sighed, watching desperately for a good place to pull

off the road. They were only a mile from Morning Star, but she couldn't steer very well with one arm around her daughter, and if Daisy got frightened by—

A horn honked loudly as a low-slung red car sped around them.

Gasping, Rose steered the horse off the county highway, onto an unpaved road. When she stopped the rig under some trees, she hugged Gracie close, praying that Sherrie would understand her tardiness. As the minutes passed, Rose had no idea what time it might be. Her no-frills rig didn't have a clock, and Plain folks didn't wear watches, so she sat helplessly beneath the trees until the rain let up and the sky began to lighten.

When Rose finally reached the Morning Star Senior Center, she parked and unhitched Daisy, tethering the mare in the yard where she could graze on the wet grass that bordered the garden. As she hurried inside with Gracie and a canvas tote filled with books and toys, her heart sank. She usually arrived by eight o'clock, and it was almost nine thirty. Breakfast was long over, and Sherrie was probably wondering if Rose had decided not to come back to work anymore.

"Let's check the kitchen first, Gracie," she said as they hurried through the unoccupied dining room. "We'll hang up our jackets and—"

"Rose and Gracie! I'm so glad to see you two," Sherrie said as she followed them into the kitchen. "I was worried that you had trouble on the road, or—"

"We was parked under the trees, coz I was scared of the lightning," Gracie blurted. She rushed over and threw her arms around Sherrie's thighs. "But we're safe now!"

As she watched Sherrie heft Gracie into her arms, Rose chose her words carefully. "I'm so sorry, Sherrie. We were already on the way when the storm caught us, so I couldn't call you—and it was slow going while the rain was beating down on the buggy and our poor horse. I'll stay later this afternoon to make up for—"

"Remind me again, how long does it usually take you to make the trip in the morning?" Sherrie asked with a concerned expression.

Rose sighed, trying to relax after the difficult drive. "On a *gut* day, I can make it in forty minutes. Maybe I should leave earlier, or—"

"Or maybe you and Gracie should stay here at the center during the week—drive in on Monday and go home on Friday," the director mused aloud. "We have a couple of vacant apartments. I'm sorry I didn't think of this sooner."

Rose's eyes widened. It would be a relief not to rush around every morning, getting Gracie ready and hitching up the rig for the long drive. But could they be away from home all week, and tend to all the chores and the laundry on Saturdays?

"What do you think?" Sherrie asked, hugging Gracie before letting her down to the floor. "I wouldn't charge you for the apartment, because you'd be here to cook all three meals. You could do your laundry in the machines our residents use, and Gracie would have a place to nap if she wanted to—"

"Nah, I'm too busy helpin' Mamma to nap," Gracie insisted. Her eyes sparkled and she gazed up at Sherrie. "But we could have our own place? Just like Gladys and Flo and Zelma?"

"You could," Sherrie replied. "Let's take a look at the empty apartments right now, so your mamma can think about them today while she's working."

Rose followed the director through the dining room and

down the wide hallway, her thoughts whirling. "It would be easier if we stayed, but what would I do with our mare?" she asked. "It's one thing to let her graze for the day, but we'd need a place to stable her—"

"We can ask Matthias!" Gracie blurted. "He said he wanted to help us, Mamma."

Rose's cheeks blazed when Sherrie looked at her. "He's just a friend—a fellow we know here in Morning Star," she hastened to explain. "He and Gracie are *gut* buddies."

"I think everyone Gracie meets becomes her buddy," Sherrie said kindly. She took a key ring from her pants pocket as they approached a door near the end of the hall. "And here we are. This apartment has a sitting area, a separate bedroom, and, of course, a bathroom. What do you think?"

When Sherrie opened the door, Gracie raced inside ahead of Rose. "Look, Mamma! A fan on the ceiling and carpet everywhere," she exclaimed. Then she stopped in the doorway to the bedroom. "Do we gotta sleep on the floor, Sherrie?"

The director chuckled. "We have some basic furniture in our storeroom," she replied, looking at Rose. "You could each have a bed, and we'll find a couch and some easy chairs. One of our former residents even left a TV, if I recall—"

"We'll not be needing that," Rose insisted before Gracie could get excited. Her little girl was fascinated by the televisions they saw when they made occasional trips to the discount store in New Haven. "And we could bring a couple of battery lamps from home, and the small pendulum clock my husband gave me. . . ."

Rose walked slowly into the bedroom and then peered into the bathroom, which was smaller than they were used to. But it had a shower, and it would work fine for the two of them during the week.

"Think it over," Sherrie said. "The other unoccupied apartment is across the hall."

As they looked around the other apartment, reality began to set in. Would the house be all right if it sat empty all week? And what would happen to the garden? Saturdays would be very busy, if Rose had to tend to all the chores in one day—

*And what will I tell Bishop Vernon? He and Sam won't be happy when I admit I've taken a job—and when they hear I'll be out of town all week, that'll really snap their suspenders.*

"Look at this big ole closet, Mamma!" Gracie said as she stepped inside it and held her arms out wide. "If it storms, I can just come in here! I'll be snug as a bug in a rug!"

Rose blinked. Her body was still taut from the tension of driving in the downpour this morning, and she felt tired. She hadn't slept very well lately, trying to do the cooking and cleaning and laundry in the short time she had in the evenings.

"Staying here seems like the logical thing to do," Rose heard herself saying. "*Denki* for such a thoughtful suggestion, Sherrie. We'll bring a few things with us on Monday—and we'll figure out where to keep Daisy."

"Excellent!" Sherrie smiled widely. "Which apartment would you like?"

Rose glanced at her daughter, who was peering out the window at the garden. "This one," she replied. "We'll have a nice view—and a big closet," she added when Gracie grinned at her. "It's not like we'll fill it with clothes, but it might be a fun place for Gracie to play—and to keep her toys in, so they're not scattered all over the place."

Sherrie feigned surprise. "Gracie! Surely, you don't make a mess with your toys."

"Not me," Gracie insisted with a vigorous shake of her head. "I'm a little angel!"

By the time Rose had prepared two large pans of tuna noodle casserole and put them in the oven, she felt less harried—and very grateful for Sherrie's offer of an apartment. Staying at the senior center would save her more than an hour on the road every day, not to mention the trouble of hitching the mare to the rig and hurrying through breakfast after getting Gracie dressed. She felt certain God had whispered the suggestion in Sherrie's ear. This arrangement would also save her money on groceries, because she and Gracie would be eating at the center.

After lunch had been served and the residents had raved about the tuna noodle casserole, Rose followed Sherrie into the hallway. "You know, your offer of an apartment is awfully generous," she said. "If you need to pay me less to make up for this arrangement, I'll understand."

Sherrie's eyes widened in surprise. "I wouldn't dream of paying you less, Rose," she insisted. "Everyone loves the way you cook—and they're crazy about your little girl. You and Gracie have settled into our routine without a single hitch. Let's consider the apartment and your meals a much-deserved bonus."

Rose's heart fluttered with gratitude. "*Denki* so much, and God bless you," she said as she turned toward the dining room.

"He sent you to us," Sherrie replied without missing a beat. "I consider us all blessed because you're here."

Rose returned to the kitchen, humming, her heart lighter because Sherrie had said such a wonderful thing. Gracie was seated in the little school desk with a manuscript tablet, practicing her alphabet letters with a fat pencil Sherrie had given her. Alison was loading the dishwasher. All was right with her world, and Rose felt extremely grateful to God for providing this solution to her financial problems. She checked the week's menu, which was taped to a cabinet door, and began mixing hamburger, chopped onion, and rice for the stuffed peppers she would serve for supper.

"Mamma, can I go look at the fishes?" Gracie asked. "I'll sit real still and I won't bother nobody."

"Won't bother *any*body, *jah?*" Rose smiled as she removed the stem and seeds from a green bell pepper. "That'll be fine, sweet pea. I'll come out with you as soon as I'm finished here. I like looking at the pretty fish, too."

When Rose had placed the stuffed peppers in baking pans, she spooned spaghetti sauce over the tops of them, sprinkled them with shredded cheese, and then slid the pans into the refrigerator. The dishwasher was whirring and Alison had gone to launder residents' towels, so Rose slipped out to check on her daughter. True to her word, Gracie was seated in a big chair near the aquarium, gazing at the fish that swam lazily in the bubbling water.

"How are the fish today?" Rose asked as she pulled a chair on rollers next to Gracie.

"They're *gut*. Swimmin' and swishin' their tails. See this pretty yellow one?" Gracie asked as she rose to point at it.

At the sound of the front door opening, Rose glanced behind her to see two Plain women carrying large plastic bins. As they set their loads on a bench in the lobby, Sherrie came out to greet them.

"Good afternoon, ladies! I'm glad you could come today," the director said as she removed the lid from a bin. "Oh, these colors are so cheerful—as always," she exclaimed as she held up a pair of crocheted slippers.

"Mamma, can I go see?" Gracie whispered excitedly. "Look at the pretty stuff they brought!"

"We'll both go," Rose suggested, taking her daughter's hand. It was a blessing that Gracie wasn't intimidated by strangers, but sometimes she became more exuberant than she realized.

Sherrie was holding up another crocheted piece as Rose and Gracie approached her. "Isn't this a pretty shawl?" she asked, stooping so the little girl could admire it. "Rose and Gracie Raber, I'd like you to meet Anne and Martha Maude Hartzler from down the road."

Martha Maude, the older and larger of the two women, immediately bent low to take Gracie's hand and chat with her, but Rose was too stunned to watch them. *Anne Hartzler.* The name stole her breath away. As Rose gazed into a freckled face framed with brown hair—the very image of the water-color painting she had, with minor adjustments for age—she felt totally tongue-tied.

"It's so nice to meet both of you," Anne said, nodding at Rose and then at Gracie.

"Rose is cooking for us now that Frieda Yutzy has re-tired," Sherrie explained. "Gracie is everyone's friend—our very own ray of sunshine."

"*Jah,* I can see that," Martha Maude said. "Even if she wasn't wearing a pretty yellow dress, her smile would warm everyone she meets and make them smile back."

Gracie giggled, gazing up at the older woman as though thoroughly enchanted with her.

"These ladies donate the lap robes, shawls, and slippers they make, so our residents can enjoy them," Sherrie explained to Rose, as though encouraging her to join in the conversation.

"Summer's coming, and these folks tell us they get chilly in the air-conditioning," Anne said pleasantly. "They don't go outside much or get a lot of exercise to warm them."

Rose was aware of nodding and excusing herself to the kitchen, hoping Anne and Martha Maude—and Sherrie—didn't think she was behaving oddly. As soon as she reached the safety of the kitchen, she inhaled repeatedly to still her hammering heart.

*That was my mother! Except for a softening around her jaw and a few slight wrinkles, she looks exactly like Joel Lapp's portrait.*

Rose pressed her hand against her chest, straining to calm herself. She needed to fetch her daughter before Gracie got too caught up with those two admiring women.

*And how will you explain this situation to Gracie?*

Rose sucked in another big breath and released it slowly. It was too soon—too dangerous—to tell Gracie that Anne Hartzler was her grandmother. Gracie was missing her *mammi* so much, she clung to every woman in the same age bracket.

*Did Anne have any idea I'm the daughter she gave away? Was there any sign of recognition?*

Rose reviewed the moments after Sherrie had introduced them. She couldn't recall any telltale signs that Anne had recognized her . . . but if Rose continued working at the senior center, and the Hartzler women kept donating their quilted and crocheted gifts, it was only a matter of time before they met again. How could Rose possibly keep her identity a secret, considering the way she yearned to know her birth mother?

"Mamma!" Gracie called out as she entered the kitchen's swinging door. "Them ladies are gone now. Sherrie says I can go get Gladys so's she can pick somethin' pretty out of those bins! And Zelma and Flo! Come with me, Mamma!"

Rose focused on her little girl, setting aside her jumbled thoughts about meeting Anne Hartzler. At this moment, the only thing that mattered was Gracie's plump, warm hand gripping hers and the eager expression on her daughter's face.

*Remember that*, Rose warned herself. *It's all about taking care of Gracie. Now that your financial problems will soon be behind you, don't jump into a can of worms you can't get out of.*

That afternoon, as Anne prepared dinner with Martha Maude, her thoughts wandered away from the potatoes she was peeling. Could the Rose she'd met at the senior center be *her* Rose? Was it her imagination, or did Rose have her father's bold eyebrows and olive complexion—along with Joel's dark auburn hair? Rose was about the right age, from the looks of her. Anne had tried to study the young woman's features unobtrusively, but Rose had retreated to the kitchen— *Because she's read those letters I wrote? Because she knew who I was after Sherrie said my name?*

"I can't get that little Gracie out of my mind." Martha Maude leaned down with a meat fork to check the pot roast in the oven. "Such a sunny disposition she has, but it can't be *gut* for her that her *mamm* is working. Do you suppose Rose is widowed?"

Anne had heard about Myron Fry's sawmill burning to the ground with him and his son-in-law in it, and more recently she'd seen Lydia Fry's obituary, but she didn't want to seem too familiar with Rose's situation. "That would be my guess," she hedged. "We could ask Sherrie, next time we take our shawls and lap robes."

Martha Maude's short laugh suggested that she wasn't satisfied with Anne's answer—and that she might take it upon herself to learn more about Rose and Gracie sooner rather than later. She was headstrong that way.

Anne went to the bin for a few more potatoes, seeing Rose's face in her mind again, wondering if God could possibly have brought the two of them together. But why would He do that?

"Well, now," her mother-in-law said as she peered into Anne's big pan of potatoes. "I've heard that *some* folks mash the skins right along with the potatoes, but I don't know that *we* like them that way."

Anne blinked. When she saw that several of the potato quarters in the water still had skins on them, her cheeks turned hot. She'd been peeling mindlessly, thinking of a more interesting topic than potatoes. Anne thought about pointing out that the skins were the most nutritious part—and she wanted to tell Martha Maude to peel the potatoes herself if she didn't like the way Anne had done it. But years of living in the Hartzler household had taught her to keep her mouth shut. She certainly couldn't tell Martha Maude that she might be very closely related to the Rose they'd met today.

"What was I thinking?" Anne murmured as she began plucking the unpeeled potato chunks out of the water.

Martha Maude raised one eyebrow. "I sometimes wonder."

# Chapter 19

As Rose hung their dresses on the clothesline early Saturday morning, she thought back to her meeting with Anne Hartzler. In the stillness of the dawn, while Gracie was still asleep, Rose tried to decide how best to deal with the birth mother who'd shown up so unexpectedly in her life.

*Was it really so unexpected? What if God had a hand in this?*

Rose shook a little blue jumper until it snapped, then pinned it to the line. How could she act as though Anne was just a local Plain woman who donated handmade items to the senior center? How could she *not* reveal her identity to Anne and fulfill her longing to reconnect with her mother?

When she'd hung her last two black dresses, Rose carried her laundry basket into the kitchen to think about breakfast—and to decide what food to freeze so it wouldn't spoil while she and Gracie stayed in town. Meanwhile, she realized—as Bishop Vernon had warned her—that engaging Anne Hartzler in a relationship might have consequences she couldn't control.

There was Martha Maude to consider, first of all. Rose

suspected Saul's mother, so tall and stalwart but without an ounce of fat on her, was a woman to be reckoned with. What if Martha Maude chastised Anne for bearing a baby out of wedlock? It might tarnish their relationship—and she would surely tell her son about Anne's secret. Rose had wondered what sort of mother would name her son Saul, reminiscent of the biblical man who'd persecuted Christians, rather than Paul or Sol—after King Solomon. Again she had the feeling Martha Maude was a woman of strong will and purpose.

*What if Anne becomes so upset, she wants nothing more to do with me? What if she stops bringing her crocheted and quilted items to the senior center to avoid me? If Sherrie finds out Anne has stopped coming because I revealed my identity to her, Sherrie might not want me to work there anymore—*

"Mamma, let's have French toast! I'm starvin'!"

Gracie's exuberant request brought Rose out of her troublesome thoughts, and for that, she was grateful. Gracie had put on a green dress, and her *kapp* strings mingled with the strawberry-blond hair that hung loosely over her shoulders.

"We can do that," Rose replied as she took eggs and milk from the refrigerator. "We have to plan ahead today, thinking about what clothes we'll take for next week," she told her daughter. "But first we'll wind your hair into a bun, in case the bishop or other folks stop by."

"Or 'Rusalem," Gracie said in a hopeful voice. She climbed into her chair and removed her *kapp*. "I gotta tell her 'bout movin' to Morning Star! She'll be really surprised!"

*She's not the only one,* Rose thought as she smoothed her daughter's silky hair and began braiding it. Should she insist that Gracie not tell anybody about her job and their new arrangement to live at the senior center?

*That would be like telling a robin not to sing.*

Rose deftly wound Gracie's braid into a bun at the nape of her neck, deciding to see how the day went. If she insisted that Gracie keep quiet, her daughter would demand to know why Rose's new job was such a secret—and maybe nobody would stop by the house, anyway. If Bishop Vernon and Jerusalem did come, and Gracie blurted out their new living arrangements, the adults could have the discussion and be done with it.

It wasn't as though Vernon could make Rose quit her job. She was working of her own free will—that two-sided gift of God's the bishop had reminded her about. On the one hand, Rose felt she'd found a perfect solution to her financial problems, even if the bishop believed she was putting Gracie's welfare—and her own salvation—at risk by working.

After they ate breakfast, the day went quickly because they had a lot to accomplish before Monday morning. In the garden, Rose snipped the lettuce that was of edible size, assuring Gracie that they would enjoy fresh peas in a couple of weekends, when they were home. As she checked the radishes, she also hoed weeds—realizing that her extended absences meant the garden would get even weedier.

"If you like helping," Rose said as Gracie pointed out weeds for her, "you can go out with Alison and pick the peas in the senior center garden. I bet we'll be eating some of those this week, because they got their garden planted sooner than we did."

Gracie gazed at her with a serious expression. "Coz we was bein' with Mammi, right?" she asked softly.

Rose blinked back sudden tears. "*Jah,* we were, sweetie. It's important to help folks who can't do anything for themselves."

Gracie pointed to another dandelion, and Rose removed it with the pointed corner of her hoe. "And when we're stayin' at the center, we can be helpin' all those people more, huh, Mamma? I like that."

"I like it, too, Gracie. And it'll be easier for us because we don't have to make that long drive every morning and afternoon," Rose replied.

"You better call Matthias, so's he'll keep Daisy for us."

Rose thought for a moment. She did want to talk to Matthias, but she was hoping for a conversation without Gracie's excited interruptions—and her keen ears. "Let's take those clothes off the line," she said as they headed toward the house. "While I'm ironing a few things, I want you to pick out the toys and books and clothes you'll want this week. Put them on your bed, nice and neat, so we can pack them and put them into the buggy before Monday morning."

"Do we getta use suitcases? Like for a big trip?" Gracie's eyes lit up with the idea, for she'd seldom been anywhere that required luggage.

Rose chuckled as she gathered the sun-dried clothing. "*Jah,* it'll be a big adventure," she said. "You don't have to take all of your toys and dolls, you know. That way you can play with some things this week, and take different toys for the next week."

Gracie's face lit up. "I'm packin' right now, Mamma! See ya later!"

As Rose stood in the kitchen, pressing Gracie's little dresses, she decided to place her own aprons, capes, and dresses on hangers—an entire outfit together—and take them in the garment bag. If she put her underthings on the bottom of their largest suitcase, she'd have enough room for Gracie's clothing and their toiletries in that bag.

On impulse, Rose decided to tuck the letters from her birth mother into the suitcase, as well. She'd been weighing the consequences of talking with Anne Hartzler, and maybe if Anne had doubts, she would surely remember the letters she'd written when Rose was a tiny baby. Trying to envision how this reunion would come about was beyond her, however. Rose yearned to reveal her identity, even as she suspected the Hartzler household would never be the same after she did. Would Anne be willing to risk a relationship with her long-lost daughter?

Rose turned off the burners where she'd been heating her two irons. She was folding the old ironing board, wondering what to have for supper, when she heard the rapid patter of feet in the hallway above her head.

"Mamma! Mamma, it's Matthias!" her little girl shouted ecstatically. "He's comin' up the lane in his rig!"

Rose looked quickly out the window as Gracie raced through the front room and out the screen door, letting it bang shut behind her. When Rose recognized the fellow in the buggy, her heart stood still. She was eager to see Matthias, to discuss the events of the past few days with him. However, she also recalled the way she'd stalked off when he'd told her to leave well enough alone—not to meddle with the Hartzlers' marriage by seeking out her mother.

*But it's different now. My mother showed up without my having any say about it. And if Matthias is here, he must've gotten over our disagreement.*

When Rose stepped out onto the porch, her heart flip-flopped. Gracie was clutching Matthias around the legs, chattering as though she hadn't seen him for months—and then Matthias swung Gracie up in the air, making her giggle in sheer delight. What a sight it was, the two of them so wrapped up in one another.

And there would be no dealing with Gracie's disappointment if Rose didn't invite Matthias to stay and eat with them. As Matthias strode toward the house with Gracie riding on his shoulders, Rose realized that *he* might be just as broken-hearted if she didn't ask him to stick around for a while.

"You've arrived just in time to choose what we'll have for supper, Matthias," Rose teased as he stopped at the bottom of the porch steps, in front of her. "The choices aren't fabulous, but we could have grilled cheese sandwiches, or peanut butter and jelly, or—"

"Fried eggs with bacon, Mamma! You said we gotta use that up before—"

"Fried eggs with bacon sounds wonderful," Matthias agreed as he gently put Gracie on the ground. "I really didn't come for a free meal—and I brought some fresh peas for Gracie—"

"Yay! I *love* peas, Matthias!"

"So you've told me, peanut," he said, tweaking her nose. "How about washing your hands and we'll shell them for your mamma?"

When Gracie shot into the house, again letting the door bang, Matthias climbed the stairs to the porch. He searched Rose's eyes for a moment. "I've got something to tell you when a little somebody with big ears isn't listening," he said softly.

Rose's eyes widened. What could this man she hardly knew have to share with her that was so important? "Matter of fact, I've got a few things to discuss with you when Gracie's asleep, too," she said softly. "It's been a big, busy week. I'll go get a couple bowls—and *denki* so much for bringing peas," she added with a smile.

Matthias kept gazing at her as though they were going to share some important secrets later—and he appeared eager to spend time with her as much as with Gracie. He jogged to his rig and drove it to the stable, where he unhitched his horse and led it inside. He returned with a plastic sack of fresh peas, and soon he and Rose were settled on the porch swing with Gracie and two bowls between them. Gracie watched attentively as Rose showed her how to hold the fat green pod, tug on the end to pull the string, and then squeeze the peas into the bowl. She dropped the empty pod onto a towel she'd spread on the porch floor in front of the swing.

"This is fun!" Gracie said when her first podful of peas bounced into the bowl. "Can we have creamed peas and taters with our bacon and eggs, Mamma? It'll be a feast!"

Rose laughed, catching Matthias's eyes above her daughter's head. "This supper's sounding a lot better than PB and J sandwiches," she said. "We're glad you've come to see us, Matthias."

"Me too," he mouthed as he held her gaze. Then he glanced down at Gracie. "So what have you girls been doing this week? I stopped by on Thursday, but nobody was home."

"We was in Morning Star!" Gracie crowed. "Mamma's cookin' and I'm a ray of sunshine."

Matthias's laughter echoed in the porch ceiling as he squeezed peas into the bowl wedged between his thigh and Gracie's. "I have no doubt you're spreading *gut* cheer, little girl," he said as he shot Rose a questioning glance.

"I'm cooking at the senior center," Rose began. "I started last Monday, and after we got caught in that rainstorm yesterday, my boss offered us an apartment. We'll be driving in on Monday mornings and coming home Friday afternoons now—and if there's a way you could stable Daisy for us—"

"Of course I will, Rose."

"—I think we've got all our bases covered," Rose continued in a rush. "So you can see how it's been quite a week for Gracie and me. The folks at the senior center adore her."

"I bet they're glad to have you cooking for them, too," Matthias remarked. "*Gut* for you, Rose. I know the bishop's not keen on your working, but because Gracie can be with you all the time, well—I'm not a bit surprised," he added with a smile. "I didn't figure you for a gal who'd sit around moping, depending on other folks for every little thing."

Rose's cheeks tingled. Matthias was taking her side, complimenting her for the action she'd taken.

"Ooh, look at this fat pea pod!" Gracie said happily. "Did you grow these peas in your garden, Matthias?"

Was she imagining it, or did Rose detect a secret as Matthias considered his reply?

"I've made some new friends in Morning Star," he replied. "When they heard I wouldn't have time to plant a garden, they felt sorry for me and gave me a bunch of fresh stuff from their garden—last week and again yesterday."

"Eat your veggies!" Gracie teased.

Matthias chuckled. "*Jah,* I am—and, by golly, we've shelled every one of our peas now," he said lightly. "I'm sure glad you asked for creamed potatoes and peas, Gracie, because I just love those two together."

Rose started into the house with the bowls of peas. "You can feed those empty shells to Daisy and Matthias's horse," she suggested to her daughter.

"*Jah!* Let's go, Matthias," Gracie said, hopping out of the swing. "You and Daisy can get to be friends, before she stays at your house next week."

In the kitchen, Rose rinsed the peas and put them on to boil. As she was peeling potatoes and cutting them into chunks, she watched her daughter showing Matthias the garden and the flowers around the yard. What a pair they were—and what a patient man Matthias was, allowing a five-year-old chatterbox to lead him around. By the time they returned to the house, Rose had bacon frying in the skillet and was making white sauce for the peas and potatoes. She'd taken a cake from the freezer, too—a neighbor's gift after Mamma had passed.

As the three of them ate their simple supper, Rose couldn't remember when bacon, eggs, and creamed potatoes and peas had ever tasted so good. Matthias was telling them about all the places he'd visited in Morning Star, and about a fancy saddle he'd been making for a rodeo cowboy. When they'd eaten their cake, he offered to help with the dishes and Rose didn't turn him down.

It was nice to have a man helping in the kitchen, and Rose was feeling more comfortable with Matthias as she and Gracie chatted with him. As the sun sank behind the barn, Rose was thinking about the best way to get her daughter tucked into bed so she and Matthias could talk. "It's Saturday night, Gracie," she said. "We should get you into the bathtub—"

"But I don't want Matthias to go! We're havin' *fun,*" her daughter insisted. Her lower lip began to quiver.

Matthias smiled. "Tell you what, young lady," he said as he tweaked her nose. "If you'll take your bath like your mamma says, and get into bed, I'll read you a story before you go to sleep."

Rose bit back a laugh. Gracie's eyes widened and she grabbed Rose's hand. "I'm likin' this, Mamma," she said excitedly. "Let's go upstairs *now!*"

In short order, without any further fuss, Gracie finished her bath, hurried into her nightie, and hollered down the stairs, "I'm ready, Matthias! I'm gonna pick out a book now!"

For Rose, the next half hour was nothing short of amazing. Matthias seemed totally comfortable stretched along the edge of Gracie's bed, reading the book of Bible stories by the light of the nightstand lamp. Gracie listened intently, as though Rose hadn't read these stories to her dozens of times. She was leaning against Matthias and his arm was around her; and when he closed the book, he kissed the top of her head.

"Time for prayers," he said. When he knelt at the side of the bed with his hands folded, Gracie slipped down to the floor beside him, bowing her head.

Rose's mouth dropped open. It was the sweetest sight . . . Nathan had always left the bedtime routine to Rose, so watching a man perform this ritual so smoothly and comfortably was a new experience. And when Matthias gazed at Rose over his shoulder, his smile inviting her to join them, Rose was in awe. She knelt on the other side of Gracie, bowing her head.

"Whom shall we pray for, Gracie?" he asked quietly. "Let's say a prayer in our heads, and then I'll pray for someone out loud, and you can pray for someone, and then your mamma can, too."

Keeping her eyes closed tight and her head bowed, Gracie nodded.

After a few moments of silence, while Rose wondered if her daughter and their guest could hear the hammering of her heart, Matthias spoke quietly, reverently. "Dear God, please bless Rose and Gracie and the time they spend at the senior center. Amen."

Rose peeked between her eyelids, to see Gracie's face glowing with angelic purpose and deep thought. "Dear God," she whispered, "please bless Gladys and Zelma and Flo—and Sherrie," she added, "and the two ladies who brought the pretty stuff they made. And bless Mamma and Matthias, too. Amen."

Rose licked her lips, hoping her prayer sounded half as de-
vout as the two she'd already heard. "Dear Lord, I thank You
for this quiet time with Gracie and Matthias, and I thank You
for the opportunities You've brought us this week. Bless us all
as we try to do Your will. Amen."

Rose waited for Gracie to get into bed and arrange the sheet
and the quilt the way she liked them. "*Gut* night, angel," she
whispered, leaning down to kiss Gracie's cheek. "Sleep tight
while God watches over you."

Rose started for the door, figuring Matthias would be behind her—and then stopped. Matthias, too, leaned over to
kiss Gracie's cheek. "Close your eyes and sleep, sweetie. I'll
see you on Monday when you come to Morning Star." He
flipped the switch on the battery lamp and then followed
Rose from the darkened room.

As Rose went quietly down the stairs, she wondered how
she would tell Matthias about meeting her birth mother . . .
how she would ask his advice about what she should do next.
She was still feeling uplifted by the way Matthias had read to
Gracie and prayed with them; it seemed a shame to spoil the
mood by talking about her birth mother. However, this was the
only time Rose could talk to him without Gracie listening in.

"Shall we sit out on the swing with some lemonade?" Rose
asked when she and Matthias reached the kitchen.

For the first time this evening, Matthias appeared a little
nervous. "*Gut* idea," he replied. "For what I've got to say, I
might need to wet my whistle a time or two."

# Chapter 20

Matthias sipped gratefully from his glass of lemonade as he sat at one end of the swing, a respectful distance from Rose. He felt as nervous as a kid asking the girl of his dreams if he could give her a ride home from a singing, knowing that the topic he wanted to discuss carried a lot more weight than asking a pretty girl for a date. He was still floating from the idyllic time he'd spent tucking Gracie into bed, bathed in her sweet, clean aroma as she gazed so lovingly into his eyes. The child he and Sadie were expecting would've been a few years younger than Gracie, had Sadie lived, and Matthias still ached for both of them.

But the ache was ebbing now . . . and Matthias knew he was wading into a relationship that might either suck him down with the undertow or leave him high and dry, lonely again. He sensed Rose was waiting for him to open the conversation, so he cleared his throat.

"I, uh, met Saul Hartzler and his wife this past week," he began in a tight voice. "Saul has offered me a full partnership in his carriage business, and I accepted."

When Matthias stole a glance at Rose, the darkness couldn't

camouflage her shock. Her mouth was an O, but no sound came out as she stared at him. "Well, now," she finally said, "I met Anne—and Martha Maude—Hartzler this week, too. And I don't know how to tell her who I am—or how I'll be able to act as though I don't know who she is," Rose continued hoarsely. "Anne and her mother-in-law bring their crocheted and quilted items to the senior center every now and again. Gracie has already wrapped Martha Maude around her little finger, so that complicates matters even more."

It was Matthias's turn to stare. "They just walked in?" he asked. Then the more obvious question came to him. "Did Anne realize who you were, Rose?"

"I—I don't think so. But it was all I could do not to blurt out my maiden name," she confessed. "I had to go hide in the kitchen, to settle myself down."

"Wow. I can't imagine how tough that must've been." Matthias thought hard for a moment, considering whether Rose's revelation would affect the way he told her the rest of his story. "After all the talking Bishop Vernon and I did, telling you not to go looking for Anne, it's quite a coincidence that *she* found *you*. But I still—"

"I'm not so sure it was a coincidence," Rose murmured. "I believe God always knows what He's doing."

Matthias blinked. "There's that," he said with a sigh, "but when I went to the Hartzlers' for dinner last week, I became even more certain that you shouldn't pursue a reunion with Anne. Saul's a big, bold fellow who's used to having things go his way—no doubt the wealthiest Amish fellow in Morning Star, by the looks of the assembly line and all the employees in his carriage shop."

"And then there's Martha Maude," Rose mused aloud. She gazed out over the porch railing as though she could find a solution to this problem in the velvety darkness of the night sky. "Just from the few minutes I spent with her and Anne, I had the feeling Saul's *mamm* might have the upper hand. She seemed much more outgoing."

"*Jah,* she is. She and Saul have a lot in common," Matthias agreed. "But here's the deal—Saul and Anne have no children . . ."

Rose's eyes widened in surprise.

". . . and that's why Saul asked me to become his full partner," he continued earnestly. "I was shocked that he'd consider somebody he'd just met a few days before, but he asked around in Willow Ridge about me and the quality of my work. He says he's got no employees who could keep the business profitable after he dies."

"Oh, my." Rose's pretty green eyes widened. "That's quite an honor, Matthias."

"*Jah,* I thought so, too. I knew in a heartbeat that my harness business would grow by leaps and bounds if I associated with Saul's shop," he said with a nod. He longed to reach over and take Rose's hand, but he wasn't sure the moment was right. "Turns out Martha Maude is the company's bookkeeper."

"I'm not surprised. But I'm wondering if Anne's as meek as a little mouse, or if she ever puts her foot down—ever speaks her piece if she disagrees with Saul and his *mamm.*" Rose inhaled some cool night air and let it out. "I figured she'd have kids to look after, though—and grandkids by now. That puts her marriage in a different light altogether."

Matthias heard the yearning in Rose's voice and figured he'd better spell out his feelings. "Rose, the way I see it, if Saul gets word about you being Anne's daughter by another man, and he realizes I'm a link in this chain, he'll tear our partnership papers to shreds and send me packing. I hope you don't think I'm selfish, seeing things this way."

Rose gazed forlornly at her hands, clasped in her lap. "I suspect Martha Maude would side with her son and be upset about Anne having a baby out of wedlock. If it's two against one, my mother will be backed into a corner . . . with no place to go, even though Saul can't put her out."

Matthias tentatively scooted toward the center of the swing and took Rose's hand in his. "I'm sorry this situation is so complicated," he whispered.

"Me too." Rose gazed at their two joined hands, making no effort to remove hers. "But what am I to do, Matthias? If Anne is my mother—the only relative I have left—"

"But, Mamma, Mammi Lydia's your *mamm*!" Gracie protested as she rushed out of the house to stand in front of Rose. "Anne is that nice lady who makes those pretty things for the folks at the senior center."

Matthias kicked himself for not checking to be sure Gracie was sleeping before he began this conversation. Rose looked as bewildered as he felt. It was clear she hadn't told her daughter about being born to a mother different from the one who'd raised her—and obvious that Rose had no idea how to explain the situation, either.

*What can I do to help Rose out of this awkward spot?* Matthias wondered. *Depending on how much Gracie heard, she might lose all her trust in me if I don't handle this openly and honestly. . . .*

Rose frantically tried to keep her composure and say the right thing. Gracie was only five, but she was bright and she never forgot a name, a face, or a story. Rose was grateful that Matthias hadn't released her hand or said anything questionable that Gracie might bring up to them later—or that made the two of them appear guilty of lying to her. Rose was also relieved that when her daughter placed both of her little hands on top of Matthias's larger one, Gracie acted as if it was perfectly normal for Matthias to be clasping Rose's hand while they sat on the swing together.

Bless him, Matthias leaned forward and opened his arm, and Gracie crawled up into his lap. "How long have you been listening to us, Gracie?" he asked gently. "What did you hear that you want to ask questions about?"

Gracie snuggled against his chest even as she nipped her lip. She knew she was supposed to stay in bed once she'd been tucked in, unless she was ill. "I dunno," she hedged. "I was just seein' if you was still here, Matthias."

Rose closed her eyes, sighing. She couldn't be angry, because Gracie adored Matthias and didn't want to miss out on anything. "What do you want to ask me, sweet pea?" she repeated. It was better to have her daughter express her doubts than to try to second-guess them.

Gracie nearly put her thumb in her mouth, but thought better of it. "Why did you call Anne your mamma?" she asked. "Does Mammi know, up in Heaven?"

Rose reached over to stroke Gracie's cheek, praying for the right words. "Your *mammi* told me about Anne right before she passed on, Gracie. When Mammi was a young woman, she had cancer and wasn't able to have babies, so she adopted me from Anne when I was only a few days old."

Gracie considered this. "It was the cancer?"

"*Jah.* Mammi had it when she was young, and it came back last year." Rose blinked back sudden tears. "The cancer is what she died from, remember?"

After a moment, Matthias gazed at Rose before taking

their explanation along a more pleasant path. "The lady you met—Anne—hasn't seen your mamma for a long time—"

"Nearly thirty years," Rose murmured with a nod.

"—because your mamma was just a wee little baby. She looks a lot different, now that she's a grown-up," Matthias continued patiently. "That's why Anne doesn't know that your mamma was her little baby, once upon a time. And Martha Maude doesn't know, either."

Gracie's eyes lit up. "Can I tell 'em? They'll be real happy to find out who Mamma is, *jah?*"

Rose's hand fluttered to her mouth before she could blurt out a *no*. If the situation in the Hartzler household were different—as uncomplicated as five-year-old Gracie assumed it was—it would be much easier to explain. The last thing Rose wanted was to cast Anne into an unbecoming, immoral light, because her words would probably come back to haunt them at the wrong time. Gracie didn't understand about how babies were made or why it was best for a woman to be married before she had one.

"No, Gracie, this is your mother's story to tell," Matthias insisted gently. "There's a right time to talk about this with other people, and your mamma's the one who should decide when that is."

When Gracie sat up to gaze into Matthias's eyes, assessing what he'd said, Rose wanted to hug him hard. She had a feeling that because Matthias had been the one to insist Gracie should keep quiet, Gracie would be more likely to do it. Rose had no idea how she'd manage her daughter the next time Anne and Martha Maude brought handmade items to the senior center, but at least Matthias was helping her. He realized how Gracie trusted him and believed in him, and he would hold her responsible for what she might say or do. And because he'd become Saul Hartzler's partner, his future and livelihood might be directly affected by how well Gracie kept this information to herself.

Rose squeezed Matthias's larger, stronger hand. Like it or not, they were united now by a common purpose. While Rose still longed to have a relationship with her birth mother, she also understood how high the stakes were for Matthias—and for Anne—if Saul Hartzler learned that Anne had birthed a baby out of wedlock.

*You've got to help us with this, God—please,* Rose prayed as she gazed at her little girl. *Gracie's too young and innocent to understand—*

"So if Anne is your *mamm*," Gracie pondered aloud, "who's your *dat,* Mamma?"

Rose sucked in air, exchanging a startled gaze with Matthias. She didn't feel it was appropriate to mention Joel Lapp's name, because she sensed he would never be a piece in this puzzle they were all trying to put together. Heat crept into her cheeks. This topic seemed awfully intimate to be discussing with her five-year-old. The silence of the night stretched on as Gracie gazed steadily at Rose from Matthias's lap.

Matthias cleared his throat. "Gracie, some things are meant for adults to know—"

"But Mamma tells me everything," Gracie insisted with innocent confidence. "I can go back to bed now and she can tell you his name—and then I'll hear it, too, through my window—or she can just tell me now," she added sweetly.

Rose nearly choked. Where had her daughter attained this all-knowing attitude? Did Gracie believe Rose told her everything because she was the only other person in her family now? Or was Gracie playing Matthias against her, confident that he would do anything because he adored her as much as she adored him? "Young lady, it's time you went back up-stairs to bed," she said firmly. "Matthias is right. Some things are for adults to know—"

"I should be going, anyway," Matthias added with an apologetic glance at Rose. "Tomorrow's Sunday, so we should all pray about this situation—and pray for Anne and Martha Maude," he added. He released Rose's hand to turn Gracie's face gently so she was looking at him. "And we should pray for each other again, too, so God knows we're paying atten-tion to the way He wants us to live together and . . . love each other. *Gut* night, Gracie. Mind your mamma. I'll see you Monday."

Gracie threw her arms around Matthias's neck. "Don't leave us," she whimpered. "Me and Mamma, we—"

"Gracie, that's enough." Rose stood up as Matthias did, and opened her arms.

Instead of leaning toward her mother's embrace, Gracie wiggled to get down. When Matthias set her on the porch floor, the little girl walked resolutely into the house, careful not to let the door slam behind her. Rose heard the patter of running feet on the hardwood floor of the front room, and then ascending the stairs.

Rose smiled sadly at Matthias. The moon had come out from behind the clouds and the night had a beautiful, roman-tic glow to it. Matthias pointed upward, toward Gracie's open window, a questioning expression on his face.

"*Jah,* who knew she could hear us? She must've been listen-ing through the screen door as well," Rose whispered. "I'm sorry if Gracie was pushing your buttons—"

Matthias gently grasped her arm, remaining under the porch ceiling. "She's just being curious, amazing Gracie," he insisted. "*Gut* night, Rose. It was a wonderful evening. I'll wait for you at the senior center Monday morning and take your mare and rig to my place. Happy to do it."

Rose nodded, hugging herself. It was too soon to be having such thoughts; yet she had the urge to wrap her arms around Matthias, to be enveloped by his warmth, his strength. He nodded, as though he knew what she was thinking, and then strode across the moonlit yard to the stable. Rose suddenly felt very lonely. She waved as Matthias drove down the lane toward the road, and then went back into the house.

Upstairs, Gracie was in bed with the sheet and quilt pulled over her head, so Rose left her alone. She went to her bedroom to get ready for bed. In her nightgown, as she ran a brush through the dark auburn hair that fell below her bottom, she gazed out the window. The stars glimmered in the clear night sky, filling her with a sense of peace and promise despite the way the evening had ended. She wouldn't sleep much, but tomorrow was a Sunday without church, so she and Gracie could rest up for the coming week at the senior center.

*What are You leading us to, Lord?* she prayed as she thought back to her time with Matthias. *My life is confusing now, and a little scary—but I thank You for new opportunities that sparkle like the stars in Your Heaven.*

# Chapter 21

Sunday dawned sunny and bright, and when Rose took Gracie to the stable to tend to Daisy's feed and water, she carried luggage to their surrey—a double-size buggy—as well. "Tomorrow we'll go to Morning Star for five days," Rose reminded her daughter. "We have our clothes packed, and a box of your toys and books. Have we forgotten anything?"

Gracie thought for a moment while Rose arranged their belongings in the back of the rig. "Are we takin' feed for Daisy?"

"*Gut* idea! I hadn't thought of that," Rose replied. "We'll take this half sack of rations with us, and a couple bales of hay, and we'll ask Matthias what else we should bring. It's nice of him to help us with Daisy."

"Matthias is awful nice," Gracie remarked sadly. "But he leaved us."

"He *left* us last night," Rose corrected, "because he had to go home, sweet pea. Here—put the hose in the trough and I'll turn on the water."

Gracie walked over to the galvanized tank and obediently

positioned the hose over it, but Rose thought her daughter seemed withdrawn. She'd only eaten half of her French toast at breakfast, and she'd been uncharacteristically quiet all morning. When a stream of water made the hose jump, Gracie didn't giggle as she usually did.

Rose finished tucking the mare's rations into the buggy and joined Gracie at the water trough. "Are you all right, Gracie? You seem sad today."

Gracie's lower lip popped out as she blinked rapidly. "Matthias thought I was bein' bad last night," she whimpered. "I just wanted to be with you and him insteada up in my room all by myself."

Gracie's heartbroken expression made Rose's heart shrivel. She stooped to wrap her arms around her daughter—who couldn't comprehend the consequences of the information she'd overheard last night. "I know, sweetie," she murmured, kissing Gracie's cheek. "And I know how much you like Matthias—and how much you liked Anne and Martha Maude when you met them, too. But Matthias was right," she insisted. "Some things are for grown-ups—like drinking coffee and shoveling Daisy's poop out of the stable."

Gracie turned up her nose, trying not to smile.

"So, do you understand why Mamma should be the one to talk to Anne about me being her baby—not you?" Rose continued in a serious tone.

"You're not a baby, Mamma. Me neither," Gracie replied.

"*Jah,* that's true. But you will always be my little girl—even when you're grown up with little girls of your own," Rose explained gently. "Anne will always wonder what happened to the baby girl she gave to Mammi Lydia all those years ago. And if she finds out it's me, she might need some

quiet time to think about it without anybody else around—
just like you needed time to think last night when you pulled
the covers over your head."

"Quiet time," Gracie said. "I used to need a lotta quiet
time when I was little, huh, Mamma? When I needed to settle
down and stop talkin' coz Dat was mad at me."

Rose considered this. While it was true that Nathan hadn't
always known how to tolerate Gracie's tendency to chatter
and tease him, he'd never remained angry with her. Truth be
told, Nathan had had such a soft spot for Gracie that he'd
sometimes distanced himself from her so he wouldn't let her
get away with too much.

"Your *dat* loved you so much," Rose insisted, whispering
directly into Gracie's ear. "He's looking down at you from
Heaven, seeing what a big girl you're getting to be, too. He
knows you don't need quiet time nearly as often now."

Gracie considered this pensively. "Will Dat be mad because I like Matthias? And because you like him?"

Rose blinked. Sometimes the connections her daughter
made amazed her. "Your *dat* wants us both to be happy,
sweet pea. He knows you'll need another *dat* as you grow up,
because he knows how important it is to have a family—if
not with Matthias, with another man someday."

Gracie gripped the hose, glancing up at Rose. "Does
Matthias wanna be in a family with us, you think?"

Rose smiled. The yearning on Gracie's precious face reminded her how much she, too, admired Matthias Wagler. It
was too soon to be drawing conclusions, though. "It'll take
us some time to figure that out," she replied. Glancing at the
water level in the trough, Rose released Gracie and stood up

straight. "It's another one of those things for adults to decide, but we know you have feelings, too."

Rose turned off the faucet at the wall. She had a flash image of the future, when Anne and Martha Maude visited the Morning Star Senior Center again, and Gracie rushed across the lobby to greet them. She shut out the daydream, returning to the reality of Gracie and the way she was gazing out the stable door. In the excitement of seeing those women again, would her little girl blurt out what she knew about Rose being Anne's daughter?

"Somebody's comin', Mamma," Gracie said with a big smile. "I gotta go see who it is!"

As her daughter scampered off, Rose glanced at the filthy floor of Daisy's stall. The manure and dirty straw would remain there all week because she hadn't had time to muck it out—a job that was inappropriate on Sunday. When Rose reached the door and saw the couple getting out of the rig, her heart stilled. Bishop Vernon and Jerusalem were both exclaiming over Gracie, delighted to see her.

*Will they be happy to hear my big news?* Rose wondered as she walked across the weedy, uneven lawn. She had a feeling that the bishop was here for more than a Sunday visit—and that Gracie was already telling them where she'd spent her days this past week—so there would be no concealing the fact that Rose had defied Vernon's wishes and done things her own way.

Rose returned Jerusalem's wave, noting how the bishop's wife took Gracie's hand as the two of them headed toward the garden—which left Vernon free to speak with Rose alone. The white-haired bishop smiled kindly at her as he crossed the yard, his hands clasped behind his back. "It's *gut* to see you looking well, Rose," he said as he stopped in front of her.

"I came by a few times this week to see how you and Gracie were doing, but you weren't home."

His tone was cordial, but when Vernon's baby blue eyes twinkled, Rose wondered if he already knew where she'd been. "I found a *gut* job and started working this week," she admitted. "I'm cooking at the senior center in Morning Star, and Gracie goes with me. They call her their resident ray of sunshine. She even has a little school desk in the corner of the kitchen."

Vernon's brows rose. "That didn't take long. How did the director there know you were looking for work?"

Again, Rose sensed no traps in the bishop's question, merely curiosity. "I, um, posted index cards on some of the bulletin boards in the area," she replied. "I was really surprised when Sherrie—the director—called me so quickly. It's a wonderful place to work, Vernon! Sherrie was concerned about us making the drive twice every day, so she offered us an apartment there," she added happily. "We'll be going in on Mondays and coming back home Friday afternoons."

"I'm relieved to hear you'll not be making that drive twice a day," Vernon said with a nod. "English drivers seem to take more daredevil chances on the county highways these days, thinking they won't get caught." He glanced around the yard, and then watched Jerusalem pushing Gracie in the swing, which hung from the old maple tree near the house. "I have to wonder, however, if you'll be able to keep this place up—"

"*Jah*, the grass is getting long and a lot of fixing needs to be done," Rose agreed. "But I can't do the repairs myself—and I can't afford to pay for that work. And now that I can stay in town, I've given some thought to selling the place."

Vernon's eyes widened. "That's an awfully big step to take this soon, Rose."

Rose shrugged. "The way I see it, I have a lot of big steps to take now that I'm on my own," she murmured. "I know what you said about me working, Bishop, but I believe the Lord helps those who help themselves." She glanced across the yard, to be sure Gracie was still flying high in the swing. "I had another surprise this week, when my birth mother, Anne Hartzler, came to the senior center with her mother-in-law. She didn't know who I was, but I certainly recognized her."

Vernon's bushy eyebrows rose. "Oh, my. I know how you yearn to reconnect with her, Rose, but I still believe it's best not to intrude upon her marriage—her family."

"Matthias says the same thing. Saul Hartzler has just taken him on as a full partner in his carriage shop," Rose said. "He says Saul's not a man who'll tolerate news of a baby Anne had before she married him . . . especially because they have no children."

The bishop exhaled loudly. "My word, what a week you've had! Matthias has partnered with Hartzler Carriage Company—which is no small undertaking—and you've come face-to-face with Anne at your new job."

"You know the Hartzlers, don't you, Bishop?"

Vernon's mouth opened and then shut again. "Fair enough. I've had some dealings with Saul, as he's the deacon in the Morning Star district, where my *gut* friend Jeremiah Shetler is the bishop," he replied. "Matthias's impression of Saul runs along the same lines as my own—so if you won't heed my warning, I hope you'll respect Matthias's opinion. Sounds like he might have a lot at stake."

"*Jah,* so he's told me," Rose said softly. "I can see that it's best if I don't introduce myself to Anne, but the challenge will be to keep Gracie from spilling the beans. Saul's *mamm,* Martha Maude, took to Gracie right away . . . and Gracie overheard Matthias and me talking about Anne being my mother."

"Gracie's an easy girl to love," Vernon pointed out as he watched his wife pushing the little girl in the swing. "She might blurt out what she knows next time she sees Anne, just because she's excited."

"That's what I'm thinking." Rose sighed. "What do you think I should do, Vernon? I've been over this again and again in my mind, in my prayers. But I can't anticipate what might happen—or when."

When Vernon closed his eyes and lifted his face to the sunshine, Rose remained quiet. After a few moments, he focused his blue eyes on her. "I know of bishops who would chastise you for going against their wishes by finding work—and they would point out that if you'd not taken the job in Morning Star, you wouldn't have met up with your mother," he said gently. "But I understand your motivation, and you're able to keep Gracie with you, so it serves no purpose to shake my proverbial finger at you."

Rose smiled, feeling as though Vernon had blessed her with his benediction.

"And it wasn't as though you went looking for your mother," he added gently. "I advise you to keep asking God what He's got in mind for this situation. Keep Gracie close when you're working. Perhaps if you see Anne coming into the center, you can have a place in mind to take Gracie—"

"That would be easier if she wasn't already crazy about Anne and Martha Maude," Rose mused aloud. "And Gracie usually sees people coming much sooner than I do. It's a knack she has."

Vernon chuckled, squeezing her shoulder. "Gracie's a busy bee, interested in everything that goes on around her," he agreed. "We believe all things work to the *gut* for them that love God, but it can't hurt to pray that He's watching over all of you closely, so this situation won't backfire."

Rose nodded. Her smile brightened as she watched her daughter hop from the swing and run toward her.

"It would be one thing for Gracie to tell Anne who you are," Vernon continued in a faraway voice, "but if Saul somehow finds out about you, the consequences will be far-reaching. Not a one of you who's involved will emerge unscathed, I fear. Even Gracie might bear the brunt of Saul's anger—ah, but here she comes."

"I saw you flying high on that swing, young lady!" Rose called out as she opened her arms. It was sweet relief to catch her excited daughter, to hear Gracie's giggle as she wrapped her arms around Rose's neck.

"'Rusalem's a *gut* pusher! We was havin' fun, Mamma!"

Bussing Gracie's downy cheek, Rose was aware that *fun* had been scarce in their lives lately—and she was glad Bishop Vernon would deliver no more of his dire warnings about the Hartzler family. "I bet you and Jerusalem worked up an appetite," she said as she smiled at the steely-haired woman, who was joining them. "Shall we go inside for coffee and milk—"

"And more of that 'nana bread with the blueberries, Mamma!" Gracie insisted with a big smile.

"Oh, but that sounds tasty," Jerusalem said, tweaking Gracie's nose. "And I get the piece with the most blueberries."

"Nuh-uh!" Gracie squealed with laughter when Vernon tugged lightly on her earlobe.

"I'm the oldest and the biggest," the bishop joined in as the four of them headed toward the house, "so that means *I* get the biggest piece of banana bread *and* the most blueberries. By the time I taste all the pieces to figure out which piece has the most berries, the rest of you might not get any at all!"

Rose smiled and hugged her daughter close. Her life would be a lot easier if the toughest issue she faced was deciding who, indeed, got the most impressive piece of blueberry-banana bread.

## Chapter 22

Rose got off to any early start on Monday morning, partly because Gracie was so excited about getting to the senior center and unpacking her toys, she was out of bed before dawn. All the way to Morning Star the two of them chatted happily, as though having an apartment during the week—a new home away from home—was a fresh start for both of them.

As they pulled into the parking lot, Rose saw that Matthias was waiting for them. Gracie was all smiles as he came over to help her out of the rig, and she wrapped her legs and arms around him in a huge hug.

"We haven't seen you in forever, Matthias!" the little girl exclaimed.

Matthias winked at Rose as he enjoyed Gracie's attention. "*Jah,* it's been a whole day and a half, honey-girl," he teased.

"You can come see us anytime you want now," Gracie prattled on, "coz we live here! We can play in the park and—and have picnics and all sorts of fun stuff!"

"That's a happy thought. I'll think on it while I work in my shop this week," Matthias replied as he lowered her to the pavement. "And I'll take real *gut* care of Daisy, too. She'll have my horses for company now, so she won't be all by herself."

"And *denki* for helping us this way," Rose put in. "There's half a bag of feed and a couple bales of hay in the surrey—"

"And luggage I can carry in for you before I go," Matthias added. His smile did funny things to Rose's stomach. "I've never known women to travel without a bunch of clothes and *stuff*—"

"*Jah,* the *stuff* is mine!" Gracie crowed. "I brought my chalkboard and *everything*!"

Rose grabbed the garment bag, watching Matthias heft the big suitcase and the duffel of Gracie's toys without any apparent effort. Why did he appear so handsome today? He was wearing a purple shirt and gray trousers with black suspenders—nothing out of the ordinary for a Plain man—yet something about his smile and his manner seemed different. She walked ahead of him to open the door with her free hand.

"Gracie, do you remember how to find our apartment?" Rose asked as they stepped inside the senior center. "You lead the way—but remember that some folks are still sleeping."

Gracie pressed her finger upon her lips. Without a moment's hesitation, she hurried down the hallway ahead of Rose and Matthias.

"She's excited about this move," Matthias said as he strode beside Rose. "But truth be told, so am I. I hope it'll be all right if I stop over now and again? Maybe after you've finished serving these folks their supper?"

Butterflies fluttered in Rose's stomach. "Oh, Gracie will love that!"

Matthias smiled knowingly. "And what about you, Rose?"

Rose felt like a little girl who'd been offered an extra dessert after dinner. "I—I'd like that, *jah*," she whispered. "I don't think Sherrie will mind if I visit with you now and again."

Matthias glanced up to see where Gracie had gone, his expression thoughtful. "If you'd rather not visit with me where the residents can watch, we could go for walks or—or even go to my place. It's just down the road."

Rose's eyes widened. "Oh, I don't know about that," she said worriedly. "It seems awfully private, awfully soon, to be at your place—"

"Rose." Matthias stopped before turning down the next hallway and gazed into her eyes. "We're adults, both of us married before," he reminded her gently. "It's not like we need a chaperone, and if Gracie comes along, that'll be fine, too. But once in a while—when you feel all right with it—I'm hoping to see you, just the two of us. I like you, Rose. A lot."

For a moment, she couldn't breathe. What would it be like to spend time with a man who wasn't her husband? She'd married Nathan when she wasn't yet twenty, and she hadn't dated many fellows before he'd started courting her.

Gracie's exaggerated whisper brought Rose out of her swirling thoughts. "Mamma! Here we are!"

Rose looked down the hall, where Gracie was bouncing up and down in front of a door, pointing at it as the strings of her little *kapp* fluttered around her face. "Sometimes this little girl amazes me," she murmured to Matthias as she started walking again.

"Wish I had half her energy," he said with a chuckle. "Just think about what I said, okay?"

Rose felt her cheeks turning pink. She was grateful that none of the residents were opening their doors to peer out at her. "I will," she assured him. "I just need a little time."

Matthias nodded and carried the big suitcase into their

apartment, but Rose could tell her response had disappointed him. After Gracie gave him a quick tour, he left so he could drive Daisy and the rig to his place before he started work in his harness shop. When Rose caught sight of him out their side window, she suddenly realized she had no way to reach Matthias if they needed the horse and rig during the week. Without a word to Gracie, she sprinted out of the apartment and down the hall.

"Matthias!" Rose called out as she raced out the door. "Matthias, wait!"

Daisy had just turned onto the street, but with a word from Matthias, the mare began to back up. Laughing, Rose waited on the sidewalk for the rig to reach her.

Matthias tugged on the lines to stop the horse. He opened the window, smiling. "Seems I've left you breathless, Rose," he teased.

"Maybe you have," she admitted. "I should probably have your phone number, in case I need the rig before Friday. There's a tablet and a pen under the seat."

"Do you think I give my number to just any woman who asks?"

When Matthias leaned down to find the paper, Rose thought hard. It had been a long while since she'd teased a man, or flirted. . . .

"I had your number the moment I first ran into you at the mercantile, Matthias Wagler," Rose asserted boldly.

Matthias sat up and gazed at her. He jotted his number and address on the top piece of paper, tore it out with a flourish, and handed it to her. "Running into you is the best thing I've done in a long while, Rose," he murmured. "Have a *gut* week. And don't think you can't call me for something besides your horse. Got a phone in your apartment?"

Rose blinked. "I don't know. There's one in the kitchen, but—" When she glanced toward the building, Gracie was watching them with her hands and nose pressed against the window, so she waved.

"We'll figure it out. Hope to see you real soon, Rose."

She watched Matthias drive down the driveway. When she glanced at the piece of paper, she sucked in air. After the phone number and address, he'd written *XXOO*, in large, bold strokes.

*Hugs and kisses.* When she could catch her breath again, Rose folded the paper twice and tucked it into her apron pocket. If Gracie saw what Matthias had written, Rose would never hear the end of it. Ever since Nathan had written *XXOO* in the flour on the countertop where Rose had been making bread, Gracie had known the meaning of those letters—even before she'd known the letters of her name.

*Hugs and kisses . . . maybe those are* good *things, coming from Matthias,* Rose thought as she started for the door. *Maybe this move to Morning Star is the start of something more wonderful than I can imagine.*

On Tuesday, when Rose had helped Alison clean up after lunch, she agreed with Gracie that they should take a walk. It was a bright, cheerful day—warm for the last week of April—and they both needed the fresh air and exercise. "Let's go out the front way, Mamma," Gracie suggested eagerly. "It's closer to the park and the swings!"

Gracie forgot all about playing outdoors, however, when she saw the two Plain women who were coming in the front door. The little girl sucked in her breath, looked to Rose for permission—and then ran full tilt toward Anne and Martha

Maude Hartzler. Rose prayed fast and hard that Gracie wouldn't say anything she shouldn't.

"Well, look who's here! It's our amazing Grace," Martha Maude quipped as the little girl stopped in front of her. "We came back for our plastic bins today—but I also have a special job I want to do in the flower garden at the side of the building. Will you come with me, Gracie?"

When Gracie gazed back at her, Rose nodded. "*Jah,* this girl needs a special job," she teased. If she said no, Martha Maude and Anne would surely suspect something was amiss. She watched the two of them go out the front door, hand in hand and chattering as though they were old friends.

Rose smiled shyly at Anne. What could she say that wouldn't get her into trouble? She noticed the plastic bins stacked near the aquarium—probably where Sherrie always put them after she'd emptied them. "Looks like all your pretty pieces have found homes," she remarked. "That's a very thoughtful project, bringing lap robes and slippers and such."

Anne was gazing steadily at Rose as though quilted and crocheted pieces were the furthest things from her mind. "Last time we came here, I thought you looked very familiar," she murmured. "Do I know you, Rose?"

Rose thought she might pass out. If she didn't answer Anne's question truthfully, she would never get another opportunity to discuss their relationship. But if she did answer . . .

"I'm sorry," Anne murmured, shaking her head. "I get these silly notions about folks sometimes, thinking I know them from—"

"Yes, you do know me," Rose interrupted nervously, "but it's been about thirty years since you saw me . . . after you weaned me at Lydia and Myron Fry's house."

Anne's mouth dropped open. She pressed her hands to her cheeks, leaning forward to gaze closely at Rose's face. "Oh, my word, I—I . . ."

Rose swallowed hard, tears filling her eyes when she saw the intense emotion on Anne's pale, freckled face. When she reached out, Anne clasped her hand as though she might never let it go.

"Rose! Oh, Rose," she murmured. As she wiped her eyes, she quickly looked around the lobby. "When I saw your facial features—your eyebrows and your father's hair color and complexion—the other day, I couldn't help wondering if you might be my Rose. Oh, praise God! I—I never dared to hope I'd see you again," she whispered. "But please understand, Martha Maude knows nothing about—"

Rose glanced nervously toward the door. "I don't want to cause you any trouble with your family," she assured Anne. "But if we could find a time to talk—"

"*Jah,* we must," Anne agreed, searching Rose's face as though to memorize every line and eyelash. "But it has to be when my Saul is at work and when little Gracie isn't around and—oh, my! Now we have to act as though we don't know each other," she continued with a jittery laugh. "But it's really *you.* My very own Rose from so long ago. Oh, how I've loved you, sweetheart. Every day of my life."

Rose blinked back her tears. Even though she'd yearned for this reunion, she hadn't anticipated the intense range of emotions she felt in her soul—and saw on her mother's face. "I read your letters right after Mamma passed—"

"*Jah,* I saw her funeral announcement in the paper. I'm so sorry, Rose."

"—and I didn't know what to think, but—oh, here comes Gracie," she whispered.

Anne squeezed her hand and released it. "Martha Maude won't be far behind. Oh, my. We have to be very careful, daughter."

Rose had a feeling her birth mother was having the same frightening realizations Vernon and Matthias had warned her about, when Anne considered the consequences of her husband and his mother finding out about the baby she'd given up. Rose composed her face with a firm smile, leaning down with her hands on her knees to welcome her little girl.

"Gracie, where'd you get these pretty tulips?" she asked brightly. "Look at all these colors—red and yellow and purple and pink! They're like a rainbow in your hands."

"Me and Martha Maude picked 'em—for *you*, Mamma!" Gracie crowed as she thrust her bouquet at Rose. "There's a whole buncha pretty flowers on the other side of the building. I'll hafta take you there sometime!"

"Oh, *denki*, sweet pea," Rose murmured as she took the fresh, fragrant flowers. "What a thoughtful gift. We'll put them in water right away so they'll stay nice. And *denki* to you, Martha Maude," she added as the older woman came through the lobby. "These tulips will really brighten up our apartment."

Martha Maude smiled. "Gracie was telling me that you'll be staying here during the week," she said with a nod. "We'll have to have you girls over for supper sometime."

Rose smiled, knowing better than to look at her mother's face. But what could she say, other than to act as though she appreciated Martha Maude's idea?

"*Jah*, let's go, Mamma!" Gracie pleaded eagerly. "They got goats and chickens! And peas in their garden!"

Rose couldn't help laughing at her daughter's endearing enthusiasm. "Did you tell Martha Maude that she likely won't have any peas left if she lets you pick them and eat them for supper?"

"We talked about that, *jah*," Martha Maude replied with a chuckle. She glanced down the hallway. "I guess Sherrie's not around? She usually comes out when she sees we're here."

"She stepped out for a few errands. I'll tell her you stopped by." Rose found the nerve to smile at Anne then. "The folks who received your shawls and slippers really appreciated them. The residents look forward to your visits."

"Happy to make things for them," Anne replied softly. "Some of them don't have much in the way of family. We enjoy talking with whoever happens to be in the lobby, and—well, we go away feeling grateful that God has blessed us with a bountiful life."

"Amen to that," Martha Maude put in. "We'll get our bins and head on home now. What's for supper, Gracie?"

Gracie looked up at Rose with shining eyes. "I dunno! What're we cookin', Mamma?"

"Creamed chicken—with celery, onion, carrots, and peas—over mashed potatoes," Rose replied. "And peach cobbler for dessert. We'll put this pretty bouquet of tulips on the sideboard so everyone can enjoy it before we take it to our apartment."

"That sounds tasty! Give everyone our best, and we'll see you again," Martha Maude said as she picked up the stacked bins. "Enjoy the rest of your day, girls."

Rose nodded, her heart welling up with emotions she couldn't discuss. She watched Anne precede her mother-in-law so she could open the door for her—and after Martha

Maude had gone outside, Anne turned in the doorway. The love light on her face sent goose bumps up Rose's spine. All she could do was wiggle her fingers in a wave.

Anne waved back. Then she followed Martha Maude.

Rose blinked rapidly, because if Gracie saw she was crying, there would be no end to her curious questions. When they entered the kitchen, she challenged her little girl to find something they could use as a vase. The short red pitcher Gracie pointed to was the perfect size. After Rose ran water into it and arranged the tulips, she let her daughter carry the bouquet into the dining room.

The afternoon passed quickly with supper preparations and a chat with Sherrie. After supper, Rose and Gracie took the walk they'd missed after lunch, circling the main square in town and spending some time at the park. As she pushed her ecstatic daughter higher and higher in a swing, Rose allowed herself a moment to consider today's momentous event.

*My mother recognized me—and she was glad to see me again!* Denki, *Lord, for bringing us together again, and please, please guide us in the way You would have us go as we get reacquainted.*

When Rose and Gracie returned to their apartment, they spent a little more time hanging up their clothes and putting the toys on the shelves of the big closet. Gracie was so excited, it took two stories before she was ready to go to sleep. After her prayers, Rose turned out the lamp and went into the front room. When she could hear Gracie's deep, even breathing coming from their bedroom, she took her mother's letters from the zipped compartment of the suitcase.

Reading the lines Anne had written so long ago was different this time, because Rose could hear the words in her mother's voice. One paragraph seemed more meaningful now. More acceptable.

> *I can't tell you what a blessing it has been to stay with Lydia and Myron so I could nurse you—so Lydia and I could share the first incredible eight months of your life, dear daughter. You have no idea what a gift from God you are to both of us. It will sadden me greatly to leave you behind—I'll have a huge hole where my heart has been—but I know you'll have a secure, happy life with two generous, compassionate parents who already love you as though you are their own.*

Rose sighed, filled with gratitude. Yes, Lydia and Myron Fry had been loving, devoted parents any child would've been blessed to have—now she could set aside her resentment over the way Mamma had kept her true identity a secret. After Rose read the letters again, and gazed at the watercolor portrait her father had painted, she slipped the pages back into the suitcase.

She switched off the lamp and sat in the quiet darkness, remembering Anne's facial expressions and reactions as they'd talked this afternoon. It had felt like a holy moment, a mother and child reunion orchestrated by the Lord Himself. No matter what might happen in the future, Rose was deeply grateful for the brief time she and Anne had shared.

How would they find a chance to be together again? She wondered if Anne ever went anywhere without Martha Maude . . . wondered how this reunion would play out, and what the consequences would be. Would it make a difference that Anne had sought Rose out, rather than Rose being the one to speak first?

*You know the answers, Lord. I'll watch and wait for Your guidance. Bless Anne as she considers how we should pro-ceed—bless us all with Your wisdom and patience. And* denki, *Lord, for the love that has surrounded me all my life . . . and for blessing me with two mothers. Two mothers to love me! What a gift.*

# Chapter 23

On Thursday afternoon, Rose was making a large batch of dough for cinnamon rolls when Sherrie's voice came through the kitchen's intercom. "You have a phone call, Rose," the director said. "You can pick up the phone by the freezer and take it."

"Ah! *Denki,*" Rose replied, "but it'll take me a moment to scrape the dough off my hands."

*Who would be calling me?* Rose grabbed a damp dishrag and quickly wiped off most of the flour and dough that was clinging to her fingers.

"Maybe it's Martha Maude callin' to ask us over for supper," Gracie speculated. She was drawing flowers on her chalkboard with her colored chalk, seated at her school desk next to the freezer.

"Well, I guess we'll find out," Rose murmured as she reached for the receiver of the wall phone. "*Jah,* hello?"

"And what did I catch you in the middle of doing?" Matthias asked with a chuckle. "Sherrie said you had to clean off your hands."

Rose felt almost giddy—Matthias had called her! "I've got

a big batch of dough started for cinnamon rolls," she replied. "Enough for tomorrow's breakfast, and for Sherrie to warm up on Saturday morning as well."

"Ooh. That makes me wish I lived at the senior center—*almost*," he teased. "I've wanted to come and see you, but Saul's been showing me the ins and outs of his carriage shop the past few afternoons. The man keeps long hours," Matthias added, "so I've not gotten home until nearly seven. I told him I had plans this evening, though, so if I could stop by after supper—"

"Come and eat with us!" Rose blurted. "We're having lasagna and salad and—and there's always more than enough."

For a moment, all Rose heard was Matthias's breathing. Had she said something out of line? Maybe she should've cleared this idea with Sherrie first, but—

"Lasagna's one of my favorites," Matthias finally said, "and I know yours is probably the best lasagna I'll ever put in my mouth . . . but does this mean all the folks living at the senior center will be watching us eat together? Is that all right with you, Rose?"

Rose's cheeks prickled with heat. She hadn't thought about how Gladys, Flo, Zelma, and the other folks with whom she and Gracie usually ate might react to having a man her age, wearing Plain clothes, joining them.

"Mamma, is that Matthias?" Gracie asked excitedly. "Tell him I want a picnic in the park so's we can play! I'm tired of bein' inside."

Rose laughed, and Matthias was chuckling as well. "I suppose you heard your orders from Queen Gracie," she said. "Maybe a picnic would be a better idea, say, at six? I can bring the lasagna and some plates—everything we'll need—and we'll meet you at one of the picnic tables. Some of our residents might peer out the window at us, but at least they won't ask embarrassing questions."

Matthias cleared his throat. "Does this mean you're embarrassed to be seen with me, Rose?" he teased.

"No! I—it's just that they'll assume you're my boyfriend, or—"

"Matthias is *my* boyfriend, Mamma!" Gracie called out toward the phone. "I helped make the lemon pie, so he's gotta come taste it!"

Matthias's laughter tickled Rose's ear. "How can I turn down an offer like that? Lasagna *and* lemon pie," he said. "I'll be there at six—and how about if I bring dishes and silverware so you don't have to carry all that stuff down the street? And I've got lots of fresh salad greens from the Hartzlers' garden, too."

"That would be easier," Rose admitted.

"And it makes me feel like I'm holding up my end of the date—and you won't have to mess with the dirty dishes afterward," he said. "This sounds like a really nice way to end the day. I'll see you girls at six."

"*Jah,* we'll be there. See you then." As Rose hung up the phone, her heart was dancing. Matthias had called their picnic a *date.* Even though she wore black dresses, aprons, stockings, and shoes every day, a part of her felt alive again rather than isolated by her widowhood. Just knowing that a handsome man like Matthias Wagler wanted to spend time with her made her feel lighthearted. Almost attractive.

"It's gonna be fun tonight, Mamma. I just know it!" Gracie declared from her little school desk. "See my pretty flowers?"

Rose smiled as she returned to her big bowl of dough. "You're really good at drawing, Gracie," she said as she assessed her daughter's artwork. "I see daisies and tulips and sun-flowers, *jah?*"

Gracie nodded happily as she started drawing a large sun in the upper corner of her chalkboard. "They're like the ones in Sherrie's magazines. I'm gonna try drawin' birds next."

Once again, Rose wondered if this artistic talent ran in Gracie's blood, a gift from her grandfather, Joel Lapp. She'd seen her daughter gazing at the copies of *Birds and Blooms* from Sherrie's office, but she'd had no idea Gracie would be able to draw flowers because she'd seen photographs of them in magazines. Her flowers weren't perfect, but they were de-tailed and easily recognizable.

Rose resumed her baking with renewed energy. The pans of lasagna and the lemon pies were already made and waiting in the refrigerator, but she needed to get the cinnamon rolls in the oven and make a big bowl of salad and—

*And you'll get everything done in plenty of time to meet Matthias,* she reminded herself when her thoughts began to whirl. *Even if he has to wait for a few minutes, that's part of the game, ain't so?*

When Matthias pulled his rig into the park a few minutes after six, he frowned. There wasn't a soul in sight. The swings swayed in the breeze as though invisible kids were sitting in them, but he saw no sign of Gracie or her mother. He un-hitched Daisy and put her on a long tether so she could graze on the fresh grass in the shade. He took the cardboard box out of the rig and set it on the nearest table. By the time he'd wiped the tabletop with an old towel and set three places, he heard a familiar little voice calling him.

"Matthias! I thought we'd *never* get here," Gracie cried out as she ran across the grass.

He caught the little girl when she launched herself at him. "Why's that? Did something happen that took longer than you thought?"

Gracie tugged playfully at his beard. "Mamma had to change her dress *again*," she replied in an exasperated whisper. "She got flour on the first one, so she put on a different one and didn't like it—so she put on her clean one for tomorrow. They're all black, so I didn't think it was such a big deal—"

Matthias caught sight of Rose crossing the park then, and he tuned out Gracie's chatter. Rose was carrying a canvas tote in one hand and had a pie pan in the crook of her other arm. She appeared calm and poised as she smiled at him, yet it tickled him that she'd wanted to look her very best after a day in the kitchen. Balancing Gracie on his hip, Matthias walked toward Rose with his hand out.

"I could relieve you of that pie," he suggested. "It's *gut* to see you, Rose—and awfully nice of you to bring dinner."

Rose held fast to the pie plate. "Are you one of those guys who wants his pie first and then his meal?" she challenged playfully as she continued toward the table. "Seems to me we should eat the lasagna first, while it's still hot. To everything there's a season, *jah?*" she quipped. "A time for supper, and a time for dessert."

Something about the tilt of Rose's head and the lilt in her voice made Matthias aware that he was head over heels . . . already a goner, when it came to his feelings about the woman, with the glossy auburn hair and arched eyebrows, who was taking a glass pan from her tote. Matthias tried not to be obvious about watching her lithe body and the way she moved so gracefully as she set the pie plate on the table a slight distance from the lasagna and his bowl of salad. She had a small foil-wrapped packet as well, but Matthias didn't ask about it.

He figured it was a little mystery they could talk about later—and he hoped it was something wonderful that Rose had brought especially for him. It was shaped like a couple of large cinnamon rolls. . . .

"Set me down!" Gracie urged him. "I'm starvin', coz everybody else got to eat before we came."

Smiling, Matthias went to the side of the table where he'd placed two plates and lowered the little girl onto the bench in front of one of them. "I thought you could sit beside your *mamm,* so I could see both of you better while we eat," he said when Gracie patted the bench beside her. Truth be told, he was aware that Gracie was enamored of him—and he was crazy about her, too—but she needed to know that his bigger interest was in her mother. Matthias sensed that if he let her, Gracie would get in the habit of requiring all his attention.

After a brief silent prayer, Rose removed the foil from the glass pan of lasagna. As aromas of beef and tomato sauce and cheese wafted around him, Matthias closed his eyes in ecstasy. "I hope you girls don't want any of this lasagna," he teased as Rose dished up the largest piece with a metal spatula. "I think I can eat it all!"

"Nuh-uh!" Gracie protested as Rose placed the steaming food on his plate. "Me next, Mamma, coz I can eat all the rest of it before Matthias does!"

Rose looked sternly at her daughter, her spatula poised above the pan. "Somebody's sounding awfully bossy. How do you ask me nicely for your share of dinner?"

Gracie slumped on the bench until all Matthias could see was the top of her small white *kapp.* "Please and thank you," she murmured contritely.

"Much better." Rose cut one of the pieces of lasagna in half with the edge of the spatula and placed it on Gracie's plate.

"Now you may sit up straight and eat your supper, sweet pea. I know you're excited, but it's important to behave yourself. We don't want Matthias thinking you're a fussy, spoiled little baby."

As Gracie reached for her fork, she stole a glance across the table. Matthias winked at her and put salad on his plate. "How much would you like, Gracie?" he asked as he picked up more salad with the tongs.

"That's *gut*," the little girl murmured. "*Denki*, Matthias."

"You're very welcome."

After Matthias had passed the salad bowl to Rose and they'd shared the bottle of ranch dressing he'd brought, the three of them prayed and then began to eat. He enjoyed watching Rose cut Gracie's lasagna into bite-sized chunks, his gaze lingering on her sturdy, capable hands . . . on her patient, loving expression as she nodded her encouragement when her little girl looked up at her.

*Gracie looks up to you, too—but being a* dat *raising somebody else's child is different from being an uncle to Adam's kids. Are you ready for that ongoing, everyday responsibility?*

Matthias had no idea where this question had come from, yet he needed to answer it if he intended to marry Rose someday. He'd often had thoughts of how she would redecorate his house—redecorate his whole life—with her sweet disposition and purposeful, caring ways. But this marriage would be different from the one he'd shared with Sadie. Rose had already established her way of parenting Gracie. If he unwittingly said or did things that undermined her control—mostly because Gracie was so cute and affectionate—their family dynamics would be off-kilter from the beginning. He sighed, wondering how best to handle this situation.

"You're very quiet, Matthias. Has it been a long, hard week

keeping up your harness making while you've learned about Saul's carriage business?"

Rose's voice pulled him out of his serious thoughts. He reveled in her pretty smile and the light in her green eyes—and then realized he was supposed to answer her question. "Saul? *Jah,* he runs quite a shop," Matthias remarked as he cut another bite of lasagna. "He has twenty-five fellows on his payroll full-time, building everything from Plain rigs and courting buggies to heavy farming wagons. Saul himself makes some really fancy fairy-princess buggies for places that offer special carriage rides."

"Fairy princesses!" Gracie said in a fascinated whisper. "I could draw fairy princesses on my chalkboard, Mamma."

"*Jah,* you could, Gracie." Rose focused on Matthias with a smile that did funny things to his insides. "I can see why he wants a full partner to help him keep such a business going. It seems like quite an honor that he asked you, Matthias—but *jah,* a huge responsibility, too."

"It's all of that and more," he agreed, temporarily getting lost in her gaze. Her eyes brought to mind the windbreak of peaceful evergreens out behind his house. "And I can't forget that Martha Maude is Saul's bookkeeper, so she'll be aware of every project and purchase I make through the carriage shop."

"Martha Maude's really nice," Gracie murmured. "She'd be a really *gut mammi.* But I guess that other lady—Anne—is already my *mammi.*"

Matthias couldn't miss the flicker of emotion on Rose's face. He suspected Gracie missed her grandmother Lydia as much as Rose did—and if they weren't careful, Gracie's way of blurting out her thoughts could get them into hot water.

"We've talked about that, Gracie," Rose gently reminded her daughter. "And what did Matthias and I tell you?"

Gracie glanced at Matthias and then focused obediently on her mother. "You said to be quiet—not to say nothin' to Anne or Martha Maude."

"That's right. It's *gut* for you to remember that now, and every time those ladies come to the senior center." Rose reinforced her words with a purposeful smile.

Even as Matthias observed this dialogue, he sensed tension in Rose's voice and face, as though something important might have happened this week. He was glad their meal progressed quickly and that Rose suggested they take a play break before they ate their pie. Gracie squealed with delight and ran toward the swings. "Somebody push me!" she called out.

Rose gazed deliberately at Matthias as the two of them rose from the table. "Anne knows who I am," she whispered. "When Martha Maude took Gracie outside to the flower garden, Anne asked if she had met me somewhere and—and I knew if I said no, I could never again approach her as my mother."

Matthias exhaled loudly. "Oh, my. What did she say?"

Rose blinked as though she might start crying. "It was a quick conversation, because Gracie and Martha Maude might come back at any time. But she wants to talk to me sometime when no one else is around—and she agreed that Saul shouldn't find out about this."

Matthias slipped his arm around Rose's shoulders as they walked toward the swings. "Well, this cranks things up a notch, but I don't see how you could've said anything different. I can't imagine what you must've been feeling when she realized who you were, Rose."

"It was like nothing I've ever experienced," she said, shaking her head. "We were both overjoyed and—and she said she'd loved me every day of her life after she gave me to . . . my parents."

Matthias's throat tightened with emotion. At this time in her life, Rose needed all the love she could find, but it was obvious that she and Anne were very vulnerable. Now that they'd found each other, how were they going to keep quiet about it?

He thought about this as he pushed Gracie in the swing. Then he and Rose made a game of telling Gracie what to touch, and watched her race toward each tree and teeter-totter and picnic table they mentioned. When pink-and-peach ribbons of sunset lit up the horizon, Matthias realized the evening was getting away from him too fast. Even though he'd enjoyed watching Gracie play, he'd hoped for more time alone with Rose. "I'll bring Daisy over to the center's parking lot tomorrow at noon, so she'll be there whenever you're ready to go home," he said.

"Let me know what I owe you for her feed. I bet that bag won't last her much longer." Rose waved at Gracie, who was jogging around the tall slide in the center of the park. "Time for pie!"

When the three of them had settled at the picnic table again, Matthias took a bite of lemon pie. "Wow, this is *gut,*" he murmured ecstatically. "I like this better than the kind with meringue all over it."

"This is lemon icebox pie," Rose said, seeming pleased about his reaction. "It's easier because you make the filling and pour it into the already-baked crust. You let the fridge do the work instead of the oven," she explained.

"It makes my mouth all puckery," Gracie put in. "But I'm

happy coz we've got enough left in the kitchen that me and Mamma can have some tomorrow. No way we could split two pieces amongst all those other folks."

Matthias chuckled at her logic. "And I'm happy that you brought me a piece tonight—and that you had the idea for a picnic," he added. "I'll have to wait until next week to see you again."

When they'd finished their pie, Matthias loaded the dirty dishes into his box while Rose slipped her empty glass pans into her tote. With a mysterious smile, she handed him the rectangular, foil-wrapped packet, which had been sitting near the end of the table.

"For your breakfast," she murmured. "*Denki* for a wonderful evening—and for keeping our Daisy," she added.

Matthias longed to kiss Rose good night, but he wanted their first kiss to be a private, joyful moment they could look back on in years to come—and he felt certain that he wanted to share those years with Rose. He watched Rose and Gracie cross the park in the dusk, hand in hand, awash in affection that thrummed in every fiber of his being. When they'd entered the senior center, he hitched Daisy to the rig and made the short drive home, his thoughts filled with the delightful time they'd had tonight.

When he entered his kitchen, he could wait no longer. Matthias opened the foil packet and inhaled gratefully. Two large cinnamon rolls filled his senses with the aroma of fresh cinnamon, sugar, and yeasty dough—and before he thought about it, he was uncurling the outer layer of one of the rolls. He jammed a large chunk of the soft pastry into his mouth, moaning over the sweet glaze and the chewy raisins and the abundance of cinnamon.

"Oh, Rose," he murmured as he polished off the entire roll. "We could make a sweet life together, you and me and Gracie."

Matthias hoped Rose would agree that he could court her soon. Now that he'd met her, his life seemed vibrant and worthwhile again—an adventure he looked forward to sharing with her. He had a house, and he had his business and a lucrative arrangement with Hartzler that would see him into the future. All that was missing was Rose standing beside him as his wife. Nobody else would do.

# Chapter 24

After breakfast on Friday morning, when Rose was preparing chicken and noodles for the evening meal, Sherrie came into the kitchen. She immediately went to look over Gracie's shoulder as the little girl practiced printing the alphabet on her lined tablet.

"Gracie, your letters look really strong and neat," she remarked. "Your teacher's going to be lucky, having you in school this fall!"

"I been workin' hard at it," Gracie said, beaming up at the director.

Rose smiled. "She loves the school desk you brought her, Sherrie. That was a fine idea."

Sherrie nodded, gazing intently at the big bowl of noodles, chicken chunks, and chopped carrots on the center worktable as Rose added the sauce to it. "Oh, everyone's going to love this tonight, Rose. We're so glad you've come to cook for us."

"And I'm happy to get your weekend meals ready in exchange for our apartment," Rose remarked. "It's been so much better for Gracie and me, not having to drive back and forth. I'll have pans of beef stew and scalloped potatoes with ham in the refrigerator for you before I leave today—and your breakfast coffee cakes are cooling over on the counter."

"Wonderful! I came back to tell you that Anne and Martha Maude have stopped by," Sherrie continued. "I didn't know if you'd rather meet them in the lobby, or if I should send them back here."

Gracie sucked in an excited breath. "Mamma, can I go see 'em?"

Rose chuckled. "*Jah,* go say hello and then bring them back here," she replied. Her heart began to beat faster—because she was eager to see her mother, and because she hoped Gracie, in her excitement, wouldn't blurt something about the two women being related to her.

When Gracie hurried from the kitchen, Rose glanced at Sherrie. "I—I hope you won't mind that they've come to see us," she murmured. "I don't want you thinking I'm slacking at my work—"

"Rose, you're the woman least likely to become a slacker," Sherrie teased, hugging Rose's shoulders. "I know you'll get everything made, just as you've said you would. It's good you've got company once in a while so you aren't in the kitchen all the time. You really do get time off, you know."

When Rose heard Gracie's voice in the dining room, she glanced out to see her little girl walking between Anne and Martha Maude, her hands in theirs as she chattered happily. "I appreciate that, Sherrie—and as you can see, Gracie loves to have company."

"She does well at keeping herself busy while you work, Rose," the director said. "As quickly as Gracie became acquainted with our residents, I'm not a bit surprised that she's taken to the Hartzler women. Have a nice visit. I'll see you later."

Rose quickly finished stirring the sauce into the big bowl of chicken and noodles. Why would Anne and Martha Maude be coming again this week? Surely, they couldn't have crocheted and quilted more pieces for the residents so quickly—but as they entered the kitchen with her daughter, she kept her questions to herself. Anne's smile held special warmth for Rose, and Martha Maude was obviously delighted to be with Gracie.

"What a nice surprise to see you two again," Rose said. "Welcome to our kitchen."

"That's a *gut*-looking batch of chicken and noodles you're whipping up," Martha Maude remarked. She gazed around at the big stainless-steel freezers and the commercial-sized stove and oven. "Oh, and look at those nice coffee cakes. You've been busy today, Rose."

"*Jah,* Gracie and I will be heading home later today, so I've made most of the food Sherrie will serve over the weekend," Rose explained.

Martha Maude and Anne smiled at each other as though they shared a secret. Then Martha Maude released Gracie's hand and came around the table to stand close to Rose. "I'm going to the fabric store," she whispered, "and if it's all right with you, I'll ask Gracie to go with me."

Rose's eyes widened. "Oh, that would be fine," she replied. "I can already tell you what her answer will be."

Gracie was gazing intently at Rose and Martha Maude, wondering about their secretive exchange. "Mamma, you always tell me it's not nice to whisper in front of people—"

"And you're exactly right, Gracie," Martha Maude put in with a big smile. "But in this case, I was asking your *mamm* if you could go with me to the fabric store up the road. I need some pieces to use in my next quilts, and you can help me pick them out."

Gracie squealed ecstatically. "Can I, Mamma? Pretty please?" she pleaded as she hopped up and down.

"Have fun shopping," Rose replied as she wiped her hands. "But I'd better hear that you were a *gut* girl, Gracie. Let me go get you some money—"

"No need," Martha Maude insisted as she took Gracie's hand. "If we're not back by noon, we're out having our lunch."

"Bye, Mamma!" Gracie said excitedly. "See ya later!"

"*Jah,* I'll be here." Rose watched the two of them walk into the dining room, wondering if Anne could hear how loudly her heart was pounding. When she looked at her mother, she didn't know which question to ask first. "Does she know?" Rose whispered. "Is Martha Maude doing this so you and I can—"

Anne shook her head no as she came to stand directly across from Rose at the worktable. "This was all Martha Maude's idea," she replied. "Gracie is such a special little girl and, well . . . for whatever reason, I've not been able to have any more children," she added softly. "I think Martha Maude is enjoying Gracie like the granddaughter she's never had."

Rose swallowed hard. She stood face-to-face with her mother, who was the same height as she was, and had the same body build and facial shape and the same sturdy hands . . . and she wore the same expression of hope and joy mingled with a touch of nervousness.

"Rose," her mother whispered, reaching across the table for her hand, "I didn't intend to interrupt your work, but when Martha Maude was so set on shopping with Gracie, well—I saw this as our chance to catch up with each other. I told her I'd visit with you and Sherrie while they were gone."

"I'm so glad you did," Rose murmured as she squeezed

Anne's hand between both of hers. "Let me put the chicken and noodles in their pans, and we can go to the apartment. Nobody'll interrupt us there."

Anne nodded eagerly.

Rose worked quickly, feeling her mother's gaze following her movements. When she'd put the casserole pans in the refrigerator, she ran water into the big mixing bowl and dried her hands. "Shall we go?"

Anne walked alongside her, through the dining room and out into the lobby. After they turned down the hallway toward Rose's apartment, Anne stopped to gaze at a large painting of a horse-drawn wagon loaded with hay, driven by an Amish man while his two boys and their dog jogged alongside it. "Joel—your father—painted this," she murmured, running her fingertip along the name painted in the lower right corner. "Several of his pictures are here and in other places around town. Such a talent he had—more passion for his art than our bishops would allow."

"Do you ever see him?" Rose gazed at the painting in awe. The scene was rendered so realistically, she could almost hear the creak of the harnesses and wagon wheels and feel the summer sun on the back of her neck.

"No, he moves around the Midwest, pulling a small trailer behind his truck, as I understand it," Anne replied wistfully. "Lives on the road, painting and selling his art at flea markets and galleries—or at least that's what I read in the paper once. The article's photograph looked just like him back when he and I—well, except he's a bit stockier and his face has aged," she said with a soft laugh. Then she sighed. "Joel stole my heart and I never really got it back. But I thank the Lord that Saul has made such a wonderful home for me, Rose."

Rose considered this statement as they walked down the hallway. She opened the door and gestured for her mother to precede her inside. When she closed the door behind them, Anne turned to her with an intense yearning on her face. "Oh, Rose," she murmured. "I never thought I'd be standing here with you, seeing your dear face again—"

When Rose stepped into her mother's embrace, time and her modest front room disappeared. Anne wrapped her arms tightly around Rose's shoulders and began to quiver and sniffle. Rose realized she was crying, too, overwhelmed by the reality of finally being held by her mother. They stood in one another's arms for several moments, swaying slightly. Just holding on, savoring the physical connection.

Anne eased away, gazing raptly into Rose's eyes. Tears were streaming down her cheeks, but she ignored them. "I'm so sorry Lydia has passed," she murmured. "Such a kind, caring woman she was."

"*Jah,* she was," Rose replied. She went to the small table by the window and grabbed the box of tissues so they could both blow their noses. "Her cancer stayed away until last year, after we lost my *dat* and my husband when their sawmill burned down. Mamma must've lost her resistance with all the strain and stress, because that's when the cancer came back."

Anne shook her head as she dried her tears with a tissue. "Such a nasty disease, cancer is. So ... if you're working here, does this mean you've no one left in your family—or your husband's family—to look after you, dear?"

Rose smiled sadly. "That's what it boils down to, *jah.* But Gracie and I are doing fine here at the senior center," she said. "I suppose I'll put her in school here in Morning Star this fall. Might even sell the place in Cedar Creek, because I don't know how I'll possibly keep it up—and with that money, I'd be able to pay off Mamma's medical bills, and—well, I didn't mean to burden you with all these details."

Anne waved her off. "I would pay those bills for you in a heartbeat, Rose, but the money's not mine to spend without asking Saul."

"I wouldn't dream of—would never expect you to do that," Rose whispered. "It'll all work out, *really*. I—I even have a nice widower around my age who's been spending some time with us. Not that it would be proper to marry again so soon."

Anne squeezed her hand. "I'm so happy to hear that, for you and Gracie both. Don't wait too long, Rose. Let the dead bury the dead so you and your daughter can move on and have a *gut* solid life—a home with a man who loves you." She blew her nose, chuckling. "But here I go, giving instructions like I was your mother or something."

Rose laughed out loud. When she'd daydreamed about spending time with her birth mother, she hadn't realized that Anne Hartzler might have a sense of humor—or might sincerely wish to pay her bills and take care of her. As she gestured toward the small couch, Rose felt as though she might be able to share her most personal thoughts and dreams with this gentle woman.

As Anne sat down, her eyes sparkled. "And what sort of a fellow are you seeing, dear? Does he take to Gracie? Does he have kids from his previous marriage?"

"You've seen how Gracie endears herself to everyone she meets," Rose replied as she settled onto the cushion next to her mother. "She was crazy about Matthias from the first time she saw him, and he's totally comfortable with her. His wife died before she delivered their firstborn, but he's been surrounded with his brother and sister-in-law's kids at their home place in Willow Ridge, so children are already a part of his life."

Anne was nodding, taking in these details. "And his name's Matthias, you say? We recently had a fellow by that name over for supper—a harness maker, he is. Saul was so impressed with his work ethic that he's taken him on as a full partner in the carriage business."

Rose's cheeks prickled and she bit back a grin. "I know," she murmured. "Matthias has told me about that big surprise Saul offered him."

Anne's eyes widened. "Oh, he's such a nice man, Rose! Kind and thoughtful and—" She sighed deeply. "Does Matthias know I'm your mother, dear?"

"*Jah,* and he knows not to mention anything about us to Saul, too." Rose looked into her mother's green eyes, squeezing her hand. "It's a shame that something so wonderful as our reuniting, mother and daughter, seems to pose such a problem for other people. Do you really think Saul will object, after so many years—"

"No question about it," Anne interrupted emphatically. "Saul's a fine man, but he believes I was untouched when we married. Exposing such a deception will shake the foundations of our relationship, even though we're taught to forgive and forget."

Rose nodded sadly. "I thought as much. Every man who's discussed the subject insists that nothing *gut* will come of revealing that you're my mother. I—I'm sorry to cause you such trouble—"

"Rose, you will *never* be trouble, and I refuse to be ashamed of you or the situation surrounding your birth." Anne gazed directly into her eyes, gripping her hand. "We are who we are, and we love whom we love. It's the rules of our religion—and society, in general—that cast my relationship with Joel Lapp into a negative light."

Rose's eyes widened. She was amazed that Anne had expressed such a sentiment, for Amish girls were taught from a very young age that they were to remain sexually untouched except by their husbands. And if married women had thoughts about men in their past, they knew better than to express them out loud.

"Don't get me wrong, dear. I realize I shouldn't have given in to my yearnings to be with Joel," Anne continued in a soft voice, "but I believed God meant for us to be together—until my parents learned he was jumping the fence. They forbade me to see him anymore. Had I left with Joel, my *dat* would've considered me a lost soul and no longer a member of his family—even though I hadn't yet been baptized."

Rose nodded. This was the way of it for a lot of girls who left the Amish faith to be with the men they loved, although some families didn't ostracize their daughters as severely if they were still in their *rumspringa*.

"Needless to say, my parents were still greatly upset when they realized I'd gotten pregnant despite their dire warnings about Joel's worldly ambitions." Anne's expression grew wistful. "I'm still convinced Joel and I would've made a solid couple and raised a fine family together—but we would've isolated ourselves from everyone we loved. I didn't want that sort of separation from my family," she admitted softly. "And I've told no one else, of course, that I still have a warm spot in my heart for Joel, because that's another one of those improper feelings a woman's not to have after she marries."

Rose listened carefully, hearing more between the lines than her mother actually said. "Your feelings are safe with me," she

murmured. "And after reading those letters you wrote me—
again and again—I'm not surprised you still feel that way
about Joel. I . . . I was happy to know I was created by two
people who dearly loved each other—"

"You've got that right, Rose." Anne gazed around the
room, considering what else she would say. "I wanted to tell
Joel about you, but I decided against it. I didn't want him to
think I was using you as a hook to bring him back into the
Amish faith. And once the Frys adopted you, what would've
been the point?"

Rose sighed. "I would love to meet him sometime, but
that's probably not going to happen. How long's it been since
you saw him?"

Anne cleared her throat, gazing at their clasped hands.
"Several years ago, Joel passed through Morning Star to sell
some of his paintings—his subjects tend to run toward farm
scenes with Plain folks in them, even though that's not the life
he lives anymore," she added with a wry smile. "I went to see
his exhibit in the park, but when he saw Saul with me, he understood that I wouldn't be meeting him for coffee or anything
else in the way of us catching up with one another. I got nothing
more than a wistful smile, to show me he was glad to see me."

"Did he marry?"

"I don't think so. And that surprises me, considering how
affectionate and attractive he is."

Silence settled over them. Rose supposed it was because,
until last week, so many years had separated her from her
birth mother—and because this opportunity to meet had
come on the spur of an unexpected moment. She glanced at
the clock and sighed. "I hate to call our talk to a halt, but I
need to get dinner in the oven—"

"And who knows when Martha Maude will return with

Gracie?" Anne said as she rose from the couch. "It'll be better if I'm in the kitchen with you, or visiting with Sherrie. I don't want Martha Maude to come looking for me."

Rose stood slowly. With a tight smile, she opened her arms and her mother came to her for another warm, wonderful embrace. "I'm so glad we had this time," Rose murmured.

"Me too. We'll just have to act like *gut* friends when we're around other folks," she said wistfully. "But I hope we can talk this way again sometime."

As they headed down the hallway, Rose once again wondered if Gracie had told Martha Maude of this secret. She had a feeling, deep down, that with a handful of people knowing she was Anne Hartzler's long-lost daughter, such information was bound to slip out someday. To a person, everyone said Saul Hartzler would be extremely upset if he found out about Anne's past. . . .

*But my mother has made her peace with the past. She feels God's forgiveness, and she loves me. Why does everyone believe Saul will be unable to pardon what his wife did with Joel, so long ago? He's a deacon, a leader of the church. . . .*

# Chapter 25

A nne glanced around the kitchen once more. Their usual supper hour had passed, but Saul wasn't home. The table was set, and the meat loaf and scalloped potatoes were covered and in the oven to stay warm. There was nothing to do until her husband arrived. She went into the front room and picked up the afghan she was crocheting—which she was making to brighten Rose's room at the senior center. Anne had no idea how she would present the gift to her daughter without Martha Maude questioning her, but she would find a way.

"This dress turned out cute, if I say so myself," Martha Maude remarked. She sat at the sewing machine, near the window, trimming the loose threads. "I haven't made little-girl clothes since Saul's sister was Gracie's age."

Anne glanced up from her crocheting. Martha Maude rarely spoke of Edna, who had drowned when she was twelve, after slipping out to their farm pond alone to swim. "I like that shade of orange. It reminds me of the fresh peaches we'll pick from our trees this fall."

"Gracie chose it," Martha Maude said with a smile. "The

two of us had such a fine time at the fabric store. I'll say this for Rose—she might be working and raising her daughter alone, but she's instilled Gracie with impeccable manners and self-control. There was no whining for things she wanted, no running up and down the aisles like you sometimes see in the stores."

"English kids mostly," Anne murmured. She finished off a row of the afghan and chose a skein of deep periwinkle to work with next. "I suspect—because the rest of Rose's family seems to be gone—that Rose and Gracie are always together, so Rose spends a lot of time teaching her about proper behavior, among other things. That's probably easier because Gracie is her only child."

"And talk about *sharp*," Martha Maude put in proudly. "Gracie knows how to read price stickers! She told me that this peach fabric cost three twenty-five a yard and that the bias tape for the hem cost a dollar sixty-nine! But I still wish she had a father and a proper family life."

Anne deftly worked the clusters of double crochet stitches, nipping her lip. Martha Maude thought Matthias Wagler was a fine, upstanding man, but Anne didn't reveal that he was seeing Rose. She had visions of her mother-in-law inviting Matthias, Rose, and Gracie over sometime if she knew of their romance—and one slip of the tongue would turn the gathering into a nightmare if Saul or Martha Maude suspected that Rose was her daughter.

"Rose is young and attractive," Anne said, focusing on her stitches. "No doubt some fellow will latch onto—"

"Hullo! I'm home!" Saul hollered from the kitchen. "Dinner smells awfully *gut* and I might just eat it all myself!"

Anne slipped her hook into the skein of yarn and wrapped the afghan around it. She'd wanted to eat an hour ago when their supper had been ready, but she tempered her impatient remarks. "We've missed you, Saul," she called out as she headed for the kitchen.

"*Jah,* you're so late that Anne and I have already eaten," Martha Maude teased.

Saul stood behind his chair at the kitchen table, raising an eyebrow. "I know better," he told Anne. He watched as she pulled the roaster and the casserole dish of scalloped potatoes from the oven. "Jeremiah was bending my ear. He's received a letter from the bishop in Willow Ridge stating that Matthias is in *gut* standing and that we should welcome him as a member of our district."

Anne removed the foil from the scalloped potatoes. "When the bishop talks, we're to listen—not that I had any doubts about Matthias's standing in the church."

"And we've met a nice young widow to match him up with—and her little girl's as cute as a button," Martha Maude said. "We should have them over sometime soon, don't you think, Anne? What harm would it do, getting Rose and Matthias together?"

Anne swallowed hard. If she disagreed, her husband and his mother would both quiz her. And if she let on that Rose and Matthias were already seeing one another, they would question her about how she knew that. "*Jah,* we should think about that, probably," she hedged as she set the meat platter near Saul's plate. Anne immediately busied herself by putting a spoon in the scalloped potatoes and fetching a bowl of slaw from the refrigerator, hoping Martha Maude and Saul didn't notice how pink her face was.

*How long will it take them to notice that Rose resembles me? How long before my past with another man is no longer a secret, and Saul condemns me for what he'll consider an un-forgivable sin—and my deception?*

As she drove home late Friday afternoon, Rose let Gracie chatter about the time she'd spent with Martha Maude. She was pleased that her little girl had made such a fine friend and had enjoyed her shopping trip, yet Rose felt a worm of unease squirming in her stomach.

"And, Mamma, guess what?" Gracie crowed. "Martha Maude said I was just like a little granddaughter to her. And I can call her my *mammi* if I want! I think I'm gonna!"

Rose's eyes widened and she bit back her objections. But what was she objecting to, really? Martha Maude was only being gracious and grandmotherly . . . as she unwittingly created more opportunities for Gracie to spill the beans about Anne being Rose's birth mother.

"I really gotta lotta *mammis* now, huh, Mamma?" Gracie continued, beginning to count on her fingers. "I got Gladys, and Flo, and Zelma, and Martha Maude! And my *mammi* in Heaven, too," she added sweetly.

Emotion welled up inside Rose and she couldn't speak for a moment.

"Did Anne help you with fixin' dinner?" Gracie asked. Then she leaned closer, studying Rose's face. "What's wrong, Mamma? Why're you cryin'?"

Rose knuckled away her tears. "It's still hard to think about your *mammi* passing on," she murmured. Straightening in the seat, she tried to compose herself. "It's been quite a day, sweet pea. I'm hoping you didn't let on to Martha Maude about Anne being my mother."

"Nope! We was too busy shoppin'," Gracie said matter-of-factly. "I picked out lotsa pretty fabric with flowers and stripes and polka dots for her quilts. And then she let me pick out two kinds of fabric for dresses."

"Dresses?" Rose steered Daisy onto the county road that would take them into Cedar Creek.

"*Jah,* Martha Maude's gonna make me some dresses coz she knows you're awful busy," Gracie replied with a sunny smile. "I picked orange like sherbet and green like pickles!"

"Wasn't that nice? I hope you thanked her," Rose added, even as her heart sank a bit. It felt like a pronouncement of her failing as a mother, if she couldn't even keep her child in clothes.

"I did. And she hugged me and kissed my cheek. She's really nice, Mamma."

Rose nodded. She was grateful that Gracie's outing had gone so well and that Martha Maude had taken her to the Morning Star Café for lunch, because it had given Rose more time with Anne as they prepared the senior center's noon meal. But in the back of her mind, a flare went up, like a fiery red ball of a Roman candle.

If Martha Maude was so enchanted with her daughter, what would keep her from inviting Gracie to the Hartzlers' house, as she'd suggested before? Rose would go along, of course. Then how well could she and Anne pretend they were merely friends?

*Lord, please help me to keep this situation in perspective. And watch over Anne—just in case Saul learns the truth and he doesn't take it well.*

On Sunday morning as Matthias sat in church, with the younger fellows behind him and the older men filling the pews in front of him, he found another reason to believe that God had brought him to Morning Star. Bishop Jeremiah Shetler was preaching the second, longer sermon and his resonant voice filled the main level of Preacher Ammon Slabaugh's modest home. Removing some of the interior walls created enough space for nearly a hundred men, women, and children, and they all listened attentively as their bishop spoke to them of forgiveness and reconciliation.

"Let us again consider the key verses of the passage Deacon Saul read to us earlier in the service," Jeremiah said as his gaze swept the wide room. "First, from Paul's second letter to the Corinthians, let's revisit the seventeenth and eighteenth verses of Chapter Five. Deacon Saul?"

Saul Hartzler rose with the large King James Bible and followed the lines with a calloused finger as he read aloud. " 'Therefore if any man be in Christ, he is a new creature: old things are passed away; behold, all things are become new,' " he said in a voice that filled the room. " 'And all things are of God, who hath reconciled us to Himself by Jesus Christ, and hath given to us the ministry of reconciliation.' "

" 'The ministry of reconciliation,' " Jeremiah repeated purposefully. "Stop and think, my friends. How many times this week did you practice reconciliation with the folks you know? Did you try to reconcile with your neighbor rather than thinking harsh thoughts or saying unkind words to him or her—or about him or her?"

In the moments of silence that followed, Matthias wondered if Saul was a man who practiced reconciliation, or if he used his wealth like a pedestal from whence he could look down upon those he considered lesser souls. When Matthias had gone to the carriage shop on Friday afternoon to deliver some harnesses, Saul had stopped the assembly line and was delivering a stern lecture to one of the workers who'd done a less than satisfactory job of applying the second coat of paint to the three courting buggies they were working on.

"Jake's already on probation for a shoddy job a couple weeks ago," Saul had told Matthias when they'd gone into his office. "One more mess-up and he's *out*. And if I fire him, there won't be many other local shop owners who'll give him a job."

Matthias considered this as Bishop Jeremiah asked Saul to reread the last two verses of the fourth chapter of Ephesians. He wondered what Jake, who sat a couple rows behind him, might be thinking as his boss stood up again, cradling the big Bible in one arm.

"'Let all bitterness, and wrath, and anger, and clamour, and evil speaking, be put away from you, with all malice,'" Saul read confidently. "'And be ye kind one to another, tender-hearted, forgiving one another, even as God for Christ's sake hath forgiven you.'"

As Jeremiah continued preaching, exhorting his congregation to reconcile and forgive, Matthias was aware that Shetler was considerably younger than the bishops in Willow Ridge and Cedar Creek, but his word carried weight all around the Plain communities in this area. Matthias considered himself blessed to be in this bishop's congregation now.

After they'd prayed again and sung the final hymn, Bishop Jeremiah held up his hand to give the benediction. He remained in place to make some announcements, and then gazed at the men's side until he found Matthias. "We welcome Matthias Wagler into our fellowship, now that he has moved to Morning Star from Willow Ridge. Stand up so these folks will know who you are, Matthias."

With a rush of adrenaline, Matthias rose from the pew

bench, nodding at the men around him and smiling over at the women who faced them.

"Matthias has a harness shop, and it behooves us all to support his business," the bishop continued. "I hope you'll become better acquainted with our new brother during the common meal."

The men stood up and began pumping Matthias's hand as they introduced themselves. As the tables were put up for the meal, the women began to carry out platters of cold cuts, bowls of chilled salads, and baskets of fresh bread. Many of the members said hello to Matthias, and he immediately realized it would take a while to learn everyone's name. He sensed these folks were very friendly and were pleased that he'd joined their church district. When he waved to Anne Hartzler, Martha Maude's face lit up. She grabbed her daughter-in-law's hand to lead her through the crowd.

"Matthias, we're so pleased you're officially one of us now," Martha Maude said when they'd stopped in front of him. "I can't believe you enjoy living all alone—being new here in town, especially—so we'd like you to come for supper Friday night, to meet a very nice young woman. We're just crazy about her and we think you will be, too."

Matthias blinked. Saul was watching him with a sympathetic shake of his head. He wanted to inform Martha Maude that he already had a lady friend, but he was caught between a rock and a hard place. It didn't help that Anne, who stood slightly behind her mother-in-law, wore an expression he couldn't read. She appeared dumbfounded and embarrassed by Martha Maude's loud invitation, and Matthias thought he detected some fear on her face as well. Why would that be?

With a fleeting thought of Rose and Gracie, Matthias hoped they would understand if he felt he had to eat supper with the Hartzlers and whomever they were fixing him up with. How could he gracefully turn down the invitation while Saul was watching him, and with Martha Maude gazing at him, silently insisting upon his compliance?

"Well, you're not the first folks who've tried to pair me up with somebody," he murmured reluctantly. "It's kind of you to think of me being lonely, so *jah,* I'll come on Friday—"

"Glad to hear it!" Martha Maude exclaimed.

"—but I hope you'll understand if I don't choose to see this woman again," Matthias continued firmly, hoping he still sounded grateful. "My wife, Sadie, was the love of my life, and I'm not rushing into another relationship just to have somebody keeping house for me. Truth be told, I'm seeing a nice gal who lives in a different district."

Martha Maude smiled knowingly. "Maybe Friday's supper will change your mind," she said.

Anne flashed Matthias a shy smile. Was he imagining things, or did she *wink* at him?

"*Gut* for you, speaking your mind about this, Matthias," Saul said as he joined the three of them. "You know how women are, thinking everybody has to be matched up every minute of their adult lives. But there's a lot more to marriage than having a woman to cook for you and give you children—it's a huge responsibility. We fellows have to stick together on this, *jah?*"

"*Jah,*" Matthias heard himself say. He was touched by the expression on Anne's face when she'd heard Saul's pronouncement about wives providing children. Then her smile waxed secretive, as though she was again trying to reassure him. But Matthias knew better than to question her.

*And you know better than to cross Martha Maude and Saul, too.*

# Chapter 26

On Monday morning, Rose felt haggard, struggling to catch up after serving the residents' breakfast about fifteen minutes late. She'd been so tired Sunday night, after working all day Saturday around the house and attending church and the meal afterward, that she'd forgotten to set her alarm. Gracie had fussed at her all morning, too. Then after leaving home a half hour later than they should have, it began to rain. It was a blessing that Matthias had still been waiting for them when they arrived at the Morning Star Senior Center. When he stepped out the side door to greet them, however, Rose sensed he had something troublesome on his mind.

"See you sometime this week—and you, too, Gracie," he said after he'd walked inside with them. He'd left very quickly, too.

As she wrapped the breakfast leftovers, Rose still felt baffled by his befuddled tone. *You'd better set aside your social life and get busy on lunch and supper,* she scolded herself.

"Is everything all right, Rose?" Sherrie asked. She was rolling a cart loaded with dirty dishes from the dining room because Alison had called in sick. "Take a break if you need to, dear. Nothing drastic will happen if you leave the kitchen."

Rose smiled gratefully. "It all started when my alarm didn't go off," she murmured. "I'll be fine, really—"

"And I was bein' cranky, too," Gracie put in with a wary glance at her mother. "So I'm sittin' here drawin' birds and stayin' out of Mamma's way."

Sherrie went to stand behind the school desk, looking over Gracie's shoulder. "Look at that!" she said. "You've drawn the bluebird of happiness, and because he's here, I bet you won't feel cranky anymore, Gracie. Don't you feel happier just looking at those bright blue feathers?"

Gracie tilted her head, gazing at her drawing. "*Jah*. A little."

Sherrie smiled at Rose and crouched beside the little desk. "I've got a little present for you, Gracie. Shall we go to my office and see what it is?"

Gracie's eyes widened. As the two of them left the kitchen, Rose sighed gratefully. She felt blessed to be working for such a kind, generous woman—especially since Sherrie hadn't said anything about breakfast being served late. She rinsed the plates and arranged them in the dishwasher the way Alison had shown her. She was working on the cups and saucers when she heard footsteps coming into the kitchen.

"My word, do you know how to run that contraption, Rose?" a familiar voice asked. "Looks to me like you've nearly got those dishes washed before you put them in there."

Rose straightened to smile at Martha Maude and Anne. "That's the way it seems to us Plain women, *jah*," she replied. "The health department requires dishwashers in facilities like this because they sterilize the dishes in a way you can't when you're washing them in the sink."

"I can see how that could come in handy at canning time," Anne put in as she watched Rose load the coffee mugs. "You could have all your jars clean and sterile and hot—a bunch of them at a time—instead of having to dip them in and out of a big pot of boiling water."

"Where's your little shadow today?" Martha Maude asked, glancing at the unoccupied school desk. She brought a white plastic bag from behind her back, holding the curves of two hangers that stuck out from the top of it. "We thought we'd deliver Gracie's dresses—and invite you two to supper at our place Friday night," she added quickly. "There's a nice fellow who's joined our church—"

Rose felt her face heating up. Martha Maude wasn't a woman who took no for an answer, even though Rose had a couple of good reasons to decline her invitation before she'd even heard the rest of it.

"—and we thought if you met him at our place—neutral ground—maybe you and Gracie could see him again sometime." Martha Maude gazed intently at Rose, obviously expecting an answer that would keep her plans for Friday evening—and probably for Rose's future—intact.

"That's very kind of you," Rose began hesitantly, "but Gracie and I head back to Cedar Creek on Friday afternoons so we can—"

Martha Maude waved her off. "No reason you couldn't stay over, since you've got an apartment here," she insisted. "The fellow we've got in mind has already agreed to come."

*But the fellow I've got in mind already thinks in terms of* XXs *and* OOs, Rose thought frantically. She glanced at Anne, who stood a few steps behind her mother-in-law. Anne was smiling and nodding as she silently mouthed, "It's Matthias."

Rose pressed her lips together so she wouldn't laugh out loud and expose her mother's little trick. She wondered if Martha Maude had approached Matthias the same way, not revealing Rose's name—which might explain his odd behavior this morning. Or did he already know these women were fixing him up with her, and he was nervous about eating with her and Gracie at the Hartzler place . . . with her mother? Her relationship to Anne was getting trickier by the day. She was about to answer when Gracie skipped into the kitchen, smiling brightly, gripping a large tablet in one hand and a box of colored pencils in the other.

"Mamma, look what Sherrie—oh!" Gracie cried out when she saw their guests. "I was hopin' to see my *mammis* today! I prayed about it, and here you are!"

Rose noticed Anne's face growing pale as Martha Maude stooped to hug Gracie with her free arm.

"Look what I've brought you," Martha Maude said, shaking the plastic bag to make the dresses whisper inside it. "What do you suppose it is?"

"My dresses! Yay!" Gracie replied, hopping on her toes. "Lemme see 'em!"

"Gracie," Rose warned her daughter.

Her little girl immediately stood still. "Please may I see 'em?" she asked contritely. "And *denki* for makin' me some pretty dresses."

"You're very welcome," Martha Maude said as she lifted the white plastic sack over the dresses. "Green and orange, just right for springtime."

"Pickles and sherbet," Gracie murmured. She set her tablet and pencils on the worktable so she could finger each dress.

"*Denki* so much for taking the time to make these dresses, Martha Maude," Rose said as she admired them. "Gracie's growing like a weed, and once my mother took sick with her cancer last fall, I fell behind on making her clothes."

"We all need a helping hand now and again." Martha Maude smiled knowingly at Anne and Gracie. "So, back to our other subject, we'd really enjoy having you girls over for supper on Friday—"

"Mamma, let's go!" Gracie blurted. "We don't even hafta go home for more clothes, coz I've got two new dresses!"

Rose had to laugh, even though she suspected that Martha Maude had used Gracie's presence to get her way. "All right, then, we'll come," she murmured. "But I'll be wearing black for several months yet, so that fellow you've invited might as well understand—"

Gracie sucked in her breath. "Is it Matthias? Is Matthias comin' on Friday, too?"

Rose nearly choked. Anne's eyes widened in surprise, mingled with fear. They both were watching Martha Maude's reaction as she teasingly placed a fist on her hip.

"You have a friend named Matthias?" she asked Gracie. She glanced at Rose. "What's he look like?"

"Matthias looks just like Jesus!" Gracie crowed. "I'll get my book and show ya!"

As Gracie raced out the kitchen door, Anne stepped up to the counter where Martha Maude had laid the two little dresses. "If this is Matthias Wagler we're talking about," she said, sounding pinched but determined, "it should be a lovely evening. Matthias is Saul's partner now, so we've gotten to know him and we like him a lot."

Aware that Martha Maude was studying her closely, Rose smiled. She hoped she and Anne could speak of this situation in a way that wouldn't make her stalwart, steely-haired mother-in-law suspicious. "Matthias Wagler was kind enough to dig my mother's grave, and he looks after our mare now that we stay here in town all week," Rose explained. "I haven't known him long, but he's crazy about Gracie—"

"See there?" Martha Maude interrupted with a chuckle. "I

knew he'd be a *gut* fellow for you to get acquainted with, and you're a few steps ahead of me. That'll make things a lot less complicated Friday night, since the two of you won't be nervous about meeting each other—and Gracie will enjoy having him there, too."

Rapid footsteps crossed the dining-room floor. Gracie hurried into the kitchen, clutching her new Bible storybook. "See?" she exclaimed as she held a page open for Anne and Martha Maude. "It's Jesus, and He's got long reddish-brown hair and a beard, but He's got a nice smile, just like Matthias."

Anne gazed at the page in the book, a smile warming her face. "*Jah*, you've got it right, Gracie," she murmured. "Do you suppose Matthias has a halo, too?"

Gracie giggled, delighted that Anne and Martha Maude agreed with her. She handed Anne the book and then put the thumb and digit fingers of her hands into a circle above her *kapp*-covered head. "I'm a little angel, so I can let Matthias share my halo, *jah*?"

Rose laughed along with her two visitors, grateful that Gracie had a way of making everyone relax and share her happiness.

But on Friday night, once they sat at the table with Martha Maude, Anne, Matthias—and especially Saul—an unwitting slip of Gracie's tongue could place Anne in a very difficult position. Especially if Saul quizzed his wife about how Rose had come to be her child.

*Be with us all, Lord,* she prayed as the Hartzler women took their leave. *We have gut intentions, all of us . . . but the road to Hell is paved with those, they say. Please help us follow Your will rather than the wrong road.*

As Anne walked out of the Morning Star Café, she felt full and grateful. It was their wedding anniversary, and Saul had taken her—and Martha Maude, of course—out for dinner. Although she sometimes wished for time alone with her husband, she'd long ago become accustomed to the fact that Saul didn't like to leave his mother home alone. Anne smiled when he took her hand—a rare show of his affection in public—as they strolled along the sidewalk.

"Seems to be a lot of folks in town for a Wednesday evening," Martha Maude remarked as she walked behind them.

"The merchants are hosting a customer appreciation week in honor of last Sunday being May Day," Saul explained. "Some of the stores have special sales, or goodies for customers who come in. I don't know that the Plain shopkeepers are joining in, seeing's how most of them do business out in the country."

Anne wasn't surprised by Saul's remark, because she'd never known him to have a sale on his buggies or to offer any sort of price breaks. Nearly all of his customers were Plain folks, who depended upon the vehicles built in his shop, yet they never complained about paying full price—nor did they joke with him about possibly lowering what he charged. His basic enclosed buggies started at more than seven thousand dollars—quite an expense for a large family whose father earned a modest income.

Anne, however, never challenged her husband's pricing system. Martha Maude kept close tabs on the cost of parts and the labor involved in producing each vehicle, so it was doubtful that she or her son would ever back down from the amount they charged.

*And who are you to protest what Saul charges?* Anne's thoughts niggled. *You live a fine life in a large, comfortable home because he runs a profitable business. And because he's a successful businessman, he donates a great deal of money to the church, which, in turn, helps folks who need it.*

Setting aside her musings about money, Anne squeezed Saul's hand. He was in a fine mood—and he'd closed the shop early so he could take her to dinner—so she didn't want to fret away these pleasant moments of their sunny evening stroll home. As they approached the senior center, she thought about Rose and Gracie. She hoped they'd enjoyed a good meal and were taking some time off after the kitchen was cleaned up for the day.

To take a shortcut, the three of them stepped off the pavement and started across the grassy park. Anne smiled, watching several children who were playing on the swings and going down the big spiral slide. A few families sat at the picnic tables enjoying their outdoor supper. For a moment, she envisioned herself with Joel Lapp and little Rose sharing a picnic. It was a fantasy she'd occasionally indulged in over the years—and it had become more realistic and precious since she'd reunited with her daughter last week. She was drifting pleasantly along in this stream of make-believe when an excited little voice stopped her in her tracks.

"Mammi! Mammi Anne and Martha Maude! It's me, Gracie!"

The blood rushed from Anne's head. A little strawberry blonde hopped from a swing and was running toward them, her *kapp* strings flapping and her face aglow with unmistakable love. Anne couldn't meet Saul's questioning gaze as Rose jogged behind her daughter, wearing the same fearful, frantic expression that Anne felt on her own pale face. Nervously she licked her lips.

Gracie ran up to them with her arms open wide. "My *mammis*!" she cried out again, launching herself toward Martha Maude. As Martha Maude lifted her up to her shoulder, Gracie realized that she didn't know the tall, burly, black-haired man who was with them—and who was scowling at her. The little girl stuck her finger in her mouth. Gracie lowered her gaze, yet kept peering sideways at Saul.

"And how are you, Gracie?" Martha Maude asked as she hugged the little girl. She followed Gracie's shy gaze. "This is Saul. He's my son and Anne's husband. And how are you this evening, Rose?"

Rose appeared flustered as she met up with them. She shot Anne an apologetic glance. "We were just enjoying some time in the park," she replied in a tight voice. "I hope we didn't interrupt—"

"So is Saul my *dawdi*?" Gracie gazed at him with fresh curiosity despite his intimidating expression.

Saul's eyes widened. Anne couldn't miss the way he was studying Rose's features as his grip around her hand tightened painfully. "Who is this?" he demanded in a low voice.

Martha Maude smiled, seemingly unaware of the drama that had robbed Anne of her ability to speak. "Saul, this is Rose Raber and her daughter, Gracie. We met them when we took our shawls and lap robes to the senior center—"

"And they're my grandmas," Gracie put in happily.

"Your *honorary* grandmas," Martha Maude clarified gently. "That means we love to spend time with you, like grandmas would, even if we're not really kinfolk—just like you call Gladys and Flo and Zelma your grandmas."

Saul nodded curtly at Rose, his eyes narrowed. "Shall we go?" he demanded.

Anne clenched her teeth to keep from yelping when her husband's grip crushed her knuckles. He strode briskly across the park without a thought for Rose, Gracie, or his mother. Behind them, Anne heard Martha Maude speaking apologetically to Rose.

"What was *that* all about?" Saul demanded in a low voice. "Who *was* that woman, wife?"

"I might ask the same of you, Saul," Martha Maude muttered as she caught up to them. "What *was* that all about, that you acted so rude—staring at Rose and Gracie as if they had two heads—or they were some sort of threat to you?"

Saul glared at his mother. He opened his mouth to respond, but he closed it again. He focused on the street as they crossed it, walking faster as they reached the unpaved road that ran past their home.

*This isn't going well, Lord,* Anne fretted as she struggled to keep up with her angry husband. *My face—and Rose's— surely gave us away after Gracie called me her* mammi. *Bless her heart, she loves us and we love her, so please, Lord, soften Saul's wrath if he's guessed the truth. Don't let him break that little girl's heart.*

# Chapter 27

When Saul slammed the door closed behind them, Anne knew better than to flee the kitchen. All she could hope was that if he got more demanding—if the truth of her past came out—Martha Maude's love for little Gracie would keep this heart-wrenching moment from becoming the worst nightmare of her life. How careless she'd been to succumb to Joel Lapp's charm so long ago, but how deeply she loved her daughter and how grateful to God she was that Rose had come into her life again. She had to hold this love—a mother's love, which knew no limits or boundaries—firmly in her heart as she endured whatever accusations her husband might hurl at her.

Anne went to the far end of the table to stand behind the chair, gripping the top of it in anguished silence.

Saul stopped in the middle of the kitchen, crossing his arms over his bearlike chest. He stared at Anne and then at his mother. "Seems to me that there's more to this situation than a child declaring you two her *honorary* grandmothers," he muttered. "If that's the case, why do you look like a whipped dog, Anne? And why did that Rose woman seem as frightened as you did?"

Martha Maude frowned. "Saul, I think you're reading more into this situation than—"

"I was reading faces, Mother," he interrupted tersely. "And anyone can see that Rose Raber bears a *very* close resemblance to Anne. I find that extremely . . . *interesting*. Especially because that little girl insists that you're her grandmothers."

Anne's hand fluttered to her mouth, even as she realized her actions were incriminating her as much as Saul's words. Her throat was so tight she couldn't talk.

Martha Maude let out an impatient sigh. "Sometimes, son, your imagination goes so far astray, I don't understand—"

"What's to understand?" Saul demanded, walking over to where Anne still gripped the chair for support. "Rose's complexion is darker and her hair is red instead of brown, but otherwise she's the very image of Anne when she was younger. They've got the same body build and the same green eyes, the same tendency to duck a situation rather than look me in the eye and—"

"Enough!" Anne sobbed. She knew her tears would further condemn her, but she couldn't stop them from falling. "It's your attitude—your arrogance—that frightens me, Saul, even more than what you think you saw in the park."

The flare of Saul's eyes told Anne she'd overstepped, but there was no taking back her words. Her truth.

"My *attitude*—my *arrogance*—hasn't been an issue before," he snapped as he glared at her. "But your fear, now that's something worth discussing. You wouldn't be shaking like a leaf, looking ready to pass out, if what I said about your resemblance to Rose didn't strike a note of truth. And maybe it's time for some cold, hard truth, eh?" he added archly. "Who is Rose, really? It's a sin to lie, Anne. I suspect Gracie stated the facts, whether she knew them or not."

Saul looked ready to strike her, and if Martha Maude hadn't placed herself between them, Anne suspected he might have. But her mother-in-law had her own reason for standing so close. She, too, began gazing directly at Anne's features, probably comparing them to Rose's.

"There might be a resemblance," Martha Maude murmured with a shrug. "But let me take the blame for planting the idea in Gracie's mind that I could be her *mammi*. She wouldn't have called me that if I hadn't first—"

"But, Mother, you don't appear *guilty,* as though that little girl blurted something you had hoped to keep hidden." Saul kept his gaze on Anne's face as he said this, as though he intended to stare at her until she confessed. "If I recall correctly, the girl called you both her grandmothers. Is that how you remember it, Anne?"

Anne's pulse was pounding so loudly she barely heard Saul's question. Her throat had constricted to the point she couldn't swallow, much less talk. She knew her husband wouldn't let up until she answered him . . . yet she believed that the greater sin would be to lie to God by forsaking her daughter. Thirty years of silence and keeping secrets weighed heavily on her soul now. For no matter how good her intentions had been when she'd let Myron and Lydia Fry adopt Rose, she realized there was still the matter of allowing Saul to believe he was the only man she'd ever lain with.

Anne cleared her throat, praying desperately for strength and the right words. "*Jah,* Gracie called us both her *mammis,*" she replied hoarsely.

"And why has that upset you so badly, wife?" Saul continued sternly. "If it's as Mother says—a case of being honorary grandmothers—I can't imagine why you turned as white as a sheet when that little girl ran up to you, obviously delighted to see you both. Give me a *gut* answer and we'll be done with this. The truth will set you free."

Anne had always felt blessed that such a handsome, healthy, successful man wanted to spend his life with her—a man who was deeply committed to his church as well. Yet, over the years, it had been Saul's tendency toward self-righteousness that made her wonder where his loyalty would lie if he ever found fault with her, or doubted her. She knew of employees he'd fired without a thought for what would happen to their families. Would Saul cast her out—emotionally, if not physically—if she told him a truth he didn't want to hear?

"Rose is my daughter," Anne admitted in a whisper.

Martha Maude sucked in her breath and stepped away. Saul's eyes widened and he appeared ready to lash out, but Anne went on in the firmest voice she could manage before either one of them could interrupt her.

"Long before I met you—when I was barely sixteen—I gave Rose up for adoption. Once she was weaned, I never intended to see her again," Anne explained. Even as the words left her mouth, Anne knew Saul found them to be weak and pathetic. "Your mother and I met Rose and Gracie at the senior center last week—totally unexpectedly—"

"What happened last week is not the issue here, *wife,*" Saul interrupted. His face was the color of raw steak and the sound of his ragged breathing filled the kitchen. "If Rose is not my daughter, but she is yours, what does that mean?"

Anne resented the way Saul sometimes asked questions to which he knew the answers, to test her. To put her in her place. But this wasn't the time to comment on his irritating habit.

"Saul, it's perfectly obvious what it means," Martha Maude said curtly. "Anne had a child out of wedlock. She has led you to believe she was untouched when she married you, but there was obviously another man in her life when she was young and . . . very foolish."

"Is that how it was, Anne? Answer me!" Saul demanded.

Anne knew that no answer was the right answer at this point, but something inside her refused to accept the way her husband was treating her. "*Jah*, that's how it was," she retorted. "I did nothing different from what any other unmarried Plain girl would do. My parents refused to let me keep my child."

Saul's mouth dropped open. "Oh, so it's fine that you had a child by another man, yet you've given me no children? And you accuse *me* of being arrogant?" His words rang in the silent kitchen for several seconds before he spoke again. "This is more sin and deceit than I can handle alone. I've got to talk to Bishop Jeremiah—and you're going with me, Anne, to confess your sins. Then we'll see what he recommends, as far as confessing on your knees to the whole congregation."

A fierce defiance welled up inside her. Anne had long ago confessed to God, and she believed He had forgiven her youthful passion—and that He didn't expect her to suffer for the rest of her life because she'd given herself body and soul to Joel Lapp. This idea of hers flew in the face of what the church leaders taught about the necessity of public confession, yet Anne held tight to her beliefs. She suspected she would say things to Saul she would regret. However, if she didn't speak her mind now, when would she ever get the chance to set things straight?

"I'm staying right here. I was unbaptized when I delivered Rose, and God washed me clean when I joined the church," she said softly. "Talk to the bishop, if you need the reassurance another man will give you. The truth about my past is out now—and I refuse to be ashamed that I gave birth to the fine young woman Rose has become."

Saul clenched his hand into fists, a blatant reminder that he could discipline her—could punish her physically and be within the rights their faith afforded him, because wives were to obey their husbands.

Anne waited, unable to breathe, as Saul considered his response.

With a final glare at her, he pivoted. As the door slammed behind him, Anne clung to the chair that had supported her. She feared her knees might buckle now that her past had been brought to light and her husband intended to share it with the bishop—and now that she was alone with Martha Maude, who appeared rooted to her spot in shock.

"I can't believe Saul figured it out, yet I never saw it coming. Didn't even notice the resemblance," Martha Maude murmured, shaking her head. "This changes everything. *Everything.*"

As her mother-in-law left the room, Anne gave in to her shaking legs and dropped into the chair she'd been holding. *What happens when Saul gets home? Should I move my clothes into a guest room, or should I pack and find someplace else to go until this blows over? Oh, Rose . . . no matter what comes of this, I will always love you. None of this is your fault, or Gracie's. . . .*

# Chapter 28

"Mamma, whatsa matter?" Gracie whimpered as Rose led her swiftly across the park toward the road. "Why did that man look so mean? Where we goin', Mamma?"

"We've got to talk to Matthias," Rose answered more impatiently than she'd intended. "There's going to be serious trouble—"

"Am *I* in trouble, Mamma? Why did that man get so mad?" Gracie asked plaintively. "Why did Anne look like she was gonna cry?"

When Rose realized her little girl was practically running to keep up, she stopped on the roadside. As she swept Gracie into her arms, Rose knew she needed to clarify her own thoughts—because Gracie was asking all the right questions after she had unwittingly stirred up an emotional hornet's nest.

"Sweet pea, do you remember when Matthias was at our house, and we told you not to tell anybody that Anne is my *mamm*?" Rose asked gently.

Gracie's brow puckered with thought. "*Jah*. But I didn't tell nobody—"

"You didn't," Rose assured her daughter as she hugged her close. "And Martha Maude told you it was all right to call her your *mammi* . . . not knowing what would happen when Saul was with them. It's not your fault that he got upset, Gracie," she continued with a sigh. "But now he's angry with Anne, because he looked at me and he heard what you called her, and he figured out that Anne is my mother. He knows our secret now, and he's not happy."

"Oh."

The finer points of this dilemma were beyond Gracie's comprehension, but Rose's main concern was helping her mother endure the accusations and bitter words Saul would probably hurl at her. Rose sensed that Saul was a good man at heart, sincere in his commitment to the church and to his wife. Still, the Amish faith was tilted in favor of men. It was only a matter of time before the district's bishop and preachers got involved and her mother was outnumbered—and Martha Maude might decry the sin Anne had committed in her youth as well. Her mother would be left totally alone, defenseless against so many accusers.

"So why're we gonna see Matthias?" Gracie murmured.

Rose set her daughter on the unpaved road again and walked more slowly. "Matthias knows Anne and Martha Maude because he has eaten supper at their house—and because he is Saul's business partner now," she explained. "He knows how angry Saul can get, so I'm hoping he'll think of a way to settle everyone down. It's complicated."

"*Jah,* it is," Gracie murmured, reaching for Rose's hand. "But Matthias will fix it! I just know it!"

As the small white house on the corner came into sight, Rose was glad she'd asked Matthias where he lived in case she wanted to fetch Daisy and the rig. She led Gracie across his neatly mowed yard and onto the small porch, and then pounded on the front door. Her thoughts were swirling as she thought about what her mother might be going through this evening.

The door swung open and Matthias's face lit up. "It's *gut* to see you girls," he began happily—and then he read their expressions. "What's wrong, Rose? You look worried."

"I am," she replied as they stepped into the house. "We just met Anne, Martha Maude, and Saul at the park—"

"I was real excited, and I called 'em my *mammies,*" Gracie put in dolefully.

"—and by the way Saul was looking me over, considering how I must've appeared every bit as startled and fearful as Anne did," Rose murmured, "I suspect he figured out who I was. And I bet he's nailing my mother with questions, now that they're home, and I—I'm really worried about her, Matthias. I doubt Martha Maude will stand up for her."

When a little sob escaped Rose, Matthias took her in his arms and held her close. Dozens of times he'd imagined holding her this way—but not while he was caught on the horns of the dilemma he'd hoped to avoid. If he helped Rose and Anne—took their part against Saul—he had no doubt that Hartzler would tear up their partnership papers and send him packing. He could also convince other folks not to come to his harness shop. Saul might even consider Matthias almost as deceptive as Anne, because he'd known about her secret baby and hadn't found a way to inform Saul of his wife's duplicity.

*Oh, what a tangled web we weave,* he thought as he reveled

in the warmth of Rose's sturdy body. When Gracie tapped insistently on his thigh, Matthias scooped her up so she could share their hug. Her expression was pinched and her lower lip quivered. The poor little girl seemed to sense the gravity of Anne's situation, even as she realized she might have played a part in it.

"I think we should pray about this—pray for Anne and Saul and Martha Maude," Matthias murmured. "Then we can consider what to do next."

Rose nodded, closing her eyes, and Gracie bowed her head until it was resting on Matthias's shoulder. In the stillness of his new home, in the presence of the woman and little girl he so dearly loved, Matthias prayed silently for a few moments.

Then he cleared his throat. "Lord, we ask Your forgiveness for all we've done that has displeased You," he said softly. "And we ask Your presence with the Hartzlers as they deal with this difficult situation, that the truth may be revealed— and that Your will for them be made plain as well," he continued. "Bless Rose and Gracie and Anne with Your steadfast love. Help us all to bring this situation to a peaceful resolution. Amen."

"Amen," Rose murmured. Her eyes remained closed for a few moments more, and when she looked up at Matthias, he shared the anguish that was making her cry. It seemed so unfair that just when she'd been reunited with her birth mother after losing the mother who'd raised her, she and Anne would both suffer these consequences of Rose's birth thirty years ago.

Matthias sighed, swaying with Gracie on his hip. "I'm sorry this has happened, Rose—and sorry Saul has become upset about it," he murmured. "I can understand why he'd feel he's been deceived, but I hope he'll be able to put Anne's relationship with another man behind him and focus on the love she feels for you and Gracie instead."

Gracie nodded solemnly. "Martha Maude loves me a lot. I just know it."

Rose smiled sadly and opened her arms. "You're right, Gracie," she said as she hugged her daughter close. "And maybe that's the key to unlocking Saul's heart. Maybe Martha Maude will realize how much she enjoys being with you, and she'll convince Saul to like us, too. But we can't get our hopes up," she added with a sigh. "Saul might decide that Anne and his mother should never see us again."

Gracie's lower lip quivered. She nestled against Rose's shoulder, catching herself before she stuck her thumb in her mouth.

Matthias smiled. "Shall we sit down in the front room? Can I make you some coffee?"

Rose glanced into the room he gestured toward. "That would be nice, but if we're keeping you from your supper—"

"I was just deciding which can of soup to open when you knocked," he admitted ruefully. He eyed Gracie, and a better idea came to mind. "But you know what I'm really hungry for? Pizza."

Gracie's head popped up. "I love pizza!"

Rose chuckled. "You ate a big piece of chicken and a mountain of mashed potatoes for supper, young lady," she teased, rubbing Gracie's tummy. "Where will you put pizza?"

Matthias was pleased that his suggestion had lightened everyone's mood. "How about going to the pizza place, and I'll order a large pizza and you girls can eat whatever you care to?" he said. "Eating by myself gets old . . . and maybe we'll come up with ideas for helping Anne."

It felt good to walk into town with Rose holding the crook of his elbow and Gracie grasping his hand. Matthias let his mind wander, considering the ways they might assist Anne during this difficult time. He had no doubt that Martha Maude would be incensed and that Saul would hold Anne's unwed pregnancy against her if someone didn't convince him to forgive her and focus on all the years she had been a faithful wife to him.

As they sat in the back booth waiting for their large Canadian bacon pizza with the extra cheese Gracie requested, Matthias smiled at the little girl. "That's a very pretty green dress, Gracie. Is it new?"

Her little face lit up and she nodded enthusiastically. "I picked the fabric and Martha Maude sewed it for me," she said. Her smile dimmed a little. "She made me one that looks like orange sherbet, too . . . but maybe now she won't wanna make me no more dresses."

When Matthias reached across the table for Gracie's hand, he felt an overwhelming urge to propose to Rose—to become a family now, even though she would be in mourning for her mother for several more months. Holding Gracie's tiny hand made him aware of how vulnerable she was, and how dependent she was upon whatever the grown-ups in her life decided. He had a fierce urge to protect both of them, but he didn't want to speak too soon—especially now that Rose was caught up in this drama with her mother.

"Martha Maude seems very nice," he said softly, "and she's a strong lady who does what she believes is right. If she thinks you're special enough that she sews dresses for you, Gracie, I bet her feelings for you won't change. But we need to give her some time while Saul and Anne settle things between them."

"Do you suppose Saul will demand that Anne make a confession before the whole church?" Rose asked. Her eyes widened with concern. "I was only around Saul for a few moments this evening, but I could tell he was assessing Anne's reaction—and mine—when Gracie ran up to them. Frankly, I thought he seemed very stern and judgmental."

"He was scary," Gracie murmured.

Matthias considered what Rose had said. "I suspect Saul won't be content to keep this matter within the family—*jah*, I think he'll expect a confession from his wife. And that means he'll be going to see Bishop Jeremiah . . . so what if I speak with Jeremiah as well?" he mused aloud. "He seems like a fair-minded fellow. Maybe he'll have a better perception of all that's involved if he hears from you, too, Rose. Would you be willing to go with me?"

Rose met his gaze in a straight-on way. "Of course I would. This is my mother we're talking about, and I'll do everything it takes to help her through her time of trial," she said with an emphatic nod. Then she sighed. "But if you think it would be better to speak with the bishop, man-to-man, I'll understand. And I'll be forever grateful for your help, Matthias."

"*Jah*, you might have a point." Matthias's insides tingled as Rose continued to gaze at him, her expression resolute. What a joy it would be to have this woman with him all day, every day . . . yet it wouldn't be fair to propose until she could give him her full attention, after her mind was at ease about her mother's situation. He loved Rose so much that if she was standing by him, he could endure anything—even if it meant Saul tore up their partnership papers because Matthias appeared loyal to Anne. He didn't relish challenging Saul on Rose and Anne's behalf; but if his support would help these two women, then he was ready to throw himself into the fray.

"I'll visit with Bishop Jeremiah this evening, then," Matthias said. He smiled at the waitress as she set the large, steaming pizza in the center of their table. "We'll go along with whatever he thinks is best."

"I think that's wise," Rose agreed. She inhaled the aroma of the pizza, placing a slice on Gracie's plate and then taking a slice for herself. "Maybe I have room for a slice of pizza, after all. I feel much better about the Hartzler situation now, Matthias. *Denki* for your wisdom."

Matthias smiled and took a big bite of pizza. If Rose felt better—and believed he was wise—he was a happy man.

After he walked Rose and Gracie over to the senior center, Matthias strode down the main street of Morning Star and turned his steps toward Jeremiah Shetler's home. After a few minutes, he passed a vast green pasture, where sleek Black Angus cattle grazed with the last pink ribbons of the setting sun on the horizon behind them. It was Saul's herd. Another source of income most Plain men could only envy, because these cattle were probably registered and very expensive to raise and maintain—and they would bring top dollar when they were butchered.

*Is a man's worth measured by his possessions—his success as a wage earner—or by the amount of love in his heart?*

Matthias recalled Jesus' story about the man who decided to erect huge barns to store his bumper crop, when the Savior admonished his listeners not to lay up treasures on earth that could be destroyed or stolen, but to lay up treasures in heaven. " 'For where your treasure is, there will your heart be also,' " he murmured aloud.

As Matthias walked up the lane to the Shetler home, he hoped Saul's heart was in the right place.

He knocked on the front door. A few moments later, Jeremiah opened it, smiling at him. "Matthias, it's *gut* to see you on this beautiful spring evening. Come on in."

"I was hoping I could have a word with you," Matthias said—and then he stopped short. Swallowed hard.

Saul was seated on the blue corduroy sofa in the bishop's front room, looking none too cheerful. His thick eyebrows rose and he sat up straighter. "Wagler. I don't mean to be rude, but I was bending the bishop's ear about a rather . . . personal matter."

Matthias removed his hat. He didn't relish speaking about Rose's mother in front of Saul, but he sensed God might've led him here at this moment so his business partner could be present when he spoke to Bishop Jeremiah. The bishop wasn't asking him to leave, after all.

Had Anne or Martha Maude told Saul that he and Rose were seeing each other—or that the three of them were coming to supper Friday night? Judging from Saul's puzzled expression, Matthias didn't think so.

"Your private matter concerns me as well," Matthias began, praying he would say the right words in the right way. "Rose Raber and I are . . . close, and she's asked me to speak with Bishop Jeremiah about this situation between you and her mother."

Saul came up off the sofa, scowling. "What business is this of yours?" he demanded. "The fact that my wife had a child out of wedlock and never told me is none of your concern."

Jeremiah chuckled softly. "Well, Saul, you have now made it Matthias's business, *jah?* I sense he has come on a mission of peace and compassion, which have been sadly absent in the account you've given me." He gestured toward a chair. "Let's all sit down and discuss this, please. Calmly. Rationally."

Matthias chose the armchair across from the sofa, because the bishop was taking a seat in the rocking chair near Saul. He sensed his business partner had been—understandably—blowing off steam, but perhaps in a loud, negative way.

"Matthias, do you have any idea how long ago Anne and Rose found each other?" Jeremiah asked.

He thought back. "About a week ago," he said. "Rose has taken a job cooking at the senior center. She was really surprised when Anne and Martha Maude walked in that day."

"You can't tell me they just instantly knew each other!" Saul protested. "This whole story smells like rotten fish, if you ask me."

Jeremiah cleared his throat. "From what I can tell, Saul, you don't really know much of Anne's story," he said in a low voice. He looked at Matthias. "Any idea how Rose knew Anne was her mother?"

"*Jah*," he replied, glancing warily at Saul. "When Rose was just a little baby, Anne stayed at Rose's adoptive parents' house until the baby was weaned, and meanwhile she wrote Rose a couple of letters. Rose didn't find them until the *mamm* who'd raised her passed on—"

"And you *believe* that fairy tale, Wagler?" Saul blurted.

Matthias stopped talking. He gazed steadily at his business partner, not liking what he saw. "I do," he said firmly. "Rose's adoptive *mamm*—and Anne's letters—firmly insisted that Rose was not to go looking for Anne because she knew it would upset the apple cart at your place. But there was also a painting of Anne—"

"Well, finally! A glimmer of truth," Hartzler said as he sprang from the couch to pace. "Any man would understand how such information would upset a whole lot more than some stupid apple cart."

Bishop Jeremiah sat with his fingers tented beneath his chin, watching Saul walk over to stare out the window. "Saul, the more I hear, the more concerned I become about your emotional state," he said. "Because the welfare of our church district—and the welfare of your household—rests in your hands, Deacon, I want to hear this story from all concerned parties before I decide whether Anne should endure the shunning you have requested."

Matthias's mouth fell open. Had Saul really asked Jeremiah to shun Anne before she'd even had a chance to speak with the bishop, or to confess to the congregation and abide by its recommendation? He had anticipated harshness on Saul's part, but not such a blatant separation that would make Anne pay so dearly for her behavior thirty years ago.

"I have affairs to attend to out of town tomorrow, but I'll be at your house Friday evening at seven, Saul," Jeremiah said as he stood up. "We will hear Anne's side of this story— and, Matthias, I think it would be beneficial if you and Rose were present as well."

"All right, we'll be there," Matthias said. It would be a far cry from the supper date Martha Maude had arranged for them, but at least everyone would be able to speak their minds with the bishop guiding the conversation.

"Meanwhile, Saul, I hope you'll heed the advice from Ephesians that tells us not to let the sun go down on our wrath," Jeremiah said firmly. "You married Anne for forever—for better or for worse—and until now, I've not known of a single instance when she let you down. A little patience is in order, I think."

Saul scowled and left very quickly, leaving an air of emotional turbulence and strife in his wake.

Jeremiah smiled ruefully at Matthias. "Bet you didn't figure on getting tossed into the lion's den, eh?" he said. "I'm sincerely glad you showed up, Matthias. God's hand is at work, and we'll arrive at His solution if we approach this situation honestly and prayerfully. See you Friday evening. I'm looking forward to meeting Rose."

# Chapter 29

After Rose was certain Gracie was sleeping soundly, she slipped out of their apartment and down to the kitchen. It was around nine o'clock, about an hour after Matthias had walked them home from the pizza place. The hallways were lit, and as she passed some of the rooms, she heard the blare of residents' televisions. The dining room and kitchen were dark, but she made her way through the dimness and flipped on the light at the rear of the kitchen.

Rose picked up the receiver of the wall phone, glad she'd written a list of some vital phone numbers before she and Gracie had decided to live in Morning Star during the week. After she dialed, she waited for the cue that would tell her when to leave her message—but someone picked up after the second ring.

"*Gut* evening, this is Vernon."

Rose let out a nervous laugh. "Vernon, it's Rose Raber and I—I wasn't figuring you'd answer right off. How are you?"

"Couldn't be better. Just watched one of my cows give birth to a healthy set of twins," he replied in a glowing voice.

"That's why I'm out here in the barn where the phone is. How are you? And Gracie?"

Rose let out a sigh, considering her response. "We're both doing fine, but we've . . . hit a snag, and I'm hoping you can give me some advice."

"Untangling snags goes with the territory when you're a bishop," Vernon said with a chuckle. "What can I help you with, dear?"

"Well, I told you about my birth mother, Anne, coming to the senior center," she began, "and she realized who I was, and we had some time together to talk, and—"

"Oh, my," Vernon murmured. "You sound very excited about this, Rose. And again it seems Anne found you, rather than you seeking her out, am I correct?"

"That's how it was, *jah.* Martha Maude—Saul's mother— took Gracie shopping for fabric and has made her some dresses now, so Anne and I had a nice long visit," Rose said, her words tumbling out in a rush. "But this evening Gracie and I saw the three Hartzlers in the park, and . . . well, when Saul saw Gracie running up to the women, calling them her *mammis,* Saul, um, got ideas about who I was. The way he marched Anne home, I'm afraid she's catching a lot of grief from him—"

"Slow down, dear. Let me get this straight," Vernon murmured. "When Gracie called the two women her grandmas, Saul figured out you were Anne's daughter? Just like that?"

Rose thought back to the moment she'd described to Vernon. Had it only been a few hours ago? As much as she'd been fretting about it, she felt like days had passed. "We look a lot alike," she explained. "And when Saul saw how frightened and upset Anne became—and probably read the same emotions on my face—he realized something wasn't as it seemed."

Vernon's sigh thrummed with regret. "Saul's a sharp man. If you resemble your mother, he probably put one and one together and came up with a lot more than two."

"Do you think he'll hurt her?" Rose blurted. "You and Matthias have both told me how stern he can be—"

"He has a temper, *jah*."

"—so after the Hartzlers left, Gracie and I went over to tell Matthias what had happened," Rose continued in a tight voice. "Matthias thought it best to talk with Bishop Jeremiah, so I thought I should let you know what was going on as well. You're the wisest man I know, Vernon, and—and you understand why I'm so overjoyed to be with my birth mother again—"

"Even though your presence has caused the problems we anticipated earlier," Vernon finished her sentence. He paused for a moment. "Tell you what I'll do, Rose. I'll get in touch with Jeremiah—I'll call him as soon as you and I hang up—and I'll see what he has to say about Saul and Anne. Could be he hasn't heard from either of them yet."

"Oh, *denki* so much. I'll try to be patient," Rose whispered. She felt a great weight being lifted from her tired shoulders.

"I'll keep you posted. Meanwhile, you should keep believing that God already knows what He wants to make of this Hartzler situation," Vernon suggested. "We humans perceive it as a frightening, ominous problem, but our Lord knows what lessons we're to learn and how we're to proceed. He'll bring us through the darkness and into the light."

"*Jah. Jah,* He will." Rose let out a relieved sigh. "I feel a lot better now—and I'll get some sleep thanks to you, Bishop."

After she hung up, Rose shut out the kitchen light. On her way back to the apartment, she paused to gaze at the aquarium. Except for a table lamp, the fish tank was the only light in the lobby and its soft glow and the gentle bubbling of the water soothed her. It occurred to her that those small, colorful fish were dependent upon someone to feed them and to keep their glass tank clean—just as people relied upon God's providence in a crowded, busy world that surely kept Him so occupied, she and Gracie and the Hartzlers must seem as tiny and inconsequential as these fish.

Yet in that quiet moment, Rose knew that God was watching over her and her daughter, just as He knew of the strife that Anne, Martha Maude, and Saul were experiencing.

*"If God be for us, who can be against us?"*

Rose smiled as that important Bible verse came to mind. "And if Bishop Vernon and Bishop Jeremiah are doing God's work, who can be against us?" she murmured.

She returned to the apartment, smiled at her sleeping daughter, and drifted off to sleep as soon as her head hit the pillow.


Anne sat on the sofa with her head bowed, clasping her white-knuckled hands in her lap as Saul vented his fury. Although his diatribe had already lasted longer than his visit with the bishop, she had a feeling he wasn't nearly finished with her.

"As if it hasn't been enough that we've met that Rose and her chatterbox daughter," he continued, his strident voice filling the room, "Matthias Wagler came in while I was at Shetler's house. He wanted to put in a *gut* word for you and Rose—tried to convince me that none of this deception was your fault or hers, as though I should just sweep it under the rug and forget about it! I almost told him to take a hike. I don't need a partner who'll side with my wife instead of with me."

Anne hugged herself, a new wave of anxiety roiling her stomach. Martha Maude had gone upstairs to bed, but she couldn't help hearing every word of Saul's rant—and she was probably ready to end the partnership with Matthias as well. "What do you want me to do?" Anne rasped. The tears streaming down her face were making Saul angrier, but she couldn't hold them back. "I've told you the truth—"

"*Jah,* and lucky for you, Bishop Jeremiah refused to shun you, as I requested," Saul interrupted.

"—and no matter what I say, you keep yelling at me," Anne continued doggedly. "I'm sorry I've upset you, but how was I to tell you about my daughter? Would you have married me if you'd known about Rose when we were courting?"

"Absolutely not!"

Anne squeezed her eyes shut against a welling up of despair. "Please, Saul," she murmured, "will you forgive me? May we please reach a truce so—"

"It's all or nothing," Saul stated harshly. "The way I see it—"

"I've heard enough," Martha Maude insisted as she came down the stairway. She was still dressed, with her hair still pulled back tightly beneath her *kapp,* even though she'd gone to her room when Saul had left the house. "We need to sleep on this matter so we'll be better equipped to deal with it in the morning."

"You're not sleeping in my bed," Saul said, pointing his finger at Anne.

Anne nodded. Her head was throbbing and she was grateful to Martha Maude for coming downstairs to quiet her son. "Let me just get my nightgown—"

Saul's brow furrowed. "I see no reason for you to set foot in my bedroom—"

"Saul! For the love of God, stop arguing!" Martha Maude planted a fist in her hip and glared at her son. "I'm going to ask Bishop Jeremiah to come over tomorrow and—"

"He's leaving town. He'll be here at seven o'clock Friday night."

Anne saw her chance to fetch a few things from the bedroom, but as she walked quickly toward the stairway, she didn't miss Martha Maude's deepening scowl. "Fine. And when were you going to tell us about this?" she demanded. "Truth be told, we'd already invited Rose and little Gracie and Matthias here for supper Friday, before this ruckus blew up—"

"Are you out of your mind?" Saul demanded loudly. He exhaled, struggling for control of his emotions. "Well, you get your wish. Jeremiah told Matthias to bring Rose over when he's here, anyway. Oh, it's going to be quite an evening—as though we're one big happy family, *jah?*" he added sarcastically.

Anne paused at the top of the stairs. She was relieved to know the bishop would be coming over, but how could she endure Saul's wrath for two more days before Jeremiah arrived? She was aghast at the tone her husband was using with his mother as well, for the two of them were usually of one accord.

"It would be a major improvement if we behaved like a happy family," Martha Maude finally said. "I'm as appalled as you are to hear about what happened in Anne's past, but what's done is done, Saul. Go to bed. And don't you ever raise your voice to me again."

Anne scurried down the hallway to grab her nightgown and clothing for Thursday. As she left the bedroom, where she'd slept nearly every night of her married life, she prayed for wisdom and the strength to face her husband at the breakfast table. She decided to sleep in the guest room that was farthest from Saul. As she passed Martha Maude's room and the two other guest rooms, she was again reminded that their five-bedroom house had been built to accommodate the children that had never blessed their marriage.

*Does Saul think I've secretly used some form of birth control? Does he believe I stopped wanting children because I'd had a daughter by another man? Lord, I don't know what to do—how to respond to his demands.*

When she heard her husband's heavy footfalls on the stairs, followed by his mother's, Anne quickly shut the door of her guest room. Plenty of times she'd witnessed Saul's impatience with people who fell short of his high mark, and she'd occasionally felt the sting of his irritation when food wasn't cooked to his liking or she didn't make decisions quickly enough to suit him. This current flood of his wrath, though, threatened to pull her under until she drowned in anguish. . . .

Anne knelt at the side of the bed and began to pray. In her mind, she saw Rose and Gracie. When she found the strength to give thanks for their presence in her life, a sense of hope filled her soul. Somehow she would get through tomorrow and Friday until Bishop Jeremiah and the others arrived to decide her fate—and Saul's, too.

*Saul must come to a point of forgiveness, or at least quiet tolerance. Right now, Lord, quiet tolerance sounds wonderful. Your will be done.*

## Chapter 30

Matthias was startled when someone banged on his door Thursday morning. The sun was barely a peach-pink ribbon on the horizon, and he'd just showered and dressed after tending the horses. He turned off the burner beneath his eggs before going to the front room to answer the door. A tingle of nervous goose bumps raced up his back when he glanced through the glass. Saul was standing on the stoop.

"*Gut* morning, Saul," he said as he opened the door. "I wasn't expecting—"

"*Jah*, well, a lot of things have happened that I wasn't expecting, either," the tall, broad-chested man snapped. Saul stepped inside before Matthias could invite him. He held some rolled-up papers, and while he gazed around the front room—as if to decide whether the house and its furnishings met his expectations—he tapped the papers against the palm of his hand.

"Come on back to the kitchen. I was just frying up some eggs," Matthias said, gesturing for Saul to precede him.

"Add three more to your skillet. We need to talk."

Matthias's stomach rumbled with more than hunger as they headed into the kitchen. Why hadn't Saul eaten breakfast at home? Were those rolled-up papers their partnership agreement? As he went to the refrigerator for more eggs, he wondered how to tactfully ask these questions—but Saul wasn't one to beat around the bush.

"Call me crazy, but until I get this story about Anne straightened out—and the bishop prescribes her punishment—I don't trust anything she puts in front of me," he said as he sat heavily in the chair at the head of the table. "If she kept her sordid past and her illegitimate daughter such a secret, who can say what she might put in my food?"

Matthias turned from the stove to frown at Saul. "That's the last thing I'd expect of your wife," he asserted, lighting the flame under the skillet again. "Far as I can tell, Anne doesn't have a mean—or vengeful—bone in her body."

"So much for what *you* know about her," Saul retorted. "How long did you figure to keep Anne's secret from me, Wagler? We're partners—or at least these papers say we are. If I learned something relevant about *your* wife, I'd certainly let you know so you could deal with it—*fix* it—before all hell broke loose." Saul slapped the papers against the tabletop with a flourish, crossing his muscled arms after the pieces of paper fanned across the wooden surface.

Matthias flinched. He focused on cracking four additional eggs into the skillet without getting pieces of shell in them . . . decided to scramble them all, because the whites of his original eggs were already opaque. "The way I see it, such matters should remain between a man and his wife," he said cautiously. "I didn't know you were at Jeremiah's when I went there last night. I was going to speak to him on Rose's behalf, because she was worried about her mother."

"Worried about Anne? That's rich," Saul said with a snort. "You've seen the life she lives in the home I've provided her."

Scowling, Matthias turned to look at Saul. "You know what?" he murmured. His heart began pounding so loudly he could barely hear himself think, but he had to state his case. "After what I witnessed last night at Jeremiah's—and what I'm hearing now—I'm seeing you in a whole different light, Saul. A man who's become such a successful carriage maker has to have a lot of business smarts and be savvy about people, yet you've lost all sense of reason where your wife's concerned," he continued in a rush. "You've blown Anne's one mistake, committed during her *rumspringa,* completely out of proportion."

"Huh." Saul rose and began to pace around the kitchen, going from window to window. "Are you saying you want out of our partnership? Saying you don't trust my judgment?"

Matthias stirred the eggs with the edge of his spatula and liberally seasoned them with salt and pepper. He wasn't surprised that Saul had brought up their partnership—it was probably the reason he'd come over. Matthias was in no hurry to end it, so he spoke carefully.

"I've said no such thing, Saul. I suspect you're questioning my loyalty merely because I showed up at Jeremiah's when I did," he reasoned aloud. "Had I arrived fifteen minutes after you'd left, you'd be no wiser and you wouldn't be doubting the solidity of our relationship. This situation has nothing to do with your carriage business or our being partners, Saul."

"*Jah,* it does," Saul countered loudly. He snatched up the papers, tapped their bottom edges on the table, and ripped the stack in half, side to side. The sound of the paper tearing made him smile. "I don't tolerate insubordination from my employees, and I won't have a partner who deliberately keeps important details from me. It's a matter of trust. A matter of respect."

Matthias pressed his lips tightly together, struggling to keep a straight face. Although he might be better off personally if he didn't have to deal with Hartzler's mercurial moods, he saw his new harness business limping along like a lame horse. Saul would now tell his carriage customers that Wagler Harness and Leather Shop was not a reliable place to buy their tack. In the small town of Morning Star, where Plain folks from all around did their shopping, Matthias would have a hard time staying in business.

*If I were a severely injured horse, you'd put me out of my misery, Saul.* The stray thought startled Matthias—and he realized he was playing into Hartzler's flair for drama. At this moment, he couldn't foretell the future of his business or his relationship with Saul, but they both needed to eat.

Matthias divided the eggs between two plates and carried them to the table. He grabbed the loaf of store-bought bread from the counter and sat down, waiting for Saul's response. When Hartzler looked at his plate as though he might not eat what he'd been offered, Matthias bowed his head, hoping Saul would do the same.

*Stick with me, Lord. I've been tossed into the lion's den, and I need to keep my head on straight. Denki for this food and Your presence in every moment of our lives.*

When Matthias opened his eyes, Saul did, too. Saul poked at his scrambled eggs before taking a bite, and then took a slice of bread from the bag. His expression lightened a bit.

"You could use a wife, Wagler," he teased. "You do all your own cooking?"

Matthias wasn't sure how to take Saul's remark—or his apparent change of mood—but he decided to answer straight on. "*Jah*, I do. In Willow Ridge, I had a sister-in-law cooking for me, and before that, my wife, Sadie," he replied as he spread apple butter on his bread. Martha Maude had given him the apple butter, but he wasn't going to mention that. "Since Sadie died, while carrying our first child, I've learned how to make do without a wife. But I don't recommend the single life. From where I sit, the wealth you've accumulated from your carriage shop is *nothing* compared to the rich life you live with Anne. Just my opinion."

Saul appeared ready to start in on another diatribe, but something made him back down. "*Jah*, whatever," he muttered as he took another bite of his eggs.

"I intend to marry Rose someday," Matthias continued in a purposeful voice. What did he have to lose by expressing his intentions? "I believe Anne and Rose should be free to enjoy a close mother-daughter relationship—and include little Gracie in it—without any backlash from you, Saul. Again, just my opinion. But there you have it."

Saul's eyes widened. He slathered a thick coating of butter and apple butter on his bread, not saying anything.

Had Saul begun to see reason? Matthias wasn't going to stake the future of his harness shop on it, but at least his partner had stopped ranting. Their meeting with Jeremiah would tell the tale.

"I've told you that Gracie and I will be staying over tonight, *jah*?" Rose asked Sherrie as the two of them began setting the tables for supper. "I should drive home early to-morrow so I can get our household chores done, but—"

Sherrie gently grasped her arm. "Don't worry about a thing," she said, gazing kindly into Rose's eyes. "You can do your laundry here, in our machines—I'll show you how they work, if you need help. If it's easier, stay the entire weekend and relax, because by this afternoon you'll have already prepared our meals for the weekend. That room is yours for whenever you and Gracie want to stay in it."

"*Denki* for offering again to let me do our laundry here," Rose whispered, shaking her head. "I—I didn't want to push the wrong buttons and mess up the washer."

Rose swallowed hard. In the quiet of the dining room, where just the two of them worked while Gracie practiced writing her letters at her desk in the kitchen, she felt the urge to confide and confess about more serious matters than laundry. Sooner or later, Sherrie would hear that Anne Hartzler was her mother, so it might be best for Rose to break the news herself. She'd been so keyed-up these past couple of days that sharing her situation with Sherrie might make her feel more confident about the outcome of tonight's meeting with Bishop Jeremiah.

"Gracie and I will be going to the Hartzlers' house tonight," Rose began hesitantly. "We were originally invited for dinner, but now we're meeting there with the bishop because—because Anne's husband figured out that she's my mother. My birth mother, anyway," she added quickly. "Anne gave me up for adoption when she was only sixteen, and now her husband's really upset about—well, he'd had no idea she'd borne a child before she married him."

Sherrie gaped. She set her stack of plates on the table so

she wouldn't drop them. "Have you always known this, Rose? Did you know Anne and Martha Maude that day they came with their shawls and lap robes?"

Rose shook her head. "I recognized her because of some letters and a portrait of her I found after my adoptive mother passed. I had no idea Anne lived in Morning Star, or that I would ever see her—"

"My word, Rose, what a revelation!" Sherrie said in an excited whisper. "This is surely God's hand at work—Him leading you here, and then bringing Anne into your life again as well."

Rose smiled ruefully. "Saul doesn't feel that way," she murmured. "When Gracie and I go there tonight with Matthias, I can only hope Bishop Jeremiah will somehow soften Saul's heart. Gracie will be crushed if she's not allowed to see Anne and Martha Maude anymore."

Sherrie wrapped her arms around Rose's shoulders and hugged her tight. "I'll keep you all in my prayers. Tonight's meeting sounds like one of those scary, life-altering events that we dread, but sometimes we have to go through the valley of the shadow in order to come out in the light on the other side."

Rose nodded, comforted by Sherrie's wise words. "*Denki* so much for understanding," she whispered. "And *denki* for all you do for Gracie and me. I hate to think about where we'd be without your support and this job you've given me. I've started paying off some of Mamma's long-standing medical bills, thanks to you."

Sherrie smiled as she released Rose. "No matter what happens tonight, everyone here loves you and Gracie, and we consider you part of our family," she murmured. "It'll all work out the way it's supposed to, Rose."

As they finished setting the tables in companionable silence, Rose prayed that their time at the Hartzler house would be positive and productive. Sherrie's gracious acceptance meant so much, and it gave Rose a reason to believe that everything would indeed work out, because God had a plan for them. And He never failed.

# Chapter 31

"I'm glad you've brought your colored pencils and paper tonight, Gracie," Matthias said as he drove his buggy out of the senior center's parking lot and onto the street. "Your *mamm* says you're a *gut* artist, and I'm looking forward to seeing your pictures."

As Gracie beamed up at Matthias, Rose took a deep breath to settle her nerves. "I've explained to Gracie that tonight's conversation will be very serious, so she's to keep quiet unless someone speaks to her."

Matthias's smile stilled some of Rose's anxiety. "Could be that because Gracie's there, Saul's temper won't get ramped up as much," he remarked. "I don't know how Anne has been doing since you met the three Hartzlers in the park, but I can't imagine that Bishop Jeremiah—or Martha Maude—will allow the discussion to get out of hand."

"That's a *gut* thought," Rose whispered. Even though Matthias seemed cheerful, the furrow between his eyebrows made her wonder if he might be keeping something from her.

Gracie gazed up at her, her expression troubled. "Is it okay if I say hi to Martha Maude and Anne, Mamma? Or do I gotta be quiet?"

Rose slung her arm around her daughter and pulled her close. What a shame it was when a little girl hesitated to show her affection for her grandmother and her great-grandmother, simply because the man of their family was upset by what she'd said a few days ago. "Let's see how it is when we get there, sweet pea," she murmured. "If they smile at you and open their arms, it means they really want to see you. And if they look sad or scared, maybe you should just smile at them and say a little prayer that things will get better because of tonight's talk with the bishop."

Gracie nodded, hugging her tablet of paper and the box of colored pencils to her chest. She seemed wise beyond her years, but Rose prayed that her daughter's feelings wouldn't be hurt by anything she would hear.

The trip to the Hartzler house didn't take long. As Matthias drove up the long lane toward a large, well-kept white house, Rose gazed at the green pastureland dotted with black cattle, and at the abundance of dogwood and redbud trees just beyond the peak of their blooming season. "It's so pretty here," she murmured.

Matthias nodded as he pulled up beside two other buggies and horses already parked near the barn. "Saul's done well with his carriage shop and those Black Angus cattle," he said. "I wonder who's here besides Jeremiah?"

Rose inhaled deeply again, smiling as Matthias stepped out of the buggy. He lifted Gracie out and then reached in to help her down. "*Denki* for coming to be with us," she said. "Your presence will surely help everyone remain calm and considerate."

Matthias's gaze made butterflies flutter in Rose's stomach

as he kept his hands at her waist for a few extra moments. "Jeremiah asked me to be here—but for you, Rose, I would've come even if I hadn't been invited."

Rose wished her relationship to Anne hadn't put Matthias's partnership in possible jeopardy, but there was nothing she could do about that—Saul's decision was beyond her control. When Matthias reached down for Gracie, she wrapped an arm around his neck while clutching her paper and colored pencils. He carried her against his hip as they started toward the house. They had almost reached the large front porch when Martha Maude stepped outside to greet them.

"Gracie, it's *gut* to see you, honey—and don't you look pretty in your new peach dress," she said.

Gracie wiggled happily; and when Matthias set her on the porch floor, she raced into Martha Maude's arms. "I brung my colored pencils so's I'll be real quiet," she said as Martha Maude swung her up to her hip. "I'm gonna be a busy bee."

"You'll be the best girl ever," Martha Maude affirmed. Her smile for Rose and Matthias was more reserved. "We're all here now, and with Bishop Jeremiah and Bishop Vernon from Cedar Creek—and the *gut* Lord—to guide us, we're in the best possible hands."

Rose's heartbeat accelerated as they all entered the large, comfortable house. Had Vernon come because she'd sounded so worried when she'd called him? As they passed through the beautiful kitchen into the front room, she felt more confident just knowing he was present—and it didn't hurt that Martha Maude was carrying Gracie, either, as though her feelings toward the little girl hadn't changed.

"*Gut* evening, Matthias and Rose and little Gracie!" Vernon exclaimed as he rose from an intricately carved rocking chair. "We're pleased you've joined us—and if you've not met him, Rose, this is Jeremiah Shetler, bishop of the Morning Star district."

Rose nodded at the tall, dark-haired man who stood to greet her. Jeremiah was a lot younger than Vernon, with a head of thick, dark hair just getting some gray at the temples. He had an air of calm authority about him—and his gracious smile was quite a contrast to the scowl on Saul's face. Rose took in Saul's glossy black hair and beard, his robust build—and the fine furnishings with which he'd filled his home—and she realized that if he would smile and acknowledge how blessed he was, he would be a very handsome man.

"*Gut* evening, Saul," Rose murmured with the warmest smile she could manage. "I've prayed long and often that we might reconcile our differences this evening. God's will be done."

Saul grunted and looked toward the footsteps coming from one of the back rooms. Anne entered, appearing older and more fragile, her face pale with dark circles beneath her eyes. She smiled wanly at Rose and held out two Amish-style cloth dolls, a boy and girl, as she gazed at Gracie.

"I thought you might like some friends to play with while we grown-ups talk," she said. "And we've got chocolate chip cookies for later, too."

Gracie wiggled down from Martha Maude's embrace. "We'll all be real quiet," she said as she tucked the dolls under her arm. "Can I sit in the kitchen and draw on the table?"

Rose's heart swelled as Anne and Martha Maude accompanied Gracie to the kitchen and got her settled. Matthias was seated on an upholstered love seat near the fireplace, so she joined him. From where she sat, Vernon was at her right, Saul was in a large upholstered chair, and Jeremiah sat in the matching chair on the other side of a glossy walnut table.

Anne and Martha Maude took their places on the remaining sofa.

The front room was quiet, except for the ticking of a large grandfather clock in the corner. As it struck the hour, Rose marveled at the elaborate song its music box played and then she counted the seven stately, sonorous chimes that made conversation impossible. *Bong . . . bong . . . bong . . .*

As the final chime died away, Jeremiah sat forward in his chair and gazed at each of them in turn. "Shall we pray?" he asked as he bowed his head. "Dear Lord, we request Your presence and Your guidance as we hold our important discussion this evening," he said earnestly. "Grant us Your wisdom and Your peace as we seek Your will for the Hartzler family. *Denki* for Your love and forgiveness when we've gone astray and wandered from the path You would have us follow. Amen."

They were just opening their eyes when Saul started in, his face growing ruddy and his tone terse. "To set the record straight, I resent the way we're airing the family's dirty laundry with strangers present," he said, glaring at Rose. "I'm also displeased that Matthias has come, because he's so deeply involved in this sordid situation that I have severed our partnership."

Rose sucked in her breath. Matthias acknowledged this news with a rueful smile as he wrapped his hand around hers.

"And, Mother," Saul continued vehemently, "I can't believe the way you were clinging to that little girl as though—"

"As though she's a member of our family?" Martha Maude challenged. One of her eyebrows rose as she gazed at her son, her voice as cool and calm as her demeanor. "You know, Saul, after two days when you've chosen not to be here except to sleep, I've had a lot of quiet time to think and pray. And you know what? This isn't about *you*."

Rose nearly choked. She had figured Martha Maude to be more outspoken than most Plain women, but she hadn't anticipated the way this mother confronted her son. The two bishops were looking at one another as though they, too, were stunned by what Martha Maude had just said.

"So do I understand correctly, Saul, that you've spent your time—and eaten your meals—away from home since you and I talked?" Bishop Jeremiah asked. "It doesn't sound as though you've made any effort to understand your wife's situation, or to reconcile with her."

Saul's eyebrows shot up. "Don't you see how it is?" he snapped. "With two women in the house, I barely get a word in edgewise—especially when they've banded together against me."

"That's not true, and you know it." Anne's voice shook with fear, yet her conviction rang true. "More often than not, you and your mother take up with each other and leave me out."

"I see that more clearly now," Martha Maude agreed, "and I apologize, Anne. My son has not been at his best during these past two days. Frankly, his absence was much easier to take than his presence."

Saul sat up very straight, his eyes narrowing. "And do you forget whose home you share, Mother? Do you not recall how I saw to the sale of the poor old farmhouse I grew up in, and brought you here to a better life after Dat died?"

"Puh," Martha Maude said as she shook her head. "Your father made an honest living and he loved us with all his heart. You don't take after him in some important ways—but again, this isn't about you, Saul." She smiled briefly at her daughter-in-law. "When Anne was forced to give up her baby, she was obeying her parents and following the Old Order ways by keeping the birth a strict secret. And I suspect the young fellow who got her in the family way refused to take responsibility."

"He didn't know," Anne murmured. "We loved each other— I intended to marry him—but I was naïve . . . about how babies were made, among other things."

Saul coughed as though preparing to launch into another lecture—until Martha Maude rose from her chair. She stared at him until he met her gaze. "I heard you accuse your wife of holding out on you, not giving you children, so I should point out that you, too, are probably a victim of some Old Order ways."

The room got very quiet. Rose glanced at the faces around the room, noting the wary surprise in her mother's eyes and the patient, interested wisdom Vernon and Jeremiah exuded as they witnessed this exchange between mother and son.

Saul could stand the suspense no longer. "How's that?" he finally muttered. "Far as I can recall, you and Dat were faithful, model Amish parents, even if you could never seem to get ahead."

Martha Maude smiled gently. "Remember how your *dat* refused to go to the doctor when he was sick? And remember when you were a young scholar, and you became terribly ill with a high fever—and we kept you out of school for nearly two weeks?" She pressed her lips together as though this memory still bothered her. "Because your father wouldn't let me take you to the clinic, I suspect that nasty fever destroyed your ability to father children. A midwife I know says she's heard of such a thing happening."

Saul sprang from his chair, glaring at his mother. "Why on

God's *gut* earth must you reveal such personal—hurtful—information in front of all these other people?" he demanded. "This is an outrage!"

"Maybe so," Martha Maude put in, "but for all these years, you've blamed Anne for your childless marriage. Now that Rose has appeared, you must face a different truth." She held Saul's gaze when he appeared ready to protest again. "Sometimes it's the unexpected details that bring us to our knees. Goliath might've been a giant, but a tiny stone felled him."

Rose gripped Matthias's fingers. It was embarrassing, yet liberating, to hear the reason that this large home had never rung with the laughter of children—and to learn why Anne and Saul had no grandchildren by now. Her heart ached for her mother, even as she watched understanding dawn on Anne's pale face.

"That doesn't change the fact that Anne sinned with another man, and she never admitted it to me," Saul retorted.

"And I heard you tell her—in no uncertain terms—that you wouldn't have even considered marrying her, had you known about her past. Think of the years of happiness you—and I—would've missed." Martha Maude crossed her arms beneath her ample bosom, not nearly finished with what she had to say. "Again, Anne was following Plain customs when she gave up her baby and kept quiet about it. Do you think she hasn't suffered every single day since she gave away her only child? Do you think she hasn't been sorely disappointed that you've given her no children to fill the hole in her heart?"

Rose let out the breath she didn't realize she'd been holding. Never had she expected to witness this frank discussion between mother and son, nor Martha Maude's impassioned, unconditional support of her daughter-in-law. A sense of hope wrapped around her heart, and she could see that Anne seemed amazed and relieved as well.

"I've done a lot of soul-searching while you've stayed away, son," Martha Maude continued in a lighter tone. "Remember how, in the Bible, Saul persecuted Christians until the Lord knocked him down and blinded him to get his attention?" she asked with a knowing smile. "The day you were born, I sensed you had a defiant streak—like your namesake, Saul—and I figured that someday a major, life-altering encounter would take you down a peg or two. Well, here it is."

Saul appeared ready to argue again, but this time he turned his back on his mother and the rest of them.

Martha Maude cleared her throat. "If you can forgive Anne, you might enjoy welcoming Rose and her delightful little girl into your workaholic world, my son. Lord knows we could use a heaping helping of *grace* in this family."

Near tears, Rose glanced toward the kitchen. She wasn't surprised to see Gracie peering at them from the doorway, her face alight with curiosity as she clutched a doll and some pieces of paper. Bless her, she'd been so quiet and well behaved. When Matthias crooked his finger, Gracie hurried across the front room as though she'd been invited to a party. She crawled into Matthias's lap, smiling at Rose, but remaining quiet as the conversation continued.

Jeremiah rested his elbows on his knees, tenting his hands as he looked at Anne. "Do you have anything to add? You've remained quiet while we've taken in what your husband and his mother have discussed, but I believe your story has remained untold for long enough."

Anne licked her lips, holding the bishop's gaze. "As I mentioned to Saul the other night, I gave birth to Rose while I was still in my *rumspringa*," she said softly. "When I joined the church a year later, I believed that God had washed my sins clean with the blood of Jesus our Savior, and that I no longer carried the guilt of my sin. I rested in the comfort that my child was being raised by a faithful couple who longed for a child they couldn't have."

She paused, glancing at Rose as she considered her next words. "Maybe I shouldn't have written those letters to you, Rose," she said in a quavering voice. "But I wanted you to know how much I loved you."

Rose sniffled and swiped at tears. "You and Mamma both told me not to look for you, and I tried to abide by your wishes—but it seems God had a different idea when you came into the senior center that first time."

"*Jah*, He did," Martha Maude put in.

"And what a blessing it is that Rose has come into your lives again, quite unexpectedly," Bishop Vernon said. He scooted forward in his chair, smiling at the Hartzler women. "Anne, I was pleased that you—back when you were known as Roseanne—could stay with Myron and Lydia Fry long enough to wean your child, and that you didn't want Rose to find you when she grew up. I, too, insisted that Rose never needed to know she was adopted. However—"

Vernon paused for effect, as he sometimes did in his sermons, until Saul turned to see why he'd grown silent. "However, I've changed my mind," the bishop continued, his blue eyes twinkling. "Seeing the sweetness of little Gracie being held by her great-grandmother and welcomed by her grandmother, I'm reminded that Jesus insisted that little children be allowed to come to Him. The Bible also tells us that in God's peaceable kingdom, all His creatures will coexist without jealousy or hatred or separation, and a little child will lead them."

"A little child has led us to this moment—even if what she said has caused us some discomfort this week," Rose whispered, gently stroking Gracie's cheek. "And I'm glad."

"*Jah,* me too," Anne put in, sounding much more confident now.

Saul was following this discussion with a doubtful expression. "So now I'm hearing that Anne isn't even your real name?" he demanded. Saul sounded quieter, less confrontational.

Anne met his gaze. "Roseanne was my given name. But when I gave away my Rose, half of my heart—and half my name—stayed with her," she explained calmly. "I apologize for keeping yet another secret, fearing you wouldn't understand it. Will you please forgive me for this, Saul, and for keeping my daughter a secret?"

When Saul appeared ready to protest, Bishop Jeremiah spoke first. "It's the issue of separation that concerns me most," he began. "It warms my heart to hear you speak of forgiveness and unconditional love, Martha Maude, because your son came to my house Wednesday evening, demanding that I shun his wife outright."

Martha Maude's mouth fell open. Rose sucked in her breath. It was unheard of to shun a member of the Amish church without first giving that person a chance to confess to the bishop—and then confess before the entire congregation if he thought it was necessary. No one member could order another member to be shunned. It was a decision of the entire congregation.

"What were you thinking?" Martha Maude demanded in a low voice. "You're a deacon of the church, yet you've taken it upon yourself to pass judgment and order punishment without anyone else's input? I raised you better than that, Saul."

Saul had the sense to appear sheepish as his mother glared at him. "Okay, so I was upset," he muttered.

"Your wife has also asked you to forgive her," Vernon pointed out with a nod at Anne. "Forgiveness is a two-sided gift. The one who requests forgiveness is admitting a need for it, while the person who grants forgiveness has freed his own soul of any lingering doubt or distrust."

"And once a person has asked another for this gift of forgiveness," Bishop Jeremiah continued, "he or she deserves an answer. Forgiveness is not a one-sided situation that leaves the requester hanging until her accuser gets around to a response. It is an urgent, sincere appeal that demands an immediate, positive response, if we are to follow the path Jesus would have us go down."

Saul glanced warily at Anne and then focused on Bishop Jeremiah. "Are you saying my wife won't be going before the congregation to confess?"

Rose bit her lip. Why didn't Deacon Saul forgive his wife instead of ducking the bishops' remarks about forgiveness?

Jeremiah's lips curved. "I believe Anne confessed long ago, Saul, and unforeseen circumstances have brought her daughter back into the picture. You're dodging the real issue."

Once again, the front room got so quiet that only the ticking of the grandfather clock broke the silence.

Gracie tapped Matthias on the chest. "Wanna see what I drawed?" she whispered.

Matthias smiled and looked down at the two pages she showed him. Rose leaned closer to take a look, and tears came to her eyes. One drawing was a large blue bird and the other had a big red heart in the center with the letters *I* and *U* on either side of it.

Gracie grinned. "This one says, 'I love you,'" she murmured, "and this is the bluebird of happiness!"

Rose saw Anne and the bishops smiling at each other,

while Martha Maude came to stand behind the love seat so she could look over Matthias's shoulder. "A little child shall lead us, indeed," she said as she smiled at Gracie. "Show everybody what you've drawn, honey. We all need to be reminded that we do love each other—and that we need the bluebird of happiness in our lives every single day."

After Gracie held up the pages for the others to see, she turned and handed the heart drawing to Martha Maude. "This is for you," she said sweetly. After Martha Maude took it, near tears, Gracie climbed down from Matthias's lap. She paused for a moment, looking from Anne to Saul and back again, before taking the picture of the bluebird to Saul. "This one's for you, Dawdi," she said shyly. "You could use some happiness, *jah?*"

Rose pressed her fist against her lips to keep from crying. What a picture it made, her little girl handing a gift to the man who'd gotten so upset when Gracie had revealed Anne and Rose's relationship—because she loved her grandmother and Martha Maude.

Saul's eyes widened. He seemed struck dumb by Gracie's unexpected gift. When he finally took the page from her hand, the whole room breathed a sigh of relief. Gracie smiled shyly at him and then went over to hug Anne's knees. As Anne lifted Gracie into her lap, the little girl kissed her cheek with noisy gusto. "I'm gonna draw one for you next, Mammi," she said.

"I can't wait to see it, sweetie," Anne said as she held Gracie close. "You are such a blessing—to every one of us."

Bishop Jeremiah cleared his throat. "Well, I can't add a thing to what Gracie has just shown us," he murmured. "Of such is the kingdom of Heaven, and we'd all do well to follow her example of generosity and kindness."

"She takes after her mother," Vernon said as he smiled at Rose. "I believe you Hartzlers will be richly blessed by accepting Rose and Gracie into your family."

"*Jah,* it's a hard-hearted soul who can resist Gracie," Martha Maude said with a chuckle.

With a purposeful gaze at Saul, Bishop Jeremiah cleared his throat. "I believe forgiveness must be freely given to be sincere. So for all practical purposes, I'll call this meeting to an end. The ball's in your court, Saul. God be with you as you decide what comes next, and as you live as an example to the members of our church."

As the bishops stood up, Martha Maude spoke. "*Denki* for your presence with us, Jeremiah and Vernon. We hope you won't run off before you enjoy some cookies and coffee in the kitchen."

"Cookies!" Gracie crowed. "Can I help?"

"Of course you may, Gracie," Martha Maude said as she held out her hand. "I couldn't do this without you—and first we'll tape your picture to the fridge."

As Rose watched her little girl heading toward the kitchen with Martha Maude on one side of her, and Anne on the other, her whole body relaxed. She was still holding Matthias's hand. When they stood up together, she gave it a squeeze. "I'm so glad you came with me," she whispered. "But I wish you'd told me that Saul had—"

"I'm guessing you two will be setting a date in the near future?" Vernon asked as he came up behind them and squeezed their shoulders.

Rose's cheeks prickled with heat. "Why do you ask?" she teased.

Matthias shrugged, feigning surprise. "I have no idea what you're talking about, Vernon," he said with a telltale smile. "I think I'm doing really well at living single and keeping house—ain't so, Saul?"

Saul stared blankly at Matthias, but when he laughed, years fell away from his face. He joined them, walking toward the kitchen, carrying the drawing Gracie had given him. "From what I've seen of your place—and your cooking—Wagler, you can't get hitched soon enough."

Rose took a seat at the kitchen table with the others to enjoy some cookies and coffee. It seemed a good sign when Saul taped his bluebird drawing on the refrigerator beside the page his mother had posted. Gracie's artwork added a homey touch to a kitchen that was beautiful, yet a little too tidy and perfect, to Rose's way of thinking.

She noticed Anne and her mother-in-law whispering at the kitchen sink, and then Martha Maude came to stand behind Rose and Matthias.

"Sunday is Mother's Day, you know," she began as she placed her hands on their shoulders. "Anne and I would love it if you two and Gracie would join us for dinner. What a blessing it will be to have four generations of mothers and daughters at the table together—"

"And it'll be a treat to have Saul and Matthias clean up the dishes afterward, too," Anne put in, her eyes sparkling.

Saul's eyes widened. He shoved a cookie in his mouth to avoid answering.

"Count me in," Matthias declared. "I'm an old hand at washing dishes. Great way to keep your fingernails clean, Saul."

A subtle smile softened Saul's face. "We'll flip a coin to see who washes and who dries."

A short time later, the bishops departed; not long after that, Matthias took Rose and Gracie back to the senior center.

When Gracie raced down the hall to their room, Rose murmured, "Well, the evening turned out pretty well, all things considered. But I feel bad for Anne that Saul's having such a hard time forgiving her."

Matthias chuckled. "I suspect he'll come around pretty soon, because Martha Maude won't let him leave the issue hanging," he said. "I was really surprised she talked to him in such a tone, and that he let her speak to him that way."

"To me, that says Saul may strut like a proud, powerful rooster, but his mother rules the roost," she said. "And thank the Lord she's taken Anne's part. My mother would have a difficult time in that household if mother and son teamed up against her on this issue. A dark cloud would hang over that family forever."

Matthias peered around the corner to see where Gracie was, and then stepped back into the shadows of the hallway. When he took Rose in his arms, her heart began to pound rapidly. She couldn't look away from his ardent gaze.

"Rose, I didn't tell you that Saul tore up our partnership papers because . . . well, I'm hoping that when he forgives Anne, he'll reconsider our business relationship," he explained. "I have a feeling his moods get the best of him—and he was in a *mood* when he came to my place yesterday."

She sighed. She was hoping they'd left the subject of Saul behind them in favor of a more personal topic. "He did seem to be softening by the time we all left. And maybe—if you don't want to ride on his emotional roller coaster—you'd be better off just tending to your own harness business."

"I've thought about that," Matthias said. "And I've also thought about the damage he might do if he badmouths me and my shop. But right now, Rose, I'd rather think about, well—" He gazed into her eyes until she wondered if he was peering all the way down to her soul. "Rose, I—I love you," he whispered. "And I do want to set a date, as soon as you're ready."

She felt twenty again, as giddy as when Nathan had proclaimed his love—yet this time the words sounded even sweeter. This time, Rose knew what marriage required and she understood the consequences of commitment, just as she longed to belong to a steady, faithful man again. "We'll talk about that soon, *jah*," she said lightly. "Come tell Gracie *gut* night and we'll see you on Sunday."

# Chapter 32

R ose held her breath. She knew she was dreaming because the events she felt caught up in were out of kilter and out of order—and she'd experienced this same dream for the past few nights without seeing how it came out. She was at the house in Cedar Creek, the home where she'd grown up, and when Mamma stepped off the porch, calling Rose's name— calling her to supper—Rose held her breath.

Lydia Fry looked young and vibrant and healthy, as she had when Rose was a girl. Rose wasn't nearly finished gazing at Mamma—felt compelled to run up and hug her hard— when Dat came out of the barn. He waved at her as though he was delighted to see her—as though he'd never died in the sawmill fire. His body was muscled and firm, and he walked to the tire swing in the big tree, inviting her with his eager eyes to sit in it so he could push her higher and higher until she squealed in delight.

Rose held her breath, wishing this moment of seeing her youthful, healthy parents would never end. The house was freshly painted and the flowers flourished in the beds around its foundation. The vegetable garden thrived, with neatly hoed rows of green beans, ferny carrot tops, and vines full of yellow blooms that wound around the hills of zucchini and butternut squash. The heat intensified the smell of the plants and the earthy scent of soil that had recently received rain, and the breeze brought her the heady scent of lilacs from the bush beside the house.

It all felt so real—too beautiful to be true—that Rose longed to stand in the sunshine beneath the clear blue sky forever. If only she could go back to those days when she'd had no idea how wonderful her life was—when she'd had no idea that she was not Lydia and Myron's biological child.

Rose's chest constricted. Mamma and Dat were coming toward her, their faces alight with an all-consuming love for her, their beloved only child. Her childhood came back to her in a rush—the stories they'd read to her . . . the special birthday meals Mamma had made, with grand cakes frosted in pink . . . the kitties they'd let her keep after a stray mamma cat had birthed them in the barn . . . the songs they'd sung together during buggy rides . . . the cooking and sewing and cleaning Mamma had taught her by example . . . the bedside prayers with Mamma and Dat, kneeling on either side of her.

So much they had taught her, so much of themselves they had shared—no child had been more loved than Rose Fry. No girl had been blessed with more attention and heartfelt instructions on how a faithful Amish girl should live her life. Her parents had given her everything they had, and if they had lived longer—

Rose awoke with a sob and sat up. As the dream images dissipated, she realized she was in her apartment at the senior center, with Gracie sleeping in the twin bed across the bedroom. Her heartbeat slowed. She slumped, rubbing her eyes. Why had this dream held her captive the past few nights, yet only in the early hours of this morning had she realized the message behind it?

"Slow learner," she mumbled. She felt ashamed. She'd become so enamored of her birth mother, Anne, and so caught up in the secret her parents had kept about her adoption, she'd forgotten the very foundation of her life.

Mamma and Dat had loved her with their whole hearts, their entire lives. They had forgotten she was another young woman's child because to them, it didn't matter. God had entrusted little Rose to them, and she was the blessing of their lifetime together.

"I'm sorry," she whispered. "I was wrong to question your love for me, and the secret you kept about who I was. None of that really matters. I miss you both so much."

Rose was resting her head on her bent knees, struggling to regain her composure, when a little voice at her bedside pulled her from her troubled thoughts.

"Mamma? What's wrong?"

Rose raised her head. She smiled at Gracie through her tears, stroking her silky blond hair. "I was feeling sad about your *mammi* and *dawdi* in Cedar Creek, missing them," she replied as she opened her arms. "But I'll feel all better if you'll come snuggle with me."

Her daughter hopped eagerly onto Rose's bed. They hugged and then tickled for a moment, giggling, before Gracie burrowed beneath the covers. Rose lay down and took her daughter in her arms. Gracie's eyes were squeezed shut, her expression intense as she pretended she was sleeping.

"Is Gracie playing possum?" Rose teased as she'd done since Gracie was a very little girl.

Gracie shook her head, faking a snore.

"We have a whole day ahead of us here in Morning Star,"

Rose murmured, delighting in the softness of Gracie's hair as she nuzzled it. "We need to wash our clothes, but that won't take long because we're using the electric washers and dryers here. Otherwise, we're free to do whatever we want."

Her daughter kept her eyes closed, but her expression showed a distinct spark of interest.

"With tomorrow being Mother's Day," Rose hinted, "why don't you fold some of your paper in half and make cards for Anne and Martha Maude? They'll probably put them on the refrigerator and look at them for days and days—"

"*Jah!* Let's get up and do that now!" Gracie blurted. "Or maybe after we eat breakfast!"

"*Gut* idea, sweet pea."

Rose hugged her daughter and released her, laughing as Gracie raced to the closet to get dressed. She recalled the rare and special moments she'd climbed into her parents' bed and snuggled between them, realizing that those times had been as precious to them as they were to her now. Rose remembered making cards with her paper and crayons, too, and recalled the delight on her parents' faces when she'd presented them.

What she wouldn't do to have just one more day with Mamma. Her mother's love had formed the warp and woof of her life, weaving so many important lessons, holidays, and responsibilities together to make Rose the woman—and mother—she had become. Rose smiled sadly and gazed upward.

"I love you, Mamma," she murmured. "I didn't say it enough, but I hope you know I meant it with every beat of my heart, from the moment you called me your own."

Was it her imagination, or did the room brighten with a glowing warmth that wrapped itself around her? Rose sighed, feeling much happier—ready to learn how to operate an Eng-

lish washer and dryer, and ready to lavish her love on Gracie
as they enjoyed their Saturday together.

Anne was getting ready to start a busy Saturday, winding
her long hair into a bun, when a creak made her turn. Her eyes
widened when she saw Saul entering the guest room, where
she'd spent the last three nights.

He cleared his throat. "Need to oil this squeaky door," he
murmured.

Anne remained at the dresser, hairpins in her mouth and
her arms still raised, holding the last segment of her hair. Did
she dare hope her husband had come on a mission of forgiveness? Or did Saul intend to disrupt her plans for Mother's
Day by calling off their special dinner? Considering the way
he'd gone to bed without even saying good night, she wasn't
counting on reconciliation anytime soon.

"I was hoping to talk with you while Mother wasn't
around."

Anne nodded her head toward the wall that adjoined
Martha Maude's room.

Saul chuckled softly and approached her, a cautious expression on his face. "Between you and me, I think she talks
too much for her own *gut*," he murmured. "But maybe she
made some points. She could always talk some sense into me
when nobody else could."

Anne put her hairpins on the dresser so they wouldn't shoot
from her mouth if she started laughing. Saul seemed more con-
trite this morning, but it was his place to forgive her—and she
wasn't saying anything until he did.

Saul sighed, tucking his thumbs behind his suspenders.
"Maybe I was wrong to judge you," he said in a voice so thin

she could barely hear it. "Maybe I should be more like Gracie, loving and giving—and happy—instead of casting stones when I'm not without sin myself."

Anne's eyebrows rose. In her twenty years of marriage, she had known Deacon Saul to worry over some of their friends' bad decisions, but she'd not heard him do much soul-searching. She held his gaze, silently willing him to go on.

"And maybe I should be thankful that you and Rose have found each other again," he went on softly. "She seems very nice—much like you in many ways. Lord knows she'll be a boon and a helpmate to Matthias. He needs all the help he can get."

Anne turned to face the mirror again so she could finish with her hair. From what she'd seen, Matthias was a fine man—far more self-reliant than Saul. He was crazy about Gracie and very supportive of Rose.

Saul sighed. "So you're giving me the cold shoulder? Have I said something wrong?"

Anne met his gaze in the mirror. It wouldn't be right to criticize or demean her husband, but she decided to answer his question. "Maybe, maybe, maybe," she murmured. "Maybe you were wrong, and maybe you should be more like Gracie, and maybe you should be thankful that Rose has found me. The Saul Hartzler I know didn't build his business—his successful life—on *maybe*."

He blinked. Then he came to stand behind her, barely touching her body with his, yet preventing her escape. He placed his hands on the dresser on either side of her. When he stooped to reestablish eye contact in the mirror, his damp beard brushed her cheek. "What would I do without you, Anne?" he murmured.

Hair and hairpins forgotten, she clasped her hands over her heart. "I don't know," she whispered. "You tell me."

Saul's arms encircled her waist as his body shook with soft laughter. "I'm such a donkey sometimes, hardheaded and—and—"

"Noisy. Not to mention full of yourself," Anne murmured cautiously. "But you're also strong, and reliable, and you've given me a fine life for all these years. I don't want to live without you, Saul."

His eyes widened. "But? You said that as though a *but* must surely follow."

Anne took a deep breath to steady herself. Saul smelled like the soap from their shower, and he'd chosen her favorite coffee-colored shirt, which accentuated his arresting eyes. He was a big bear of a man, winsome when he chose to be, but this wasn't the time to succumb to his allure. "We have unfinished business between us."

Saul cleared his throat. He suddenly appeared shy and unsure of himself—not an impression Anne had ever had of him. When he let out a long sigh, his bluster and pride seemed to deflate like a pricked balloon. "I'll forgive you if—"

"*If?*" she blurted.

"—if you'll forgive *me,* wife," he continued in a whisper. "I've treated you—and this whole situation surrounding your daughter—badly. I'm sorry, Anne. I'll try to do better—I *will* do better—if you'll give me the chance." He smiled hopefully, turning her in his arms. "I want tomorrow to be the best—the first—Mother's Day you've ever celebrated, because you're finally with your child and—and our grandchild."

Anne put her fist to her mouth so she wouldn't cry out—or just cry. "Of course I forgive you, dear," she murmured. "All you had to do was ask. And I'm sorry about your . . . inability to make babies. Not that it changes my love for you after all this time."

When Saul pulled her close, she felt intense relief and comfort—and joy. The rift between them these past few days had made her ache with loneliness; their separation had driven such an emotional wedge between them. Joel Lapp had claimed her heart when she was young, but Saul had given her a lifetime of love that could withstand the trials and tribulations of marriage.

Saul kissed her tenderly, thoroughly, before he embraced her again. "I feel like yanking those pins out of your hair," he said in a husky voice. "But I suppose Mother will wonder why we're not in the kitchen for breakfast."

Three firm knocks on the wall made them both laugh out loud.

Saul let Anne finish putting up her hair and they went downstairs together, hand in hand. Forgiveness flowed between them like the maple syrup they poured on their pancakes half an hour later—pancakes Martha Maude made with a satisfied smile on her face.

## Chapter 33

When Matthias steered the buggy into the Hartzlers' long lane midmorning on Sunday, Rose's heart thrummed. Puffy white clouds drifted across an incredibly blue sky, Saul's glossy black cattle grazed peacefully in the rolling pasture, and the idyllic scene reminded her of the dream scenario set on her home farm in Cedar Creek—except this vision was real and in the present moment.

*It's time to sell that poor old place,* her thoughts whispered. *You can't go back to the perfection of your childhood, so you must move forward. Move on.*

"Ah, now I see what's smelling so *gut*," Matthias said as he pulled the rig into the shade of the barn. "Saul's grilling out back of the house. Why don't you girls go on inside? I'll tend the horse and chat with him a bit."

"Never hurts to be on the cook's *gut* side," Rose teased. When Matthias had helped her down, she glanced toward the grill. "Saul's smiling at us, too. That's a *gut* sign."

"We'll believe the best and go from there." Matthias set Gracie on the ground and gave Rose a quick kiss. "I'm sure your mother and Martha Maude will fill you in on all the details."

"Mamma, quit kissin'!" Gracie cried. "We gotta give 'em these cards!"

As her daughter raced up the hill toward the house, Rose laughed—until Matthias pulled her into his arms for a longer, sweeter kiss behind the rig. "I hope you'll have a wonderful time today," he whispered. "Happy Mother's Day, Rose."

She stood on tiptoe to plant a final kiss on his cheek above his wavy, brown beard. "*Denki,* Matthias. I'm glad to be spending it with my mother, *jah,* but with you as well."

Was there a special light in his eyes as he smiled at her? Rose strode up the hill toward the porch, where her mother and Martha Maude were making a fuss over Gracie as she handed them their cards. When she waved at Saul, he waved back without a moment's hesitation and a big smile on his face. She wasn't surprised that he had a large, fancy grill with a curved top that came down over the meat.

"Gracie, you look gorgeous in green!" Martha Maude was saying. "And I will treasure this card always, honey, because you made it just for me."

"*Jah,* it's mighty special to be getting my first Mother's Day card from you, Gracie," Anne said as she hugged the little girl. "And you know what? We made a special flower-shaped cake for dessert, and we want you to decorate it."

Gracie's expression touched Rose deeply. What a joy it was to watch her daughter basking in the glory of a grandmother and great-grandmother, who already cherished her. Anne turned to smile at Rose. "It's a blessing to have you here today, daughter," she said with a hitch in her voice. "We have so much to catch up on, and it's the perfect day to start."

As Rose returned her mother's embrace, she knew immediately that the rift between her and Saul had been mended. Anne looked fresh and rested. Her face was glowing beneath her white *kapp;* her freckled complexion set off by her dress of robin's egg blue. "So all is well now?" Rose whispered as she reached over to share a hug with Martha Maude.

"*Jah*—and can you believe it?" Anne replied with a chuckle. "Saul offered to grill our dinner. He said only our best, biggest beef brisket would do. He marinated it overnight and put it on the grill this morning so it would turn out just right for our special guests."

"He's a much happier man than when you last saw him," Martha Maude remarked as they entered the house together. "I'm thinking Gracie's bluebird of happiness picture turned him around. What a blessing she is."

Gracie pivoted to smile at the three of them. "*Jah*, I'm a little angel," she said sweetly. "What else are we havin' for dinner?"

Rose entered the kitchen with them and once again realized how large and clean and perfect it appeared—as though nothing ever got spilled and no one ever cluttered the countertops with dirty dishes and the week's mail.

"We have corn casserole and fresh glazed carrots from the garden," Martha Maude replied. She pulled a chair up to the end of the table so Gracie could reach the cake, which sat on a pedestal plate. "And we have a red gelatin salad with fruit cocktail, and creamed peas—"

"Yay!" Gracie crowed, clapping her hands. "And we have this pretty pink flower cake, too. What do I do?"

Anne came to Gracie's other side with a pastry bag filled with frosting. "Here's how you hold it," she said, placing the little girl's hands on the bag, "and when you squeeze where the bag is twisted shut—"

"Dark pink frosting comes out!" Gracie finished gleefully. "Let's make lines so the flower has petals."

Rose's heart filled to overflowing, watching the two women as they guided Gracie's little hands and encouraged her. With their help, she drew the petal outlines and then began filling the flower's center with pink dots. As the men came in the back door, their laughter filled the kitchen—a good sign that the two of them seemed to be on the best of terms again.

Saul set his covered pan on the back of the stove and came to stand behind Gracie as she finished decorating the cake. "Look at that! I thought we were having plain old cake, but you made it really pretty, Gracie."

Gracie giggled. "It's pink, so it's a girl cake. You don't get any."

"*Awww.*" Saul leaned down so his face was even with hers, and whispered, "Can your *dawdi* have a kiss today?"

Rose held her breath. Anne and Martha Maude stepped aside, and Matthias came over to slip his arm around Rose's shoulders.

Gracie held Saul's gaze for a long moment as everyone around the pair held their breath. She quickly pecked his cheek and went back to squeezing frosting dots on the cake.

Saul's face turned a delicate pink, and Rose thought he might cry. "I've got a surprise for you after dinner," he murmured. "Do you feel like a princess today?"

Gracie paused in her decorating, eyeing him. "Whadaya mean?"

"You'll see," he said as he bussed her cheek. "Maybe your mamma and Matthias will want to go along, too—but *you* get the special seat. On top."

Gracie's eyes widened with wonder. "*Jah,* I can be a

princess," she said, nodding emphatically. "Let's eat *now*! I'm done with this cake."

Rose chuckled and helped her mother and Martha Maude take the glass casseroles from the oven. Saul began to slice the brisket while Matthias brought some thick books from the front room to stack in Gracie's chair. Soon they were all seated and praying, in a kitchen warm with good food and goodwill.

What a wonderful meal they shared, and what a blessed day it was for Rose to feel like part of a family again, after losing so many people she'd loved in the past year. The brisket was seasoned and cooked to perfection, and each of the vegetables Anne and Martha Maude had prepared tasted especially fresh and tender. The roll basket went around a second time, as did the platter of brisket and all the side dishes. Gracie waited eagerly in her elevated seat for the grown-ups to finish the main meal.

Saul looked around the table to see that everyone was done eating. "We decided to do our little surprise for Gracie now, and have our cake and coffee when we get back," he announced.

Rose shared a smile with her mother and Martha Maude. "Does this mean the men are backing out on washing the dishes?" she teased. "We can wait until they've finished cleaning up—"

"Nuh-uh!" Gracie blurted. Then she flashed her best smile at Saul. "Dawdi says I getta be a princess, so we gotta go now. And Dawdi's in charge."

"Right you are, little girl!" Saul said as he rose from his chair. "I think we should let Matthias and your mamma come, too. Is that okay?"

Gracie scrambled down from her chair, nodding excitedly.

As Rose got up, she leaned over her mother's shoulder. "I'll help you with those dishes when we get back. It was such a wonderful meal—"

"We're so happy to see Saul wrapped around Gracie's little finger! We'll gladly do the dishes," Martha Maude said, waving her off. "You kids go have a *gut* time. It's a special day and we should enjoy every minute of it."

Matthias reveled in the feeling of Rose's sturdy hand clasping his as they sat in the backseat of Saul's enclosed rig. He had an inkling of what Gracie's surprise was to be—and he felt gratified to be included in it. When Saul drove around behind the large metal building that housed his carriage shop, Gracie leaned forward to gaze out the windshield.

"Where we goin', Dawdi?" she murmured.

Saul smiled as he pulled Dandy, his chestnut gelding, to a halt. "This is my shop, where we make carriages and rigs, Gracie. Most of the buggies are like this one, but your *dawdi* also makes some very special princess buggies," he explained as he opened the door. Then he shook his head, teasing her. "But you probably don't want to see them, much less ride in one, so maybe—"

"We're goin'!" Gracie said, scooting toward the door. "I wanna see 'em *and* ride in 'em!"

When Saul opened the back door of his shop, Gracie raced in ahead of him. He smiled at Matthias. "You saw these coaches earlier, but with all the lights working—all the bells and whistles up and running—they're really something, if I say so myself," he said. "The wedding wagon is already shipped off—"

"It's a big ole punkin!" Gracie cried out from inside the shop. "And there's a pink princess one, too!"

Matthias laughed. The wonder on Gracie's face—and in Rose's eyes—made him even more grateful that Saul had reinstated his partnership when they'd been on the back porch. It was good to watch Saul leaning down to ask Gracie which carriage she wanted to ride—and even better to hear his laughter ringing in the shop when she wanted to ride both of them.

"I think we can arrange that," Saul told her as he slid a wide door open. "We'll hitch the pumpkin to Dandy and try that one first. You're really helping me out, Gracie, because I need to drive these carriages on the road to be sure everything's working. Watch this."

When Saul reached up to the coach's console and flipped a switch, tiny orange and yellow lights began to flash, racing around the wooden wheels and the windows, and twinkling around the coach on the grid of tiny wires surrounding it.

Gracie clapped her hands, beside herself with joy. "Oh, Dawdi!" she cried.

Saul's face shone even more brightly than the sparkling pumpkin. "We can see the lights better in here than we can out in the daylight," he explained. "Let's get you settled up on the driver's seat—and your *mamm* and Matthias can ride inside."

Matthias felt a thrill of gooseflesh as he put down the metal steps and let Rose precede him into the coach. The seats were upholstered in deep orange leather, nicely padded—and he was delighted when Rose patted the place beside her.

"What a surprise," she murmured as she gazed at the coach's luxurious interior. A few moments later, when the vehicle lurched and rolled out of the shop, she scooted closer to him. "All's well between you and Saul, I take it?" she whispered.

"*Jah,*" Matthias replied as he slipped his arm around her. "Luckily, Martha Maude had a copy of the original contract, so she wrote it out again and we'll sign it this afternoon. She gave her son quite an earful, by the sound of it—but Saul had already realized he'd let an angry moment get the best of him when he tore up our agreement."

Rose nodded. "He seems much happier today. Totally absorbed in fussing over Gracie."

Matthias smiled. "That allows me to be totally absorbed in her mamma. How has your weekend been, staying in Morning Star rather than driving back to Cedar Creek?"

As they rolled down the road past the Hartzler place, Rose's expression suggested that she had many things on her mind. She rested her head on his shoulder before she replied. "I've had a vivid dream these past few nights, and I think I've finally figured out what it means," she said in a faraway voice. "I saw my *mamm* and *dat*—both of them looking young and healthy—and so happy to be my parents," she added with a hitch in her voice.

Matthias hugged her shoulders. "*Jah,* I still dream of my folks every now and again, too. And they look much better than when they passed—although Mamm wasn't old or sick. She died in a buggy crash."

"Oh, I'm sorry," Rose murmured, touching her fingertips to his cheek. "This dream woke me up to a couple of important things. First, I realized that my parents were the best I could've ever had, even if I wasn't born to them."

Nodding, Matthias gazed into her eyes. "I can't imagine what a shock that must've been, to find out that the two people you loved and trusted most in this world had kept a very important secret about you."

"But it worked out for the *gut,*" Rose insisted, "and I'm

blessed now to be with my birth mother again—to belong to a whole new family."

For a few moments, they glanced out the coach's open windows. They heard Saul regaling Gracie with descriptions of the places they were passing in the countryside, and Rose's expression became more purposeful. As the coach turned up a side road that would return them to town, her gaze made Matthias go very still.

"Will you help me get the Cedar Creek farm ready to sell?" she asked in an urgent whisper. "In my dream, the house and the gardens were perfect and well-tended, as they were when I was a child—and I'll never be able to keep the place up, much less get it into such *gut* shape again."

Matthias's eyes widened. "This is an awfully big step, Rose. Are you sure you're ready to be rid of the place where you've spent most of your life?" he asked quietly. He was quivering inside, wondering if this thread of conversation would possibly tie in with his own desires. "Where will you live?"

Rose blinked when the carriage began backing up. They were at the carriage shop again, and when Dandy had positioned the pumpkin coach where Saul wanted it, the big man jumped down from the driver's seat.

"Everybody out!" he cried, grinning at them through the window. "Princess Gracie says we're taking the pink coach for a spin now. Hope I'm not interrupting anything," he teased.

Matthias hopped out of the coach and then lifted Rose and set her on the shop floor. He helped Saul unhitch the beautiful chestnut gelding from the pumpkin coach, and then the two of them tugged the pink coach with the white wrought-iron curlicues into hitching position.

"How was the ride in the driver's seat?" Rose asked her little girl.

Matthias paused to take in the sight of mother and daughter as they gazed happily at each other. More than ever, he hoped to take them into his home soon, as they already held a place in his heart.

"We saw Dawdi's cows, and the creek at the bottom of his hill, and *everything*!" Gracie exclaimed. "It was so much funner than ridin' inside!"

"And Saul tied your strings so your *kapp* wouldn't fly off?" Rose asked, tugging on the neat bow beneath Gracie's chin.

"*Jah*. It was fun feelin' the wind in my face!"

"Ready, Gracie?" Saul asked. He reached up and flipped on the lights, which twinkled with a soft white glow all around the elaborate pink coach.

"*Oooh!* That's really pretty." Gracie's mouth dropped open as she took in the wondrous sight.

Saul extended his hands and Gracie rushed into them, giggling when he held her up over his head. After he carefully set her on the driver's seat, he looked at Matthias and Rose. "Ready for another spin? We'll go a different way this time—"

"A longer way!" Gracie put in. "*Please,* Dawdi? Pretty please with sugar on top?"

Saul's sparkling eyes rivaled the lights on the carriage. "The princess has spoken," he murmured. "Hope you don't mind riding around with us."

"It's fun to see how these fancy rigs turned out," Matthias put in. "Don't worry about us—we'll be your quality control inspectors for the interior."

When he and Rose were settled inside the pink coach, the horse took off at a trot. The carriage was obviously geared toward little girls, because everything was bright pink leather, trimmed with white, and a grid of tiny white lights flickered on the ceiling. Like the pumpkin coach, this vehicle's windows had no glass, so the sunshine and breeze came in freely.

"Saul builds these specialty carriages himself," Matthias murmured when he noticed Rose gazing at the interior details. "Truth be told, his work's as *gut* or better than any I've ever seen."

Rose nodded. Then a girlish grin brightened her face. "I was asking you about selling the place in Cedar Creek," she reminded him. "I can't think having an auction will be worth the preparation time or the expense, considering how—except for our clothes, the dishes, and a few items I want to keep—all the furniture's seen better days."

"I'll contact the real estate fellow who helped me find my house," he said softly. "He'll be able to help you with those sorts of details. And I was asking *you* where you were going to live, honey-girl."

Rose's face turned a pretty shade of pink—or maybe she was reflecting the interior of the coach, but Matthias couldn't stop gazing at her. Would it be appropriate to propose to her now? Would Rose think he was pushing her, or that he could choose a more romantic place and a time when they were completely alone? He could hear Saul and Gracie chattering about the pool hall and the car dealership they were driving past. They were paying no attention to their passengers, so if he kept his voice down—

"Sherrie has given us that apartment at the senior center for as long as we want it," Rose replied with a lilt in her voice. Then she smiled shyly. "Or . . . maybe you would consider, um, taking us poor girls in."

Matthias's pulse galloped. "Are you saying—I don't want to rush you while you're in mourning for—"

"Life is for the living, Matthias," she whispered. She gazed steadily at him with her glimmering green eyes. "Ask me. Ask me anything."

Matthias pulled her close, reveling in the way she wrapped her arms around him and hugged him back. He swallowed hard, wondering why it wasn't any easier to get a proposal perfect than it had been when he'd asked Sadie—

*But Sadie said yes, and so will Rose. Don't sweat the small stuff, Wagler.* He let out the breath he'd been holding so he could gaze into Rose's wide eyes. What had Nathan said to her to win her heart?

*You're obsessing again. Just do it!*

"Rose, I love you so much," he murmured, running a finger along her silky cheek. "Will—will you marry—"

"*Jah,* I will, Matthias!" she replied, beaming at him. "I want to tend to the farm—or at least get it up for sale—first, but then I'd be silly not to hitch up with you. I've loved you for a long while—"

Matthias kissed her gently, gazed at her, and then kissed her for a long, lovely time while everything else around them disappeared. She felt so perfect in his arms, in his life, that he wanted nothing to disrupt this moment when she was his entire world.

"What a beautiful day it's been," Rose murmured as she hugged him again. "Saul has reconciled with my mother, and Martha Maude accepts us, and now I have you, Matthias."

"And we have cake waiting for us whenever you two lovebirds are ready to go."

Matthias gasped, turning quickly. Somehow, they had returned to the carriage shop and parked without his being aware of it. Saul was gazing through the open window at them, holding Gracie as though it was the most natural thing

in the world for him to do. Gracie's eyes were huge with curiosity—and hope—as she gazed from Matthias to her mother.

"Whadaya doin', Mamma?" she asked softly.

Rose blinked back a few tears, but her smile rivaled the sun.
"I've just told Matthias I would marry him, sweet pea, so—"

"Yay!" Gracie blurted, clapping her hands. "I told you he
loves us! Now we gotta go eat that cake, likes it's a birthday.
A birthday for us bein' a family!"

"I'm honored to be the first to hear, and to congratulate
you two," Saul said, sticking his hand through the window to
shake Matthias's. "This princess carriage must be a magical
place where dreams come true—right, Gracie?"

"*Jah!* Now we gotta go home and tell Mammi and Martha
Maude," she replied. "Everybody's gonna be really happy!"

That evening after Matthias had driven them back to the
senior center, Rose delighted in his strength, his joy, as he
lifted Gracie to his shoulder and then hugged them both.
"What a great day," he murmured as he bussed the little girl's
cheek. His smile made Rose shimmer inside. "Maybe while
I'm helping you with your farm sale, you can help me get my
house ready for a wife and a child."

"Can I have a pink room, Mamma?"

Rose laughed along with Matthias as she tweaked Gracie's
nose. "If we tell your new *mammis* that's your color, I have a
feeling they'll want to help you decorate it—maybe with a
quilt for your bed and curtains."

"It'll be *beautiful*," Gracie said with a happy sigh.

"It will be," Rose agreed.

Later that evening, after she'd tucked Gracie into bed, Rose
gave thanks to God that her entire life had been beautiful.
Thanks to the love of two mothers—the one who'd given her

life, and the one who'd blessed her with the bedrock foundation of faith she'd relied upon—Rose had come through a tough year.

She'd come full circle, too, back to her birth mother and into another family who'd welcomed her and Gracie—and Matthias as well. Saul was extremely pleased that his partner would soon be his son-in-law. Anne and Martha Maude were overjoyed that Rose and Gracie would be living in Morning Star, just a short walk away from their home. It had been a Mother's Day none of them would ever forget.

"Only You could've made it all work out, Lord," she murmured as she stood in the moonlight coming through the window overlooking the garden. "*Denki* for standing by me, for seeing me through—for every *gut* and perfect gift."

When Rose went into the bedroom to stand beside Gracie's bed, her little girl stretched up her arms in the darkness. "I love you, Mamma," she whispered.

"And I will always love you, sweet pea," Rose said. She kissed Gracie's cheek, and as she left her daughter's bedside, her heart overflowed with love and joy.

*Love and joy,* she thought as Matthias came to mind. *Love and joy—and a happy family—make life worth living.*

Have you read all of Charlotte Hubbard's Seasons of the Heart series, set in the little Amish town of Willow Ridge? They're available in print or digital format from Zebra Books.

*Welcome to Willow Ridge, Missouri! In this cozy Amish town along the banks of the river, the Old Ways are celebrated at the Sweet Seasons Bakery Café, and love is a gift God gives with grace . . .*

## SUMMER OF SECRETS

Summer has come to Willow Ridge, but Rachel Lantz is looking forward to a whole new season in her life—marriage to strapping carpenter Micah Brenneman, her childhood sweetheart. When a strange *Englischer* arrives in the café claiming to be the long-lost sister of Rachel and her twin Rhoda, Rachel feels the sturdy foundation of her future crumbling—including Micah's steadfast love. As the days heat up and tempers flare, Rachel and Micah will learn that even when God's plan isn't clear, it will always lead them back to each other . . .

*The leaves are falling and there's a chill in the air in Willow Ridge, Missouri, the quaint, quiet Amish town where love, loyalty, and faith in the Old Ways are about to be put to the test . . .*

## AUTUMN WINDS

Winds of change are blowing through Willow Ridge, and they're bringing a stranger to the Sweet Seasons Bakery. At first, widowed Miriam Lantz has misgivings about Ben Hooley, a handsome but rootless traveling blacksmith. But as she gets to know the kindhearted newcomer, she wonders if his arrival was providential. Perhaps she could find love again—if only there weren't so many obstacles in the way. With Bishop Knepp relentlessly pursuing her hand in marriage and the fate of her beloved café at stake, Miriam must listen to God and her heart to find the happiness she longs for and the love she deserves.

*Snow is falling, cookies are baking, and Christmas is just around the corner in Willow Ridge, Missouri, where a new season marks fresh beginnings for the residents of the tranquil Amish town . . .*

## WINTER OF WISHES

As another year draws to a close in Willow Ridge, life seems to be changing for everyone but Rhoda Lantz. Her widowed mother is about to remarry, her sister is a busy newlywed, and soon Rhoda will be alone in her cozy apartment above the blacksmith's shop. An ad posted by an *Englischer* looking for someone to help with his mother and children may offer just the companionship she's looking for, but if she falls for the caring single father, she may risk being shunned by her community. Certain she can only wish for things she cannot have, Rhoda must remember that all things are possible with God, and nothing is stronger than the power of love.

## AN AMISH COUNTRY CHRISTMAS

*In Willow Ridge, Missouri, the Christmas season is a time when faith brings peace, family brings warmth, and new romance brings sparkling joy . . .*

## THE CHRISTMAS VISITORS

For spirited Martha Coblentz and her twin Mary, the snow has delivered the perfect holiday *and* birthday present to their door—handsome brothers Nate and Bram Kanagy. But when unforeseen trouble interrupts their season's good cheer, it will take unexpected intervention—and sudden understanding—to give all four the blessing of a lifetime . . .

## KISSING THE BISHOP

As the year's first snow settles, Nazareth Hooley and her sister are given a heaven-sent chance to help newly widowed Tom Hostetler tend his home. But when her hope that she and Tom can build on the caring between them seems a dream forever out of reach, Nazareth discovers that faith and love can make any miracle possible . . .

## BREATH OF SPRING

As a bright season brings a fresh start to Willow Ridge, Annie Mae Knepp feels she can never make peace with the past. Her disgraced ex-bishop father is furious she has taken her five siblings to live with her. She's never been truly at home in her faith . . . or believing in herself. And Annie Mae fears no man will want to take on the responsibilities she's gladly shouldered. True, her quiet neighbor Adam Wagler has been steadfast and unshakable helping her through her trials, but he surely couldn't think of someone so lost as more than a friend. Believing she is unworthy because of her doubts, Annie Mae will find in a moment of surprising revelation that God can work impossible miracles—and that love makes all things new.

## HARVEST OF BLESSINGS

The tranquil little town of Willow Ridge is facing a startling challenge. Wealthy Nora Glick Landwehr is determined to make it her home again—and put her past to rest. Cast out by her own family, Nora can't reconcile with Old Amish ways or her strict father. But she'll do anything to help her community embrace the future . . . and make amends to the daughter she had to give up. So, she certainly has no time for her reckless new neighbor Luke Hooley. They disagree about almost everything. And how can she trust him if he always seems to believe the worst about her? Somehow, though, his unexpected support and passionate heart are helping her find her own way in faith. And Nora will discover that even in the face of insidious lies and unyielding judgment, God creates unexpected chances for forgiveness—and love.